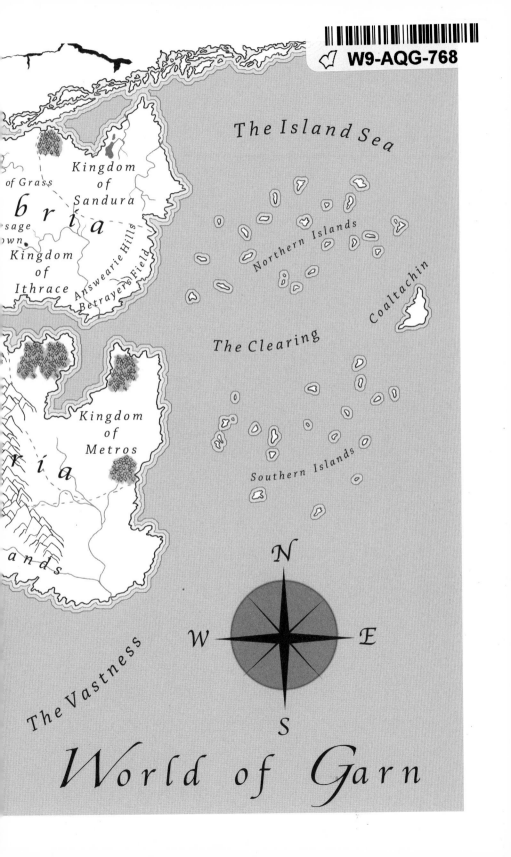

The Island Sea

Kingdom
of Grass   of
          Sandura

b r i a

sage
own

Kingdom
of
Ithrace

Answearie Hills

Betrayers Field

Northern Islands

Coaltachin

The Clearing

Kingdom
of
Metros

Southern Islands

r í a

a n d s

N

W   E

S

The Vastness

World of Garn

MASTER OF FURIES

MASTER

OF

FURIES

FIREMANE: BOOK THREE

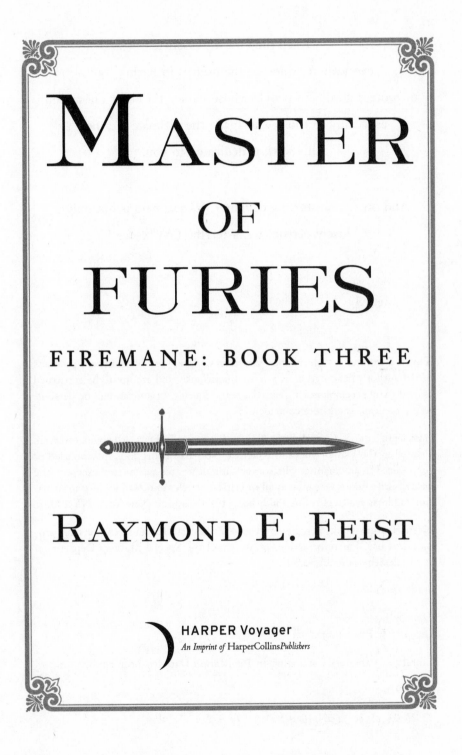

RAYMOND E. FEIST

HARPER Voyager
An Imprint of HarperCollins*Publishers*

To all the First Responders,
everywhere, who put themselves in harm's way,
to protect us all. To people whose names I'll never know, and
especially to those who made the ultimate sacrifice,
this work is dedicated to you.

And once more for my daughter, Jessica, who is not only a
lovely person, but a terrific first reader.

HarperCollins books may be purchased for educational, business, or sales promotional use. For information, please email the Special Markets Department at SPsales@harpercollins.com.

FIRST EDITION

Maps by Jessica Feist
Designed by Paula Szafranski

Library of Congress Cataloging-in-Publication Data has been applied for.

ISBN 978-0-06-231582-3

22 23 24 25 26 LSC 10 9 8 7 6 5 4 3 2 1

CONTENTS

ACKNOWLEDGMENTS

ONCE AGAIN, I SAY THANKS to people who made this career of mine possible, beginning decades ago with all my gaming friends, and to the thousands of readers I've been privileged to meet in person and online. It only feels like I'm doing this alone at times, but in truth I have many people who make this life possible and rewarding. I would especially like to thank Jane Johnson and Vicky Leech for editorial wisdom and a lot of hard work during very difficult days.

PROLOGUE

REACTIONS AND OUTRAGE

Toachipe, the Hour Marker of Akena, struck the marble floor twice, and the door guards opened the massive ornately carved portal to the Camera, allowing entrance to the Lord of the Golden Pride. The Hour Marker stepped aside as Tarquen entered ahead of the four leaders of the other most powerful Prides in Nytanny. As was customary, the leaders of the lesser Prides stood to either side of the entrance, each resigned to their lower station or secretly plotting how they might one day be part of the procession. As was his habit, Toachipe surveyed the group quickly, compiling a mental tally of who was in the capital. His duties comprised more than marking the passage of time; he was also a chronicler of every detail of governance, for one never knew which small element might prove critical in the future. Accountability and blame were vital to surviving in his office.

The Pride Lords entered in specific order, a tacit agreement as to their influence and power. Much of the governance of Nytanny came down to unspoken tradition, conventions created from centuries of living under constant threat from the Dark Masters. Centuries of living just moments away from inconceivable retribution for any transgression had created a ritual observance of social norms to become hardened into inflexible institutions. All were designed to reduce conflict among the families and Prides, despite the myriad of murderous feuds and rivalries that had endured between them for generations.

Toachipe's office was one of many that had evolved over this time to ensure that this brittle peace stayed in place. Toachipe's primary virtue was patience, as it had been for his predecessors: the only name for his duties was "tedium." Yet with that tedium came privilege, and few outside the Prides could claim such advantage. The nations were allowed only as much or little bounty as the Prides above them were allowed, and only office holders like Toachipe were free from such control.

Occasionaly he wondered who the first Hour Marker had been and how he had contrived that station. Toachipe was ignorant of this fact because, while there were records of every order of business going back to the farthest memory of any ancestor, the study of such history was forbidden to him, despite his office.

Urias, the Lord of the Tiger Pride, followed Tarquen, and behind him came Mioscomi, the Lord of the Onyx Pride, Jakanda of the Eagle Pride, and Shono of the Jaguar Pride, each in turn peeling off to right and left, until the five most powerful men in the nation had taken their appointed seats.

Following them were the five recorders—women blessed with a remarkable ability to retain details, each responsible for transcribing every word their own specific lord uttered. They operated under seal of death, not just their own but that of their entire families, should one word of what they recorded be uttered outside the Camera. Collective punishment was assumed among the people of Nytanny: it was part of the rigid code that kept the peace under the eyes of the Dark Masters.

Last to enter was the First Speaker, the one man not of the ruling class trusted to hear all that was said and whose sole role it was to act as chief arbitrator. Following tradition, he paused for a moment and turned to face the Hour Marker, indicating that it was time to shut the doors.

From the moment the sound of the closing portal stopped reverberating, only those within this room would know what was discussed; the population would learn what had been concluded by whatever edicts emerged from the Camera: all the deliberations, debates, arguments, and occasional threats, that were spoken within were closely guarded secrets.

Each Pride Lord retained his own recorder so that no later claim could be made predicated on misinformation or faulty memory. Should two recorders differ in their recounting, it fell to the First Speaker to decide the correct version of words or events. As a result of this great power, the First Speaker occupied a position of authority unequaled by any other below the lords. His family was kept in luxury, though he would never see them again, and when he grew unable to discharge his duties, he would be painlessly put to death, and his family would continue to prosper.

The Lord of the Golden Pride looked at each of the other four Pride Lords and then to the First Speaker. The latter gave a slight bow and then said, "The Camera is sealed, and now I yield to the Lord of the Golden Pride."

Tarquen was a man at the height of his power, both physically and politically. He stood up slowly. He was an imposing figure at six and a half feet tall, with wide shoulders and a narrow waist, and his face, with its chiseled cheeks and square jaw, looked as if it had been carved out of flawless obsidian. His eyes were as dark as his skin. Tarquen's stature was enhanced by the formal robes he wore: red, embellished with golden embroidery and shoulder patches. Against his dark skin the robes were dramatic,

as he had intended when he first commissioned them, ten years
before. He hated wearing them, for they were hot and heavy and
the climate in Akena demanded light, loose garb, which all other
citizens of the city wore on most occasions, but he understood
that such magnificence enhanced his aura of power. The other
Pride Lords knew that despite his size he was all lean muscle and
sinew, the strongest and fiercest warrior among them. Truth be
told, many of them had not held a weapon in years.

Tarquen was the third of his line to be the paramount Pride
Lord, a burden he embraced as his fate. His grandfather had
crushed rivals to achieve supremacy in the Camera, at times risking retaliation from the Masters, and his father had withstood
several attempts to dislodge the Golden Pride from their position of power. In the history of the nation, no Pride had stood
so high for so long.

Despite his relative youth (he had turned thirty-six a month
previously), Tarquen had been schooled since childhood in governance and understood both the public and covert methods
of maintaining control. Moreover, he had mastered the art of
persuasion, convincing the other Pride Lords to follow his lead,
knowing when to bow to alternative solutions in order to gain
socially while losing in different ways, and when to hold firm to
his own position.

His rule had been far less tumultuous than that of his fore-
bears, as the other leaders in this chamber had grown up with
the Golden Pride being the paramount one for their entire lives.
Should Tarquen bequeath the premiership to his eldest son, this
might be the beginning of Nytanny's first dynasty. No Pride
in history had endured for four generations. It was an outcome
Tarquen fervently desired.

He gave a slight bow, barely more than a nod, to Nestor, the First Speaker.

"We have begun," Nestor intoned formally.

TARQUEN SAID, "THE REPORTS CIRCULATED"—THEN paused for effect—"as well as those from those agents you chose not to share, have been considered."

There was a slight shifting by some of the Pride Lords, evidence that Tarquen's jab had struck home.

His temper had been at the fraying edge of self-control as he had read his own agent's report, which had been personally conducted to him by trusted go-betweens, before dressing for today's Camera. That report was the source of his quietly controlled ire.

Someone had captured *Borzon's Black Wake*, the Golden Pride's treasure ship, not only depriving him of abundance for years to come but turning a profitable undertaking into a financial disaster of monumental proportions, potentially weakening his Pride enough to render it vulnerable to its most powerful rivals, the Onyx and Tiger Prides, or even ambitious newcomers like the Jaguar Pride.

Tarquen said, "The *Queen of Storms* was taken, from a well-equipped Azhante crew."

Most of the Pride Lords had received the same report, but a few hadn't bothered to read it before this meeting. There was a collective intake of breath.

"That is a certainty? Could she not have been lost at sea?" asked Mioscomi, Lord of the Onyx Pride.

"A certainty," said Tarquen. "We have verifications that the *Queen of Storms* was lying in ambush should anyone unwisely attempt a run north of Elsobas . . ." He sighed. He realized they knew where the ship had anchored. "And there were dead bodies. Which you would know if you had read the report." He took a breath: his temper was threatening intemperate words. There were times to rail and times to inform, despite one's own mood.

Urias, Lord of the Tiger Pride, who was sitting to Tarquen's left, leaned forward slightly, his greying hair and deepening lines revealing his advancing age, though his gaze was still focused and hinted at an intellect not yet dimmed. "Who would dare such a thing?" he asked.

Tarquen looked at his greatest rival. "I intend to find out. What little information our agents have discovered so far is that seafarers from beyond the Border Ports, perhaps early arrivals from the raids on the Twin Continents, were seen at Elsobas." He paused: he did not wish to confirm the loss of his Pride's treasure ship. He would equivocate should anyone inquire how the strangers had arrived. "They were observed and were seen speaking to locals. One oddity: some local boys, street urchins, vanished after being seen with these incomers."

"Slavers?" asked the Lord of the Tiger Pride.

"Unlikely," Tarquen replied. "Perhaps someone who saw a monetary opportunity to capture some boys, but practiced slavers would know better than to get that close to the Homeland."

"Perhaps those boys were spies?" suggested Jakanda of the Eagle Pride.

Urias said, "We should leave it to the Azhante to unravel that mystery. What of our destruction of the Northern Twin?"

Relieved that the discussion had turned away from the loss of *Borzon's Black Wake*, Tarquen said, "As we expected, those who survived fled to Marquensas; Sandura is isolated, and the inhabitants of Zindaros and Metros are staying cloistered in their cities along the shore of their homes on the Southern Twin or fleeing southward from the unprotected towns and villages; chaos is sown, plunder is being acquired to please the raiders and all goes according to design."

"They expect invasion," said Urias in a satisfied tone.

"Soon chaos will befall those left in Marquensas, as refugees flood their lands. Famine and disease will reduce them even more. The slave nations are basking in the glory of their victories and luxuriating in the wealth of their plunder. We should have peace on the Homeland borders for a year or more. Ample time to plan the next assault."

"What of Sandura?" asked Mioscomi.

"Prepared. The Church is now ours, and Delnocio has fled; his collaborators are dead, or soon will be. The Church is moving against Lodavico, and the people of Sandura are trained to obedience like whipped dogs. They will welcome us as liberators when we take Lodavico and hang him, or burn him, or whatever they do with their criminals. When we crush Marquensas next year we will control both coasts of North Tembria. We can leave the land in between ungoverned for decades while we relocate the excess population of the slave nations and relieve the pressure here. After that we shall see to the Southern Twin."

"Twenty years," said Urias. "I was a young man, not much older than you, Tarquen, when we destroyed Ithrace, and ended the last of the line of the Firemanes."

Tarquen refrained from mentioning the rumor of a surviving Firemane child. He simply said, "It is our way to be patient."

"But never before have we seen such restlessness among the slave nations," said the Lord of the Eagle Pride. "We must cull them."

"Many were culled in the raids," replied Tarquen. "The men of North Tembria are not without valor and resolve. It was a victory, and when it is time to colonize the Twins we must ensure there are enough people left behind to serve, and enough sent forth to conquer. It is why we must hold for another year or two"—he paused, then continued—"and when we do colonize, we will add to our abundance."

Considering what he knew about the massive raiding of the Twin Continents, information that might not have reached the other Pride Lords, Tarquen defaulted to his customary practice of letting the others choose the matters they wished to discuss while planning his own later course of action in secret. He nodded to the First Speaker, indicating that he had finished speaking on that matter, and Nestor held up his hand, signaling that the lords were free to raise other questions.

The Lord of the Golden Pride was not surprised that it was Shono of the Jaguar Pride who started to speak as if he had been recognized by Nestor, and he was mildly amused that none of the others objected.

The business of the morning passed slowly.

At last, after the final point of discussion had been raised, Nestor stood up and declared the meeting adjourned, and the Pride Lords departed in reverse order of their arrival.

As they passed through the door, Tarquen saw the lesser Pride leaders form into small knots awaiting word from any of the five greater leaders with whom they were allied. A pair of younger men moved in his direction, but Tarquen waved them off to wait for him at a distance. He turned and caught Urias's eye.

The leader of the Tiger Pride tilted his head slightly, as if in question, then moved toward his senior rival. When he was close, Tarquen said, "A word when you have the time."

Urias was silent for a moment then said, "Your pleasure."

"I will be only a short while, then I will dine. Join me?"

"I shall," said the older man. Then he turned and beckoned his small group of sycophants to follow him.

Tarquen composed himself, pushing down rising rage. It took only a moment, yet it felt like a long struggle. He had been battling what he saw as this flaw in himself for his entire life, and while the fury still seethed beneath the surface, only a few intimates knew of that continuing conflict. He took a breath, then with barely a twitch of his head, encouraged his followers to leave. His personal guards formed up around him and accompanied him back to his apartments, where he would greet the Lord of the Tiger Pride.

Striding along the corridors, Tarquen considered his choices. He had already sent word to all his trusted agents in the Border Ports to start inquiries as to who might be bold enough to capture his treasure ship, and to ferret out who was behind seizing the *Queen of Storms*, the finest ship the Azhante had ever constructed. He had no proof, but in his bones, he knew that the offenders were one and the same and that suspicion fueled a growing disquiet.

This hidden actor was an unknown, and that troubled him deeply.

TARQUEN WELCOMED URIAS AND WAVED him to sit down beside him on the plush carpet. Both men had relinquished their heavy ceremonial robes in favor of the lighter hip-length, short-sleeved tunics and the baggy knee-length trousers favored at this time of the year.

The low table had been set with a midday meal perfect for the hot weather: chilled meats, cheeses, vegetables brined and spiced, fresh fruit, and metal pitchers of chilled water.

When the servants had finished placing the plates before the two Pride Lords, Tarquen dismissed them. When the two leaders were alone, Urias said, "As pleased as I am with this lavish repast, I can only conclude that the rumors of your treasure ship being lost are true."

"Your spies do you credit," said Tarquen with a rueful chuckle.

"Spies are hardly necessary when the streets run rife with rumors," replied Urias. "Obviously we do not know details of how great a loss it represents, but as your Pride was the primary architect of that assault on North Tembria, so you bore the brunt of the expense."

Tarquen shrugged, indicating that he was resigned to that unfortunate event. "While the loss of a treasure ship is regrettable, the loss of the *Queen of Storms* gives rise to greater concern."

Urias nodded. "Who would dare?" he asked softly.

"That is exactly the question, isn't it?"

Both men were silent for a moment as they reflected on the enormity of that question.

Lowering his voice, Urias said, "Since the Dark Masters went quiet . . ." He left the sentence unfinished.

Tarquen smiled. "More than a century has passed and yet we still whisper their name."

Urias forced a smile in return. "Habit. My grandfather told stories of people mentioning them and vanishing before the very eyes of onlookers."

"And my mother told me if I didn't finish the food on my plate, a horrible creature would come steal me away after I went to bed." Tarquen's grin widened. "One hundred years and a bit more everything changed, and to this day we do not know why."

"Yet we live in daily apprehension that the Dark Masters might return in a manner as unheralded as they departed."

"May that day never come," said Tarquen. "Still, we do much in our daily lives predicated on that fear."

"I remember my grandfather telling my father and me the story his father told him about the day of tribute when the sacrifices were taken to slaughter pits for the Ritual of Appeasement, but the Dark Masters did not appear. They waited for an entire day and night, then returned the next dawn in confusion and fear." Urias's expression was masked, but Tarquen saw a hint of the lingering fear every human from Pride Lord to slave felt when the Dark Masters were mentioned. "But you did not invite me here to speculate over ancient dread."

"True. Without the sacrifices and battle rites of ancient days, this expansion of our power to the far side of the world is necessary because of the growth in our population."

"You speak the obvious."

"Yet, we face unintended consequences."

"Agreed, yet you have something specific in mind," suggested Urias.

"Our own house has fallen into . . . disunity."

"Ah," said Urias, nodding. "You fear a factional war?"

"Not fear so much as anticipate," said Tarquen.

"Shono?"

Tarquen nodded. "He is ambitious."

"As were we all once; your grandfather more so than all of us."

"Which is why the Golden Pride has endured, but with our leadership, we have contrived to keep order. Order that has kept your Pride almost our equal in wealth and power since our fathers' days."

"True." Urias studied Tarquen's face for a long moment, then asked, "What are you proposing?"

"I think we should give Shono something important to pursue, so that he is distracted from his ambitions to one day take my place in the Camera."

Urias smiled: he knew that was as likely to be true as much as it was ridiculous. He nodded. "Such as?"

"Ask him to oversee the Azhante as they seek out those who stole the *Queen of Storms*."

Urias considered this, then gave a single approving nod. "Since the success of the raid on the Northern Twin, and the collapse of the Church of the One, that will keep the Azhante busy."

"And knowing the Azhante, they will not consider for one moment allowing Shono to upset the current balance. The Azhante may not be happy servants, but they understand better than most the need for order. Without a goal, they tend to grow restless."

"They currently lack one, that is certain," agreed Urias.

"In a year, two at the most, the Twins will be ripe to occupy, and by then we shall have decided who will colonize and who will remain and return to something approaching normal order."

Urias rose. "Send word should you need my assistance."

"Between the two of us, and the uncertainty of Eagle and Onyx, we need but . . . agitate one or two of Shono's lesser Pride alliances, and that should keep him busy until it is time for the migration of our colonists."

"We can but hope," said Urias. There was only a hint of doubt tingeing his words. He departed, leaving Tarquen with his own thoughts.

First had come the obliteration of Ithrace, and the complete infiltration of Sandura and suborning of the king's authority. And then this massive raid, on a scale unmatched in history. Next would come the occupation of the Twins, and then, after generations of planning, Nytanny would rule all of Garn.

Then the doubt brought about by the loss of two ships, the *Queen of Storms* and *Borzon's Black Wake*, made the Lord of the Golden Pride return to that one troubling thought: out there was an adversary far cleverer and more daring than he could have anticipated. That worry would likely linger for a very long time, second only to his lifetime of fear that the Dark Masters would return.

I

REFIT, REEDUCATION,

AND THE UNEXPECTED

T he *Queen of Storms* eased into the refurbished berth in the
Sanctuary's harbor. The sun shone brightly, and Hava welcomed the warmth on her back and shoulders after having spent
over an hour slowly navigating the mist that frequently shrouded
this island, the mist that provided the protection needed to hide it
from all enemies. It was dense enough to dampen her blouse and
when the breeze freshened, it had chilled her.

That ring of surrounding mist had been a major factor in the
Flame Guard picking this location for their original hiding place.
Hava had navigated enough in the area now that she appreciated
the quirky weather conditions and how to get in and out of the
Sanctuary safely. That shroud of mist and fog combined with
the further difficulty of navigating the shoals, reefs, and rocks
that littered the passage from the island to open waters. It was
called "the Scorching Sea" off the coast of South Tembria, but
she had not heard any name for it here. It was just "the ocean."

The Sanctuary loomed ahead, and Hava could see a handful of
workers who had been tasked with cleaning away years of debris
and decay from the currently empty buildings just above the

harbor. One task Hava had assumed without consulting anyone was that of freeing any captives from North Tembria who had been taken by slavers. In the three short weeks since she had first arrived, she'd made half a dozen more journeys through the chain of islands dominated by the Border Ports and had returned with freed prisoners and former slaves. These had been nursed and fed, and those who were able had been put to work reviving this ancient home to the Flame Guard. The rest were cared for, and eventually they would either recover or die.

Hava had little sense of "home" from wherever she had lived. Her father had been quick enough to send her away as one less mouth to feed, so the closest place to home was the school where she learned how to serve Coaltachin, alongside her friend, now husband, Hatushaly, and other children. Coaltachin was where they had learned to murder, steal, and spy for a society of criminals and assassins. They had shared the strange quality of being part of a larger whole, perhaps a "family" in a sense—she had seen families in her travels, so she accepted hers was a strangely odd one by most measures—but no one place was "home."

Still, there was something about this place that was growing on her, even in so short a time, perhaps like Beran's Hill. That was where she and Hatu had lived in relative safety. Or at least until the horror of the assault that had destroyed the town.

Being apart from her husband had made it clear to Hava that pretending to be his wife had evolved into the feeling that she *was* his wife, though she was never going to take orders from him in the way of many women she had witnessed deferring to their husbands in her travels. At least she felt closer to him than any man she'd known and found the sex far more satisfying because of it. She had lain with a few boys, men, and a few women during her training. Much of it was pleasant, sometimes even fun, and at worst she had learned how to endure everything from incompetence to abuse, should sex be required as part of her mission.

With Hatu it was different. She hadn't quite come to understand fully what it meant. It was just better than with other men, but whatever the reason, she was planning on dragging him into their bed as soon as she bathed.

Catharian stood on the quay, waving a greeting. Hava smiled as she ordered the ship made fast, and turned to her first mate, Sabien. "Get our passengers off first." With a sweep of her hand, she indicated the ship. "Then get her cleaned up and let the men go. Have them fetch those casks of ale we looted up to the public mess and open one. They deserve some time to themselves."

"Yes, Captain," replied the former mason.

Hava watched his back as he moved down to the main deck. She repressed a grin: he rarely shouted orders, preferring to pass them along in hushed tones. He raised his voice only during rough weather or when calling to the crew aloft. This caution probably stemmed from their first escape from captivity, and she felt no need to change his manner. Sabien had blossomed into as stalwart a mate as she could have hoped for. He had risen to become her second in command, after she had given her previous first mate, George, command of a second warship they had taken while at anchor on the voyage home. Named *Sundown Raider*, it was an older ship than her *Queen of Storms*, and slower. She expected George to pull into the harbor around sundown.

She left the quarterdeck and made her way to the gangway, crossing to the quay where Catharian waited. No longer disguised as a mendicant friar of the Order of Tathan the Harbinger, he had stopped shaving his head, and now looked a bit older with his grey-speckled brown hair visible.

Initially she had been enraged by his part in the abduction

of her husband from the town of Beran's Hill, but after the number of refugees she'd encountered from the invasion of the west coast of North Tembria, she had finally come to understand that the abduction very well might have saved Hatushaly's life. She was even beginning to appreciate Catharian's dry, trenchant wit.

"Successful voyage, I take it," he said with a smile.

"Very. Those . . . well, can't very well call them landmarks, can we? Seamarks? Anyway, straight through the Shroud, then those color changes in the water are easy enough to follow after you've navigated them and know what to look for."

"Shroud?" Catharian asked.

"That shroud of mist and fog around this island?"

He smiled. "Never had a name before. I like it."

She studied his expression then added, "You were worried, weren't you?"

He tried to shrug but limited himself to a slight nod and an openly pained expression. "Very. Well, it was your first voyage without me." He looked over her shoulder. "Where is George?"

She laughed, a peal of delight. "He's bringing in the ship we took."

"Another ship?" he asked, glancing at the two now anchored some distance offshore. "More loot?"

"More Azhante," she replied.

"Another warship?" he asked, his eyes widening a little.

"*Sundown Raider*," she said. "Heard of her?"

"I've seen her, docked in the islands a few years ago." He glanced at the *Queen of Storms*, taking in the fact that she looked exactly the same as when she'd departed. "How'd you manage without . . . ?" He waved at the undamaged ship.

"We swarmed her at night. Apparently, word hasn't reached

everyone about the *Queen* being taken, so we were on top of them before they realized it wasn't another of their own."

Glancing at the retreating backs of the freed prisoners, Catharian said, "Food is going to start being a problem soon."

"We can take the *Raider*, escort one of the freighters, and spend some days fetching food." She glanced around. "If we're to get this place into proper shape we're going to need more people, and then we're going to have to start thinking more about permanent solutions."

"There are old farmsteads on the north side of this island. They've lain fallow for . . . who knows how long?"

"Bodai probably does," suggested Hava.

Catharian smiled and nodded. "Indeed. But I'm sure they're overgrown with weeds, and I don't know if we have any farm tools . . ."

"Make a list," said Hava. "We're due for a journey back to Marquensas, and there are certainly abandoned farms up and down the coast . . . and perhaps some farmers in hiding." She was silent for a moment, considering what they knew about the raiding of that barony. They still lacked an overall perspective but had heard enough stories from survivors to know that the barony might no longer exist. "Well, we'll see what we'll see when we get there." She added, "And no matter what we offer here, some of these people will want to go home."

"Yes, of course," said Catharian. "Families were separated, loved ones captured and put on other ships, or left dead back home. So much chaos. Those who are willing to stay . . ." He let his words drift for a moment, then added, "This was once a very busy community of thousands of people spread out over dozens of islands to the north and northwest. Everything we needed, grass for grazing livestock, timber, even mining I was told.

"As the Flame Guard evolved with the Firemane . . ." He fought for words for a brief moment, then said, "It's hard to explain, for a lot of our history is lost to us. That is one of the tasks Bodai has set for himself, and now perhaps with Hatushaly, to scour the library for whatever we can find to fill the holes in that history.

"Just know that whatever the cause, the Flame Guard left this island stronghold and the people who lived around here and eventually the majority of us were left in Ithrace, protectors and educators of the royal children, and guardians of secrets far deeper than what any of us today know. Most of us were lost when Ithrace was destroyed."

Hava looked at Catharian and saw that his expression was barely masking a true pain he usually kept well hidden, and she nodded. "I have a sense of far greater questions yet to be answered."

"Undoubtedly. It wasn't until we returned here that we began to appreciate how much of our own history had been forgotten." He was silent for a moment, then added, "I think we may have lost sight of our own true mission somewhere along the way."

"What makes you say that?"

"Nothing specific. Just a sense that there must have been a larger mission back when this was the center of our order." Catharian glanced around as if he was still taking in the changes the Sanctuary was undergoing. "But these are questions that may take years to answer, if even then."

Hava nodded and remained silent as she considered this. She looked at him and shrugged. "Hatushaly is part of those answers, it seems."

They both turned their attention to the crew making the ship secure, and then Catharian said, "You've been away more than you've been here. I know Hatushaly missed you."

"We've been apart before, and certainly will be again, but at least I'm here for a while before heading back to North Tembria."

Catharian nodded but said nothing.

"Besides," she added with an annoyed expression, "Bodai keeps him studying from dawn till dusk, so I hardly see him anyway when I am here." Her expression turned to one of mixed annoyance and worry. "I feel things are changing between us, but . . ."

Catharian touched her reassuringly on the shoulder. "Whatever changes will be what both of you decide. I can only imagine how difficult these separations are for you both; you've been together since you were children."

"Difficult isn't the word," said Hava tersely. "These studies of his when I'm gone are"—she shrugged—"one thing, but when I'm here it's—"

"Necessary," interrupted Catharian. "I assume he has talked to you about the incident on the ship? When he first journeyed here?"

She sighed. "Yes, he made it clear to me that without training he is a danger to all of us, even himself. But I don't fully understand."

"Bodai can explain at length—"

"Tedious length." Hava laughed. "Very tedious."

Catharian chuckled. "Yes, but he is thorough. Until Hatushaly, magic was the province of women alone. I can't grasp the concept of these powers. 'Magic,' if you will, was alien to me until I became a part of the Flame Guard, so I understand only a little." He looked as if he was fighting for words. "I think from what I've been told that men with . . . Ability? Power? Were . . . conduits, somehow linking with the . . . 'magic.' But only women could actually manipulate and use that power." He looked away over the harbor. "It's why it's so crucial that it was the Firemane line that had this power. Their magic came through the males, and the daughter who married had children without . . ." He shrugged. "I don't know how to explain it."

"Hatu explained what he could. He doesn't understand it either and from what I see, I'm not sure that Bodai does." Hava took a breath and gave Catharian a look that communicated this discussion was over. "Now, I will see the ship is secure, then clean up, and prize my husband out of Bodai's grasp!"

Catharian laughed. "I wish you luck."

Her brow furrowed.

"Both of you," he quickly added. "But mostly Bodai."

She chuckled. "I'll be gentle."

They parted company. Catharian set off to his room to start a list of supplies they needed, and Hava turned back toward the *Queen of Storms*, to make sure everything was as it should be before letting the crew leave.

HATU STOOD ATOP A LADDER, on the highest rung, as Bodai held it steady. Hatu stretched as far as he could to reach the leather-bound tome on the second to top shelf, using the tips of his fingers to jiggle it a bit. "Heavy," he said as he tried to breathe calmly and evenly. He'd been trained to ignore heights and potentially dangerous falls since childhood, but the ladder was not the sturdiest he'd climbed, and the floor below was stone. Silently, he thought he'd have to get Bodai to fetch hold of a taller, stronger ladder if they were ever going to reach the top shelf.

"Can you get it?" asked Bodai.

"I think so," said Hatushaly, as he tipped the heavy volume upward. He wanted to know what every book, scroll, manuscript, folio, or scrap of notes contained, who had written them, and whether they were worthwhile to study.

Bodai had mentioned that even though he had come to the Sanctuary years ago, he really had little idea what was in this vast library—many of its volumes were in languages he couldn't recognize, let alone understand.

Given his age and physique, he had not attempted to reach the books situated on the top two shelves of the main cases that lined the walls of half a dozen rooms. Even Hatu had considered this a challenge but had found a ladder and had been undertaking the task of getting down as many as he could over the last few days.

He took a deep breath and trusted Bodai to keep a firm grip on the ladder as he attempted to stretch himself as much as possible. He pushed up slightly and the book moved a bit toward him but mostly to the right. He pushed up again on the right side of the book and it moved, again a little toward him, but mostly to the left. Alternating such pushes brought the big book almost within his grasp. Hatu repeated the motion until the book was overhanging far enough that he could feel it teeter and he made ready to grab it.

"Hey!" Hava shouted from the door.

Hatu's head jerked around, and he felt the ladder twist as Bodai was also startled by the unexpected call. He started tilting backward and knew the ladder was going to fall. He had jumped off too many roofs to hesitate. He launched himself away from the ladder, tucked and rolled, coming to rest on the floor with a bruised shoulder.

Bodai half-hopped, half-slid sideways to avoid both the ladder and Hatu landing on him, almost toppled backward, but caught himself with an outstretched hand grasping the nearest shelf.

As the ladder struck the stone floor, Hava let out a bark of laughter at the effect of her greeting.

Hatu threw her a questioning look, finally registering the fact that his wife had suddenly appeared and broken his concentration. He had just started to rise when the large book he had been trying to retrieve began to slide over the edge.

"Oh, no!" shouted Bodai as he saw the massive volume start to fall from the bookcase.

Without thought, Hatu reached out, though the gesture was pointless: he was still on his knees, many yards away from where the book would land.

Suddenly, the book stopped falling.

Hava and Bodai both regarded the hovering book, their eyes widening in astonishment. They looked as one at Hatu who knelt on the stone floor, his right arm outstretched, his palm up and trembling slightly as if holding a weight. His eyes were also wide, and as he lowered his arm the book also slowly descended. When the back of his hand touched the stones, the book suddenly dropped half an inch, and they all heard the thud.

Hava said in a subdued voice, "How did you do that?"

As Bodai moved to inspect the book, Hatu rocked back onto his heels, as if kneeling in prayer. He whispered, "I have no idea."

All three silently absorbed what they had just witnessed. At last, Hatu stood up and dusted himself off, saying, "So, you're back!" He smiled broadly and moved toward Hava, who hesitated for a moment, before stepping into her husband's embrace.

She gave him a quick kiss and a brief but strong hug, then said, "So, is this what you're doing while I'm at sea, floating books in the air?"

He chuckled, but with echoes of concern as much as humor. "No. I've never done anything like that before."

Bodai shook his head. "At least you didn't burn the library down."

Hava shot a dark look at her husband's old, stout teacher,

indicating that she didn't find this remark humorous. Her conversation just a few minutes earlier with Catharian had reminded her of the risk Hatu posed to himself and others.

Bodai shrugged and held up his hands a little, as if acknowledging it was an inappropriate jest. "Nothing like what you're thinking about, but we have had . . ."

"Sometimes we get a spark or a bit of smoke, here and there," said Hatu, trying to keep his tone light.

Changing the subject, Bodai asked Hava, "How was your voyage?"

"Captured another ship and rescued . . . I guess about fifty? Maybe more."

Bodai nodded. "We will make room and find work for them."

"Some want to go home," said Hava.

"We'll talk about that tomorrow. Right now, I expect you two would rather be alone." He made a shooing motion with his hand and said, "Hatu, we will resume our work in the morning."

"I'll be here first thing," Hatushaly replied.

"Not too early," added Hava, in an emphatic tone.

Bodai held up his hands, a gesture of surrender. "I will not object," he said. He watched as they departed, and took a last look around the library, which was slowly becoming as it had been intended, a place of study and scholarship. He sighed. Yes, it was coming along, he thought, but there was still so much more to do.

As Bogartis's company crested the small ridge, they came in sight of the coast. Below them waited the port of Toranda. They had traveled here from Marquenet. Off in the distance to the southwest, he could see the coastline curving toward the setting sun and vanishing in the distance. Beyond the town lay what was known as the Endless Depths. Obviously, they were not endless, thought Declan, as somewhere on a distant shore lived the raiders who had killed his wife and friends.

"Looks fine," said Bogartis.

Declan nodded, feeling a tinge of relief that he was sure the others in the company shared. No one had known how far-ranging the attack on the coast had been. A few messages carried by pigeon had reached the baron just before Bogartis's company had departed on this mission.

Port Calos lay a smoldering ruin, as did the larger towns along the coast from there to Baron Dumarch's small garrison at the north headlands. They were still awaiting word from other gallopers who had been sent to the more distant coastal towns.

The attack that had killed the baron's family had come from the south. Bogartis and Declan had seen the carnage, as those attempting to flee to Ilcomen had frantically tried to turn back to Marquensas only to be overrun and butchered by raiders.

The baron's brother, Balven, had suspected that the southern ports, in Ilcomen, would also be in ruins, and that left Toranda as the most likely port to secure a large enough ship for Bogartis's mission.

As they rode down the hillside to the port city, Declan could see several ships anchored at a short distance offshore. He was relieved that Balven had been correct in his conjecture.

A short while later they topped a small rise and could see the town in more detail. Barges and boats were shuttling between the ships and the port. The closer they got, the more it became evident that ships were loading, as the smaller crafts were returning to the city empty.

When they reached the gate two guards lowered their pikes in a warning gesture as a third moved toward Bogartis and Declan. "What's your business?" he demanded.

"Baron's orders," said Bogartis, reaching into his tunic and pulling out the pass bearing both the baron's seal and Balven's signature. He handed it down.

The soldier who received it merely glanced at the seal, and with obvious relief handed it back. Declan assumed that meant he couldn't read but did recognize the seal.

"You all that's guarding this town?" asked Bogartis.

"No, there's twenty more inside the city, but we're spread thin, most watching the docks, in case . . . you know."

Bogartis nodded. "Indeed."

Declan understood. These three would have resisted had this company been raiders, but by the time help arrived, all would almost certainly be dead. Even the other twenty might not survive if confronting forty armed horsemen unless they could quickly close the gates.

The guard waved them through, and they entered the city. Toranda had existed long enough that a makeshift defensive wall had been erected over the decades. It ran as far to the south as Declan could see, bending slightly westward and out of sight. The gate was wide, as it serviced all the wagons leaving the city with trade goods, as well as farmers, woodsmen, hunters, and other locals bringing their wares into the city to sell. Declan glanced southward as they reached a small market square, and asked, "Another gate?"

Bogartis nodded. "Smaller, but there's not much trade here. Why do you ask?"

"Just want to know."

As they turned their mounts to ride along the large road separating the docks from the town, Bogartis said, "Fastest way out?"

Declan nodded. "And fastest way in."

Bogartis smiled. "You're a quick study." He pointed. "The road out of the south gate runs to all the fishing villages along the peninsula a few miles shy of the point. There are a number of deer paths, goat trails, and shallow streams running down from the hills, and those hills are lightly forested. The southern side of those hills, all the way to the border of Ilcomen, is almost barren. Just scrub, wild goats, and a few wrecked fishing boats." He pointed to the west. "If someone was coming in from there, it would be by sea, I'm thinking."

Declan nodded. There were no seaward defenses and just sailing right into the docks would prove far easier than attempting to land somewhere else and marching overland. "Why did they not raid here?"

"That," said Bogartis, "is indeed the question. Why stop where they did, when they did?" He shook his head. "We can only guess."

As expected, the soldiers at the docks were doing their best to keep order in a frenzy of activity as the majority of residents were moving what they could to the ships, to flee from the prospect of attack.

Bogartis would need one of these ships, Declan judged, so as they sought stabling for the horses, he would spread the word that the assaults were apparently over. The news the raiders had left just as these ships were ready to put out should have many of these people turning around and hauling their property back to shore. He had a vague sense of amusement at the thought.

Declan was still a small village lad at heart, but the bitterness of the past few weeks had changed any sense of wonder he might once have felt at visiting a new place. His reaction to his first sight of Ilcomen or Marquenet, the awe he had felt, was less than a vague memory. This was just a place to evaluate where best to defend should an attack come.

Beyond the issues of the moment, his purpose was simple:

find anyone responsible in any way for the death of his wife and his friends.

Then end them.

A hollowness inside was all he experienced, and it had colored his every conscious moment since he had awoken to learn that everything he loved had been taken from him. He did not speculate if revenge would fill that void. He just didn't care. He had a purpose without expectation.

They halted at the southern end of the main street into the city, where it intersected with a broad stone road that ran between the city and the quay. The quayside was almost frantic with people hurrying all over to waiting boats and barges tied up alongside, with others lingering beyond for their opportunity to dock.

Bogartis waved over a nearby guard. "What is this, then?"

He was a young soldier, barely more than a boy, with a shock of dark hair that peeked out from various places under his helm, and sun-darkened skin that looked bronze with sunlight reflecting off the perspiration on his face and arms. Dark eyes regarded the company with an expression of hope. The guard asked, "You here from the baron?"

Bogartis nodded. He flashed the paper with the seal on it, and said, "Where's everyone off to?"

"Anywhere but here, I guess," said the guard. "It's been like this since word arrived about the raids up the coast." He looked over his shoulder, then back at the captain. "You here to reinforce us?"

Bogartis shook his head no. "Order from the baron. We need a ship."

The guard's expression visibly changed at that answer. He almost sagged where he stood.

Declan quickly said, "It's pretty quiet now from Marquenet down to here. The raiders seem to have left."

Bogartis said, "Besides, by all reports, these people have nowhere else to go."

The guard looked only a little relieved as he said to Bogartis, "Finding a ship is unlikely. Every captain in the city is doing the best he can to get people and their belongings away."

Bogartis said, "We'll manage." He smiled. "Pass the word the raiders have left." He looked around. "Stables?"

"A few, but the closest is over that way," said the guard, pointing south and west.

Bogartis wheeled his horse to face his company. "Sixto, take the horses to that stable." He pointed to a handful of the others. "Go with him. The rest of you, dismount and grab your kits."

The men quickly dismounted and Bogartis said to Sixto, "See what boarding will run to, and storage for the tack." He gave a slight bob with his head. "You know what to do."

Sixto nodded and moved swiftly to take the reins of three other mounts and led the four horses south. Other men followed, and soon ten of them led forty mounts down the street, working hard to keep them under control and not let them shy at the townspeople rushing past.

Bogartis looked up and down the street, then pointed to a nearby inn. "Declan, you take that one." He indicated with his chin another inn a bit farther down the road. "I'll take that one. See if you can find a broker, or captain, shipper, or whoever can give us a lead on a ship."

Declan said, "I'll see what I can find, then come to you?"

"Yes. And keep spreading word that the raids are over." Bogartis pointed to half the men and waved for them to follow.

The remainder followed Declan toward the inn. He glanced up and saw a painted sign, faded, but still visible, with a whale jumping over an anchor. "I assume," he muttered, "this would be the Whale and Anchor."

One of the men nearby chuckled.

As they entered the inn, they were surprised to find it almost empty. It was midday and Declan had expected there would be dockworkers eating and drinking. The barman shouted, "We don't have much!"

Declan glanced to his right and then left and motioned for the men to take seats at nearby tables. Reaching the bar, he asked, "So what do you have?"

"We've got a bit of cheese, some sausages, and perhaps enough ale for a mug or two for each of ya. Bread, fruit, vegetables, everything else has been gobbled up."

"People grabbing what they can?"

"No, at least not here," said the barman. "Just we haven't had any deliveries for nearly a week now, and we were due when all the trouble started. The local farmers have cleared out."

Declan nodded. All the farms they had passed for the last few days had been abandoned.

"And the two local bakers closed up and left a couple of days ago." The barman looked at Declan's men. "Even the gamblers, thieves, and whores have fled. I'm the only one here, so you'll have to wait a bit."

Declan said, "I've worked in an inn before. I'll fetch the ale while you get the food . . ."

"Litwick," answered the barman. "Name's Litwick."

Declan moved around the bar and found stacks of mugs and began filling them from the ale tap. "Before you run to the kitchen, where do we find a broker or ship's master?"

"No broker, but the captains are usually over at the Hungry

Tiger," he nodded in the direction Bogartis had headed toward, "or here at the Jumping Whale."

As Litwick vanished into the kitchen, Declan finished filling the first four mugs. "Jumping Whale," he muttered. "Well, I got that wrong."

THEY HAD SECURED A SHIP, the *Brigida*, a trading schooner just big enough to hold the company and supplies. Forty armed men, combined with an ample purse of the baron's gold, convinced the captain that a trip across to South Tembria was just the charter he needed, and he began refunding whatever payment he had taken to the locals who had sought passage. As Declan anticipated, once word spread that the attacks were over, people turned around and started ferrying their belongings back into town. Several men who lived here had approached both Bogartis and Declan in the inns asking if it was true and the reply that they were the baron's men, come from Marquenet, had been greeted with relief.

Bogartis had spent the balance of the previous day spreading the word that the baron was offering work and a safe haven in Marquenet for any skilled workers, and a berth for soldiers and sailors. By the time the company of mercenaries had boarded, activity at the dock had ceased and a line of those who had remained in the city could be seen leaving by the gate through which Declan and the company had entered. Bogartis had words with the baron's remaining troops and suggested they send a message asking whether they should stay or return to the capital as well.

The stable to which Sixto and the others had taken the horses was empty, and a quick tour of the small city revealed no lodgings for the mounts, as the other stables—livery or traders'—were

abandoned. With no one to buy the horses, the mercenaries rode them to the edge of a nearby meadow and turned them
loose. For a brief minute Declan pondered taking the time to
remove their iron shoes but decided these animals were of too
good quality to not be caught soon. Someone smart enough to
put out a bale of sweet feed and start roping them, then tying
them to a long lead line, would have them in tow in a few hours.
Declan suspected that person might even end up selling them
back to the baron.

Bogartis arranged to keep the tack stored with the proprietor
of the Jumping Whale and they boarded the ship.

Declan took a quick tour of the *Brigida*, feeling it necessary
to understand how best to defend it as if it were a fortress or
a town, simply as something he must do. He noticed Bogartis
also was considering the possibility of a sea attack. He moved to
stand beside the captain and asked, "Pirates?"

Bogartis nodded. "Ever fought at sea before?"

Declan shook his head.

"Few in our company have. I hate it. You not only have to
worry about some bastard lopping your head off, but the deck
is rolling under your feet, it's wet, sometimes there's a fire, and
there's more than enough debris scattered across the decks to
trip over. If they see you coming, they'll even lay traps aboard
their own ship should you drive them back: poisoned barbs, trip
wires, and other surprises.

"It's why most experienced pirates use big, heavy blades—
cutlasses and falchions, even big sabres. They come at you quick,
hacking away to keep you off balance, and there's little time for
skill."

"What do you do?" asked Declan.

"Don't let them get close if you can help it and skewer the bastards the second there's an opening. If you do get close, get closer, under their swing, and look for weak spots. Most pirates don't like wearing armor; it's a quick way to a drowning."

Declan nodded. "Thanks."

Bogartis said nothing, just letting out a long breath, almost a sigh. Declan wondered if that was fatigue or something else.

HAVA AWOKE TO FIND HATU's side of the bed empty. As soon as she had got him alone she'd pulled him into bed and after sex, they had bathed together. At some point after eating and more sex, they'd both fallen into a deep, contented sleep.

She looked out of the window and saw that the sky was lightening to the east and judged the sun would rise over the sea in less than half an hour. She knew exactly where Hatu would be and found herself angry with that realization.

Their childhood together had been controlled by the school unless they were given an assignment, either training or working with a crew, and then circumstances controlled what they did together and apart. But their short tenure together in Beran's Hill had changed things.

Their false marriage had originally been created for apparently conflicting reasons by Masters Zusara and Kugal, so that Hava could watch Hatu and kill him should he become a danger to the Kingdom of Night. Bodai's reason was to keep Hatu as far from the Council as possible to ensure his safety until the Flame Guard could abduct him and bring him here. During the brief time they had acted as a young couple setting up an inn and operating it, they had fallen into the habits of a married couple. They were up at dawn, preparing for the day's business, tending to travelers, cleaning up, everything needed. That routine had turned them into what they pretended to be, a married couple. The unique experience for them was that, except when Hatu took a wagon down to Marquenet for wine, whisky, barrels of ale, and occasionaly additional produce not found locally, they were together. Every minute.

Even when they had been in school as children, the girls and boys had been segregated when they were out of class, though occasionally they had time for some play. Hatu and Hava had gravitated toward each other, Hatu pulling Donte in his wake, and the three had become inseparable. Now she understood there was some larger purpose, that just by being with Hatushaly she had mitigated his dangerous potential. She was still unclear how that worked, and pretty much didn't care, because the time with him since they had reached Beran's Hill had deepened the bond to that of marriage in truth. She had gone through with the ceremony more than willingly, even with enthusiasm, though her nature prevented her from showing how much it meant. That and her training; and from that sprang her doubts.

She knew Hatu was as adept at hiding his feelings when a mask was demanded, despite his temper as a boy. Even Donte, who had the most insolent attitude she had ever seen in another student, could master a role when required.

She got out of bed and quickly dressed, making her way down the steps from their apartment above the main floor of the structure and then heading through a series of halls to the library. As she had expected, she found Hatushaly bent over the large volume he had magically saved the day before.

Hava stood motionless for a long moment, feeling an emptiness inside that was alien to her. Part of her wondered why it was so troubling. Another part of her was becoming angry, as she felt that if this was where he preferred to be, she'd prefer to eat alone.

Just as she turned to leave, he said, without taking his eyes off the page, "Come over here and look at this."

She was slightly surprised he had noticed her arrival, as more than anyone she had met Hatu could lose himself in study to the point of ignoring any distraction around him. He had quietly read books and scrolls while surrounded by workmen banging away on wood with hammers, breaking up stone with picks, seemingly oblivious to chaos around him.

She moved to stand just behind him and peered over his shoulder. "What?"

"Can you read this?"

Hava needed only a moment. "Like nothing I've seen before."

"It's Delk."

"What is that?"

"I don't know," answered Hatu with a furrowed brow. "All I know is the moment I opened the book and looked at the first page, I knew it was a language called Delk."

There had been enough unexpected revelations about Hatu's abilities since coming here that Hava didn't doubt this. "How?"

He shrugged. "I just knew."

"Can you read it?" Curiosity drove away her annoyance at his having left their bed early. She knew it would return, but at the moment she was as fascinated by his discovery as he was.

Hatu studied the oddly shaped symbols that crammed the page and finally said, "Sort of . . ." He stared at it and then in a hushed tone said, "It's like the . . . words are . . . explaining themselves. The longer I look, the more they begin to make sense."

From behind them a voice said, "What makes sense?"

It was Bodai.

He said, "Is that—"

"The book we fetched down yesterday," said Hatu.

"The one he caught," added Hava.

"And you can read it?" Bodai asked.

"I think so," Hatu replied after a moment.

"That's nothing I've seen before," said the old teacher.

Hava said, "I'm hungry. I expect neither of you are, correct?"

Saying nothing, they simultaneously waved her away without taking their eyes off the page.

Hava shook her head in resignation. "Of course."

As she turned to depart the vaulted library, a flash of color caught her eye. She took a step over to one of the shelves and reached out, grabbing an orange. "Bodai . . ." she said.

Bodai and Hatu turned to look at her. "What?" asked the teacher.

She tossed the orange underhand to Bodai. "Eating while you work?"

Bodai caught the fruit and inspected it. "Not mine." He looked at Hatu.

"Not mine either," Hatu said. "One of the workers we had removing some rubble must have put it there and forgotten it. We've got lots of oranges from Marquensas."

Bodai nodded as Hatu returned his attention to the large tome, and Hava departed.

The old man looked at the orange again. He turned from Hatu and walked a short distance away, behind another shelf.

He gave the orange a sniff and then stuck his thumb into the skin, peeling it back. He pulled off the loose peel until the flesh within was revealed. It was a dark orange in color. A quick bite and he savored the sweetness.

He slowly looked around the library as if seeking something and then down at the partially eaten orange in his hand. Softly he said, "You are delicious, but you are not from Marquensas."

He slowly returned to where Hatu still sat on the floor, hunched over, and realized that his student hadn't noticed him moving away. With a slight shake of his head, he walked over to an old chair next to a large wooden table that had been uncovered when the debris had been removed and sat down slowly. Shifting his weight back, he let out a long breath and pulled out another wedge of orange which he popped into his mouth while he pondered the sudden appearance of this unexpected snack.

2

AN UNEXPECTED ARRIVAL,

REQUEST, AND ESCAPES

D onte looked toward the gate as a company of riders came through, dust-coated and exhausted. The horses also seemed close to ruin. For a brief moment he stood confused: they wore one sort of garb, but instinctively he knew that this was a company of trained light cavalry.

In the lead were two men, both dressed as commoners, but from the quality of their horses and tack, they were not, or they were exceptionally enterprising horse thieves. Given their armed escort, he assumed they were nobles traveling incognito.

Curiosity overcame his concern about the guards, especially as Deakin wasn't on duty today. Donte and the soldier who had tried to garrote him had unfinished business: both knew it, and when circumstances warranted one or the other would be dead. The other soldiers in the garrison had no idea of the enmity that Donte held in check, which was rare for a young man renowned for his temper and lack of impulse control back home, but when strongly motivated, Donte could restrain himself if he needed to.

He finished settling a large stone into place, having mastered some basic skills in the mason's trade, constructing new walls in the city of Marquenet. He had no love for stonework, but he had come to appreciate the skills needed to do masonry well.

Donte was not studious or as curious about how things worked as Hatu, or even Hava, but he did pick up skills quickly. It was his grandfather, Master Kugal, who had almost literally beaten into him the dictum that to do something, and not do it well, was a failure. His grandson might not do a task as well as another, but he must do it as well as he could.

Donte had also come to take personal pride in having hidden skills. He was almost as good an archer as Hava and Hatu, though only he knew that, and he could successfully play many roles, at least at apprentice level, such as cook, carpenter, skinner and tanner, blacksmith, and dyer. Now he could add apprentice mason to his list.

Seeing the stone was properly fitted, he turned away and headed down the steps to where more work remained, but instead of fetching another stone, he moved with purpose to where the riders were pulling up. He had learned very young that people who appear to be about some immediate business were mostly ignored compared to people lingering aimlessly, skulking in doorways or loitering at corners.

No one attempted to halt him as he reached the gate in the old wall surrounding the baron's castle and saw the troop of riders had reined in. He continued to walk as close to the wall as possible, then turned as if examining an item on a workbench that had been neglected since this portion of the old wall was repaired. He pretended to measure the keenness of a chisel's edge while listening.

Donte could hear voices, though not every word was clear. He put down the chisel and picked up an abandoned set of callipers, used to measure smaller stones, and then an empty sack, slinging it over his right shoulder. He moved slightly closer to the riders, pausing over a pile of discarded stones, then knelt, pretending to measure a decent-sized piece, before putting it in the sack. He slipped to the side of the gate, then moved past a guard who threw him a momentary glance and continued a short way to another pile of rocks.

A quick examination confirmed the riders were not mere mercenaries, but elite soldiers or household guards. While their manner of dress, and even their mounts' tack, varied there was a uniformity to their demeanor he'd never seen in mercenary bands. And the horses and tack, their weapons and boots were all well-tended and of high quality. If these were mercenary guards, they were better paid than any he had encountered, Donte thought with amusement, and he had met many during his youthful travels.

He lingered at the gate for a few minutes, picking up snatches of conversation, but little of what he heard made sense. He confirmed these were personal guards of someone important, from the east. That much he had assumed just by the likely origin of their travel—no one of importance close by hadn't already reached Marquenet. Still, as he meandered past the gate on his return, he did hear one word that made the hair on his neck stand on end: "church."

Like all of those from Coaltachin, Donte's distrust of the Church of the One was ingrained from birth. They were a rising power, with no apparent allegiance to a single place, but rather to a belief, and they were establishing influence in an ever-expanding sphere, with an agenda none of the Masters of the Kingdom of Night could fathom. If someone of rank from that church was here to see the baron, something even worse than what Donte had witnessed so far was possible.

His strong reaction was followed by a momentary confusion that literally caused him to stop moving, as he thought he heard something spoken in the language of his own home, Coaltachin. It had been whispered. He quickly tried to determine by whom but when he focused on it, he found silence, then muttering in the language of Sandura, answered by something in another language he didn't understand.

Shaking his head slightly as he gathered himself and moved away, he put aside his momentary distraction and concentrated on what was right before him, the retinue of a very important noble probably speaking with the baron on some critical matter.

Donte knew that soon whatever was being discussed up in that castle would be the foundation of gossip from one end of the city to the other. How accurate it was would depend on what level of secrecy the baron demanded, so the value of such gossip was dubious at best.

Donte saw that the sun was setting and knew that soon the work crews would be ushered into the large mess. While the guards might be a bit lax when the work was underway—too many prisoners in the workforce moving from one place to another—there would be a head count and his absence would be noticed. Deciding he had better return to his work, he was about to move past the waiting horsemen when a voice from behind him shouted, "Donte!"

He turned to see Balven standing next to a sergeant whose name escaped him at the moment, but there was no mistaking the tone of voice of the man who was second only to the baron in importance in Marquensas.

"Sir?"

"Drop those tools and come with me."

Donte shrugged and did as instructed, his mind racing between two thoughts: first, this gave him a perfect reason not to be at his assigned job should he be missed, and second, he wondered what possible trouble he could be in at this time, given he'd done nothing but what he was told since the last time Balven interrogated him.

DONTE SAT WHERE BALVEN INDICATED. The adviser to the baron put a finger to his lips, indicating silence. Donte thought this a strange-looking room, with a single chair, a writing desk, and a very odd metal cylinder protruding from the wall with a rubber ringed stopper in it. Balven removed the stopper, again indicating the need for silence. It took Donte a moment to realize he could hear voices through the metal tube, and he leaned closer to the opening. When his ear was less than an inch from it, those voices became clear enough that he could follow what they said. Donte had spent enough time being schooled in spycraft—even if he hadn't always paid close attention—to know that this tube was connected somehow to another room close by, so the baron's agent could eavesdrop on whoever was in that room, and the writing desk was there so he could transcribe what he heard. He smiled in appreciation.

Balven leaned close and whispered in his other ear. "Once the stopper is removed, sound from this room will carry down below, so listen closely, and mark what is said. Make notes here should you need to, but as long as that stopper is out make no sound as if your life depended on silence, because it does."

Donte let out a long-held breath as Balven left the room. He had no idea why he was the one who had to listen but suspected it would prove to be something significant. One thing he did know: if it was important, there might be a way he could turn this task to his own benefit, just as not doing as he was told would bring harsh results.

He had always been a fractious child, taking unnecessary risks for the sheer pleasure of defying authority, even when it led to a beating. Still, since he had been captured by the Sisters of the Deep and set on a new course, to find Hatushaly and kill him—for reasons he still did not remotely understand—he was learning that the rebellious behavior of his younger days was often not useful. He considered that just a year earlier he would have likely waited a few minutes, then peered out of the door to see if there was a possible escape route, even this deep in the castle.

He knew eventually he needed to leave; looking for Hatu was a slight itch, often forgotten, but always returning. If he left . . . *when* he left, he amended to himself, he'd rather do it at leisure, not running from a company of the baron's soldiers.

Donte resigned himself to learning more patience and entertaining fewer impulsive choices and turned his attention to the listening port. He heard a door opening and a voice saying, "Your Eminence. This is unexpected." Donte recognized the baron's voice.

"My lord," said another man, whom Donte presumed was the one addressed as Eminence. "Circumstances forced me to arrive as a supplicant; I, with my retainers, seek sanctuary."

There was a moment of silence, and Donte could only imagine what was occurring, but he suspected this request was shocking enough to keep Baron Daylon and his half-brother silent for a moment.

Donte adjusted his chair and settled in.

Baron Daylon Dumarch could not hide his astonishment. Since the slaughter of his family, his every waking minute had been colored by dark thoughts of revenge. Even returning Marquensas to a semblance of its old prosperity was to serve his mission, which was to build a vast fleet to carry a massive army across the sea and crush those who had taken away everything he cherished, but in this one instance his surprise was so profound even that dark desire was banished.

He turned away from Episkopos Bernardo Delnocio and looked at Balven, who clearly also couldn't conceal his amazement. They simply looked at one another for a long moment, then Balven gave his brother a slight nod, which both men knew meant, "We should talk about this later in private."

With a wave of his hand, Daylon indicated that the episkopos should sit as servants entered through the open door, bearing refreshments. The baron and Bernardo sat down. No one spoke while being served and eventually the servants departed.

Balven took up his usual position, standing at Daylon's right, and spared a moment to study the short man who stood at the prelate's right. He knew him by reputation as Marco Belli, rumored a dangerous man: spy, assassin, and master of a lethal network of agents. There were stories about him that defied belief, yet Balven knew all such stories were founded in truth.

Despite rumors about Belli, there was no doubt that his master, Bernardo, was as powerful a figure within the Church of the One as existed. That had been Balven's assumption until a few moments earlier when Bernardo Delnocio had requested sanctuary.

Balven's first concern was his brother's safety. He had Donte listening in to catch anything that might reference the part played by the Kingdom of Night, or by these mysterious Azhante, for just that reason. This Episkopos of the Church of the One currently posed no threat to Daylon, here in the heart of his own keep. There were guards outside the door who would be through in an instant should they be called, but just the mere presence of both Bernardo Delnocio and Marco Belli made Balven fear

more danger was on its way, perhaps even more than the invasion had posed.

"Sanctuary?" said Daylon at last. "I must say it's more surprising a request than any I could imagine. I've met with some of
your . . . former"—he raised a questioning eyebrow, and Bernardo
nodded—"co-religionists over the years." He paused, then said,
"You are welcome to rest, but given our recent invasion, you'll
understand that I'm cautious of any guest. We'll try to make you
comfortable for a few days, though Marquenet is hardly what it
once was, but still, we shall try to be worthy hosts.

"But sanctuary implies you're in need of protection and that
is something I'm hardly in any position to offer. Your reputation
reached even to our distant halls, and as you were reputed to
be a very powerful man within your church, I assume you now
have powerful enemies." He paused, then in an emphatic tone
added, "The one thing I most certainly do not need now is more
enemies." He paused again and continued more calmly, "So, why
don't you assume I know nothing, and tell me the story?"

"It's a very long story, my lord, and I must confess not a story
I wish to tell, but necessity drives us often in directions we do
not wish to take. That is why we are here, now.

"As I said, it's a long story but in the end, you'll know how to
best prepare for what is certainly coming next. To begin with,
I am betrayed by my allies. Or if not true allies, people against
whom I thought I had no cause, or they against me." He visibly
sagged a little in his chair and his tone indicated uncertainty.
"At least so I was led to believe."

Daylon said nothing, but with a small wave of his hand indicated that Bernardo should continue.

"So, you might understand who was behind the sacking of every
town and village along your coast, as well as the coast along the

Narrows. And . . ."—Bernardo paused—"what I suspect is their next assault, and more importantly, where they are." Again, he paused. "And who they are."

Daylon sat back. "Take as much time as you need, Your Eminence."

Bernardo picked up a cup from the tray of refreshments placed at his side and took a sip. After gathering his thoughts, he said, "To understand I must tell you of a distant . . . nation, or group of nations, far across the sea, and of a people known as Azhante."

UPSTAIRS, NEXT TO THE LISTENING tube, Donte was struggling to keep his mind on the conversation below. All his life he had heard stories of this lord or that noble betraying this friend or that ally and the two becoming enemies. Destruction and bloodshed always resulted, and all those stories revolved around the role played by the Quelli Nascosti, the Hidden Ones, the highest rank obtainable by any student in Coaltachin. As nothing said was unique in Donte's experience, he was nevertheless impressed at the depth of betrayal revealed by Bernardo Delnocio, needing to flee for his life.

A few questions from the baron and then Delnocio uttered a word that made the hair on the back of Donte's neck stand up: "Azhante."

Without thought, he jammed the stopper back into the mouth of the listening tube, and was out of his seat and trying the door, only to find it locked. He balled his fist and pounded on it to get the attention of the guards that must be stationed outside. "Hey!" he shouted.

He heard a key rattling in the lock and stepped back as the door swung open. "What?" demanded a leathery-faced guard whose wary expression indicated he was ready for any sudden move Donte might make to escape.

Another guard peered over his shoulder, also poised to fight.

"One of you get word to Balven. I need to see him as soon as he's free."

"He's with the baron," said the first guard.

"He'll get to you when he's ready," said the other.

"I know where he is. This can't wait," Donte said, his temper rising. Recognizing that a brawl with two guards was not his best choice, he spoke with his jaw tightening. "Get word to him, now. I have something he needs to hear as soon as he can!"

Donte's body trembled with barely contained anger, but he took a small step backward and in a stride was back in the chair, his ear close to the listening port. He knew Balven would come to get him eventually, once this interview with "His Eminence" was concluded, but he didn't know how soon.

"Wait just now—" said the first guard, taking a step toward Donte.

Holding up his hand, Donte hissed, "Silence. I'm listening. Get a message to Balven now, or you'll be guarding a work gang rebuilding the sewers, or worse."

The guard's expression turned from one of ire at the demand to confusion. Whatever he had expected, to be told to get the most powerful man in the baron's court, then be told to shut up so the prisoner could hear faint voices coming out of a metal cup in the wall, wasn't it. So, he hesitated. Then he chose to do what soldiers had done since the dawn of armies, find a sergeant and let him decide what to do.

WITHIN A FEW MINUTES, THE soldier returned one step behind a sergeant in the tabard of the baron's household guard. Before the man could speak, Donte held up his hand again, then turned and said, "Balven put me here to listen . . ."—he pointed at the open metal port—". . . and I just heard something he needs to talk to me about *now*! Send him a note . . ." Donte felt like he was swallowing a rock, but he forced himself to add, ". . . please, Sergeant."

Something in his tone convinced the sergeant and he said nothing for a moment but turned to the soldier who had brought him. "Stay here."

The soldier said, "What should—"

"Shut up!" demanded Donte.

The soldier looked back over his shoulder at Donte, uncertain if he should deal with that order, then at the sergeant who shook his head in a warning to not start trouble, pointing to a spot just outside the door. The soldier nodded acknowledgment and closed the door behind him, leaving Donte concentrating on what was being said in the room below.

BALVEN ENTERED A FEW MINUTES after Donte heard the meeting end, with the man addressed as Eminence being escorted to some apartment set aside for visitors, or a cell in the dungeon—Donte wasn't sure what "suitable quarters" meant.

Balven waved away the guard outside and said, "I'm assuming the note was not sent frivolously."

Donte wasn't certain what Balven meant by frivolously, but he said, "I don't know what the note said, but if you're asking was it important, yes." He paused for a moment, his brow starting to furrow as he realized he knew what he wanted to say but had given no thought to how he was going to say it. After a moment, he began, "That man, Eminence—"

"That's a form of address," interrupted Balven. "Until recently, he was a very important man in the Church of the One, by the name of Bernardo Delnocio, and an episkopos is a rank."

Donte nodded. "I think I've heard of that." He waved off that thought as soon as he said it and continued, "He mentioned the Azhante. I've heard that word before and if it is what I think it is, what it means, this is a very dangerous thing for the baron."

"What is dangerous?" asked Balven.

"Letting that man, Bernardo, stay here."

"Why?"

"I knew I should have thought more about this . . ." Donte's expression of frustration was obvious. "You know Hatushaly and Hava," he began.

Balven nodded.

"I'm not as clever as they are." Donte's declaration looked both painful and sincere. "Hava is smart, and she watches, and she listens . . ." He realized he was getting away from what he wanted to say. "Hava is smart," he repeated, "but no one is as smart as Hatushaly. He knows a lot and remembers everything he sees and hears . . ." Recognizing he was still not getting his point across, as Balven seemed on the verge of interrupting again, he said, "No matter what people think, I'm not stupid. I just like it when people think I don't know what's happening around me."

Balven fixed Donte with a narrowing gaze, then nodded.

"I always liked being around Hatu, because he was always angry about something, always impatient to know things, so I could play the part of Hatu's stupid friend Donte. One thing they teach us early is distraction. Misdirection, so people you're robbing are not paying attention. But I know things even they don't know. Because sometimes people think I'm too stupid to understand, they say things around me they shouldn't."

Balven nodded, and asked, "What does this have to do with the note you sent?"

"That word, *Azhante*. I am not supposed to know that word.

Only the masters understand its true meaning. My grandfather is a master, and has spoken of it to others, and twice I was nearby. He thought I was drunk, or asleep, but I heard.

"There are people called Azhante, and even the best students are never meant to hear that name. A few of the very highest in the nocusara, the Quelli Nascosti, know, but not even the oldest preceptor knows it; it's knowledge only the seven masters and a few others have. Perhaps ten men." He looked at Balven, and a look of genuine concern crossed his face. "I don't know exactly who these Azhante are, but they are people the highest among my people speak about in fear, and then only in hushed voices, and if that man, Bernardo, had them in his employ, they are very likely close and they are deadly."

Balven stood silently, considering what Donte said for what seemed a long time, then nodded. "I had you listening because you are from the Kingdom of Night. I knew the Great Betrayal was conceived by King Lodavico, as did the baron. Now I have some sense of the role the Church of the One played, though why they would choose chaos over order is a matter of speculation."

Donte's brashness reasserted itself and he looked at Balven with an expression bordering on disbelief. "Really? They may have specific aims I know nothing about, but it's generally true that out of chaos comes opportunity."

Balven smiled ruefully. "You are indeed smarter than you let on." His expression revealed genuine appreciation. "But the question is, an opportunity for what? And if not the Church, by whom?"

Donte sat back in the chair and nodded. "I'm not an expert on history, but it seems to me that if someone is manipulating the Church of the One and a kingdom like Sandura, they have to be very powerful, with vast riches and resources. People like that would have to be behind the raids here."

Balven conceded the validity of Donte's observations. He looked at the young man and then queried, "And then, why did they just leave?"

"Many things I do not fully understand, but this much I can work out on my own." He paused and took a deep breath. "For generations my people have fashioned myths about the Ghost Assassins, the phantoms in the night, the great danger of our Hidden Ones, legends that are based on some reality. Of all people on the Twin Continents, the people of Coaltachin are the most feared. And the only people *we* fear are the Azhante."

Balven sat motionless for a time then said, "Is there nothing more you know?"

Donte said, "No, and what I have just told you puts a death mark on me at home. Even my own grandfather, I think, would see me dead for giving you that information."

Both were silent for several minutes, then Donte asked, "Should I go now?"

Balven laughed. "Oh, no. I'm keeping you close by just in case you're of a mind not to stay here in the city."

Donte nodded. "I do have an . . . itch to be on my way," he replied honestly. He looked around the room as if seeking something far away, through the walls.

"To where?"

"Wherever Hatu went."

Balven's expression turned quizzical. "You said you were close, but why him?"

Donte looked slightly confused. "Just . . . I need to."

"We have word that he and Hava were last seen in Beran's Hill, Hatu during the battle, and Hava riding north with our advance units after carrying word to us of the coming attack. Then, apparently, she went on to Port Calos, to find him. After that, no one has seen them." Balven decided not to mention the baron's specific interest in Hatushaly, as heir to the Firemane line.

Donte cocked his head as if listening for a moment. "They're still alive." Then he quickly added, "At least he is."

"Why are you certain?"

"If he was dead . . . I would know it."

Balven looked around the small study then went to the guard standing just outside the door and said, "Get me a chair. I am tired of standing."

After a minute, the guard appeared with a chair and Balven said, "Leave us and close the door."

Oblivious to any hint of protocol, Donte said, "I'm hungry."

Balven looked at him with wide eyes, then he laughed. He said to the guard, "Send for food and wine. We may be here a while."

The guard said, "Sir," and left, closing the door.

Balven leaned back. "Well, then. Tell me everything about Hatushaly you know, what you suspect, and anything else about these Azhante that may come back to you."

Donte shifted in his chair. "I'm not going back to the work gang?"

"Not anytime soon."

Donte's smile expressed relief. "Someone needs to tell the captain of the guard detail, or they'll send people out looking for me."

"Already seen to. When I brought you here, I anticipated the possibility of needing to keep you around."

"To what end?" asked Donte.

Balven's furrowed brow and slightly pained smile hinted at both his annoyance and amusement. "Are you always this familiar with nobility?"

Donte shrugged again. "To what end, sir?"

Balven laughed at that. "You are incorrigible."

Donte nodded. "So says my grandfather . . . sir."

The door opened and the soldier reappeared with food and wine which he put on the small table, then left the room.

Balven indicated that Donte should help himself. Donte poured a goblet of wine and with the tip of the bottle to the second cup and raising his eyebrows silently inquired if Balven would join him.

"Later, I think," said the baron's brother. "Now, put aside the question of the Azhante for a moment; what do you know about Hatushaly and why are you certain he's alive?"

THE PASSAGE HAD BEEN PEACEFUL but not without tense moments. Declan had never spent this much time on a ship in his entire life, though he had spent most of that life within sight of the ocean. He had come to know the *Brigida* as well as he knew his own forge by the time they reached South Tembria.

The run from the tip of the western peninsula of Marquensas to the shore of Zindaros, the westernmost kingdom of South Tembria, was the longest leg of the journey out of sight of land. The *Brigida* was a coaster, a trading schooner which the captain usually kept close to shore, and only the promise of a rich fee had convinced him to make a deep-water run like this. He had made it once before as a crewman on another ship, and once again on the *Brigida*, and wasn't anxious to make it a third time until Bogartis had raised his offer.

After a week heading due south, they made landfall and turned westward, skirting the coastal towns, close enough to see if the raiders had come this far.

Some of the larger towns showed signs of depredation, while

some of the small villages looked untouched. Nowhere did they see any evidence of the wholesale destruction Declan had witnessed in Beran's Hill.

Ships were seen every day, mostly distant sails, but a few close enough to be identified, small- to medium-sized cargo ships; this was far more traffic in the area than was expected, according to the captain. Declan and Bogartis both assumed most were fleeing the assaults in the north, but at least three times ships put on extra sail and bore down on the *Brigida*, only to veer off when they got close enough to see forty armed men on the decks. Marauders, Declan judged, looking for easier prey.

The captain had put into a good-sized town for fresh water and purchased provisions from a local merchant. Bogartis had kept his men aboard, against the possibility of any surprises. After loading fresh water and food on the ship, they had continued west until reaching the tip of the land, when they rounded the point and headed southeast. The captain shared word that raiders had cruised this coast weeks before, but it seemed as if they were more intent on keeping people on land, than actual sacking.

Crossing a vast bay, they reached the first sight of land two days later, which Bogartis said was the Range of the Border Tribes. Nomads who were loyal to no king or baron, they were free traders and horsemen who were by reputation matchless cavalry.

"Should we be passing word to them about the baron building his army?"

Bogartis laughed, genuinely amused. "At best they'd rob anyone who approached them, or more likely rob him, then stake him out over an anthill for amusement. And they have nasty types of ants this close to the Burning Lands, big red bastards that can raise a welt the size of a jacket button.

"No, the only time you can parley with any of those marauders is if they come into a town to trade. They tend to be on good behavior then, as they want to be welcomed back, but that's the only time. They consider the grasslands, lakes, hills, and valleys from this coast to the mountains west of Metros theirs, and while they may scrap among themselves and steal each other's women and horses, feud and such, they'll band together as one against any outsiders."

Declan said, "Still, they sound like good fighters to have on our side."

"If you believe in miracles, such as the Church of the One teaches, that would be a good one to have, my friend," Bogartis said.

Declan stayed at the rail for a long time after Bogartis left his side, wondering if such a thing as a miracle existed and what it would take to arrange one.

DECLAN WAS STANDING WATCH AT the bow. To the west he could see the vague outlines of islands, and he knew from Edvalt's instructions to him after gaining his master-smith rank that among them was one special source of the rare sand that was needed to make the finest steel known to any smith on Garn. They would need a quick rest, and then he and a few handpicked men from Bogartis's company would be off to secure enough of that sand to forge swords for an army. And that army would visit vengeance on those who had taken everything Declan loved from him.

As they neared the port of Abala, Bogartis came to stand next to Declan. "Something's going on."

Declan grunted his agreement. There were half a dozen ships anchored offshore, and several boats ferrying people and cargo from the land. "This look familiar?" Bogartis asked.

"Too familiar," said Declan. "Toranda, again."

"As soon as we drop anchor, we start ferrying the men ashore. It's going to be a while before the ship is provisioned, and we need a smaller boat, from what the captain's said about those islands. This ship draws too deep to be safe. And every one of us needs to stretch our legs on dry land."

Declan nodded. "Agreed." He paused, then said, "I grew up on the coast in the Covenant. I know what type of boat to seek. We'll need half a dozen men, some shovels, and a very large lined box or a crate we can put large bags in. If I remember Edvalt's instructions exactly, it should be three or four days, there and back."

Bogartis took a coin pouch out of his belt, hefting it to determine how much he had, then took a second pouch out and compared them. He gave one to Declan and said, "Buy what you need. Take Sixto and four others. Meet back before sunset at whatever inn is closest to where we put in." He made a sweeping gesture toward the very busy harbor. "I'll go with the captain to see about provisions for a return trip north and see what all this is about."

"I think it doesn't bode well."

Bogartis looked at Declan and said, "Not much sign of attack along this coast, so let's hope this is merely as it was in Toranda: rumors stirring panic."

"I hope that's all it is," agreed Declan.

But something cold in the pit of his stomach told him that was not likely.

DECLAN INSPECTED A TWENTY-FIVE-FOOT LONGBOAT fitted with four rowlocks, three benches, a tiller, and a mast that could be easily raised or taken down while on the water. Two long spars lay next to it, and the design was unfamiliar to Declan.

He pointed it out and asked, "How's she rigged?"

The boat merchant looked surprised at the question. "Fore-and-aft, crab claw."

One of the men behind Declan said, "I've sailed them."

Declan looked over his shoulder and saw that the speaker was a man named Toombs, a tall, broad-shouldered fighter with grey streaks in his light brown hair and beard. Declan said, "I've seen square and lateen before, but I don't know this."

"Don't see them much up in the north," said Sixto. "I've seen them down along the Zindaros coast a few times."

Toombs said, "You'll get the knack after a few hours."

"It's not hard to master," offered the merchant. There was a frantic tone to his voice: apparently, he wanted the sale concluded as quickly as possible, as he might be among those anxious to leave. "I'll give her to you for what I paid!"

He was a stocky man who had apparently been given to gaudy jewelry, evidenced by several pale bands of skin on his fingers and around his neck, where rings and necklaces would have blocked the hot sun. His clothing was expensive, but dirty and sweat-stained, as if he hadn't changed for days.

Declan said, "And that would be how much?"

Before the man could answer, a voice cried out from north of where they stood, and within seconds other voices rose in alarm. It was a sound all too familiar to Declan and his companions, and as one they turned to face the source of the commotion.

"Raiders!" was repeated by several people as others started running frantically.

Declan turned in time to reach out and grab the merchant before he could flee. Yanking the man around, Declan shouted, "Is there a gate that way?" He indicated the southeast end of the city with a jerk of his chin.

"A small gate, a way to go to the shore and fish . . . to dump trash! Beyond are the Burning Lands! Now let me go!" He pulled hard and with a tear of his once-expensive shirt, slipped Declan's grasp and ran.

Declan said, "We must find the others."

"Where?" asked Sixto.

"Bogartis will head for that inn he mentioned, I think."

Declan hurried along, dodging people fleeing to the wharf. One glance toward the harbor told him those arriving there would find no escape. Boats were casting off and heading toward ships moored farther out, some of which appeared to already be preparing to depart, dropping sails and raising anchors.

Minutes later, as they neared the inn where they were to rendezvous, Declan saw Bogartis leading a party of men, the rest of his company and perhaps another dozen armed fighters Declan didn't recognize. Before Declan could speak, Bogartis shouted, "Is there a gate?"

Instantly Declan understood and said, "A small one to the south!"

"Run!" was the command, and Declan without hesitation turned and started fleeing with a few city folks who also seemed to know there was a way to leave the city. Within minutes they reached a clutch of people trying to force their way through a small gate, big enough for a good-sized wagon to pass through, but now clogged with citizens elbowing their way past each other, nearly trampling those ahead who had slowed down.

Bogartis roughly grabbed a big man who was shoving a child aside, turned him, and with a backhand blow sent him to the ground almost senseless. He reached over and grabbed the child, a small boy in shorts and tunic, and handed him to a frantic-looking woman, who gave him a brief look of thanks then half-carried, half-dragged the boy to the gate.

Through the gate Bogartis beckoned the mercenaries to turn eastward, past a mountain of rubbish and away from those fleeing south along the coast. He stopped a short distance away and when everyone had caught up with him, took a moment to catch his breath, then looked at one of the fighters Declan didn't know. "What now, Benruf?"

"They will die," said the stranger, nodding toward the fleeing city people.

Declan assumed he was the leader of the newcomers, and from his accent and dress took him to be from Zindaros. A few men like this had passed through Oncon during his days there.

"Either the men of the Border Tribes will hunt them down, or they will die of thirst. There is no drinkable water that way."

Declan understood. Drinkable water came from the mountains, or hills above the sea, but here beyond the endless field of rubbish and the tide pools filled with slops and crabs, there would be no drinkable water.

"What next?" asked Bogartis.

"Most likely, we die," said Benruf. "We have a choice. We walk into the Burning Lands and die if we don't find an oasis, or we wait here for the raiders from the Border Tribes. A slow death or a quick one?"

Another man in Benruf's group said, "We can go down fighting."

Bogartis looked around and pointed to a large rise. "We wait there."

Benruf's pained expression was accompanied by a plaintive question. "Why would I wish to trudge up that sandy slope to die, when I can wait here and rest before death greets me?"

"Because I don't intend to die," said Bogartis as he moved toward the base of the large slope.

"Then what, hide behind the ridge, as if no tracks can be followed?"

"No, I plan on standing on top of the ridge, and invite any who follow to come fight."

"Why, in the name of the gods?" asked Benruf.

Bogartis said, "Because I intend to kill them and take their horses."

Benruf's eyes widened a bit, his expression brightened, and he said, "Now that is a plan I like, Captain." By that address, he let his own men know Bogartis would be in charge. He waved to his men to follow and Declan and the rest of his company fell in next to them. Without giving his concern any voice, Declan knew Bogartis's plan would be decided by just how many horsemen came through that gate to hunt down those fleeing.

Still, it was a plan, and any plan was better than running away from riders or dying in the desert. He felt his legs starting to burn as he slogged up the slope, his feet sinking into the sand. Then he understood Bogartis's plan. In this sand, the horses would become useless. Without hardpan to cross, they couldn't charge.

Bogartis reached the crest and a moment later the others were alongside him, stretched out in a line to wait. Smoke was now rising from the city and despite the heat, a chill ran through Declan's body as the memory of the fight at Beran's Hill struck him. And with that memory came a cold from within, and he knew he would be killing men today.

He felt a smile spreading across his face.

"Bowmen?" asked Bogartis, between deep breaths from the climb. Three men unslung bows from their backs and strung them. "Stand behind the rest of us," he ordered, "and when we move out of your way, take out as many riders as you can."

Declan realized that the horses trapped up to their hocks in

sand would make the riders easy targets before they understood
they needed to dismount. It was obvious, but no one else had
thought of it besides Bogartis. Declan felt a sudden certainty that
the captain would get them through this. He looked around and
saw a few faces were missing from the company who had set out
from the north. But the newcomers had increased the size of the
waiting fighters.

They did as they were ordered, while Bogartis positioned half
the mercenaries in a single line at the peak of the rise, then the
others down out of sight a short way behind them, flanking the
three bowmen in the center. Without any spoken order, Declan
realized Bogartis was attempting to lure the raiders into charging by presenting a smaller company than they actually had atop
the rise and surrounding the archers to protect them as long as
possible. Declan looked from one end of the line to the other,
and saw they now numbered forty-nine swords, all at the ready.

They waited.

3

FLIGHT, DECISIONS,

AND PARTINGS

The sound of screaming, panic-stricken people faded, and the clatter of shod hooves striking stones grew louder. Declan realized that most of the people in this part of the city were already through the gate below or dead. A few might be hiding as best they could, but they would be silent.

He watched the gate keenly, waiting for the raiders to appear. From the sound he calculated there were probably a few dozen men in the raiding party, and a moment later as the first horsemen rode through the narrow gate, his assumption proved accurate. The riders in the vanguard slowed as they saw Bogartis's company atop the distant rise, and one shouted back over his shoulder at those following.

It took only a few moments before Declan realized these were fine horsemen, but not trained soldiers. He could tell by the manner in which they moved their excited, even fractious, horses through the gate, controlling them effortlessly with knee and leg pressure, shifting their weight on their backs as they quickly wheeled in behind the first pair of riders who had waited near the bottom of the sandy hill.

They were dressed in a simple fashion, wearing leather or cloth breeches, some cut at the knees, no heavy boots that he could see, but what looked to be soft leather slippers or moccasins, and their shirts appeared to be a mix of buckskin, cured leather, or cloth purchased from traders. A few were bare-chested or wore only waistcoats.

The first thing that struck Declan was they were all clean-shaven, but their hair had been done up in a huge range of styles. Some wore it flowing past their shoulders, some loose, some plaited, others sported shaved skulls but with a tall roach of hair down the middle, many colored with dye. And every man wore jewelry: rings in ears and noses, or tiny spikes of metal and gems pierced through eyebrows, cheeks, or chins. A few bore tattoos rather than piercings, but this was easily the most colorful company of fighting men Declan had ever beheld.

Despite his initial notice of their odd dress, he concentrated on their weapons. Two he could see had small shields on their left arms, strapped there so the left hand was free for the reins. The rest had only a sword or axe in the right hand.

"I count two bowmen," said Sixto.

Without taking his eyes from the assembled raiders below, Bogartis said to the crouching archers behind him, "Take out those two. One is directly ahead off my left side, the other is a few points to the right of him." To the rest of his company, he said, "As soon as I give word, everyone duck. Don't give those archers large targets."

The riders below parted, forming a path allowing another horse-man to come forward. Declan instantly saw he was their leader. He wore a black leather waistcoat over a bright red shirt, and alone of the men assembling below, he sported black boots. Declan judged them to be a prize taken off a soldier the man had killed.

Bogartis said to the bowmen hidden behind, "Once you take out their archers, their leader wears a red shirt and black weskit. Kill him as soon as possible."

Benruf said, "That is their chieftain. Kill him and they may withdraw." Then he took a deep breath and said, "But that may prove difficult."

As the last riders gathered below, Declan judged that his forces were outnumbered by at least a dozen men. He hoped the bowmen behind him were good. He wished for a moment that the young woman from Beran's Hill, Molly Bowman, were here. She might be a little strange of manner, but from what he'd seen and heard she would have had both archers below and the leader off their horses in no time. She might even have leveled the number of fighters by the time the attackers crested the ridge, if the praises of her skills were to be believed.

The leader of the horsemen held up his sword, then waved it above his head in a circle, and pointed at Bogartis's company, ordering the attack. As expected, after a few yards, the horses encountered deeper sand and suddenly slowed. Some sank to their withers, while others just had to pull high from the hocks, but all were halted abruptly.

"Wait!" said Bogartis.

The two horse-archers below unleashed shots which rose high and landed a few yards shy of where Declan and the others waited.

"Ready," said Bogartis. "They'll have our range next time!"

Almost before the words were out of his mouth, two more arrows were arching downward, and Declan moved a step away from the one heading in his general direction. That struck the sand a few feet from him, while the other grazed a man on the other side of Bogartis, eliciting a grunt of pain and an oath.

As the riders headed up the hill, the horses began to stumble and falter. Declan and the others crouched at the ready, as arrows intermittently threatened them. By the time Bogartis judged the horse-archers close enough, two of his company had been felled.

"Now!" he shouted, and Declan moved aside to let one of the three bowmen past. Looking over the archer's shoulder, Declan saw him take a bead on the leftmost of the two bowmen on horseback and let fly. The shot was true, and that raider tumbled out of the saddle.

Declan glanced to his right and saw two arrows missing the other archer, but one archer was very quick, and unleashed a further shaft which struck his horse and they both went down as the horse screamed. From what he could see, Declan judged that rider would be lucky if he hadn't broken his neck.

The charge had degenerated into a milling clump of mounts and riders struggling to move forward. A few horses were more adept at negotiating the deep sand, but they were spending as much time bumping into others who as often as not kicked out in response.

"Forward!" commanded Bogartis, and before Declan could react the old captain was a stride ahead of him, moving to engage the nearest horsemen.

Declan tried to turn and move forward and instantly fell, barely hanging on to his sword as he crashed into the sand, knees and hands keeping him from landing face-first. He scrambled to his feet just as a rider came close enough to swing at him. Declan realized this was a very young warrior, perhaps on his first raid, because he misjudged the distance between them, and the sword blow missed by more than a foot.

Declan jumped to the right, putting himself on the warrior's left, meaning he'd have to strike across the horse's neck. Declan saw the horse's head moving slightly toward him and reached up and grabbed the bridle. It was a dangerous move that could break fingers or dislocate Declan's arm if it went wrong, but the horse was already off-center and with a strong downward pull, the former smith caused the gelding to overbalance, and the rider found himself falling to Declan's feet. A swift strike and the young warrior stared at the sky with vacant eyes as blood fountained from his throat.

Declan held tight to the mount's reins, as the horse tried to right itself and pull away, but a quick yank on the animal's bridle, then a release, communicated that Declan was in control. As the fighting raged around him, Declan was in the saddle in a few seconds.

He barely saw the next attack, as a rider following the youngster Declan had killed came at him. Declan ducked over the horse's neck as the raider attempted a backhand strike. Declan leaned forward to the point of almost falling off the horse, and jabbed with his own blade, slicing the warrior's arm, causing him to lose his sword.

Without a weapon and injured, that rider attempted to turn to flee, but before he was able, Declan struck him across the back of his neck, dropping him from the saddle, dead before he struck the ground.

Declan wheeled his horse, which pulled at the reins and shook its head to express its distress. Just his luck, thought Declan, an untested warrior on the back of an untested horse. He dug his heels into the horse's flank, shoving his weight slightly forward, and the horse leapt ahead.

As the horse moved forward and another rider turned to engage him, Declan felt everything around him begin to slow, and the familiar cold calm washed up from within him. He welcomed the feeling for he knew he was now a finely tuned weapon, existing only in the moment, able to anticipate his enemy's moves.

The rider who had turned to meet him was to Declan's view slowly bringing back his arm to slash down, so Declan kicked his horse's left side, driving the animal slightly to his right, and he ducked over the neck, thrusting his sword at the man's exposed armpit, letting the horse's momentum drive the point home.

To Declan it was oddly comical seeing the man's eyes widen in shock and his mouth begin to open to scream, as Declan's sword nearly tore his opponent's arm completely off. He turned away.

Before that rider was out of his saddle, Declan felt his own mount stumble and start to fall. Kicking loose his stirrups, he jumped from the horse's back, landing in a tuck, rolling and coming to his feet as the horse struck the sand. The impact with the sand was distant, and he suffered no injury.

He turned in a full circle, and for a moment was in a place of calm at the heart of the fighting. He saw no nearby mount but spied a sword in the sand and picked it up. He hefted it and instantly knew it was an inferior weapon, mediocre beside his own blade forged with rare sands. He kept the found blade in his left hand.

With a weapon in each hand, he ran forward and in three strides slashed the leg of a horseman who was about to get the better of one of Benruf's men. The sudden attack from behind gave Benruf's warrior an opening and he killed the man.

Declan spotted an opportunity to remount. Moving quickly, he stashed the plundered sword under his arm and kept it pinned to his side before he sprang. Fingers twisting within the horse's mane, Declan swung his leg over the mount's back and found himself new purchase.

This mount was better trained than the previous and accepted the change of riders without trying to run or buck. Declan grabbed the loose reins, gathering them up and putting them in his mouth, freeing his left hand to hold a sword.

He steered the horse with his legs, with an ease that he now took for granted, and entered the fray again, killing the next man in moments.

As that man's horse darted away, Declan could see Bogartis confronting the enemy's chieftain, the one with the shiny black boots. One glance made it clear Bogartis was outmatched, and only his years of experience held off the furious attack by the younger and stronger man.

Declan kicked his horse's flanks, but before he could reach his captain, another raider came at him from the left. Without thinking, Declan moved his horse with his legs, and raised his left sword to take a descending sword strike, while half-throwing himself at the man, jabbing with the point of his right sword.

He took the blow to his blade with his left sword and took the man full in the stomach with his right. The other man fell across the neck of his horse, who bucked and kicked. Declan's mount shied from the kick, causing Declan to overbalance and fall. Both horses ran, leaving Declan facedown on the sand. He rolled away from harm and gained his feet. Declan turned and saw the raider's leader swinging down at Bogartis, who stood with sword upraised, and Declan noticed blood on his captain's face.

He moved as quickly as the sand allowed, and suddenly the battle seemed to speed up as his calm focus slipped away. Instantly the brighter sun, louder noise, and the stench of blood, shit, and piss assaulted his senses. Declan hesitated as if suffering a blow to his stomach.

Shaking his head, he forced himself to move toward Bogartis, who in desperation was attempting to back away from the leader of the raiders. Shouting taunts at Bogartis, only the deep sand prevented him from riding down the old captain.

Rather than the calm, clear slowing he usually knew, Declan was visited by a rising sense of rage and near-panic at his inability to move quickly through the sand. It took only a few extra moments, but it felt as if every passing second was ten, and every yard of distance was double.

He saw Bogartis fall backward as the chief raider swept down with his blade, missing his target's head by scant inches. Declan drew back his right hand and threw his sword like a dagger. It tumbled over and over then struck the chieftain across the back, bouncing off but leaving a deep gash in his waistcoat, from which blood began to seep. His blow ended as he arched backward and cried out in pain, and his horse moved to the side, missing Bogartis by a few feet.

The sideways movement of his horse caused the chieftain to lose his balance, and he fell off backward, landing in the sand with an audible thud. Declan launched himself at the chieftain as Bogartis lay still for a moment, then started to move away on his back using his elbows.

The leader of the raiders rolled away from his mount, turned and rose to his feet ready for Declan's attack, his face contorted into a snarling mask of pain and rage.

Declan felt a surge of emotion; anger, hatred, fear, and loss rushed through him. Seeing Bogartis on the ground, scrambling as best he could to get away, Declan knew he needed the clarity he had known in battle. Taking a precious moment to focus, he forced the calm to return. Instantly, the battle slowed, noise faded, and his vision became like that of a hawk, clear and focused.

The chieftain of the raiders moved toward him, and his posture and movement told Declan exactly where his attack was centered. Declan knew how this would end, and he felt more calmness than ever before, with everything around him getting slower and easier to anticipate.

The raider's leader neared and even while he anticipated the attack, Declan could see more detail than ever before. The chieftain was a man of early middle years, in his late thirties, perhaps a bit more, but by the evidence of a number of obvious scars, he was a veteran of many fights. He had a slightly crooked nose from a badly healed break, and his jaw protruded slightly as he attacked, his eyes wide enough to show the whites surrounding dark brown irises.

A part of Declan's mind was surprised by his ability to see in such detail, but he set aside this fascination to gauge every possible outcome of this attack. Without realizing he had come to any decision, Declan felt his body moving without conscious thought, as if some higher mind had seized control and he was but an observer.

He took a single step toward the leader, then stopped abruptly, as the chieftain swung hard at the space Declan would have occupied in another step. Finding only empty air, the blade continued past Declan, who then stepped forward.

As he had anticipated, a lethal backhand swing came a moment later, but Declan took that blow on his own blade. As the raider recoiled and pulled back for another strike, Declan let the glancing parry propel him in a circular motion. He spun around completely, coming back with his sword fully extended as the raider chieftain began his next strike.

Declan had expected the man to be open for a brief instant, but what he hadn't expected was that his own blow would miss the warrior's arm and shoulder by a scant inch and instead strike him in the side of the neck, cutting straight through, easily severing muscle and bone, and beheading him.

Blood fountained out of the neck stump as the chieftain's body seemed to continue the strike as it collapsed to the sand, the head landing at Declan's feet. He had an odd mixture of feelings. The unexpected hot rage was somehow contained within that slow, cold awareness he'd known previously when fighting. He'd gained a new focus.

He bellowed his victory, and grabbed the head of his enemy, lifting it high as his battle shout echoed.

Like a ripple spreading in a pond from a tossed stone, an awareness of this triumph spread through the battle and the raiders began to move away, giving ground as they saw their leader's head held high like a trophy, as Benruf had predicted.

"Let them go!" Declan shouted. His fighters paused and as distance grew between the two sides, the raiders who could turned and fled back toward the city gate. "Get the horses!"

Some of the men simply fell back, exhausted and needing to rest, but others heeded Declan's command and set out to recover whatever mounts had not run too far.

Declan quickly surveyed the scene and realized that half his company was dead or gravely wounded. Fewer than twenty men stood able to fight. He glanced to where Bogartis had fallen and hurried over to kneel next to his captain.

Bogartis had a serious wound seeping blood through his chest plate. The man Declan had just killed had sliced through the hardened leader's armor and deep enough into Bogartis's chest to deliver a mortal blow. Blood flowed from the sides of the captain's mouth so Declan knew there were only minutes of life left to the old mercenary.

Bogartis reached up with his left hand and grabbed Declan's right arm, pulling it weakly. Declan leaned over and could barely hear the old man's voice.

"Save ... as ... many ... as ..." He gasped and then his grip went lax and his head fell back, vacant eyes staring at the sky.

Declan looked down at Bogartis's body as he removed the now-limp hand from his arm. He knew this man had taught him a great deal, almost as if he were Bogartis's son, but while he admired the man's knowledge and ability, Declan found himself again devoid of grief or regret. He had been alive and still powerful despite his age one moment, and then suddenly dying upon the ground.

Sixto came over and saw that Bogartis was dead, his blank eyes staring skyward. He knelt and closed them, then turned his attention to Declan. He seemed on the edge of saying something, but Declan's expression, devoid of grief or anger, stopped him. At last he said, "What now ... ?"

Declan glanced down. "His last instruction was to save as many of the company as possible."

Both men stood, and Declan saw men bringing back mounts and some who had taken a moment to recover after the fight, now standing, waiting for orders.

Among his own company he recognized Toombs, Sixto, a newer recruit named Billy Jay who had come from Ilcomen, and other familiar faces—a reliable fighter named Giacomo, and the rest were Benruf's men. More of the original company from Marquensas would be out trying to get the horses.

Suddenly it dawned on Declan that the men were waiting for him to give orders. He had been named as Bogartis's second, and had treated that like a meaningless title, but now the reality of his responsibility struck him.

As if recognizing Declan's need, Sixto asked, "What next, Captain?"

"We have no time to bury our brothers," he said. "Gather up

whatever of value you find, weapons, especially bows and arrows, and most of all, water."

Benruf arrived leading a pair of mounts, as he said, "We must leave soon. It will only take the raiders a few more minutes to select their new leader, and they will be back, or another company with a different leader may be heading our way."

Declan said, "What are the odds?"

Benruf shrugged. "Another company may not think it worth a fight to rag-pick our dead bones, but this company, they will be back. It is a blood honor."

The men scavenged the corpses, comrade and foe alike, and quickly organized a cache of extra weapons, and every water skin they could salvage. The remaining men leading horses arrived and Declan did a quick accounting.

Only eleven of the forty men who had left North Tembria were still standing, and only four of them did he know well. The other seven were recruits Bogartis had enlisted to replace those lost in the battle at Beran's Hill. Two of them he knew by name: Jack and Mick Sawyer, brothers who had fled from some northern timber camp; but other than the names and their family's trade, he knew little of them. They seemed reliable, and were obviously strong and tough, but he didn't even know the names of the five remaining of his own company.

He knew Benruf's name only because he'd heard Bogartis address him. The mercenary captain from Zindaros had ten men with him. Twenty-two left out of forty-nine. Another man might have been overwhelmed by hopelessness, but Declan shrugged aside any doubt and simply turned to Benruf and asked, "Which way?"

"As I said to Bogartis, along the coast is death. To enter the Burning Lands may also be death, but we also may find water and live." The sound of riders in the distance came from the city. "And staying here also is death."

"How many wounded?" asked Declan.

"Three can ride," said Sixto, indicating the men gathered before Declan. "Four on the ground are unable."

Softly but firmly Declan said, "Quick mercy."

Without hesitation, Sixto pulled out his sword and moved swiftly among those on the ground, ending the lives of the four unconscious men. They would endure no torture at the hands of the raiders before they died.

Declan ordered the men to mount up and with one horse being used as a pack animal, they still had two extra. He instructed two of the men to lead the spare animals. He was certain they would need them before this was over.

With a wave of his hand, Declan moved them into the desert and as they set out at a brisk canter, he could feel the heat of the afternoon rise measurably as they left the relative coolness of the coast.

He spared Bogartis one last glance as they rode away and considered once more that the only person left in the world he deeply cared for was Edvalt, back in Marquenet. Then he realized he did not know what happened with Hava and Hatu, as they were unaccounted for. Captured, most likely, he considered, and turned his mind to what was to come. He liked the couple who had purchased Gwen's father's inn, but they were hardly close friends; yet, he wondered what had happened to them.

HAVA WATCHED THE SAILS, JUDGING the rigging properly set and the crew well about their business. She had been focused on getting through the shoals that protected the Flame Guard's Sanctuary for a day and a half, but a few minutes earlier she had broken from the underwater maze of reefs, shoals, and sandbars that surrounded that island, and set course to Marquensas. It was a long run with a following wind, so little tacking would be needed until she was more than halfway to their destination, then she would need to adjust as needed.

Without immediate distraction, her mind returned to her final two days with Hatushaly. There was a growing discomfort in her regarding the time they spent together. He was completely occupied, to the edge of obsession, with his studies. She knew that was his nature, but for the first time since childhood she felt neglected by him.

Sabien came to stand beside her and said, "Everything's secure, Captain. Why don't you get some rest? It's been more than a day since we left."

Hava's chuckle was more irony than humor. "Sometimes the winds help and sometimes they don't."

"Truth that," replied the large former mason. He dwarfed most men on the crew; Hava felt tiny when they stood side by side. Still, he followed orders without hesitation. As his predecessors had taken command of the ships she'd captured, Sabien had quickly risen from a freed prisoner to her first mate.

"We're still shorthanded for a long voyage, so I expect all of us will be losing sleep as we go."

"You still haven't named a second mate," he reminded her.

Hava shook her head. The unspoken politics of a crew was similar to what she'd witnessed in the gangs of Coaltachin, also known as "crews." It made her more uncertain than she liked. Jealousy and rivalry could poison a crew as quickly as bad food or tainted wine. If she picked the wrong man to be giving orders to a former shipmate, she could destroy harmony and their trust in her judgment. "Do you have someone in mind?" asked Hava.

"Truth to tell, the lad Willem we picked up in Port Calos, on his way to Elsobas, has the makings of a fine sailor, but the men would never take orders from a boy that young."

"Then who?"

"Probably Glyn. He's a Port Calos sailor with a lot of experience, and he knows the waters around here better than any other. I wouldn't think he could command his own ship, but he's up for looking after things if you and I are both below or ashore."

"You know them all better than I do," Hava said. Given that she was a woman, she'd elected to be even less familiar with the crew than most male captains were—she did not want to encourage unwanted familiarity. Maybe if she ever got a steady crew without all these changes . . . She caught herself and realized she thought of being a captain as her calling, and a steady crew would take months, perhaps years, to achieve with all that was happening. That also added a new issue to consider in judging her relationship with Hatushaly.

"Captain?" said Sabien after Hava stayed lost in thought for a minute.

"Yes, he'll do," she said. "Send him up here, then I'll grab a bite and turn in for some rest. Wake me at sundown. I want to see if what Catharian said about star positions stuck with me. It's different not having him leaning over my shoulder and pointing at everything."

Sabien laughed. "I think we'll be fine. North Tembria is an awful lot of land to miss. If we go too far north, we'll see ice. Then turn south and down the coast!" He tried to sound lighthearted, but he could see something was bothering Hava.

"Don't worry," Hava countered, trying to match his light tone. "I'm just tired. Go fetch Glyn and that will be the end of my watch."

He lifted his hand to his forelock in what passed for a salute among her crew. As he descended to the main deck, Hava tried to return to her concerns about Hatushaly, but found she was too fatigued for anything like coherent thought.

Besides, if she knew her husband, he was nose-deep in a book or having some sort of debate with Bodai. He had probably forgotten she had left.

DECLAN LAY ON HIS SIDE, knees drawn up, his scabbarded sword upright in the crook of his arm, the hilt driven into the sandy soil as deep as he could manage. It served as a central support for a makeshift personal tent fashioned from a large robe carried for this purpose, to provide him with needed shade during the day's hottest hours. The robe had come from a man who had died two days before, a man whose name he'd never learned.

Declan was trained as a smith. He had endured hours of heat in the forge but he always knew there was an abundance of well water nearby that he could drink as needed, and that cooler air was just steps outside the door of the smithy, even in the hottest days of summer in the seaside village of Oncon.

This was heat like nothing he could have imagined before breaching the edge of the Burning Lands. Declan breathed slowly, trying to conserve energy as waves of heat washed over his unsheltered position. He had slept lightly for a few minutes at a time, but it was a troubled doze, images and sounds in his mind jarring him awake after only moments of rest. This was not how it was supposed to have gone, he thought in mute anguish.

The silence of the still air was occasionaly punctuated by the faint sound of one of the men moving slightly, adjusting his own makeshift tent, or startling himself out of dozing off. Lack of water and fatigue were taking their toll. A few of the local men seemed able to simply sit without shade and remain upright.

Declan had no sense of time without his familiar reminders, where the sun was in the sky, the lengthening of shadows, the accustomed changes in a thousand tiny details that led him to know how soon sunset would come. Here it was continuous heat, then a short evening, then deep darkness until the moon rose. The day's scorching heat cooled, but it was still stifling, or if the wind arose, it could become a cutting chill. This desert was merciless.

The remnants of Bogartis's company sought what little shelter was available in the deepest part of a depression on the shady side of a tall dune. The shade was scant, slowly descending to cover the men huddled under their tiny tents, offering little relief from the brutal heat.

Benruf had led the escape from Abala. The attack on that city had come while Bogartis's entire company was spread out among three small inns, so almost half of the men had been lost before Bogartis, Declan, and the others had gotten through the south gate.

Declan considered the hidden purpose of their mission. Bogartis had spread a little coin around and warned the men to silence about it and to stay with the story that they were recruiting for the coming war against those who had destroyed the western coast of North Tembria. Now the mission to gather large amounts of the special sand was a complete loss, and only survival mattered. For a moment, Declan judged the expanse of sand on all sides the darkest of ironies.

The *Brigida* was to have been reprovisioned, to return north. Declan had no inkling if the ship had cast off and gotten free of the attack or been taken. He shook his head; given where he was, it was premature to say the least to consider the need for a ship back to the barony.

He shifted his position slightly, keeping the makeshift tent around him, as the sand quickly became unyielding, providing little comfort. Declan felt his eyes flicker, as if he was on the verge of sleeping, and wanted nothing more than to splash handfuls of cold water onto his face. The only water he had was a half-empty skin that he had taken from the saddle of his horse, which was lying dead two days behind them.

The horses had been staggering and near death, and it had been Benruf and two of his men who had shown them how to humanely kill the animals and insisted they drink as much blood as possible to extend the water they carried. As disgusted as Declan and his companions had been to do so, it had probably saved their lives as the water they carried would last another two days at most.

As his eyelids lowered, Declan settled for rubbing his hand down over his face. His dry, calloused palm brought little relief, though the movement revived him slightly. He resisted asking Benruf how much longer it was before sunset, for knowing how long it was would do nothing to ease his discomfort.

Declan contemplated the unknown difficulties facing him. Relying on strangers for his life was troubling. Still, Benruf and his companions were in the same situation and betrayal was scarcely a risk, though failure and death were.

The fight had been unexpected, and he still barely understood what had happened. Benruf had speculated that warriors from the Border Tribes were migrating due to pressure from those fleeing south from the Kingdom of Zindaros. If the raids in North Tembria had disrupted enough towns and cities along the coast, fleeing soldiers and countless civilians would have had nowhere else to go. Zindaros was divided by a soaring range of mountains that cut off the western third from the rest, save a narrow passage between the northwestern foothills and the sea. South would be their only avenue of escape, into the range of the Border Tribes, and the tribespeople would be forced into the Burning Lands, or southwest to Abala.

Declan nodded off a little and jerked awake as a hand touched his shoulder. "It is time," said Benruf.

Declan raised his sword, unfolded himself, and attempted to stand. Benruf grabbed his arm to steady him, saying, "Cautiously. You are weaker than you think."

Declan nodded. The smith-turned-mercenary looked around and saw the others also coming out from under their makeshift shelters. He looked to the west and saw the sun was now low in the sky, an angry red as the moisture over the distant sea turned the sky a mix of orange, blue, and indigo. In Oncon, he would have wagered that a storm was approaching, but here . . . ? He'd welcome a downpour, but doubted rain ever reached this far inland.

Inland, thought Declan. The coast was devoid of potable water, and a deep crevasse less than a mile south of Abala prevented any attempt to move farther in that direction. As the city itself was being overrun by tribesmen from the north, a run to the east into the Burning Lands had been their only option.

The crevasse had abruptly turned north, forcing them into a running fight with a small band of raiders who had overtaken them, seeking revenge for the killing of their chieftain. One of Benruf's men had fallen, but they had kept the raiders behind them for nearly an hour before the tear in the ground arched east, then southward. As if knowing the limits of their water, the pursuing raiders turned back, leaving the desert to punish Declan's band.

Every hour saw the opening in the ground widen and deepen until it became a broad canyon. Benruf had called the canyon

"Garn's Wound" and said it ran for hundreds of miles to the southeast, bisecting the Endless Desert. Common lore claimed the desert reached completely across the southern continent, ending on the shores of The Island Sea, bordering the Kingdom of Metros, on the other side of the Great Southern Mountains.

In short, there was no safe escape.

"The well is a day from here," said Benruf.

"It had better be," said Declan, his voice sounding like a frog croaking in his ear.

Benruf shrugged. "It is as the gods will it, my friend. The well will have water and we shall survive, or it will not and we will all die."

Declan looked at the others, now only sixteen of them in total, and motioned for them to follow. Lifting one tired leg after the other, he plodded after the desert-savvy mercenary.

THE DRY WIND SLAPPED AND jabbed at Declan and the others. After trudging across broken flats and pockets of sand, they were all on their last legs. If they didn't find shelter and water soon, all would die in the following day's heat.

In the few days traversing this desolation, Declan had come to understand that the rising wind was a harbinger of the sunrise and to the east the sky above the horizon was lightening. He judged they had perhaps half an hour before the sun crested and perhaps another hour before the day would be too hot to travel.

"How far?" he asked Benruf, his voice sounding hoarse and faint in his own ears.

"Soon," came an equally weak reply and Declan paused for a moment, realizing he had been plodding along without thought, his mind almost turned off as he simply applied all his energy to moving forward in the darkness, content to let Benruf and his companions lead the way. He assumed they used the stars to guide themselves, like sailors, as there were no landmarks in this desert even in the daylight.

As the sky lightened Declan saw the twisted landscape reveal itself, first as uneven patches of shades of grey, then resolving slowly into more detailed patterns of rocks and wide swaths of hardpan, mounds of sand, and deepening depressions.

"There," said Benruf, and Declan saw a dip ahead that seemed to be widening as they approached. He forced himself to pause a moment, and look around, and counted. Two men fewer than the day before. He couldn't focus enough to determine who was missing, just that at sunset there had been sixteen men with him; now it was fourteen. He was too exhausted to feel anything for those lying facedown in the desert behind him.

The dip turned into a downward-sloping depression that widened as they descended. Soon the sun was hidden as they continued down. As the sky lightened above them, they picked their way carefully among rocks, with some men stumbling and needing to be helped to their feet. Declan knew they were hours at best away from being too weak to move. He said, "If you have even one swallow of water left in your skins or canteens, drink it now." He held up his own water skin, which was damp to the touch and bulging when full but was now dry and almost empty. He pulled out the stopper and upended the canvas bag, and a pitiful warm dribble of water was his reward. Still, even that tiny amount was welcome and for a brief instant he felt a glimmer of hope.

"Don't throw those away," said Benruf. "We'll need to fill them before we can attempt to find a safe way out of here."

Declan nodded and silently questioned if the Zindaros fighter was saying water was close or just trying to keep spirits from failing, to get another few miles out of these dying men. He decided it didn't matter, for either they would reach water or not.

The deepening pathway protected the travelers from the rising sun as they wended their way down into a wide gully. The shade was welcome and seemed to give the company an added boost as did drinking the last of their water. In less than a mile, the gully had become a ravine, and both sides now rose up a hundred or more feet above their heads. In the morning light, Declan could see the striations of the walls and hints of what he took to be nickel and iron ore, a few flakes of yellow that might be gold but were much more likely to be pyrite. His attention was now focused, because if there was indeed pyrite here, there was a possibility of coal.

Then it struck him as humorous and he laughed aloud, though the sound was a hoarse croak as much as anything.

Benruf look back over his shoulder and said, "Something funny?"

Declan shook his head. "Some habits are . . . just hard to ignore, I guess. I am looking at these walls and wondering how much iron and coal are buried here."

From behind him Declan heard Sixto mutter, "Not my first choice for a place to build a forge."

Declan tried to laugh again but once more only a dry croak escaped his lips.

The sun rose and crested the distant rim of this deepening gorge. Then there was a moment when Declan felt something that brought him to a standstill. The air was different!

Benruf said, "Ahead!"

Declan looked past the fighter who had now started moving forward with purpose and more vigor than he thought possible and saw a hint of green. There was vegetation in the distance, and that meant water!

As if a silent ripple had spread, the men all started hurrying, one after the other, coming as close to a run as they could manage given their weakened conditions and the difficult rocky footing. They came to a flatter area and farther away they could hear a sound which revitalized them: birds! Birds were singing, chirping loudly.

A deep cut into the ground constricted their descent for a few yards, and then they emerged into a widening canyon, and below they saw treetops and could feel the air cooling as the canyon rose up on both sides to shelter this improbably small forest from all but a few hours of sun each day.

Benruf fell forward and Declan saw he was facedown in water, as small birds took to the wing to avoid this rushing human. Declan barely kept to his own feet until he reached the other man's side and he collapsed and submerged his face in a wide pool. He drank and felt a stab of pain for an instant as the water flooded his mouth, going up his nose and down his throat.

He rose up, coughing, and felt a strange constriction in his stomach, and swallowed hard. He did not want to vomit up the water that was now almost choking him. He took a deep breath and laughed, as the other men fell to their knees around this pool and drank.

The laugh was followed by another fit of coughing and Benruf said, "Again, what's funny?"

"It would be a tale to tell to come all this way across the desert only to drown."

Benruf barely cracked a smile. "Drink slowly, my friend."

Declan nodded and turned to take another deep drink, this time avoiding inhaling. Soon he felt revived enough to stop drinking, sit up, and take a look around.

The pool was fed from a small stream that came through a

narrow cut in the southern wall of this ravine. Declan estimated they were twenty or so feet from the opposite side, where he saw water draining into a rill that headed down into the forest below. "Benruf?"

"Yes?"

"How do you know about this place?"

"Tales, stories." The Zindaros mercenary shrugged. "The legend, if it is indeed such, is that deep within Garn's Wound lay a green world full of mystery and treasure."

Another man said, "I'll settle for this water."

Another voice said, "And food, if there is any."

"Birds," said Declan. "Perhaps some waterfowl, down below."

He indicated the canopy of treetops that spread out before them, filling the canyon as far as they could see. "This pool doesn't provide enough water down there to grow all that." He stood up and saw little more than when sitting. "There must be other water sources, and if there are birds, perhaps there are also animals." He glanced from face to face, seeing the other men all appeared to have been somewhat revived.

He noticed several still carried their bows and quivers. "Perhaps something we can hunt." He glanced skyward, and said, "This shade will vanish soon. We may be better for this water, but it will once again get hot when the sun crests that rim. Let's get below the trees and see how much shade they provide."

"Fill those skins and canteens," said Benruf. "Declan may be right about more water but it may be miles from here. This is part of Garn's Wound and it is said it cuts across most of South Tembria."

The men did as they were told and when they had all the water they could carry, they began moving down into the forest. Declan knew all were feeling relieved, but he also knew they were far from being safe. He felt a slight stirring of dark, ironic humor. With the war upon them, would they be safe anywhere?

Declan struggled to collect himself, to focus on the matter at hand. Whatever drove him, loss, revenge, or a hope of survival, he knew one fundamental truth. Nothing existed beyond life; death ended everything. If he wanted to visit revenge on those who took Gwen from him, he must stay alive.

4

STRANGE REUNIONS,

DISCOVERIES, AND TREACHERY

Hatushaly sat back, emitting a growl of aggravation. Bodai gave a loud exhalation that echoed Hatu's frustration. "Nothing?" he asked as he pushed back from the table they were sharing and stood.

"No," said the younger man, moving the large book away from him, as if an additional few inches of distance would ease his impatience. "It comes and goes as it pleases, it seems."

Bodai said, "As you know, in my younger days I was a pedagogue, but this is a subject I know nothing of, this use of your power."

"The 'magic,'" said Hatu with a sarcastic tone. "This power I never asked for," he added bitterly.

Bodai held up his hands in resignation. "I know. I know. None of us are asked if we want our parents."

Hatushaly's expression relaxed for a moment, then he chuckled. "You've come to know my moods almost as well as Hava." He shook his head. "You should have seen me when I was young."

"I did," said Bodai. "Once I recognized you for who you were, I kept track of you, even if you weren't part of my crew."

"Then you remember the tantrums?"

Bodai said, "They were heroic, even legendary. Every preceptor knew you got as angry as a storm if you didn't get every question answered."

"I got beatings almost as often as Donte did for his pranks."

"No one got beatings nearly as often as Donte," corrected Bodai with a rueful chuckle.

"True." Hatu also stood up and walked away from the table to the closest bookcase. He just looked for a moment, then said, "Sometimes I understand every word I look at, as if it was written in my native tongue. Other times I don't see anything but mysterious markings, even if it's a book I'd studied the day before. And the memory of what I read fades until I have no idea what I read just a few days earlier."

Bodai nodded. "I think having someone transcribe what you read might be the next step," he said, holding up a quill and then setting it down next to an inkwell and a stack of heavy paper.

"If I knew when I could . . ." Hatu shrugged and left the statement unfinished.

Bodai knew as well as Hatu that this coming and going of certain magical abilities was seemingly random. They had both accepted that the mastery of flames Hatu had achieved at sea had been driven by the fear and anger at the attack by Azhante raiders. Since then, he'd shown no ability to ignite a single twig, let alone burn a ship down to the waterline.

"Here's what we know . . ." Bodai began.

Hatu interrupted. "I'm the first male able to use magic, even if I don't know what I'm doing. Women use men as . . . vessels for magic? Maybe? Sabella and the other women have no idea either and they use their powers . . ." He waved his hand around to illustrate pointlessness. "We know nothing."

Bodai shrugged. "How are things between you and Hava?"

That abrupt change of subject surprised Hatushaly, and it clearly showed on his face. "Fine. Why?"

"I thought perhaps something was amiss and you might be distracted."

"Why would anything be amiss?"

Bodai spread his hands a bit and said, "Should something be amiss with your wife, that would be a serious distraction."

Hatu considered the question for a moment, then he said, "I think everything is fine."

Bodai waved him back to the table and pulled out his own chair and sat. After Hatu sat, he said, "You discovered this . . . ability to read languages you'd never seen before the night after she returned. And while she was here, it . . . faded, right?"

"Yes."

"I'm simply looking for any reasons why you've lost that ability. So if things with Hava are as they were that first night, then my question is without merit."

Hatu leaned back in his chair. "I'm . . ." He shrugged. "Certain things are fine."

Bodai nodded. He looked around and said, "We need some light. That means the sun is low, and you are probably getting hungry."

Hatushaly nodded. "I could eat."

"Go, the mess should be serving, and there'll be other young people there. Drink an ale, talk, relax. You've been working hard every day. You need to let up, get your mind rested."

Hatu stood and, with a wave of his hand indicating the hundreds of books nearby and even more beyond, said, "How can I relax with all this waiting?"

"We'll find a way," said Bodai. "Now go."

"You?"

"I'm going to stay a bit. If you want to come back after you eat, I'll be here. If you act your age and get drunk with some friends, I'll see you here in the morning."

Hatu nodded, turned, and left.

After he was gone, Bodai sat motionless until he was certain Hatu was out of earshot, then said, "You going to keep lurking?"

Across the room, from behind a long bookcase, a figure emerged from the shadow. "I thought I did a fair job of lurking."

Stepping forward, a tall boy of perhaps Hatushaly's age revealed himself. He had broad shoulders but a narrow waist. His hair was a dirty blond and cut close at the top of his ears in the way of some fighters who chose to wear full helmets.

He had a friendly, open smile and Bodai thought his blue eyes almost sparked—a trick of the light, perhaps. He was square-jawed, and Bodai felt a strange sense of the familiar, though he'd never seen the youngster before. Yet there was something about the young man's face and manner that was very amiable, as if he were a friend, and that caused Bodai some discomfort. Too many years of being the most important spy in the history of the Flame Guard made him distrust such impulses. His little reading on magic had included being beguiled.

The lad wore a white open-collared shirt with long sleeves and baggy green trousers. From the sound of leather on stone, Bodai assumed he wore boots hidden by the long trousers. He carried a dagger at his belt, and had a rucksack slung over one shoulder.

"If you want to stay hidden," said Bodai, "I suggest you refrain from snacking. That particular type of orange is very aromatic, close to pungent. I could smell it from here."

"I got hungry," said the youngster. "Want one?"

"Yes, please." Bodai felt a chill. This exchange returned memories long forgotten, of when he was very young and had met a traveler who had changed his life.

The young man swung his rucksack off his shoulder and reached in, fetching out an orange which he gently tossed to Bodai.

Rather than eat it, Bodai gave it a close inspection. "I haven't seen the like of this fruit in . . . thirty years?"

"Really?" asked the stranger as he moved Hatu's seat out from the table and sat down in it.

"This variety is not from around here."

Settling back in the chair, the young man said, "Oranges are all pretty much the same to me. I seem to remember some big ones once, with a dark, almost purple-red, pulp. Very tasty."

"Those I've not seen," said Bodai. "Where did you get this one?"

"Same place I got the last one," came the unhelpful answer.

"The man who gave that one to me, years ago, was a stranger from very far away."

"We have that in common, or perhaps I'm the same traveler."

"You don't look old enough to have been around thirty years ago, let alone sharing wondrous tales of distant worlds. You're also quite a bit taller, and he was not blond with fair skin."

Taking out another orange from his bag, the youngster jammed his thumb in and began peeling. "Looks can be deceiving. I'm certainly older than I look." His brow furrowed. "I'm older than I remember, so maybe that *was* me," he added as he gazed far away for a moment. Then he shrugged. "Or maybe it was someone else. It's hard to know sometimes."

"What brings you here—and by the way, how did you get here if you didn't arrive on one of our ships?"

"To the last, I came aboard when that woman Hava stopped to stock up on water and food at Elsobas. She'd rescued more people and was almost out of both. There were enough strangers to her crew milling about that it was easy to get aboard. And just as easy to slip away with the newcomers to the Sanctuary.

"As to why I'm here, I'm here to help."

"Help with what?"

"The boy, Hatushaly, of course. He's cursed."

Bodai slowly nodded. "The Curse of the Firemanes. Yes, terrible things will befall any who harm him."

"Seeing as a lot of people are trying very hard to find and kill him, that curse hasn't circulated much, I'm afraid. No, I was being hyperbolic. I meant he's cursed with a gift he doesn't want. I heard him say that he has powers that are untrained and dangerous." He pointed a finger at Bodai. "You're trying to help him but working at a great disadvantage."

"I don't know what I'm doing," agreed Bodai.

"That's why I'm here."

"You're going to teach him about magic?"

"Gods, no," came the reply. "He and I will eventually meet, but not for some time. That's for everyone's good. No, I will help you do what you do best, teach."

Bodai sat back. "What I do best . . . That traveler I mentioned told me when I was very young that teaching would be what I do best. I was halfway to becoming a healer when he changed my life." He thought about this for a long moment, then asked, "And how do you propose to do that?"

"Long days ahead, my friend," answered the blond-haired youngster. "After supper you and I will meet, and I will give you the next day's instructions. A few things will come easily but most will take time, so we'll be seeing a lot of one another for the foreseeable future."

"To what end? And why should I trust someone who . . . just

turned up?" Bodai pointed to the half-eaten orange he had put on the table before him. "You appear with knowledge that should be beyond your understanding, and expect my trust?"

"What if I give you the cause of his inability to read texts that he could read just days ago?"

"That would be enlightening," Bodai replied.

"I heard the story of him burning a ship at sea from Hava's crew and then observed for a while how he struggled with reading, when before the words had come to him without effort. Those actions have one thing in common."

"What is that?" Bodai leaned forward in his chair, his curiosity piqued.

"When the magic worked it was when he didn't think. He just acted."

"Really?" said Bodai.

"He saved a crew at sea from Azhante raiders, by all accounts, and just looked over at a book on the floor and could understand it."

"So, he's trying too hard?"

"He doesn't need to try at all. He just needs to learn how to do it without trying."

"And how does one achieve that odd result without effort?"

"With time and practice."

"You have me very intrigued," said Bodai. "What is your name?"

The man paused, cocking his head slightly as if listening, or trying to recall something, then laughed and said, "I am not sure. I've had . . . a few."

"I can't call you Stranger."

Settling back, the younger man said, "Names are odd." He fell silent as if lost in thought, then brightly said, "Call me Nathan."

Bodai noticed a wooden tube protruding from the top of the traveler's rucksack. "You're a musician?"

"Apparently," came the answer, and the youngster reached down and pulled out a wooden flute. He played a few notes, a jaunty tune, then stopped and returned the flute to the bag.

"A bourrée," said Bodai. "I haven't heard one since I last visited Ithra. A trio in the central market . . ." For a brief moment he reflected on all that was lost when Ithrace was destroyed.

"Maybe that's where I heard it."

Bodai was about to object, given the man's apparent youth, but decided he'd heard enough to accept that this young fellow was perhaps a great deal older than he seemed. They were talking about magic, after all, and at this point Bodai realized being open to any possibility was his best choice. "So, where do we begin, Nathan?"

"So many things, so many places to start." He crossed his arms then fell silent, again seemingly lost in thought. As Bodai was about to repeat the question, Nathan asked, "What do you know about stars?"

Bodai was startled. "Stars? What about them?"

"That's what I asked, what do you know?"

"They're little points of light in the night sky, and if you know their patterns you can steer a ship or cross open plains using them to find your way."

"Good," said Nathan. "You don't know anything. Let's start there."

DECLAN CAME TO ACCEPT THE reality of his now leading this combined company of mercenaries. He still thought of it as Bogartis's company, but realized this was his duty at least until they found a safe route home . . . He felt a sudden bitter twinge at thinking of anywhere now as "home." Since the destruction of Oncon and Beran's Hill there was no place to go "home" to, and he had no desire to become attached to another. Still, keeping these men alive was his task, and he would do everything possible to see that achieved, so his sense of homelessness would be put aside. He would lead them back to Marquenet if possible, and then he would put aside soldiering, and return to the smithy, and forge weapons with Edvalt, even if he came back without the precious sand. The weapons he would make might not be of King's Steel, but they would be the best weapons he could forge.

Mercenaries were expert foragers, and when raiding a town could find most hidden valuables, even those in cleverly concealed places. Livestock, stored food, hidden cold cellars: all were familiar to swords for hire. What Declan needed now were hunters, trappers, and fishermen. Fishing he could handle, but the rest?

"Anyone here a skilled hunter? A fowler? Trapper?"

He scanned the faces of the remaining men from Bogartis's company: the Sawyer brothers, Jack and Mick, Toombs, Billy Jay, and Sixto. Giacomo had drunk his fill from the pool, fallen asleep, and died during the night.

Of Benruf's group, six remained, some of whose names were still unknown to him, but he would make a point of knowing who they were by the end of this journey. One of Benruf's men, an archer, held up his bow and said, "I am a good hunter. But so far I've seen no sign of large animals. Small signs, yes, perhaps monkeys in the trees, but nothing that can feed . . ." He glanced around and counted. "Eleven men."

"Your name?"

"Sebastian," said the archer.

"Anyone else track and read signs?" Declan asked.

Some muttered no, and others shook their heads.

"Sebastian, you take point."

The archer slung his bow and moved to stand next to Declan.

"We may not be the first men to find this place, so we'll need to stay alert. Sebastian will break trail or find us a game trail, and we'll keep looking until we find food or starve to death. But at least no one is dying of thirst."

The men accepted his orders and began to organize themselves into a patrol line. "Keep sharp and walk softly."

They were barely at the west end of the massive canyon and it was widening as they descended.

"Keep alert for fruit or berries," Declan told them. He knew the men needed no more urging than the grumbling of their stomachs.

As they slowly moved down the slope of the narrow canyon, Declan said to Benruf, "I lived my life on the edge of the ocean, only spent a bit in a hill town. I know nothing of places like this."

Benruf said, "I've never seen a place like this in my life."

Over his shoulder, Sebastian said, "This is nothing like the forests at home."

After an hour's slow descent over rocks that offered difficult passage, they came to a small clearing, and Sebastian knelt. "Game sign," he said in hushed tones.

"What?"

"Hard to judge. Maybe a fox, or a weasel." He stood up and looked at Declan and Benruf. "But if there are predators here that means prey, and what they eat, we can eat."

A man behind Declan said, "Hell, right now I'd eat the fox or the weasel."

That little quip seemed to lift the mood, for now every man knew there was a possibility of survival. They had full water skins and signs that the forest ahead had game.

Declan said, "From now on I want silence. Even if we're the only men here, noise will scare off game." A few men with no hunting experience showed surprise, but the rest nodded and as Sebastian moved down the slope, Declan gave him five steps then followed, and Benruf also let Declan set an interval, then followed him. They would now follow trail discipline and obey. They were now Declan's company.

HATU WAS SLIGHTLY INTOXICATED WHEN he came back to the vast library, causing the abrupt end to Bodai's first instruction from Nathan. Bodai had decades of being a spy and watching the craft of the Quelli Nascosti, and he would vow he'd never seen anyone disappear as adroitly as Nathan.

In the hour or so during which they'd spoken, Bodai had realized be it charm, trinket, or spell, he now trusted the stranger as much as if they'd been friends since birth, and how much more he had to learn, despite his age. In less than an hour, Nathan had opened Bodai's eyes to a universe he could not even have imagined. But the lesson was unfinished and he had no idea how it would apply to Hatushaly.

Bodai rose. "I think age is getting the best of me. I know I said come back, but truth be told, I am exhausted and need some sleep." He looked Hatu up and down, and said, "And apparently so do you."

"I am tired," Hatu admitted. "And I didn't come back so I could fail reading again, but something you said set my mind to worrying."

"What?" asked Bodai. He gently took Hatu's arm and turned him so that they were both facing the door.

"About whether things were good with Hava." He betrayed confusion as he went on. "But what if I'm wrong? What if things aren't good and I'm too stupid to see? I mean, I'm too stupid to know how I did the things I can't do anymore."

"That's the frustration and drink talking, boy," said Bodai. He gently moved Hatu toward the door. "You are many things, but stupid is not among them." After they had gone a couple of steps, Bodai said, "I was married once."

"Really?" Hatushaly's eyes widened.

Bodai took a deep breath. "Part of my role as a master in Coaltachin was to have heirs."

Hatushaly stayed silent, waiting for Bodai to continue.

"My reason for sharing that, I suppose, is that you were raised by preceptors and trainers, ordered about by them, and crew bosses, people who felt no love for you. Maybe one or two had a touch of affection for you, but never love in any profound way. You never knew a mother or father who would put their life ahead of yours." He looked away from Hatu, and then added, "It's a love without conditions; it's putting another's needs ahead of your own."

Hatushaly listened.

"What do you know of families?" Bodai asked.

Hatu stopped dead, his expression one of open confusion. "What do you mean?"

"You've traveled, seen this and that, so I assume you've seen families who actually care about each other." He motioned for them to resume walking.

Hatu fell into step but he was silent as he weighed the question. "I suppose so. I was once apprenticed to a leatherworker who seemed really happy to see his children when they interrupted his work. I thought it was odd that he'd feign annoyance when they intruded upon his work, but actually was delighted to see them." Hatu reached up and brushed back his hair, then continued. "It was sort of a game, I think, but they really seemed to enjoy it. He'd chide them for coming into the tannery, then catch and scoop them up and spin them around the room, each in turn, then feign scolding them and shoo them out. It was a few days before I realized it wasn't a real . . . a real problem, but some sort of game they played."

Bodai nodded. "When I first came to Coaltachin, I succeeded because no one had seen the real Bodai at home for years. As I told you, once I rid myself of two older brothers—as I also said, despised by the real Bodai—I was heir to the clan's leadership. But I apparently failed to realize that by doing so I had removed two of the last three obstacles between becoming a master and my 'younger brother,' who managed to kill my wife but failed to kill me before I ended him." Bodai let out a slight sigh. "It's so commonplace in Coaltachin, killing for advancement, it's hard to believe the society has endured as long as it has.

"Anyway, the strongest survive and in a way that strengthens everyone, I suppose." He looked at Hatu in a way that suggested he was open to questions.

"You're talking about things . . . I never understood."

"Time for a bit more history, then." Bodai saw Hatu's expression cloud over and quickly said, "I'll try to be brief."

After a second, they both laughed. "I'm not going anywhere, Bodai." Then Hatu's forehead furrowed for an instant and he said, "When you first told me who you were, back on Elsobas, did I ever ask your real name?" His gaze narrowed. "That drug you slipped me played serious tricks with my memory."

"Not so. I remember I told you it was Zander, which was a lie." Bodai answered. "As for my original name, it's been so many years I occasionaly have to remind myself it is Nelson."

"Nelson?"

They reached the door to the courtyard, and both stopped.

"Nell's son, as Nell was my mother's name, and no one knows who my father is. She abandoned me and the Flame Guard took me in. But I've been called Bodai for so many years it's more my 'real' name than the one the first pedagogues gave to me here." Bodai took a breath, then added, "I expect we'll discover many histories scattered among the volumes in that library. So, if we ever get organized you can delve deeper into the subject, but what you need to know is this. This Sanctuary was once the home to the Flame Guard, and we were here for several reasons, but the key reason was to keep an eye on the Nytanny. That name is used for the land and the people who live there, though that is somewhat lazy, for Nytanny, the continent, is home to many people, many nations."

"I see," said Hatu.

"We . . ." Bodai sighed. "So many different places to start." Then he smiled. "But where we start is a question that can wait until tomorrow. Right now we both need sleep."

Hatu nodded. "Goodnight, Bodai." He turned toward his quarters.

"Goodnight, Hatu," the teacher replied. He stood for a moment watching the troubled young man walk away and then turned toward his own rooms. Whatever might be false or not how it appeared, he knew his need for sleep was as real as the stones beneath his feet.

As he neared his own quarters, Bodai realized that his conversation with Hatu had touched on feelings he had ignored most of his life. The truth was that his wife was someone he had wed for political advantage within the families of the masters, and it had put him in position so that when the time came, he had been able to replace the true Bodai's father on the Council without opposition. But even though his motives had been based on logic and politics, he'd come to appreciate his wife, and had grown very fond of her. He realized this was the closest he had come to that love, and for the first time in years felt a twinge of regret at her death.

DONTE FOLLOWED A PAIR OF porters into a section of the barracks put aside for the escorts and retinues of visiting nobles. Some must have had large escorts, judged Donte, because this company numbered seventeen men, not counting the two men who were still staying with the baron, yet they filled less than a quarter of the barracks. So, sometimes a hundred men-at-arms and servants were housed here? Donte decided there were things about life on North Tembria he would never understand. Most Coaltachin masters wouldn't let one armed retainer of any foreign noble within striking distance, let alone a hundred.

The baron had placed a company of his best soldiers around the barracks. They were members of his household guards—those they called castellans, and from the look of them, Donte judged them to be as rough and ready to brawl as any fighters he'd ever seen.

After a long discussion with Balven, who had listened closely, the second most important man in the barony had concluded that Donte needed to stay close to these men. His awareness of danger from the Azhante put him in a unique position to anticipate trouble, whoever they might be. Donte wasn't happy with the assignment, but then he was rarely happy with any assignment given him.

He knew this escort for Episkopos Bernardo was as serious a band of soldiers as those outside guarding them. He had no objection to them happily murdering one another but had a strong aversion to being caught between them.

"Supper, courtesy of the baron," he announced as the porters deposited two large trays with plates and cups, while behind Donte half a dozen other porters entered carrying food and wine.

The episkopos's company looked a bit wary until the food was placed where they could reach it, and when the wine goblets were full, any reluctance to trust strangers vanished.

Donte watched from the corner of the barracks next to the open door, outside of which Baron Dumarch's soldiers stood ready. No explicit plan had been made, but Balven had ordered the sergeant in charge to be ready should trouble erupt. Donte also suspected he had ordered the sergeant to make sure Donte didn't slip away.

The episkopos's men grabbed at the wine first, and two of them jostled, and one swore at the other without thought, and the word he used was one Donte knew well.

Donte wasn't averse to a brawl, but he also was nobody's fool when it came to being outnumbered by trained soldiers. He stepped outside and shouted, "Subdue them and keep everyone alive if you can!"

The sergeant in charge didn't hesitate. Normally, he would never take orders from someone like Donte, but Balven's instructions had been clear enough and he was ready for just this sort of problem.

The men inside were momentarily surprised, and most were holding food or drink, and their weapons were next to the bunks in the far end of the barracks. The baron's guards swarmed in, and half the men were on the floor being pummeled senseless by the time the others reached their weapons.

Several turned to find soldiers of Marquensas holding swords poised at their throats, and others were struck from behind and slammed against the wall. A few managed to grab their weapons and lashed out at the baron's troops, and two others saw that it was hopeless and threw down their arms.

Three men attacked Dumarch's men, and one was the soldier

who had uttered the curse that set Donte off. Donte had no weapon, but he pushed through those between him and the man he had singled out, and at the last jumped high, slamming into the back of the soldier engaged with that man, knocking both of them into the wall.

Donte unceremoniously put his knee into the back of the baron's soldier, and lashed out with his fist, sticking the targeted man as hard as he was able. "Swarm him!" Donte shouted, and within seconds three other Marquensas men were throwing themselves upon the target.

Donte jumped up and almost overbalanced, falling back, then catching himself. He desperately searched for something to use, grabbing a dirty road rag used to wipe dust and sweat from a rider's face, then leapt onto the pile of soldiers squirming in the corner.

Donte reached down and jammed the rag into the target's mouth, shouting, "Be wary of poison!"

The outbreak of fighting had rapidly brought more of the garrison's troops to the fray, and while Donte tried to keep the man at the bottom of the pile subdued, the flood of Dumarch's soldiers resulted in clubbing and kicks that rendered the episkopos's retinue senseless in good order.

A big hand grabbed Donte by the shoulder and pulled him off the top of the pile.

Without a weapon, Donte was ready to strike with balled fist, till he saw that the man hauling him off was one of Dumarch's senior sergeants. "Strike me and I'll beat you within an inch of your life, boy, and apologize to the baron after!" he shouted at Donte.

Donte took a moment to gather his wits. Looking down, he saw the man he suspected of being a sicari had been completely immobilized by the weight of bodies upon him, as well as the rag jammed in his mouth. His eyes were starting to bulge as he fought for breath, and Donte found that amusing.

Suddenly he found himself gripped by giddiness, and looked back at the sergeant who said, "Easy there, lad."

"Easy . . ." said Donte, not understanding what had occurred, then looked down and discovered a dagger was protruding from his side, just above his hip.

He found that even funnier, and started to laugh, but pain seized him and drove the breath out of his lungs, and he gasped as he fought to refill them. "Damn," he said as consciousness fled and he fell into the sergeant's arms.

5

ENCOUNTERS,

EDUCATION, AND HOPE

Baron Dumarch was overseeing the training of new recruits, many of whom were experienced brawlers, but few with soldiering experience. All the accounts of the raids that had destroyed the western coast detailed massive swarms of raiders, who pillaged and took captives, but there were no reports of organized forces under any field commanders.

Daylon had consulted with every experienced soldier he could, his own officers and sergeants, and some fleeing from Ilcomen and the Copper Hills whom he had enlisted into the army he was building. Command came from somewhere in that massive fleet, and there were only two orders: first to loot, burn, and take captives; then to retreat back to the ships. Despite the simple organization, they had effectively sacked every community from Port Calos down to the border of Marquensas, driving the Baron of Copper Hills into hiding, and turning the Kingdom of Ilcomen into a failed state. Other reports suggested they had raided along the northern coast of South Tembria, keeping the big fleets from Zindaros and Metros safely at anchor in deep harbors.

He decided that no matter how big his new army grew, at

its center would stand a large company of well-trained soldiers who could be directed to a specific target of his choosing: that being whoever had been responsible for the destruction of his family. No matter what else, the author of that horror would die at Daylon's hands.

"Ship coming in!" came a cry from a rider galloping through the gate.

Daylon waved the rider over. The man's horse was lathered, its nostrils flaring, but Daylon could tell this had been a fast gallop and not a long, hard ride. "North Point?" asked the baron.

"Yes, m'lord."

Daylon turned to the sergeant overseeing the training, a Copper Hills man named Haskel whom he knew from his visits to Rodrigo, the Baron of Copper Hills. "Continue the drills," he instructed. He then motioned to a groom and said, "Saddle my horse."

He hurried to the barracks where Balven was interrogating the men Donte had identified and could hear shouts and grunts of pain from within as he came nearer. "Tell Balven there's a ship approaching North Point. I am going there," he told the guards at the door.

The guards saluted, and by the time the baron had returned to where Sergeant Haskel was drilling the gathered fighters, he found his horse saddled and waiting for him.

"Escort, m'lord?" asked the groom.

"Have half a dozen riders catch up with me, if they can."

The baron urged his mount out of the castle gate and down through the city streets toward the north gate. Life was becoming more settled in the city, though it was hardly back to normal. There were still food shortages, hoarding, and fights erupting between those who had fled returning to find squatters in their

homes and places of business. Still, progress was being made on
a daily basis. It was as if Marquensas was becoming what Daylon
demanded by his force of will alone.

He rode at a good canter, having to avoid only a few people
as the population was still half what it had been, and once out of
the gate, he set his mount to a gallop. He ran his horse for a little
over a mile, then reined him back to a trot. Daylon had seen more
than one mount ruined by a rider demanding too much, and his
personal horse was the finest he'd ever seen. He estimated that
the messenger who had carried news to him had galloped the last
mile or two into the city, but also had spared his mount.

Daylon had visited the North Point countless times since he
was a boy, as it was one of the first places his own father had
taken him when he began his military lessons. Literally, a lifetime
ago, he thought ruefully. Bitterly he then realized he had no one
left to teach as his father had taught him.

A cascade of memories threatened to come flooding in, from
his boyhood up to recent attempts by his brother Balven trying
to remind Daylon he was still young enough to take a third wife,
start a new family, all of which he rejected equally, as nothing
would detract him from his need for revenge.

After trotting, cantering, and galloping in rotation, Daylon
crested a hill and saw the North Point tower come into view. A
ship, barely more than a white blot on the distant blue sea below,
was anchored a short distance out from the shore. Daylon slowed
his mount to a walk, resisting the urge to get to the tower as
fast as possible.

This was the first ship to approach any port or landing in
Marquensas since the raids. And while the barony had been spared
direct assault, the impact of the raids was still devastating. Daylon
knew that the arrival of this ship was important.

* * *

SABIEN SAID, "TAKING THEIR TIME, aren't they?"

The *Queen of Storms* had sailed into view of the North Point tower more than four hours earlier, hoisted a white parley flag, and dropped anchor a short distance offshore.

Hava said, "Seems that way. Then they sent a rider off to the baron, and whoever's up in that stone tor is not willing to take the responsibility of inviting us ashore. Probably a sergeant, maybe a corporal."

"Corporal?"

"In between a sergeant and regular soldier here."

"Oh." Sabien's expression was one of boredom. The journey had been easy and uneventful, but tedious as once they got north of the equator the winds changed. A great deal of tacking and rigging of sails had been involved, and progress had slowed.

"Don't they have signal fires?"

"Whoever's in charge probably didn't want the baron bringing his whole army with him. Better to send a rider."

Sabien shrugged. "Makes sense, Captain."

After a few more minutes, Hava asked, "How are the people below holding out?"

"Anxious to know if it's safe to return home, and restless."

"They've been restless since we cast off at the Sanctuary."

"True," agreed Sabien.

Hava had been surprised that so few people wanted a quick return. Less than a hundred of the more than four hundred she'd freed on repeated raids of Azhante ports and ships had requested a trip back to North Tembria. Hava suspected it was fear, the realization that Port Calos and Copper Hills were in total ruin, and the promise of fresh farm- and pasture-land on the countless islands surrounding the Sanctuary. She thought many of them looked at that part of the world as a new beginning, a way to turn their backs on a horrifying happening in their lives, one where they'd lost all they owned, the lives of friends and families. She knew she'd never feel that way, but she did understand how they felt.

"I see a rider," said Sabien, as he pointed to a distant speck coming over a ridge and heading toward the tor.

"Maybe someone will answer our parley flag."

"Maybe," said Sabien.

The distant rider seemed in little hurry as his horse trotted the final quarter of a mile from the ridge to the tor. There, he vanished into the structure and as they watched a company of riders came over the hill, moving quickly as if to overtake the first rider.

"I wonder what that's about?" said Sabien.

"I have no idea," began Hava, then an answering white banner was hoisted atop the tor and waved from side to side to ensure that it was seen.

"Maybe we're about to find out," said Hava. "Ready the longboat."

"It's been ready for about four hours, Captain," said Sabien with a chuckle.

Hava moved down to the main deck, where four sailors waited to crew the boat. Hava felt confident leaving Sabien in charge: she had seen enough to know that they were in safe waters.

She watched as the crew deftly housed the boat, turned a pair of hoists, and lowered the craft until it was even with the railing and the rowers entered, Hava last of all.

The boat was lowered and within minutes they were rowing toward the breakers. Hava was pleased with how the crew was shaping up, after months of combat, deft sailing, and the routine day-to-day care of the *Queen of Storms*, and what pleased her most was her crew retention. At first it had been a makeshift collection of some experienced sailors and those willing to serve in exchange for a voyage to a safe haven. Now she had a crew who understood their captain, knew their jobs, and worked well without the need of bullying from a mate.

Sabien was large enough a presence to intimidate all but the most foolhardy, or dangerous, members but his quiet manner made it unnecessary for him to be a bully. A few times she had had to resort to discipline—usually a few days on hardtack and water or night duty aloft in bad weather—but from what she'd been told, the amount of punishment she dished out was light compared to most large ships' crews. Given her lack of previous experience next to that of her crew who'd been sailing for many years, she still felt pleased.

Her initial "I want to be a pirate' impulse was proving to be a revealing insight into her nature that she had not expected. She remembered how it had been boredom that had driven her to demand something to do aboard a ship—seemingly ages ago, yet here she was, captain of a ship she'd captured, from people who would label her a pirate, and no doubt hang her without hesitation.

They quickly rowed ashore, riding the breakers into the sand, and when Hava jumped out of the longboat she saw Baron Dumarch standing on the beach, arms akimbo, while his bodyguards surrounded him, ready for danger.

She approached Daylon and when she was a yard away said, "M'lord."

For a moment, the baron looked unsure. Then he said, "I know you."

"I'm Hava, Hatushaly's wife."

"Yes," said Daylon. "Balven would know you on sight." He spent a moment regarding her. "So, here we are. You want a parley. What are we to discuss?"

"First, I have nearly a hundred people who want to come home, so can I move them ashore?"

Daylon was silent for a moment then said, "If they are my people we'll find something to do with them." He glanced north along the shoreline. "I guess they're all my people, given there seems nowhere else for them to go."

Hava's expression revealed that this was not the answer she had expected, but she replied, "Can we disembark them here?"

"We can't feed them here."

"They can carry enough ashore to eat for the next two or three days. That should get them down to the city."

"Then this is as good a place as any." He turned and said to the lieutenant leading his escort, "Get ready to receive those coming ashore." Turning to Hava, he asked, "What else?"

"We have much to talk about."

"Ride with me back to the castle?"

Hava smiled and said, "If there's a bath involved, a good meal, and clean clothes, then yes."

Daylon smiled. "We can see to that." He looked skyward and said, "We're going to be short of daylight, so perhaps spend the night here, and depart at sunrise?"

Hava nodded. "I'll go back to my ship and I'll be here at first light tomorrow."

"Good," said the baron. "Should I send for healers and wagons for those coming ashore?"

"No," said Hava. "They're all fit and can walk to the city in a couple of days."

"A carriage?" He smiled as he asked.

"I can ride," she said.

"That you can," he answered. "I'll have fresh mounts here in the morning, waiting."

"Until then," she said, both anxious for word how the rest of the coast fared and desperate for a meal and sleep. She had taken a long arc to steer clear of any raiders' ships that might remain, and had edged closer to land for two days, moving carefully until she was convinced there wasn't a warship or slaver anywhere near Marquenet, and decided to put in near the North Point tor. She knew it was the last fortification on the coast since she had ridden past the cut-off road between the main highway to Beran's Hill and the sea.

Still, she wished she wasn't on her last legs from three days' sailing with only a couple of short naps and could magically be at the castle now, for there were so many things to share with the baron and as many questions to ask.

She waved for her rowers to launch the longboat and waded in to jump in when it was far enough out. She took a deep breath of relief, for until she saw the answering flag to parley, she never knew from moment to moment if she was sailing into a fight.

She kept her rowers in the longboat as they came alongside the *Queen of Storms* and quickly climbed up the rope ladder to the railing. Sabien waited at the rail. "Start ferrying the passengers ashore," she said as she cleared the railing, and then added, "I'm for a meal and sleep. You're in command until morning."

"Aye, Captain," he replied, his expression showing relief that nothing was amiss.

Hava went down a companionway to the crew's mess and found it unattended. She foraged a little and came away with a small round of cheese, some hardtack and a half-empty wine skin. "That will have to do," she muttered, realizing that her first proper meal would probably be eating with the baron. She hoped he'd set a better table.

She made it back to her cabin, nibbling along the way, and once sitting on her bunk she managed to get her boots off, finish the wine, before falling sound asleep with the remaining cheese and dried bread on the floor, still wearing the clothes she'd worn for three days.

DECLAN CHOSE TO STAND WATCH while the others stuffed their faces with raw, bloody liver. Sebastian had spotted deer tracks in a muddy wash above a watering hole and Declan had moved the men back while Sebastian created a makeshift hunter's hide and waited.

Near sundown a small group of deer had come to drink and Sebastian had felled a young male. He had called for the men and by the time they'd come down the wash he had already turned the deer on its side and sliced it open, cutting off a piece of the liver. He was chewing on it when they reached him. He started cutting more pieces and said, "It will keep you alive while we cook the rest!"

The men had gladly taken the bloody nourishment and two had started a fire while the rest went looking for sticks upon which to roast the meat. With night falling and the cooking fire alight, Declan decided that sentries were needed. The men were as exhausted as he was but he felt the need to stand the first watch. The smell of deer meat sizzling on sticks above the fire was making him ravenous, but he could wait.

Toombs rose up and said, "I can stand a watch, Captain, while you eat."

"Thanks," said Declan and he approached the fire.

Sixto saw him coming as the sun set and grabbed a skewer

stuck into the ground near the edge of the fire and handed it to Declan.

"Appreciated," said Declan and he sat down and began to nibble the still-sizzling meat.

"It's funny," said Sixto, "but when I was a child the one thing I hated most was when my mother fed us liver." He shook his head as he wiped grease off his chin. "She'd be amazed to see this."

"Can't say as I fancy the taste, but it fills the belly," said Declan. He lowered his voice. "Over my left shoulder, do you see anything?"

Sixto smiled, and nodded as if Declan had said something amusing, then, keeping his face still, he shifted his weight slightly and looked to the left over Declan's shoulder. After a few moments, he said, "Something."

"Animal or man?" asked Declan.

"Can't tell. I only know because there are a few parts of the brush that aren't moving as they should."

"Well, we're damn close to that watering hole and the fire sent up some smoke, so it could be either."

"Yes," Sixto agreed.

"So," said Declan, "keep watching and . . . tell me more about your mother's love for liver."

Sixto didn't have to feign amusement as he said, "She could get it cheaply from the butcher in our village. I never tasted beef, lamb, or pork until I left home. It was liver with vegetables, fried kidneys, sweetbreads, whatever the butcher would give to her in barter."

"What did she barter?" asked Declan with a few hand gestures to make the conversation look animated should someone be watching. He also knew there could be nothing there and all this was for naught, but as the old expression went, better safe than sorry.

Sixto's eyes stayed fixed on the distant woods as the light faded. "We had a small plot and she grew vegetables. She was good at it, knew when to plant and when to change what was planted. There was always something growing and something ready to pull out of the ground. Carrots, turnips, onions, other plants."

"What about your father?"

"He was a mercenary, like me. He would be gone for months, even over a year once. I never knew him well. He'd come back and my mother would welcome him. There were six of us, and I was oldest, so he tossed me out when I was about thirteen years of age. He drank a lot when he was home, and now that I've been in this trade I know that he spent most of what he made fighting on drink and whores. But he brought home enough that my mother could pay for a few things, like fabric to make clothing, or a new pot." Sixto shrugged. "When my father told me to leave, he said something about being the age he was when his father threw him out." His eyes stayed fixed on the distant brush and trees now fading in the gloom. "One of the reasons I vowed never to marry. I've seen too many children left homeless and alone from too many battles."

Declan nodded, remembering the dead children he had seen lined up for a mass grave at Beran's Hill. "I wanted to have sons and daughters . . . once."

Sixto spared him a glance and whatever question he might have had about that last statement went unsaid. Eventually, he said, "I can see nothing now."

Declan nodded, briefly gripping Sixto's arm. "Set the watch, in case."

"Me?"

Declan motioned for Sixto to follow him, and when he neared the campfire said, "Heads up."

The men who were chatting stopped, those who were eating paused, and two who had fallen asleep were awakened.

When he had all eyes on him, Declan said, "Tomorrow we move deeper into this canyon. Sixto and I saw . . . something. Perhaps nothing, but if we're being watched by someone, I don't want any surprises. So, trail discipline and no talking. Sixto will set the watch." He looked at Benruf. "You've been a staunch ally so far, but I don't know you that well. Sixto is now my second, and if we get safely out of here, you can stay or leave as you see fit." He took a deep breath and added, "Bogartis's last words to me were to save as many as I could, so that is my goal, right now. The sand we sought is lost, but I can still fashion good weapons without it. I intend to return to Marquenet and make fine blades for the baron. And when he sails to find the source of all this butchery, I plan on standing at his side."

The men glanced from face to face but no one said a word.

When he heard no objections, Declan said, "Sixto, for the watch two men, two hours each." He looked each man in the face in turn and said, "We have a chance to survive."

Still no one said a word.

Bodai waved Hatu to sit opposite him at the table that had become their makeshift desk.

"Good morning." Hatu shook his head. "You were right. I fell into bed and slept like the dead."

Bodai said, "That's good." Then he yawned.

Hatu laughed.

"Late night. But I did read some things that bear on our studies." Bodai was an adroit liar, and unless he was maladroit Hatu would have no hint that this was information he had gleaned from Nathan the night before. "So, let me return to one of our more pressing concerns: magic."

"My powers?"

"Yes," said Bodai, "but your peculiar situation is only part of a question. Imagine a world where magic is . . . everywhere, used by many people, to different levels of success, both for good and ill."

"A world other than Garn?"

"Yes." Bodai nodded.

"Such as in the wonder tales told by minstrels?"

"Exactly."

Hatu sat back as if considering something then said, "When they said 'faraway lands' or 'wonderful lands' I just assumed they were speaking of some place here on Garn, but very far away, or very far back in time." He shifted a bit in his chair. "After I got older, I realized they were imaginary places because everywhere I traveled, well, it was as if everywhere was something like everywhere else."

Bodai nodded. "It's true that people do have more in common than is first supposed. They have babies. They seek wealth or at least sufficiency, and some fight while others pray to gods, some stay home for safety while others travel to seek new vistas; but at heart people are people."

A sudden memory of his capture by the Sisters of the Deep sprang into Hatu's mind and he said, "And some are very evil."

"I've seen enough to agree with that," replied Bodai. "But let's return to our imaginary land."

Hatu nodded.

"What if I told you that there are different worlds beyond Garn?"

Hatu's forehead furrowed as he weighed the question. His

expression alternated between appearing to ponder the idea and doubting it, as if Bodai was somehow testing him. "Seriously?"

Bodai said, "Seriously."

"What, you've been to other worlds?"

"No," said Bodai with a laugh. "But I've seen things . . ." He held up his hands, palms out. "I'm tempted to go off into another of my long explanations, but I'll save that for questions you may have ahead. Just suspend your doubt and agree that there is a world far away with people on it who are much like us, and other creatures that are very different."

"Like those water creatures that serve the Sisters of the Deep?"

"Those poor souls that were once men, monstrously fashioned by blood sacrifice and dark arts. Yet in a way, perhaps something like that, but natural beings, having their own language and manner of living. For want of a better way to say this, animals but with minds and souls and . . ." Bodai shrugged, struggling with the explanation. His tutelage from the night before had overwhelmed him and he struggled to remember half of what Nathan had shared with him.

Hatu let out a long breath. "Very well, for the sake of this exercise, I'll accept a world somewhere out there"—he waved his hand—"where people and other creatures live and magic is everywhere."

"I sense your doubt, but we'll put that aside for a moment." Bodai feigned that he had more to share, but his simple hope was that Hatu didn't ask questions for which he had no answer.

"I'll try," said Hatu with a barely contained smile.

Bodai's gaze narrowed. "You fail magnificently in hiding your disdain. What is the problem with imagining magic in large amounts, given what you personally achieved?"

"Magic, if you want to call my powers that, I'll accept, though I'm still uncertain what it really is, but other worlds? If there are other worlds, why don't we know about them, or visit them, or . . . where exactly are they?"

"Ah, I keep forgetting you were never raised as the Firemanes were, but rather as just another student of Coaltachin." Bodai visibly slumped in his chair. "The fault is mine, Hatu, not yours." He drummed his fingers on the table and then sat upright. "Stars. What do you know about stars?"

Hatu smiled. This was a subject he presumed to have some knowledge of, mostly taught to him by Master Bodai himself. "Lights in the night, but they move in a predestined pattern. They travel slowly across the sky in a procession, and if you understand the pattern and the time of year and where you sailed from, you can plot a course and land reasonably close to where you want to." He sat back with a smug expression, obviously relieved to have remembered that lesson.

"True," said Bodai, "but that's not the answer. Those are suns."

"Suns?" repeated Hatu, seriously confused. "There's only one sun, and it rises every morning and sets every evening."

"They're suns," said Bodai flatly.

"But they are tiny."

"Because they are very far from here. Some are many times as big as our own sun."

"And you know this?"

"Yes."

"How?"

"I was . . . taught, I suppose you would say, by someone"—he paused for a moment to refine his story, then went on—"a long time ago . . . actually, just before you were born. He was an odd fellow, but I quickly came to understand that he had traveled much farther than I, had seen far more than I had, and had actually visited those worlds."

"Impossible," replied Hatushaly.

Bodai sat motionless, then said, "Sometimes I forget that just because you are very clever and curious doesn't mean you have a developed imagination."

"What is a developed imagination?" asked Hatu.

As Bodai's eyes widened and he was poised on the edge of a major rebuttal, Hatu started to chuckle, the first genuine sound of delight Bodai had heard from him. After a moment, Bodai began to chuckle as well. "You are a pain in my arse, Hatushaly," he said a moment later.

"I can imagine many things, Bodai," said Hatu as his mirth subsided. "You underestimate me."

Bodai settled back in his chair, then suddenly barked out a laugh. "I hate it when my students challenge me, and they're right." He looked at Hatushaly. "What do you need to know?"

"I need to know, what has this to do with my problem?"

"Context."

"Context?"

"Yes, so many things are not understood unless you know the context."

"Such as?"

Bodai paused for a moment then said, "Imagine you have a goat."

"Very well."

"Now," said Bodai, "imagine that goat has wandered off your property and devoured your neighbor's garden."

Hatu nodded.

"So, are you responsible for the damage done to your neighbor?"

Hatu weighed the question, then said, "That would depend—"

"Yes!" Bodai shouted, startling Hatu with the interruption. "It would depend on the context. Was your goat tethered? Did your neighbor have a fence? Did he leave the gate open? Had this problem existed before?" He sat back, pleased with where the lesson was heading. "So, we have too many . . ."

"Unknowns," supplied Hatu.

Bodai grinned. "So, you did pay attention."

Hatu shook his head slowly in amusement. "Of all the masters you were the only one I looked forward to learning from. The others gave useful instructions for all the tasks given to students, but your lessons were the most interesting."

"Really?" Bodai's expression showed genuine surprise.

"For me, anyway," said Hatu with a chuckle. "Most of the students thought you a windbag in love with the sound of your own voice."

Bodai looked abashed.

Hatu held up his hand. "Not me. What I found the most interesting was how you . . . made things connect."

"How was that?" asked Bodai.

"You'd say things like . . . there was a bad crop here so people would be looking for grain somewhere else and we could be advantaged . . . by doing something where there was ample grain . . ." Hatu shrugged. "That's a bad example."

Bodai laughed. "No, it's what I tried to teach. Coaltachin needed smart agents. Not just those wicked with a dagger, or able to gull the right targets, but those who could see a bigger picture. How everything is linked in some fashion or another."

Hatu smiled and nodded. "Cause and effect. That's it, like ripples in a pond. What happens in one place may have an impact somewhere else. It was not lost on me, apparently."

"Wonderful," said Bodai. "So, now we can accept that things

we don't understand are not necessarily understandable at first glance, but eventually can be understood."

Hatu sat back, a rueful expression on his face. "This is going to be a long session, isn't it?"

Bodai nodded. "The first of many."

Hatu gave out a soft groan. "So, sooner begun, sooner ended, right?"

Bodai said, "Exactly. Now, where was I? Oh, yes. Stars, and the universe being so much vaster, so much more than we imagined . . ." He smacked the table and added, "So, let us begin there."

6

REALIGNMENTS,

DISCLOSURES, AND DISCOVERY

———⊹———

Hava was surprised and pleased to see the baron waiting for her at the base of the tor. Behind him, her passengers were climbing into wagons, enough to carry all of them to the city.

She jumped out of the boat and was standing in front of Daylon even as her crew was turning the longboat back toward the *Queen of Storms*. "You sent for wagons," she said.

"After we talked, I thought it's a long walk, even if these people are fit, and I was going to ride with you anyway, so I can bring half a dozen wagons up here at the same time as a coach for you."

"A coach?" she scoffed. "I thought you said you knew I could ride."

"Yes, but a coach affords us some privacy to talk. There are many things that must be kept to a small group of trusted people. Come, we'll talk more about this once we're underway. Would you care for something to break your fast?"

"I would, but perhaps something we can share in the coach?"

"There is food in a basket, in the coach," said Daylon, motioning her to follow him.

A footman waited next to a well-built, but not particularly ornate, coach which was designed to carry as many as six people, with a guard next to a driver and small seats for two guards at the rear. The baron entered first, an entitlement of his rank, and Hava followed.

Once seated, Baron Dumarch pulled back a cloth covering a large basket and Hava looked in to see fresh fruit, cheese, and sausages, as well as cloths to clean their hands, and a porcelain pot.

"The tea should still be hot. I had it brewed on the stove in the tor. The rest is as fresh as I could manage. I'm sorry to say food is a serious problem now, since most of the farms in the barony were deserted and are only just resuming their work."

She fetched out a mug and asked, "Tea?"

"No, thank you." While she filled a mug for herself, he said, "Seeing you wading ashore from that ship was both a surprise and a relief. I got a report back from Beran's Hill that you'd vanished after the sacking of that town and later someone said they'd seen you and another woman heading north. When I reached Port Calos and saw the utter destruction there, I assumed you were either dead or captured by slavers."

"The latter," said Hava. "Molly Bowman is the other woman. We contrived a revolt by the prisoners and took over their treasure ship."

"Whose?"

"I should start at the beginning."

He nodded.

As they moved at a good pace down the highway to Marquenet, Hava began to tell her tale from the moment she and Molly had set out for Port Calos to seek Hatushaly.

The baron settled in and listened.

* * *

HATU SAT DRINKING A MUG of coffee, having discovered a large bag of roasted beans plundered from one of the Azhante ships that Hava had captured. The boys running the kitchen hadn't understood it was for a drink, so Hatushaly had conducted an impromptu lesson in how to grind the beans, and filter hot—just shy of a boil—water into a pot. He threw half a dozen hard biscuits into a small sack and tossed in a still-fresh apple and carried them all into the library.

The study sessions over the last few nights had been fascinating, but fatiguing. Still, he was eager to press on. The topics Bodai had chosen seemed to have nothing to do with the immediate problem of his powers having gone for no apparent reason, but the concepts and subject matter were challenging. He was forced to think hard, to challenge his assumptions about how things were. To his surprise, he found he welcomed that challenge.

"I have some hardtack biscuits, if you're hungry," he said, entering the area of the library where he and Bodai had been holding their sessions.

"I ate earlier," Bodai said. "Besides, that ship's fare always gives me a sour stomach."

"Well, the boys in the kitchen say the masons will have the big ovens back in working order soon, so we'll have real fresh bread!" Then with a sarcastic tone, he added, "If we can get flour, baker's yeast, and the rest of whatever they need."

"If we get that, I'll pillage some eggs from a henhouse and show them how to bake egg-bread!" Bodai gazed off into the distance as he savored a memory. "Truly delicious and nourishing!" He sighed loudly. "Rebuilding a functioning society, even a tiny one like on these islands, takes time. We have farmers who've cleared their land and Hava said she'll bring back whatever she can by way of tools, plants that can be repotted and planted here, and workers she can find to join us . . . but I wonder how many of those who traveled with her will want to come back?"

Hatu shrugged. "It depends on how bad things are. She'll return with the first reports of what happened after people were captured."

"True," said Bodai. He motioned for Hatushaly to sit down and took the chair to his right. "So, what do you think about what we discussed yesterday?"

"I pondered, and at last realized that your claim that stars are suns, but so far from here that they look like tiny lights, is no more unlikely than assuming they are little lights that are close." Hatu started to chew on a biscuit and then took a sip from his coffee mug. "So, I don't *know* that either explanation is true, but either might be."

"A fair beginning. For the moment assume my claim is the true one, that the universe is this vast expanse, so big we don't have a number for how far away things are, or how many stars there are. That stars are gathered in what are called galaxies, and that when you're out to sea or alone in the mountains that incredible number of lights you can see is countless, and more, that beyond what you can see there are more and more galaxies stretching so far that the light vanishes before we can see it. Stars that outnumber the grains of sand on all the beaches on Garn."

Hatu laughed. "You gave me a headache last night with all this, Bodai. It's far too early in the day to be drinking! I am not sure I believe any of this, but I find it fascinating and beyond that, the idea of worlds circling the stars? Most people I know think the sun circles Garn."

Bodai waved away the comment. "What I told you the first day, that our world rotates, explains the apparent—"

"Yes, I know," interrupted Hatushaly. "You spent a good hour explaining the entire relative point-of-view and perspective thing. I'm not entirely sure I fully understand, but it explains it in a way that, like the stars question, is equally reasonable as an answer."

"Very well," said Bodai. "My belaboring the point about the vastness of the universe is to help you understand that a great deal of what we take for granted is based on assumptions. We do not feel the ground beneath our feet move, so we assume it's motionless, just as a tiny gnat clinging to a piece of fruit doesn't sense it's being moved in a wagon bearing that fruit to the market."

Hatu gave an inclination of his head, conceding the point.

"Because of that assumption, we then decide that because the sun moves across the sky during the day, it must be revolving around us."

"A point you made repeatedly yesterday, Bodai. What's next?"

"What's next is that we can't assume those other stars and the worlds around them are like Garn."

"Fair point."

"Some stars will be small, some worlds frozen, unable to host life. Others may be very hot and will also be uninhabitable. But let's assume that some are enough like Garn that life thrives there. Moreover, some of those worlds have living beings there, rational beings with logical thoughts."

Hatu chuckled. "I like where this is going." He seemed genuinely delighted. "Why couldn't our classes have been more like this?"

"Because that was Coaltachin." Bodai's tone was somber.

Hatu lost his smile. "Knowledge to serve the Kingdom of Night. Never knowledge for knowledge's sake."

"Yes."

"Just knowing," said Hatushaly, "is . . . worthwhile, sometimes." His expression hinted at a sense of loss, a moment of "what might have been," then he resumed his usual manner. "So, what more?"

"Magic," said Bodai.

"Magic?" Hatu gave a shrug of his shoulders.

"What if what we call magic, what is told in the minstrels' songs and travelers' tales, and your powers, what if that is merely a name for things we don't understand?"

Hatu slowly nodded, accepting that proposition.

"Why does a rock fall from your hand when you drop it?"

Hatu's eyes widened and he said, "I don't know. It just does."

"There's a force that pulls it to the ground, just as if you fall from a ladder—"

Hatu put up his hand. "A phenomenon I know all too well."

Bodai smiled. "Yet a mote of dust can float."

"And birds and insects can fly," added Hatu.

"Yet we do not know how."

"They have wings?" suggested Hatu.

Bodai raised his finger. "But motes of dust do not. Leaves from trees can be carried for miles by a very strong wind."

Hatu was silent.

"Things we do not understand," said Bodai.

"Yet!" exclaimed Hatushaly.

With a laugh, Bodai said, "Yes, yet!" Then he said, "The force that makes you and a rock fall to the ground is called gravity."

Hatushaly nodded, his face set in an expression of delight at new answers to questions, almost the opposite of his frustration and anger at questions left unanswered when he was a child.

Reflecting Hatushaly's delight, Bodai could adequately play out the lesson from Nathan the night before. "Gravity is a force, agreed?"

Hatu nodded. "We see it all the time—" He halted. "Is this a perception thing?"

Caught a little off guard, Bodai said, "Not as I think you mean, like assuming the sun revolves around Garn. As you said, we see it all the time. A baby knows about it before he can speak, simply by landing on his backside while learning to walk."

"Fair enough," agreed Hatu.

"There are many other forces we take for granted but see every day. The heat that comes from our sun along with the light. Both heat and light are forces. Wind is a force. When the ground below our feet shakes as it moves, that's a force.

"We may not understand why those forces manifest as they do, but we do have some sense of the underlying reasons."

Hatu's attention was now rapt.

"All forces in the vast universe are caused by a conflict between positive and negative furies."

Hatu's brow knitted.

"Consider magnets. They attract metal," Bodai went on, and Hatu nodded. "Yet if you put two magnets opposite each other, with the same poles facing one another, they repel each other."

Hatu's expression changed as he pondered that. "So when they attract . . . identical ends of a bar magnet . . . face opposites . . . Yes, I think I see."

"We call one end of the magnet positive, the other negative. We could as easily have said black and white, male and female, good and evil, but whatever the label, it's the force that's real."

"I think I see."

"Some furies are like one end of the magnet, while others are their opposites. Some push against each other, while others are drawn toward each other. The furies are countless, smaller than those dust motes that float in the air, unseen, but pulling and pushing constantly."

"Unseen?"

"Can you see air?"

"Sometimes . . ." began Hatu.

Bodai cut him off. "No, you sometimes see what's in the air, dust or smoke, steam in the kitchen, but never the air itself. Yet air is real. Without it, we die." Hatu nodded. "The furies are just as real as air, and they are always creating a force, creating power. Magic is the manipulation of that force."

"So my powers are manipulating that force, the tension between the furies?"

Bodai stood. "Yes, and that ends our lesson for this day."

Hatu said, "But—"

Bodai silenced him with a wave of his hand, and a reaction learned from years of being taught by the masters caused Hatu to fall silent instantly. After a moment he said, "Very well, tomorrow."

Bodai patted his shoulder and said, "Curb your desire. All shall be made clear eventually." Silently he wondered if that was true. He also needed to explain to Nathan that he would need much longer lessons if Hatu was to be kept busy.

DECLAN MOVED SLOWLY THROUGH DEEP undergrowth as Sebastian tried to cut away serious impediments with a big belt-knife. What they needed was a pair of machetes. Still, they were making progress down into the valley.

The plants were slowly changing as they descended. The canopy of treetops soared higher, and the valley widened. The thorny plants were thinning out while a lusher, thicker undergrowth grew more prevalent.

The day after they took the deer, Declan had the men rest as best they could to regain their strength. Here there was shade and the high walls of the deepening cleft in the ground had the sun directly overhead for only a few hours rather than from sunrise to sunset, and they could drink their fill from the nearby watering hole before refilling their water skins to move on. As a result, the heat of the day was bearable. So instead of pushing on at first light, he had them rest until the sun cleared the easternmost rim.

Declan couldn't escape the feeling that they were being watched, a sense that had begun the evening they'd felled the deer two days earlier. Still, no stalkers were seen as Declan's company trekked deeper into the Wound.

With water and the promise of more food, his next concern was focused on returning to Marquensas. He had ruled out trying to go back to Abala, for even with the provisions and water they could carry, they couldn't withstand the desert again without horses, so they continued along this deepening gorge. It was heading southeast, away from Abala, but Declan hoped they'd find another such passage leading to a way out.

What little Benruf knew of this area offered scant reassurance. Apparently, there were other smaller canyons, some of which might rise back to the surface, but they emptied into what was known as the Scorched Coast and miles without drinkable water, or the Endless Desert. While the desert wasn't literally endless, it was vast enough. Without knowing where water could be found, it offered only a certain and miserable death.

Sebastian was seeking a game trail or a stream they might

follow downward. He had proved to be a competent trailbreaker and they'd only had to double back once so far this day.

Declan stayed alert for any possible ambush as they slowly descended the long canyon and watched for any signs of illness. The newest and youngest man from Bogartis's recruitment up in Marquenet, Billy Jay, obviously had the most trouble, as he was unused to the privation of the trail, but he seemed to be managing. He was learning from the more experienced members, and other than hunger, the men seemed to be holding up.

Declan was glad to be moving forward, for that was the only plan, to keep going lower into Garn's Wound, to a cooler place where the small group of survivors could regroup and find a way out.

They pushed on.

HATU LAUGHED, AND SAID, "AGAIN, you amaze me with these speculations."

Bodai scowled. "I thought we agreed yesterday that for the purpose of your education you'd put aside your disbelief and accept what I say as fact."

Hatu held his palms out in a gesture of surrender. "It's been a long day. The sun is setting and I'm getting hungry."

Bodai's expression turned dark. He had endured a tedious, long session with Nathan the night before in order to keep Hatu occupied.

"I'm trying," Hatu said in mock-plaintive tones, but then he started to laugh. "I can accept the idea of furies, power, forces, energy, although I barely understand what they mean. I can even accept the idea that the stars are suns so distant that they look like points of light, and certainly it would be reasonable that some suns are larger or smaller than others, but suns so vast that the fastest horse couldn't run around their . . . circumference, right?" Bodai nodded. "In . . . what was that number?"

"A million." Bodai's expression revealed that he was on the edge of exasperation.

"The fastest horse ever couldn't run from one side to the other in a million lifetimes!" Hatu shook his head as his mirth subsided. "I'm sorry, but some of it is absurd . . ."

"Nathan!" Bodai shouted. "This isn't working!"

Hatu's eyes widened and he sat back. "What?"

"If you don't come out, this is over!"

After a moment, the blond stranger stepped out from behind a bookcase on the other side of the library. "Very well."

Hatu shot to his feet, but Bodai put up his hand and said, "It's all right. This is the source of all these new ideas."

"I don't understand," said Hatushaly, not a hint of humor remaining in his manner. "How long were you hiding over there?"

"Long enough," said the newcomer as he reached the table and pulled out a third chair. Sitting down, he said, "Though you did last a bit longer than I'd imagined."

"What?" asked Bodai.

"You were right. It was too brief a lesson yesterday. I thought there was a moment when you were going to give up or Hatushaly was going to walk out on you."

"There was," both Bodai and Hatushaly said, almost in unison.

Nathan laughed, and it was almost musical. Hatu felt uncomfortable, knowing that this stranger had been hiding a few feet away, and having being unaware of his presence, yet he found himself reacting much as Bodai did. His concerns seemed to drop away by the moment, and he felt himself relax. There was just something about this man that fostered a sense of the familiar, a feeling of friendship and trust. Like Bodai, Hatu's background and training made him suspicious at first, but then, as if he'd been given a drug of some sort, this trained reflex to question, to look for lies, just faded away.

"You're both tired," said Nathan. "It's been a long day, so perhaps one quick demonstration and a simple exercise and we can begin in earnest tomorrow. Is that acceptable?"

Both men nodded.

"Why all this nonsense if you were going to meet Hatu, anyway? You said something about it was imperative that he not meet you now."

Nathan said, "I let you infer something dire would occur because I needed to convince you"—he pointed his finger at Bodai—"before I could convince him." He hiked his thumb at Hatu.

"Why?" asked Hatu.

"Human nature," answered Nathan. "If I tried to convince both of you together that I could unravel the secrets to your problems, you would simply have convinced each other that you both were right, and I was a charlatan, an agent of some dark power seeking to keep you from finding the truth." He gave a dismissive wave. "That sort of nonsense. Now that I've convinced you, Bodai . . . I did convince you?"

Bodai gave a slow nod. "I'm not completely convinced, but you've given me so much to ponder. And what you have shared is reasonable yet seems so impossible."

"Well, I was hoping to spare myself this next bit. It's rather hard work." Nathan stood up and waved his hand in a sweeping arc aimed at the ceiling. Abruptly the vault of the library darkened as if night had suddenly dropped upon them and a shimmering circle of darkness with sparkles inside it appeared. It resolved itself rapidly into a stunning field of stars and Nathan said, "Hatu, pick one."

"What do you mean?" Hatu asked in a near-whisper.

"Magic!" gasped Bodai. "Real magic."

Nathan shrugged. "Some people call it magic. I think of it as tricks, just of a higher quality than you find from a mountebank at a street festival. Both of you, being from Coaltachin, know exactly the sort of sleight of hand and mummery I mean. So pick a star, Hatu, and learn."

Hatu considered. "That slightly blue one near the center, just above those three smaller white ones."

"Ah!" said Nathan, obviously enjoying his performance.

He waved his hand and suddenly it was as if they were flying forward at a terrible speed until the star began to resolve itself and in moments a roiling mass of what looked like blue fire hung above them, its light blotting out all but a few of the very brightest stars at the edge of the image.

"It has a name, I dare say, from those who are capable of seeing it, but for us it's just a blue star. I'm no expert on the subject of stars, though there are beings across the universe who study them, I know, but this one is many times the size of your own sun," Nathan continued. He looked at Hatu. "That number you struggled with, Hatu?"

"A million."

"What's the highest number you've experienced in real life, say counting gold your crew has stolen?"

Thinking back to his days as a thief, Hatu said, "A hundred. I've seen a hundred coins. It's a lot."

"A full purse of coins," Nathan agreed. "Now, ten hundred is a thousand."

Hatu nodded.

"A thousand thousands is a million."

Hatu sat back, his eyes wide, as Bodai said, "I should have thought of that example."

"A thousand millions is a billion," said Nathan, and even Bodai's forehead furrowed.

With a wave of his hand, Nathan made the image change. Hatu and Bodai sat transfixed as a round ring of a star with long lances of white light blaring through its hole unfolded. "This too is a star, though one you'll never see through even the best sailor's spyglass. From one end of that fine lance of light to the other measures billions of miles."

He looked at Hatu and said, "Doubt your own senses, but do not doubt that this universe is so much vaster than you could ever have imagined."

Hatu sat motionless and after a moment said in a whisper, "Show me more."

Nathan waved his hand and suddenly the image sped across the vault of the ceiling and centered on an angry red point of light. As it came forward they beheld a ball of what looked to be pulsing red gas. "This is a type of star I know little about," he said. "I just know that this is an old one, and it's dying."

"Stars die?" Hatu asked, glancing at Bodai.

His former master and current teacher sat wide-eyed, moisture gleaming on his forehead, apparently moved to speechlessness.

Nathan said, "There are probably some books in here about stars." He waved his hand and the image vanished.

"How did you do that?" asked Hatushaly.

"As I said, tricks, but . . . honest ones." He sighed and sat down. "That was tiring." Leaning on the table, he said to Hatushaly, "You are . . . a nexus. Powers surge through you, whether or not you wish it, and either you just let it happen or you learn how to tap into those powers."

Hatu slowly let out a deep breath. "What am I?"

"Unlucky, I guess," said Nathan. "Everything you saw is many times larger than what I showed you. Everything in the entire universe comes into being, is moved, and dies because of tension." He held his fists in opposition before his chest. "Like magnets pushing against each other or pulling together. Positive and negative furies."

"Furies," agreed Bodai.

"That star we saw, the great spewing of . . . energy. The essence of that star is the product of furies at work. Everything within you is a tool," he said to Hatu, "a way to harness that power, to make it obey you . . ." Then he laughed. "Up to a point. There are always limits. If you were truly able to control all furies, you would be a god."

Hatu was drained. "How did you do all that?" he asked weakly.

"Pay attention and you'll be able to do the same, and more, but . . ." Nathan paused. "If you live long enough. That seems to be the immediate problem."

"I need a drink," said Bodai.

"Later, and I'll have one with you," said Nathan. "We have one more thing to do before the day's over, so the faster we do it the sooner we can have that drink. All right?" he asked Hatu.

Hatu nodded his agreement.

"Sit over here," said Nathan, pointing to the chair he had vacated.

Hatu complied and when he was seated Nathan said, "Get up a moment."

Hatu did as he was instructed, and Nathan moved the chair

a few feet farther from the table. "That's better," he said. "Now, please sit."

Hatu sat down and Nathan said, "That was an easy exercise. So, have you seen people who are required to hold their arms above their heads for a long time?"

"What do you mean?" asked Hatushaly.

"Someone pushing against a tall ladder, while someone else is at the top? A soldier being punished so he has to hold a pole arm high above his head? Something like that?"

"I suppose so," said Hatu.

"There's a trick to that. I will teach you. This is your first lesson. All right?"

Hatu nodded and waited.

"First, close your eyes."

Hatu did so.

"Now, put your right hand above your head."

Hatu moved in the chair a bit, leaning to the left, and lifted his right hand above his head.

"Now, Bodai, close your eyes, too."

Bodai hesitated for a moment, then nodded and did as he was instructed.

A moment passed in silence, then Nathan said, "Hatu, imagine a string, strong and unbreakable, is gently pulling your hand up. Can you feel it?"

After a moment, Hatu said, "Yes."

"Now, passing through your hand that string touches the top of your head. Do you feel that?"

"Yes," said Hatu.

"So gently tug up on that string, lifting your hand and your head."

Hatu moved as instructed and another long, silent moment passed.

"Very well," said Nathan. "Tug up a tiny bit more, just to make sure that string is taut."

Hatu pulled and felt a tug in his hand and his head.

"Keep it pulling upward! Feel it lift! You feel lighter as it pulls up!"

Then after a moment, Nathan said, "I have to move a chair. Keep your eyes closed and just relax and let the string pull you up."

Hatu did as instructed and heard a chair scrape across the stone floor. Then Nathan said, "Very well. Relax a little, then do as I tell you."

A few moments later, Nathan said, "Feel the tug upward, relax, and let it pull you . . . now, open your eyes."

Hatu and Bodai both opened their eyes and Bodai gasped. Hatu looked down and saw the chair below him had been pulled out by Nathan, and he was floating three feet above the floor.

Hatu exclaimed in surprise and suddenly fell, landing hard on the stone floor. Breath exploded out of his lungs and he cursed as shock ran through his body.

"What was that?"

Bodai said, "You were floating above the floor." He shook his head in wonder. "What was that?" he asked, echoing Hatu.

"It's about not trying, but just doing. You have powers that will elude you if you seek them." Nathan smiled and moved to stand over Hatu. Looking down, he said, "You need to let those powers come to you, calmly let them flow toward you. If you learn to clear your mind, we can move forward and get where you wish to go. So, now that I've shown you . . . things . . ." He looked from Hatu to Bodai. "Let's go get a drink."

7

ENCOUNTERS AND SURPRISING

REALIZATIONS

"A remarkable tale," said Daylon, after Hava had finished recounting all that had occurred since the sacking of Beran's Hill. "What troubles me most is the nature of the assault by these people. They hit as if it was an invasion, at multiple locations, all timed to spread defenses to the thinnest, then they looted, took slaves, and ran. Had they dug in to the north and east, I would have had no means to root out either front without leaving Marquenet open on the other front. I could only defend, and not all that well."

"The people at the Sanctuary probably have more information than I do," said Hava. "I got as much out of them as they could tell me before I left, but a lot of things are still unknown."

They had talked for hours. The coach was moving at a steady pace and would be stopping at the well halfway between North Point tor and the city gates. They were on track to reach the city at about sunrise.

The baron said, "I forgot to mention, a lad claiming to be friends with you and Hatushaly arrived just after the battle, by the name of Donte."

Hava's eyes grew large and she gaped. "Donte! He's alive! He's here?"

"He's something of a proposition, that boy."

Hava laughed both at the news of Donte being among the living and the baron's remark. "A proposition?" She grinned. "That's Donte. Have you had to lock him up?"

The baron looked fatigued and older than Hava remembered, but he smiled as he said, "I think twice now."

"I have to see him."

"You will. He was injured in a struggle." He saw a look of concern pass over Hava's face. "He'll live. A wound that sliced meat and gristle, missing anything vital, but he may limp a bit. My man Balven is finding him useful. We have . . ." He waved his hand. "That can wait. You're tired and I can spare you tales of eastern politics and plotting. We have a great deal to speak of, as I intend to carry the war to those murderous jackals and what you know about that area may be vital. So rest if you can." He stood up and moved to the opposite bench so that Hava could stretch out.

She put up no argument: fatigue swept over her. She lay down and quickly fell asleep.

Daylon Dumarch, Baron of Marquensas, sat silently, pondering how he could use Hava's information to his advantage and what sort of staging area those islands she mentioned might afford. Since the revelation of where the attacks had originated, from the continent named Nytanny, he and Balven had spoken many times about the simple fact that building an army was one task but getting it safely across a vast ocean was another matter entirely. Daylon's only response had been that if the raiders could conceive of a way, he could as well. Even when he had said it, it had rung hollow, but Hava's mention of seizing ships had planted the seed of an idea, and Daylon was waiting for that idea to blossom.

DECLAN MOTIONED FOR THOSE BEHIND him to pass by, and when Sixto caught up with him, he asked, "Did you see anything?"

"I think someone is on our left side, but I can't be sure."

"If they are," said Declan quietly, "they must know this part of the valley well. There would have to be a trail parallel to this one that we didn't find."

"Or they're very good at dodging through trees," said Sixto.

"We're too exposed here." Declan glanced around and realized that the price of taking the path of least resistance was being relatively out in the open.

They were moving through a part of this valley where the floor was dotted with clumps of trees and brush, but there were also open patches of grasses and small plants. It was easier to forge ahead but it offered a predictable route to anyone following, which meant a tracker might not be behind them or to one side but hurrying ahead to where they could lie in wait.

The light was fading as they went deeper into the canyon. For the entire day both canyon walls had been shrouded in shadow and revealed only for a short period when the sun crested the opposite side until it was directly overhead. Those few hours had shown Declan bare stone faces, difficult but not impossible to climb, but leading only up to the unforgiving sand and sun of the Burning Lands.

Declan judged it would be time to make camp in another hour or so. "When we stop for the night, I want to be close to that northern cliff face."

"I think that's where our watcher lurks, if we have a watcher," Sixto said.

Declan let out a deep, silent breath and he clapped Sixto on the shoulder. "My mind may be playing tricks, conjuring up phantom enemies. But I don't think both of us have the same phantoms."

Sixto replied with a dark chuckle. "Though we could both be crazy."

Declan gave his shoulder a friendly squeeze. "That could be true," he replied softly. "Start looking for somewhere we could defend tonight."

Without further comment, Sixto nodded and Declan started ahead more quickly, to catch up to where Benruf was breaking trail.

Hava awoke as the coach rolled in through the castle gates. She yawned and stretched, seeing that Daylon had finally succumbed and dozed off, arms crossed over his chest while sitting upright in the corner. She still needed one good night's sleep, but it would have to wait for another day. She uncurled herself and Daylon's eyes opened as the coach slowed.

He was fully awake as the door opened and he leapt out, his boot barely touching the fold-down step.

Hava likewise exited deftly and saw that the sun had risen, though it was hidden behind the buildings to the east. It was going to be a bright, clear day and Hava got a good view of the city below, despite the morning's shadows. It looked surprisingly untouched by the ravages she had seen everywhere before she had been carried away by slavers. In days gone by the streets had been empty just like this at this hour, so for one tantalizing moment, it was achingly familiar.

Her momentary reverie was interrupted by the baron asking a guardsman, "Where's Balven?"

"If he's not breaking fast, m'lord, he should be in the escort barracks, talking with the prisoners."

"Where I left him," said the baron. Turning to Hava, he said, "Knowing my brother, he's already started questioning those prisoners."

He hardly noticed as a small squad of castellans, his household soldiers, fell into place behind him, but Hava noticed. It appeared that the baron needed to be guarded in his own citadel.

When they reached the barracks, the guards at the door saluted and Daylon said, "Is Balven inside?"

"Yes, m'lord," answered the nearest guard.

The guards opened the door and Daylon and Hava entered.

Two bound men were sitting on the floor, one of them obviously unconscious, and both showing they had been subjected to severe beatings. Balven turned to see the baron enter, and Hava behind him.

"M'lord. Nothing so far."

"It appears that they soon may not be able to answer, even if they wish to," Hava observed.

Balven nodded at her. "Good to see you well. With so many lost, we assumed the worst. Hatushaly?"

"He's fine, sir," she answered. "Safe."

Balven glanced at his brother, who gave a short negative shake of the head which Balven understood well: this was something to be discussed later, in private.

Hava looked past Balven at the two prisoners, saying nothing.

Balven watched her for a moment, then said, "Given your . . . place of birth, have you any methods in mind for getting information out of recalcitrants?" He turned to look at the two men on the floor and added, "They seem determined to endure punishment and remain silent, no matter the threat."

Hava slowly shook her head. "I've heard of potions and the like, but it was not part of my education. Those of us who were selected . . . well, you know . . ."

They knew that she had been a member of a crew, a criminal gang, working for Coaltachin. What they did not know was how complex that system was. Due to Hatu's keen knowledge of the inner workings of Coaltachin, Hava was expected to be ready to kill him if orders came. Her refusal would instantly put a death mark on her as well. Still, Hava was reluctant to speak of some things, even though the baron and Balven knew more than most outsiders. "The interrogators, men we call *inkuiri*, train for years."

At that word, the conscious prisoner's eyes widened and he stared at Hava.

"We rarely risk abductions, but if we do, my people—"

The prisoner could barely speak through his swollen mouth, but he managed to rasp, "*Baci*?"

Hava instantly stopped speaking. Balven and Daylon turned to look at the man. "What?" said Balven.

Hava put her hand on Balven's arm and stepped past him. To the prisoner she said, "*Gaerma*?"

Despite being in obvious pain, the man became animated and in pleading tones launched into a long sentence, an effort which appeared almost to overwhelm him. He repeated it, falling back against the wall. After a moment, his eyes closed and he passed out.

"What was all that?" asked the baron.

"He called me 'sister,'" said Hava, showing confusion. "So I called him 'brother.' His accent is very different, and some of his vocabulary . . ." She took a deep breath as if calming herself, turning to Balven and Daylon. "He asked me"—she gestured to herself—"if I'm serving you and why you"—she indicated Balven—"are torturing him."

Balven regarded Hava. "Donte said they were something called Azhante."

She stared at him, then said, "I only know what Hatu told me about them, but . . . I don't fully know what it means. Where's Donte?"

"Still asleep, most likely," answered Balven. "He was wounded—"

"I already told her," interrupted Daylon. He turned to the nearest guard and said, "Go fetch Donte here, now."

"M'lord," replied the guard and he hurried away.

A few minutes later the man returned, followed by Donte, who was hobbling, supported by a simple wooden crutch. He saw Hava and shouted, "Damn!"

She stepped forward and embraced him. Tears ran down her cheeks. "Hatu told us you were dead!"

Donte laughed as he tried hard not to fall sideways as a result of her embrace. "Looked dead enough, I'll warrant." He paused. "You can let go now."

She stepped back and wiped the tears off her cheeks. "Damn," she said. "I've missed your stupid face."

"And I've missed your cute face. What about Hatu?" he asked.

"He's well. He's with Master Bodai, studying."

"What?" Donte hobbled over to the bench closest to him and glanced at the baron, who nodded permission for him to sit. Wincing as he eased himself down, he said, "I don't know which of those bastards stuck that dagger in me, but when I find out, I'll use this crutch to show him how I feel about it."

Looking back at the two prisoners, the baron said, "That'd put an end to him, if it's one of these two."

"It was a bit of a free-for-all there for a minute," agreed Donte.

Balven whispered something to his brother, and the baron nodded once and said, "See to it."

Balven motioned to a guard and pointed to the prisoners.

"These are to be kept here, but send for a healer. No one besides you and the healer—and the four of us here—is permitted in here. Understood?" The soldier nodded. "Tell the sergeant outside my order, and that when either of them awakes to send word immediately."

"Yes, m'lord."

As the guard hurried off, Donte said, "So, is Hatu back at Coaltachin with Bodai, or around here somewhere?"

"It's a long story," said Hava.

"Apparently we have several long stories," said the baron. "I'll see you all when these men are fit to talk with again." To Balven he said, "I have some road dirt to be rid of and could stand a meal. See to these two."

"M'lord," Balven replied as his brother left the room.

"I'll see to quarters for you, Hava, and the two of you can catch up." He regarded her keenly. "You also look as if you could do with a bath and a meal."

"And more sleep," she replied, her fatigue flooding back after the shock of the prisoner speaking the language of Coaltachin and seeing Donte.

Donte levered himself upright using his crutch and moved out of the way so that Hava could pass. "I'm glad you and Hatu are alive as well!" he said as they passed through the door. A guard posted outside closed it behind him.

He navigated down the two steps and Hava waited for him. Balven was a few yards ahead when she asked, "How did you survive?"

"I don't know," Donte answered. "I was grabbed off that boat with Hatu and when I revived . . . I don't remember much except being alone, cold, and wet." He grimaced and Hava didn't know if it was pain from his wound or his memories. "That part was blurry.

Then I was underwater, surf over my head and walking toward the shore . . . south of here, it turns out. I didn't know who I was."

She looked at her childhood friend with concern but stayed silent. She'd seen Donte in many moods but this sense of something painful was new to her. He had always hidden any hint of trouble behind a mask of cheerful bravado.

"What is it?" she asked.

He sighed, then forced a smile. "I don't know. It feels like something was taken from me, and there's something now missing inside me."

Hava paused as they overtook Balven, who had stopped to give instructions to a servant regarding Hava's quarters. He turned. "I'm going to join the baron. This man will see you to quarters." To Donte he said, "Catch up, then let her rest. You go back to your own room and wait until you're called." Without waiting for an answer, he walked quickly away.

Donte and Hava followed the porter and soon came to the door of the room to be used by Hava.

"Lord Balven gave instructions, m'lady—"

Hava almost burst out laughing at being so addressed by the porter, assuming the man had afforded her an honorific in case she was of some rank.

"And I have sent for a tub and hot water for a bath, and a meal will be brought to you soon after. Is there anything else?"

She said, "No, this will be fine."

The porter pushed open the door and stood aside so that Hava and Donte could enter.

The room had windows overlooking a rolling green patch of land upon which several horses cropped grass in a leisurely fashion. A long window seat ran below it, and Donte sat down there gingerly.

"Should you be hobbling around with that wound?" She pointed to his side.

"If I tear a stitch the healer will just sew me up again."

She gave him a look of mock dismay. "Nothing ever changes with you."

"Oh, one or two things, maybe. Now, what is this about Hatu and Bodai?"

Hava explained what had happened from when she got to Port Calos to finding Bodai and Hatu at the Sanctuary, and how Bodai was an impostor who was spying on the masters of Coaltachin.

Donte laughed, then winced from the pain. "We can never tell Grandfather!"

Hava threw him a questioning look.

"It would give him a heart attack!"

Hava laughed.

"Zusara and Bodai are the two masters he trusts the most!"

"I wasn't planning on telling him," said Hava. "In fact, I was planning on never returning to Coaltachin. Hatu and I have turned our backs on that life. We're married."

"Married? Really?" asked Donte in delight. "You two were always an odd pair, but a good pair."

"Thank you, I think."

"I mean, Hatu is like my brother, and you're sort of like my sister, but if you'd got me drunk I'd have slept with you."

Hava laughed. "I've seen you drunk!"

He waved off her comment. "All right, so maybe I think of you as a sister." He pointed his finger at her. "But I have seen you naked!"

She laughed again. "Not since we were babies!"

He nodded. "True. But you do have a very nice body."

Hava shrugged. She couldn't think of anything to say to that.

"It will be good to see Hatu again, and to trade some stories. I've missed that hot-tempered, crazy man. He's been one of my truest friends, no matter what." His expression grew dark. "Then I'll kill him."

"What?" Hava's eyes grew wide for a moment, then narrowed as she said, "Are you joking?"

Donte shrugged. "Maybe. I don't know. When I got my memories back, some parts were jumbled; some still are. I just had this strange feeling that I'm supposed to kill Hatu . . . somewhere far from . . ." He shook his head. "It's those Sisters of the Deep." He gave a sigh. "The feeling comes and goes, but it's not as strong as it was before."

"That's my husband you're talking about killing," she said with menace.

With a forced smile, Donte said, "Well, then maybe I won't kill him after all."

HATU FLOATED A FOOT ABOVE the floor, his eyes closed and his head tilted back, arms outstretched. His mind was flooded with images that were cascading in rapid succession.

He imagined himself in a void, but within that void lines of power sped by, like countless threads, and he simply waited as they coursed through him. He felt their touch, knowing for a brief instant where they came from and where they were going, but the moment he almost apprehended them enough to understand those facts, they faded, to be replaced by new threads.

Nathan had instructed him not to try to understand, but just to experience, to let the threads pass through him. At first it had been difficult, and several times he had felt the contact with all this power start to wane, but he found it easier each time to fall back into the "not trying" mindset that Bodai and Nathan had attempted to teach him. Practice was beginning to take hold, and when he almost fell out of his awareness, he managed to struggle back into it.

He was elated. His senses were abuzz, and he felt vibrations wash over him that were as stimulating and pleasant as having sex with Hava, taking the first sip of a cold beer on a hot day, or the first time a puppy had licked his face when he was barely more than a baby. Those comparisons were close, but nothing could fully explain the exact, almost perfect, thrill of the power racing through him.

He was on the verge of understanding the idea of being a nexus, of having access to countless lines of energy, yet being able to simply be in the moment, to just let things occur and to witness, not participate.

The experience was timeless. He had no concept of how long he had been in this void, yet he didn't care. It was simultaneously an instant yet also endless. He was living it, yet could barely understand it, nor explain it to anyone else.

Hatu reveled in the experience, then began to sense it fading. He didn't know if it was instantaneous or took hours, but he found himself floating downward, and when his feet touched the stones of the library floor, he blinked. A sharp pain struck him in the head, and his knees threatened to buckle. Bodai was standing next to him and grabbed him, preventing him from falling.

A shiver ran from his feet through his skin to his scalp, and his hair stood up for a moment. Hatushaly felt energized. "That was amazing," he said, his voice a croak.

Nathan offered him a cup of water and he drank, realizing he was very thirsty.

"How long?"

"You were suspended in the air for almost an hour," Bodai answered.

"It felt so much longer . . ." Hatu shook his head as if clearing it. "And yet at the same time it felt like seconds."

Nathan slowly smiled. "Time. It's difficult. It makes no sense."

Moving to the table where they shared lessons, Hatu felt his strength returning. "What do you mean?" he asked as he sat down.

"What is time?" Nathan asked.

Hatu reached for a mug of wine and took a drink. "After several of these lessons, I know better than to waste time answering. So, what is time?"

Nathan smiled at having his question thrown back at him. "For a moment," he began, "imagine a moment, because we need to pretend . . . there is no time. There is no space. Suddenly, everything we know now comes into being. Matter like earth, rock, air, everything comes into being, and all the furies are unleashed, with all those lines of energy being created, and time comes into being. What is time?"

Hatu concentrated on the question, and when Bodai started to speak Hatu held up his hand to silence him. For a long few minutes Nathan and Bodai watched Hatushaly as he sat there, eyes locked on something only he could see, his arm still outstretched and his hand held upright, and then after more than a few minutes, he said, "Time keeps everything from happening at once."

Nathan shouted joyfully, leapt from his seat, and danced in a circle. "That's right. Now, again, what *is* time?" His joy fled.

Hatu hesitated, then said, "I know what it does. I don't know what it is."

Nathan's eyes shone as if tears were gathering. Softly, he said,

"That is the only right answer." He returned to his seat, and motioned that he needed his cup filled, and when Bodai had done so, Nathan grabbed it and drank deeply.

Nathan looked from Bodai to Hatu, then back again. At last he said, "We mark time. We say one rotation of the planet, from sunrise to the next, is a day. We say so many days as the world revolves around the sun to the place we marked as the first day, that is a year.

"We divide time into hours, minutes, even parts of minutes, measured by the progress of the sun across the sky, by drips of water, by mechanical devices, by any means we can dream of . . . but what *is* time?"

Bodai looked quizzical.

"Those marks we create, locations relative to the sun, progress measured by seasons, how long it takes for a volume of sand to pass through a tiny aperture, those are our creations, not time's. Time can drag slowly, or pass quickly, and our perspective is shaped by how we experience those moments. So how can we measure exactly, when we see time as relative to our mood?" Nathan shrugged. "In the end we are always left with that one question." He pointed his finger at Hatushaly.

Hatu said, "What is time?"

Nathan smiled. "When you find out, tell me."

Bodai laughed. He slapped the table. "I love a good question. Now, drinks and dinner?"

"Yes!" both Nathan and Hatushaly replied at the same time.

DECLAN MOTIONED TO SEBASTIAN to come and sit beside him at the fire. "Did you see him?"

The mercenary said, "I thought I saw someone move just for a moment at the edge of the light."

"Can you get behind him?"

Sebastian shook his head. "Even if I feign going for a piss, I have no chance." Declan realized the archer looked years older than when they had met just two weeks ago. He wondered if he had aged that much as well.

Sebastian continued. "Near my home village, in the forests where I hunted as a boy, perhaps. This forest belongs to whoever is out there. Even without traps and snares, I could injure myself in the dark, or walk into an ambush; he would hear me coming. No. It's best we wait for sunrise and then you decide what to do next."

Declan felt frustration, an urge to do something. Too long now they'd been shadowed by one or more men. His inability to act was pushing him to the brink of rashness and he needed to rein in that impulse.

He forced himself to remain calm. Taking a deep breath, Declan said at last, "Very well. Get some sleep. Someone will wake you for your watch."

The archer nodded, rose, and went over to his makeshift sleeping pallet, a cloak once owned by a man now dead many miles back.

Declan stood up and turned his back to the fire, the better to see in the dark. He was at the point of welcoming an attack: anything to reveal what was going on. He was certain Bogartis would have had some sage advice on how to deal with this situation, but Bogartis was dead, left for the scavengers and weather to dispose of his corpse. Declan felt utterly alone.

8

THE UNEXPECTED,

SHOCK, AND ADJUSTMENTS

D eclan hardly needed to hold up his hand to order a halt, for every man reacted as he did. A lone figure walked out of the forest into a clearing, a longbow shot away.

He was a tall man, broad-shouldered. His hair hung to his shoulders, and, like his long beard, was mostly grey. Even so, he looked able, and wore what appeared to be old leather armor. A longsword was casually slung over his shoulder as he waited for Declan's company to approach.

Without instruction, the men fanned out and kept their hands close to their weapons. Declan said, "Watch the flanks. I think he wants to parley."

When they reached the center of the clearing, the man held up his left hand, palm out. "Far enough. Wouldn't want any misunderstandings."

Declan said, "Steady," as the men halted. To the stranger he said, "We've had our share of misunderstandings lately, so let's not have another. Who are you?"

"My name is Tobias Winters. And you?"

"I'm called Declan Smith."

"You're the captain?"

"Not by choice."

Tobias laughed. "No one comes here by choice, Declan Smith." He looked over the company, squinting a little. "You've come out of the Scorched Coast, which I would have wagered was impossible. How'd that happen?"

Declan said, "It's a long story. Abala was sacked by nomads and we didn't have a lot of choices as to where we could run. There were forty or so of us when we started. You?"

Tobias pointed vaguely to the north and said, "We were run down here from the grasslands, by the same damn nomads. Years ago." He said, "Forty or so you say?"

Declan nodded.

"That's a grim trail you took. Still, you're here now." He turned and said, "Come along. I can see you're hungry and there's enough to share." He looked back and saw that Declan and the others were following. "I needed to judge you in haste, so you don't turn the wrong way."

"Wrong way?" asked Declan as he caught up with Tobias and the others fell in behind as they entered the woods.

"Game trail ahead about a mile," said Tobias, pointing. He pointed to his left. "There's another you've been paralleling for a good while now. Where they meet is something like a border."

"Border?" asked Declan.

"That way"—Tobias pointed roughly north—"is where our camp is."

"Our—"

"You'll see," interrupted Tobias.

Close up, Declan could see that Tobias Winters was a man of advancing years, despite his bearing and powerful frame. The way he squinted implied that his eyesight was fading.

They continued on a southeast course, and then the trail bent to the east. As Tobias had said, they quickly came to the intersection of two game trails. He stopped and said, "Lads, never go that way," and he pointed south.

"There are some people down there you never want to meet. Me and mine did some serious damage to them before they came to understand we'd leave them alone if they let us be."

"Who are they?" asked Benruf.

"Can't say what they call themselves. They have no civilized tongue any of us have heard. We call them 'eaters' because they'll eat you as soon as a fine side of beef, if they'd ever come upon such a thing down here."

"Cannibals," said Declan. "How'd you—"

Tobias held up his hand, and Declan stopped. The old fighter said, "Time enough for questions once we get to our camp." He looked from face to face. "From here till I tell you, walk in single file, each man staying exactly behind the man in front. Because of them eaters we've got everything from these two trails rigged with some nasty snares, spiked pits, deadfalls, and the like. We like to change things around from time to time, so even if they figure out a bit of it, they come on a surprise sooner or later. Everyone understand?"

Declan checked the faces of his men and saw uncertainty there. "He could have let us turn the wrong way," he said quietly, and various among them nodded.

Then he pointed to Billy Jay. "Stay right behind me, boy." The newest member of Bogartis's company nodded and stepped closer to Declan.

"You see the man in front start to wobble, grab him," instructed Tobias, "but if he falls, don't go with him." He smiled and said,

"If he's lucky, he'll get up and dust himself off, but if he's not, no sense you going with him. Right, Declan?"

Declan couldn't argue, and now was almost certain Tobias had been either a soldier or a mercenary before he had landed here. This was a story he wanted to hear. If this old man and some others could survive here, then they could too. And maybe it was possible that there was a way out, even if they hadn't found it yet.

When everyone was in a line, Tobias Winters led them between two distinctive trees, so Declan knew where the starting point was. He had no doubt Benruf and any other man with even a little tracking experience were also noting every significant landmark along the way.

"If you see a snake, don't jump," said Tobias. "The ones around here are, mostly, harmless."

"Mostly?" said Declan.

"Well, there's this one bastard with a shovel-shaped head with a red diamond on it. Him, you should avoid best you can."

"Venom?"

"A-yep."

They moved with purpose, but Tobias's pace was measured rather than slow. As they passed certain spots Declan could make out signs that traps had been laid but realized he only saw them because he'd been warned. He had no doubt a fair number of those "eaters" had found out the hard way that this was not a safe course.

With a guide who knew the way, and a clear passage, it took Declan and his men little time to leave the field of traps. Tobias turned and said, "It's safe going from here, boys, and you can draw an easy breath."

Declan was pleased that none of the men had faltered and something akin to a safe haven lay ahead.

Benruf pointed up ahead. "Smoke."

Tobias Winters said, "Boys'll be cooking. Gets dark early down here."

"We noticed," said Declan. "Can't say as I like it much."

"You get used to it," said Tobias. "Can't say you'll ever get to like it, but you'll get used to it."

"I hope not," replied Declan.

"Planning on getting out, no doubt."

"If there's a way," Declan answered.

"Oh, there's a way, two ways actually, three if you count just killing yourself outright, by going back the way you came. You're the first we've seen come that way, from the Scorched Coast. The other two are less risky than certain death, but the risk is high enough you'd better think long and hard about trying."

They exited a copse of trees and in a large clearing saw a collection of huts. Several men were tending to a cooking fire, upon which sat a large iron pot. Tobias raised his hand and shouted.

The men tending the fire waved back, and others came into view, exiting the huts. Tobias said, "Monkey stew, again."

"Monkey?" asked Billy Jay.

"Rabbit mostly, but we toss a monkey in from time to time, so we call it that. Some of those big chaps make a pretty fair meal. That deer you took was being tracked by Mack over there"—he pointed at one of the cooks—"and he was the one came back to tell us we had visitors. Deer are rare here, so one wanders up this way, we go after it." Tobias put down his sword, leaving it on a large log, one of several in a semicircle near the cooking fire, and sat down. "Supper will be ready soon. Sit and rest, and then we can sort out some stories."

Declan sat near Tobias and saw more and more men arriving

to see the newcomers. Within minutes Declan estimated two dozen or more men had gathered. They appeared curious but because it was Tobias who was bringing strangers into their camp, they seemed to reckon it was safe. Most were older, like Tobias Winters himself, but a handful were younger, about Declan's age or a bit older.

Tobias explained that two groups had survived trading endeavors with the nomads that had gone badly wrong, and they were the only ones to escape slaughter.

Declan sat back and took a deep breath, letting it out slowly. At least for the moment, his small band was safe. And Winters had mentioned a possibility of escape from the Wound. He refused to indulge in optimism, but he felt pleased to have a bit of hope.

DONTE'S REVELATION THAT HE PLANNED on killing Hatu had taken Hava completely by surprise. For a short time she had thought he was making one of his terrible jokes. Then she realized he actually meant it, but after questioning him, she was still confused.

Donte had returned to his own quarters, to rest until summoned, and Hava had taken a hot bath. It should have been an enjoyable luxury, for she had been keen to rid herself of days of grime, but Donte's odd fixation on killing Hatu worried her.

He hadn't said it with any specific purpose, just that they'd see one another, get caught up on all the events since they'd been taken by the Sisters of the Deep, and then when they had done that, Donte would kill Hatushaly.

Donte had gaps in his memory, but felt it had something to do with the Sisters, though he wasn't precisely aware of what, and his offhand manner suggested that he wasn't fully engaged with the task on any sort of level that made sense to Hava. Recalling some lectures from Bodai, she remembered the word "motive." There was no apparent reason why Donte should want to kill Hatu.

After eating, Hava lay down to rest, yet as tired as she was, Donte's odd behavior stopped her from falling asleep. She couldn't conceive of what could possibly warp Donte enough for him to consider for an instant killing his best friend, and to be so indifferent to that goal.

Finally, sleep pulled her down.

In the morning a loud knock on her door woke Hava and she sat up, finding that her travel clothes had been taken and cleaned for her. Fresh clothing was welcome after so many days in her own dirt, and while the sleep had helped, the struggle with Donte's statement had prevented it from being fully restful. In addition, she was also intrigued by the Azhante prisoners and wondered what they might reveal.

She dressed quickly and opened the door, finding a page waiting outside. "The baron requests you join him in the guests' barracks." He moved to the side and with a sweeping motion indicated that he would escort her, and she stepped through the door.

Hava found it amusing that the prisoners were now "guests," even though their situation remained unchanged.

She followed him to the barracks, her concerns over Donte beginning to fade as her strong desire to know more about the prisoners pushed those worries aside.

Entering the barracks, she saw that the baron and Balven were already there, and Balven waved her forward. She went to stand next to him and saw that the two prisoners had been given beds and had their wounds dressed.

The one who had spoken to her the day before was awake, though how alert he was remained to be seen.

The baron simply said, "Talk to him."

Hava moved closer to the bed and softly said, "*Gaerma?*"

The man's bloody clothing had been replaced by a long, clean nightshirt, and one wound on his face had been bandaged, while his bruises had been salved. He moved slightly and his eyes focused on Hava. He tried to speak.

"Water?" she asked.

One of the guards moved quickly and provided her with a cup of water, which she gently lifted to the man's lips. This appeared to revive him a little and he at last said, "*Baci.*"

There had been a time in Hava's life when she would never have dared to speak the native tongue of Coaltachin in front of anyone who had not been born there, but those days were far behind her and she quietly began talking with the man.

It was clear that there were enough differences between the two languages spoken by Hava and the prisoner that questions had to be repeated and often he paused to regain some focus before he could speak.

After half an hour, she sat down on the side of the bed and they continued, slowly, but gaining more familiarity with one another's accents, strange expressions, and words, and the exchange quickened.

"He thinks I am somehow part of his . . . tribe?" she said to the baron and Balven. "This is my language, but it is as if it were spoken on one of the outer islands of my nation, by people who have changed it here and there."

"Or perhaps you're speaking his language, and your people have changed it," Balven replied.

Hava considered what Balven suggested and nodded. She returned to her discussion with the prisoner. After a minute he asked a question, and Hava paused before answering, then gave a long response, ending with the word, "Coaltachin."

The man's eyes widened and welled up with tears and he tried to sit up, reaching for Hava. The guard standing next to him prevented him from touching her. The prisoner openly wept and tried to grasp Hava's hand: it was clear that he wasn't trying to harm her, but to embrace her.

Hava slowly reached forward and gave his hand a squeeze. She let him hold her hand for a moment, then pulled it away and stood up. She turned her back to the prisoner and took a step toward Daylon and Balven.

"What is it?" asked the baron.

"If I understand what he said," she began, "he's . . . his people have . . . been seeking *our* people for ages."

"Say on," said Balven.

"I will have to speak to him more—his name is Sepisolema, Sepi for short—and he told me some things about 'Prides' I don't quite understand, but I think what he's saying is . . ." She turned to Daylon. "Can we step outside? I could use some air."

The baron turned and moved to the door which a guard had opened for him. Balven and Hava followed him outside.

Hava took a deep breath of the morning air and paused to let the breeze refresh her. She looked at the two men. "From what Hatu told me of his encounter with the Azhante when he was accompanying Master—" She stopped herself, then continued, "Bodai when he was up in Sandura, they encountered some Azhante working with the king, and they had something to do with the Church of the One." She stopped. "You can dig through that with your prisoner, the episkopos—"

"Guest," interjected Balven.

"Say on," said Daylon, annoyed by his brother's interruption.

Hava held up her hands, then said, "All that is not the point. The point is, Hatu felt there was some fear of the Azhante, that they were hunting us for some reason, and for whatever reason, the masters of Coaltachin were doing everything possible not to be discovered by them. It's something going back to when the Kingdom of Night was founded by the seven masters who sit on the Council." Hava looked away for a moment then back at the two men, as if struggling to find the words. "If I understand Sepi, they weren't seeking to hunt us to hurt us . . . They were seeking us to somehow *save them.*"

Balven and Daylon exchanged a glance.

Daylon asked, "Save them from what?"

"I'm not sure," she answered.

Daylon frowned. "Balven, you and Hava find out what this is about." He gazed out over his city. It was now fully awake. "I have mouths to feed, an army to raise, and our treasury is nearly empty. I have no one to tax, so what will we do when I run out of gold?"

Hava stood silent a moment, then said, "Would a very large ship full of treasure help?"

Daylon looked at her in astonishment. "A very large one, yes."

"I happen to know where one is hidden, and it could ferry a few hundred soldiers and horses as well." She pointed to a distant gate. "From there to here. It's that big. And it's got two decks full of loot."

"Where did you find that?" asked Balven.

"Well, I didn't find it. I stole it."

Both men were speechless.

AFTER A LONG MEETING WITH Hava, Daylon and Balven waited for her to go off for a midday meal with Donte. When she had passed through the door, Balven said, "If her description of that ship is accurate, it must contain most of the wealth of Port Calos."

Daylon said, "Remember we said we'd have to take Port Calos and garrison it?"

"Soon?"

"Now," said Daylon, as he stood. He stretched: sitting hours in a chair was not his first choice. "I want to see how the lower walls are coming along. Start setting up a plan to send a garrison to Calos, as well as some sort of fortification at Beran's Hill."

There was a knock at the door, and Daylon said, "Enter!"

A page appeared, holding a message. He handed it to Balven, who scanned it and said, "No reply," and the page quickly left again.

"What is it?" asked Daylon.

"Well, we've finally found Rodrigo."

"He lives!" Daylon said with pleasure. Of all the nearby nobles, Rodrigo Bavangine, Baron of the Copper Hills, was one of the few he would name a friend. The assault had driven him and his family into hiding.

"He, his family, and a hundred men-at-arms hid at a hunting lodge in the northeast corner of the barony."

"I know that lodge," said Daylon. He laughed. "It must have been crowded and uncomfortable. It's a small one."

"Rodrigo says his city has been reduced to ashes, and his populace have fled. He seeks sanctuary."

Daylon shook his head. "Another sanctuary request." He crossed his left arm across his midriff, cupping his right elbow while tapping his right index finger on the side of his chin.

Balven said, "All right, what are you plotting? I know that look."

"What would Father do?"

Balven gave out a sigh, expressing acceptance of whatever Daylon had planned, even if it was something he would not agree with. The two brothers had argued enough throughout their lifetime that both knew the answer to Daylon's question, so Balven indulged his brother with a reply. "Father would seek to turn this entire mess to his own advantage."

Daylon nodded. "And how would he go about that?"

Balven thought about it for a moment, then said, "Put Rodrigo so deep in your debt that he effectively becomes a vassal, and seize Port Calos."

"The latter is already underway. So, about Rodrigo?"

Balven smiled. "Give Port Calos to Rodrigo to command a garrison of our troops."

"Father would approve." Daylon returned the smile.

Balven looked amused. "I think you're right."

"Send a message back to him explaining in vague enough terms that it won't be obvious we're bending him to our service, but assure him that ample provisions, workmen, whatever else, will be there by the time he arrives," Daylon instructed.

"At once." Then, dryly, Balven added, "I'll hold off on having the mapmakers redraw the boundaries. Once we've annexed Copper Hills, Port Calos, and the important parts of Ilcomen, shall we become the *Kingdom* of Marquensas?"

Balven asked the question lightly, but Daylon's expression was not at all humorous. He said, "Should we survive what we must do, why not? There isn't a standing kingdom on North Tembria now that the Church has seized Sandura, and Zindaros and Metros are in no position to object. We need ships and that's what they're good for. With Hava's treasure ship . . ." He took a breath, and added, "Yes, again, why not? It's what Father would have done."

"I can't argue with that," Balven conceded. Then he asked, "Can you spare me tomorrow?"

"I don't need you with me to inspect the fortifications. Why?"

"There's something I want check on, and I've been putting it off because of other things."

"What is it?"

"I need to do some tallies on what we have in stores, and what we need—which is everything—pen some messages to some nobles out there we've tracked down, and after I do all that, I need to speak with Edvalt Tasman about his progress producing armor . . . and some other things."

"Yes, of course. Shouldn't the company of Bogartis and Declan be back by now with Edvalt's 'magic' sand?"

"I don't know about the magic, but I've seen those blades and they're worth having." Balven thought for a moment then added, "Yes, if nothing went amiss, they should have been back by now, or perhaps in a few more days."

"Discuss it with Edvalt, what we're going to do about forging weapons if they don't return."

"I will," said Balven, and he watched his brother leave.

There were several things Balven needed to discuss with the master smith whom Daylon had put in charge of manufacturing weapons, and one of those things was a question he'd been wanting to ask ever since he'd first met Declan, a question made all the more vital now that Daylon had revealed that his ambition was to create a new kingdom.

As he moved toward the door, Balven realized that the question was only important should Declan return. He wondered if the company had encountered trouble.

DECLAN WOLFED DOWN THE "MONKEY stew," which consisted of some meat and plenty of vegetables, not that he recognized what they were, eaten off roughly cut boards with a scooped-out

center. The stew was a little salty, which Tobias said was due
to them having uncovered a salt lick about a half-day's walk to
the north. They chipped off pieces of that and a tiny bit in the
stew gave it a touch of flavor. To Declan, after a week of cooked,
then dried, venison, and whatever berries they could find, the
stew was as good as anything his foster mother, Mila, would
cook when he was a boy. She used seafood, mostly, and she had
a wicked command of spices, and would add onions, carrots, and
whatever else she could find. He had loved her cooking, but at
this moment this concoction matched her best. As Mila had said
more than once, "Hunger is the best seasoning."

Declan, his company, and the residents of this village had been
discussing the raids on the northern continent up to the attack
on Abala and their being chased into the Wound. Declan had
explained briefly about recruiting fighters for the baron, with
a brief mention of the search for the special sand. He fielded a
few questions. As they finished the meal, Tobias asked, "So, you
survived a fight with some of the Border Tribes?"

Sixto, sitting next to Declan, said, "He beheaded their leader
and they withdrew, giving us time to get away."

Toombs, sitting beside Sixto, said, "It was impressive. Declan
wheeled in a full circle and took the chieftain's head right off
his shoulders. He grabbed the head by the hair, and the others
ran away. It was a hell of a blow."

Tobias sat motionless for a moment, then said, "You idiot!"

Out of any possible response to that story, this was not one
Declan expected. "Idiot?"

Tobias put his hand up in a peace-making gesture. "No offense!"

Declan was exhausted and his fatigue and the constant fear
had worn his nerve endings to raw nubs. "What do you mean?"

"If you don't know the ways of the Border Tribes, then what

you did makes sense. If you kill the hetman, the chieftain, of a tribe, you claim his power. They retreated to decide who would challenge you. Had you stayed and when they returned . . ." He waved his hand as if he wished to begin again. "When they found you gone, they decided that you have no honor and that was when they gave chase. Had you remained and stood with their hetman's head in your hand, one of two things: either the next big war-chief-in-waiting would have come at you in single combat, or they would have all bent the knee and you'd have been their leader!"

Declan was silent.

"If you'd done that, you could have ordered them back into Abala, and maybe you'd have had to fight another chieftain, or maybe the other bands would have just shrugged it off and ac-cepted you as one of their own, and your men, too.

"But if you'd been accepted, or if you'd killed a challenger, you'd have had . . . a hundred? two hundred? fighters at your side. You could have simply ordered them to seize a ship and sailed back home to your baron." Tobias leaned back and shook his head in dismay. "What we don't know, right?"

Declan was silent for a moment then said, "My captain didn't know that, so I didn't know that."

"I get it," said Tobias. "I left North Tembria years ago, seeking my fortune down here, and I ran companies for Metros to the edge of the Swamplands for a few years before I learned some of the ways of the Border Tribes. They're an honor-bound people with all sorts of strange ways, but if your captain wasn't familiar with them, no way you'd know."

"Bogartis said he'd been south before, but the ways of the Border Tribes were not discussed. All I knew was they were a tough bunch and they behaved themselves when they came to Abala to trade."

"Bogartis?" asked Tobias.

"I was his second. He was killed in that fight."

"Damn me," said Tobias. "I rode with him twenty . . . maybe twenty-five years ago, when we were both young bucks trying to make a name for ourselves." Winters looked reflective, then added, "He was a young captain, just starting his first company, and he was smart. Best thing about him, he learned from his mistakes and worked hard to keep his men alive. Some captains spend lives like crazed gamblers spend coins, but not Bogartis. His men were loyal."

"Why'd you leave?" asked Declan, putting aside his own feelings about Bogartis.

"I was young and stupid." Tobias laughed ruefully. "I wanted to be his second, and someone else was chosen, and I took it personally." He fell silent for a moment. "I can't even remember the name of the man he chose; he's probably long dead, and I don't remember how long I wandered before I got myself together enough to claim a captaincy. So I came down to South Tembria and learned what I should have known years earlier."

Declan felt moisture gathering in his eyes and wiped it away. "He was a very good man."

"Now that I'm over my stupid envy," said Tobias, "I can say, yes, he was."

Surprised by this moment of emotional connection, Declan retreated to the dark place of emptiness that had filled him since Gwen's murder. "Tell me about how we escape this place."

Tobias shook his head slowly and finally replied, "You're not the first to ask. There are two canyons rising to the north that empty out near the southern border of the grasslands, just at the edge of the Burning Lands. Still desert, though not as brutal as what you've traversed, but the chance of survival there is not much better than the way you came. It's not as hot, but you're much farther from Abala.

"The one to the east is the easiest to navigate for fit men with some gear, but it empties out farther into the range of the Border Tribes. It's luck that decides if there are marauders nearby who will hunt you down and kill you for sport.

"The western route empties out just south of a range of mountains. It's a steep climb, and you end up right at the edge of the nomads' southern route; if you go around to the south you're back in the Burning Lands—"

Declan interrupted. "That's the way we came."

Tobias nodded. "So, the other way is a climb over mountains; not so big as mountains go, but they're a bitch to traverse, or to chance the southern pass the tribes use."

Declan glanced at Sixto, who eyed his captain closely. At last Declan stood up and looked at every man in the camp, then asked Tobias, "Which way can get every man out?"

"Every man?" asked Tobias.

Declan nodded. "You took us in and fed us, so we'll not leave any man behind. You're all coming with us."

Tobias shook his head slowly and gave Declan a rueful smile. "Damn me if you're not cut from the same cloth as Bogartis."

9

UNEXPECTED ALLIES AND OPPORTUNITIES

———†———

Hava had spent her third straight day with Sepi and his fellow Azhante agent, Firash, who had now regained consciousness.

Both men had been held under guard but were now housed in another room in the castle, with better beds, food, and care. Both were young and strong and likely to fully recover.

Now Hava sat with the baron and Balven as their dinner guest for the third night as they made plans. The first night she dined at the baron's table, she'd been almost overwhelmed. A servant coming or going almost constantly, and more than one plate! At one point, Balven had said something about meager fare, almost an apology, and Hava had wondered exactly how lavish the fare had been before the raids.

Now she took the servants and food for granted, as she was drawn deeply into devising several options with them based on what she knew of Nytanny and her home islands.

Balven had finished describing how they'd sent companies out to explore the communities to the north and east. Daylon had sent messengers ahead to urge people to come to Marquenet, but now he had companies out looking for anything abandoned but still usable to melt down for weapons, from plows to kitchen pots.

The first wave of returning refugees had created chaos and had finally been resettled. But now more people were arriving, from farther away, and Daylon found himself with more mouths to feed than before, and less food to distribute. The closest farms were being worked again, but many would be a year away from producing food. The majority of the orchards and groves were still standing, so there was some fruit, mostly oranges, grapes, and pears. Some herds in distant corners had survived and they were being resettled closer to the city, but many would be spared the butcher so they could be bred from.

"We really need to send someone to the Sanctuary, to speak to your Bodai," said Daylon.

"I can leave in a few more days," said Hava. "I need some new rope and canvas, not a lot, but there's not much to be found around here. Some was found down at a town called Toranda, and it got here this morning. Anyone you want to send with me is welcome. I could use a few good sailors—half our crews had other trades before we freed them."

"We're sending a company of guards," said the baron.

Hava had half-expected this but hadn't decided exactly how she felt about it. She knew that with the *Queen of Storms* anchored off North Point she couldn't stop him from seizing the ship, and they were effectively allies given the current circumstances, but she still wasn't happy to hear this. "Very well," she said, her tone less than enthusiastic. "We could use some help with our defensive fortifications." She looked at Daylon for a minute then asked, "How many?"

Balven answered, "Twenty. In case of attack, we're detailing ten archers. The other ten are engineers and logistics men." He pointed at Hava. "You're the only expert we have in the ways of the Kingdom of Night; how you move your agents from place to place, deploy your spies, gather information. We need to learn the ways of these Azhante, and it seems these must be related to the ways of Coaltachin."

That surprised Hava a little and she said, "Catharian and Bodai can teach your men what they need on those subjects."

"We have no designs on your Sanctuary," Daylon said, "unless you invite us in, but from what you've said there are hundreds of islands—"

"Thousands, more likely," interrupted Hava.

"Very well," said Daylon. "And you say some are large enough to launch an attack of size."

"I suppose so," she replied slowly, seeing his drift. She realized that if everything came together, the baron planned on moving an army to locations within the countless islands off the northeast coast of Nytanny, and at the right time launching a retaliatory attack as massive as the one North Tembria had endured the previous year.

The baron sipped from a mug of wine then said, "Our plans are in their early stages, so we need much more intelligence. Your friends here"—he pointed in the general direction of where the two Azhante were housed—"were almost certainly the source of information as to where the massive raid was to strike, and how best to coordinate the attacks to the north, the destruction of the southern ports in Ilcomen, and harassing the ports on South Tembria to keep the Zindaros and Metros fleets from sallying."

"Most likely," agreed Hava. "Not those two specifically, but other Azhante. Sepi and Firash were insinuated into the Church some years ago, on the continent of Enast, so they speak that tongue—and no one here does—but they know some Sanduran from their time there, and I'm beginning to fully understand what they're saying with a little work."

"How much of what they've told you, about seeking out Coaltachin for some sort of salvation, sounds likely?" asked Balven.

"I think they believe what they say," Hava replied. "But I'm still uncertain if I've understood entirely what they've told me. As best I can make out, they are much like Hatu and I were in importance to the masters. We were tasked to play the part of husband and wife, to go to Beran's Hill to wait and report back." She shrugged.

"You were kept out of the way," said Balven.

"I assume the masters had hints that something might be on its way, but I think it may have been concerns that Sandura and the Church were going to attempt to take Marquensas, not an attack from a distant land across the sea."

"So, how are our two guests like you?" asked Daylon. "They were insinuated into the Church as hired bodyguards, not their military."

"The Church Adamant," supplied Balven.

"Yes," Hava acknowledged.

"The Church Adamant is a martial order, which owes no allegiance to people like Bernardo," Balven added.

Dryly, Hava said, "That is now apparent. In any event, the two Azhante are not prime agents like Coaltachin's Hidden Warriors." She took a drink of wine and continued. "These two do not appear particularly dangerous as spies or assassins, but at the right moment they could be. Their duty is to watch and report.

"If we of Coaltachin are indeed descended from the Azhante, and our practices of spycraft are similar, then they must have someone in Sandura they could get a message to. That agent would then get the message back to whoever was in charge of what was going on in Sandura." Hava took a breath. "It's so distant from Nytanny, I have no idea how they could get messages back and forth in a timely fashion. So, there must be someone very important and powerful in Sandura." Then a thought hit her. "When you searched them, did you find any sort of . . . a token? A necklace or something hanging from a thong around their necks?"

"I don't believe so," said Balven.

"Hatu told me that the Azhante that he had encountered in Sandura wore a token, a black lacquered square of metal. Those must be their equivalent of our Quelli Nascosti. So much of our success is . . . our lies. We have convinced many people we are ghosts who can pass through walls—"

Balven held up his hand. "Since I was a boy, being taught my role by our father, I've learned all I could about every danger to our barony. When as a baby Hatu was secreted within Daylon's tent, I was sure Coaltachin must be involved in the betrayal of the King of Ithrace, and got word to your people. I had no idea Sandura was also employing agents of . . . whoever, these Azhante." He paused, then added, "Perhaps Lodavico had no idea, either. He may have thought, wrongly, he was dealing with your Hidden Warriors."

Daylon said, "Speculation is a waste of time. Someone was manipulating the Church, setting it to destroy Sandura while the rest of North Tembria was overrun, except for us."

Hava could see his ire rising. "Why were we spared?"

"A fair question for the two Azhante, though I suspect they may not have any knowledge. Still, I will ask."

Balven said, "I think I should accompany Hava to the Sanctuary, and speak with this Master Bodai."

Daylon said, "I need you here." To Hava he said, "I suspect you're correct about how much our prisoners know. Bring your Master Bodai here."

Hava chuckled. "I can ask, but he may say no. He was very busy with matters he considers vital when I left."

Balven said, "He's not one of your subjects, brother." When Daylon looked to be on the verge of an outburst, Balven added nonchalantly, "At least not yet."

The baron stared with a startled expression at Balven, then suddenly he laughed. Hava let out a slow breath of relief, and realized that like her, Hatu, and Donte, these two men had grown up together and Balven had the added responsibility of preventing his brother from acting rashly.

"Besides," said Balven, "I met him briefly when he brought Hatushaly and Hava here, so I'm a known face, if not a familiar one, and with Hava with me, he may say yes."

"How long would a trip there and back take?" the baron asked Hava.

"With full sails and good weather, and considering *Borzon's Black Wake* is a wallowing slug compared to *Queen of Storms*, the return voyage would take much longer . . ." She calculated. "A month or so, two if weather is against us."

"You can spare me for two months," said Balven.

"Very well," Daylon agreed at last.

"And a week or so for me to get a good look around those islands," Balven added in an offhand tone.

"Do not linger," instructed the baron, wagging an accusing finger. He scowled. "I know how you get when something interests you. What we're discussing is promising, but we still have people to feed, and no matter how much treasure you"—he pointed at Hava—"can bring to our cause, people can't eat gold."

Hava was silent, then said, "We can salt fish."

"Salted fish?"

"I've never seen fishing so abundant as around the Sanctuary. Perhaps it's because not many people have lived on those islands for so long, but we send out a small boat and it comes back filled to the gunwales. We can't send you fresh fish, but we can dry and salt it."

Balven said, "Marquensas will take as much food as you can send." He rose. "If you'll excuse me, I have a few things to attend to before I leave."

Daylon waved him away, then turned to Hava. "You'll keep him safe, of course."

"Of course," she replied.

Daylon seemed more tired than Hava could remember having seen him. In a year he seemed to have aged ten. His eyes were becoming darkened, sunken in their sockets, and his hair was now noticeably greyer than when they had first met, only a few years earlier. He was silent for a long time then said, "I never used to mind waiting. I was once a very patient man." His gaze grew distant. "I don't know if I truly loved my second wife, or just needed someone to give me heirs."

Hava realized the baron was slightly drunk. She hadn't paid much attention to how much wine he had consumed, and assumed part of this was his exhaustion, but he was speaking more like a man lost in memory than the avid planner she'd come to know in the last three days, during which he'd been focused and discussed all manner of options and contingencies. She had been impressed with how he and Balven worked together anticipating problems and coming up with potential solutions, though she couldn't judge if any of the plans were those of a madman or a genius. And now he was an injured man, lost in painful memories.

"But I adored my children," he added after a long silence. She saw a tear gather in his eye and before it could run down his face, he absently rubbed it away.

"I should probably go, Baron," she said, starting to rise.

"No," Daylon said, reaching out to hold her wrist.

Her training had her on the verge of a violent reaction to that grasp, but he released her before she acted and said, "Just stay . . . until Balven returns." He sighed and it sounded as if something deep within him was fighting to let go. "You don't have to say anything. Just sit here for a while."

She saw now that he was overwhelmed, by countless days of loss and pain, by the responsibility and challenges before him. She knew nothing about nobles, and only a little more about people not from Coaltachin, but she could see he just needed someone to sit close for a while. Settling back into her chair, she said, "Of course."

They sat quietly for a long while.

BALVEN KNOCKED ON THE DOOR to Edvalt Tasman's lodging and in a moment it opened. The old smith looked at the baron's brother and said, "I suppose you want to come in."

"Just for a moment," said Balven, and Edvalt stepped aside for Balven to enter.

The baron had given the master smith command of all metal-work for the barony, yet rather than basing himself in a smart house, Edvalt had picked a small room near the forges and small foundry that would be the center of weapon production until a larger structure could be built close by.

There was a bed, a freestanding wooden wardrobe over a set of drawers, and a table bearing a single large candle. Balven glanced around as Edvalt said, "You can sit on the bed." There was no chair.

"I'll stand. I won't be long." Again he glanced around the room. "You could have had better quarters, Edvalt."

"To what end? I'm alone, and this is close to work and the workers' mess, and it's also close to the jakes, and at my age I find I need to get up now and again and go piss."

Balven couldn't argue with that logic. Eventually, he said, "There are matters afoot I can't speak of yet, but there are things I need to know."

"Yes?" said Edvalt as he took the liberty of sitting on his bed.

"Declan. I need the truth. How did he come to be with you?"

Edvalt said, "I've told the story. A wagon came along with a pair of unpleasant people who claimed the boy was a foundling, and wanted to sell him to me." He laughed and shrugged. "In the Covenant? Slaves? But Mila took one look at the lad and said we'd take him. So I raised him as if he were my own, and he became as fine a smith as I could imagine my own son being. Truth is, I love him as I do . . . did my daughter."

Balven recalled that Edvalt's wife and their daughter's family had died during the attacks on North Tembria.

"If he doesn't return," said Edvalt with an unhappy edge to his voice, "I'll have lost everything."

No words sprang to Balven's mind. He was watching his brother go through the same loss, after his wife and children had been burned alive in their coach, trying to flee the attackers.

At last, Balven said, "I know you . . . wish for his safe return, as do I."

"Even if he doesn't make it back, I'll still see you get the finest swords and armor we can make," the smith said gruffly. "I'll look over the shoulder of every damn smith and tinker in Marquensas if I have to."

"It's about more than weapons," said Balven. "You must tell me a thing, and this time, the truth, and when you do, I will share a secret that will help you understand."

Edvalt looked up at Balven, his eyes narrowing as if he were measuring the man. "What would you know?"

"You were given your freedom after the betrayal of King Steveren. Your daughter was born a year later, yet you claim she was already born when Declan was sold to you. The ages do not match up. Where did you truly find Declan?"

Edvalt rubbed a calloused hand over his face and sat silently for a long while. At last, he said, "Very well. You're too clever a man for me to gull. He wasn't the toddler we claimed, but we told him the story so often that he came to believe it more than his own experience." Edvalt let out a sigh. "The truth is, his mother came to us, looking for a safe home in the Covenant where no noble held sway, where a common boy raised as a smith would not attract notice."

"His mother?"

"A fine lady," Edvalt said. "Mila was with child and I had no apprentice, and was hoping for a boy to train, but there was always a chance we'd have a girl, which we did." Mentioning his daughter was visibly difficult, but Edvalt went on, "Declan's mother was, as I said, a fine lady, in a rich carriage, stopping for some wheelwork—at least that was the story. She was fleeing to Marquensas because her father was seeking the boy. She was Lady Abig—"

"Abigale Lennox of Tumar," finished Balven.

"You knew?"

"I surmised," Balven replied. "She was Father's last lover before his death." The noble shook his head and went to sit down next to Edvalt, who moved over to make room. He put an arm around the old smith's shoulder. "Her father wanted her married to Father, but he didn't want a bastard in his household, so she fled, to bring him to Daylon for safety. He's our younger brother."

Edvalt's face remained impassive, save for a tightening around his eyes, as if he were confronting something he didn't wish to see. At last, he admitted, "He does have the look, but I put that out of my mind."

"As I told Daylon, he looks more like Father than either of us."

"So, the lady changed her mind I guess, and if the boy vanished, maybe her father wouldn't be looking to find his bastard grandson and kill him."

Balven nodded. "She wed some minor baron, I forget where, then she died young."

"So, now what do you plan?"

"A vow of silence?"

Edvalt nodded. "I swear."

"The secret you share with no one is if we survive this coming war, my brother plans on annexing . . ." He stopped himself. "You don't need to know the details, but after we deal with those who murdered your family and my brother's, Marquensas will become a kingdom. If Daylon survives he will be king. Declan's mother was nobility. Even as a bastard, with Daylon having no sons, that makes Declan heir to the throne of Marquensas."

Edvalt remained silent, his face still set in a mask. After a moment, he said, "I'll take that secret to my grave, if needed."

"I'm going on a journey in a few days, to what ends you need not know, but I will leave with you a document to hide. Should I fail to return, and should anything befall Daylon, it will be Declan's claim to the throne. Will you accept that charge?"

"Willingly, if not gladly," said Edvalt. "I spent enough time before and after the Betrayal to know that being king means countless enemies."

"Yes, that it does," said Balven, standing.

He and Edvalt shared a look that affirmed understanding. Without another word, Balven opened the door and left Edvalt alone.

The old smith sat quietly for a long time, aching to know if Declan was safe. His mind raced at the thought of what he had learned, that Declan might be king one day, should he survive. Eventually, he extinguished the candle and lay down, wishing for a dreamless sleep.

DECLAN AND TOBIAS CAME INTO camp, exhausted and covered in trail dirt. Another stew was boiling and Declan said, "More monkey?"

Sixto said, "Rabbit. Young Billy Jay is quite the hand with a snare. Got six fat coneys, with some wild onions and carrots."

"Sounds delicious."

Declan and Tobias sat down, waiting for the meal to be passed along.

"What'd you find?" asked Sixto.

"It can be done," said Declan. "As a boy, I often had to climb the bluffs looking for eggs, from terns, gulls, and other birds during nesting season. Sometimes we'd rig bird snares. I've been climbing since I was a lad."

Tobias said, "Standing at the bottom of the rocks, Declan showed me point by point a route up. Tricky, but he reckons we can do it."

"How?" asked a man named Oscar, the oldest fighter in the village. "I came down that way, chased by those damn grassland raiders. They only stopped chasing us because they wouldn't risk their horses. I damn near broke my leg scrambling down those rocks. Climbing back up them without ropes and gear?"

Declan said, "Benruf, those vines we saw coming down from Abala?"

"Lianas. They can be cut down from the trees and braided. If we do it right they're as strong as ropes woven from hemp or jute. I've seen them all my life used by sailors along the Zindaros coast. Hard to cut, though."

Declan said, "Blades are the one tool we have in abundance."

"I don't know," said Oscar. He looked at Tobias. "We've been stuck here . . ."

"Close to ten years," said Tobias.

One of the younger men, named Case, said, "It's been almost five for us."

"There are now thirty-eight of us," said Declan. "If we all work together, we can make it."

"I'm old, Declan," said Oscar in a plaintive voice.

Declan said, "That's all right. If we have to throw a rope around you and drag you up behind us, the younger lads can take turns."

Some of the men laughed loudly.

"It's dangerous, I know, but we're a large enough company now to stand a chance should we run across any raiders, and if we can get to those mountains to the northwest of here, we'll be rid of them. Then we can take stock and figure out the best way over the hills—there must be some sort of pass or gap, some way to Abala."

"It's nice having a captain again," Tobias said, looking at Declan. "Even if he's going to get us all killed." He laughed. "We try now, or we just sit here and die of old age, or until the eaters take us."

His men slowly nodded and began to agree.

"First," said Declan, "we'll send a group of you up the way we came to start cutting lianas, and then we'll see what we can contrive to use as tools." He stared at the big cooking pot. "If I had a forge, I could use that to fashion tools." Then he looked at Tobias and said, "Where exactly did you get that pot?"

Food was being scooped out by a narrow-handled wooden spoon carved years before, ladling hot stew onto the boards. Tobias said, "Now, that's a long story. I'll tell you while we eat."

10

PREPARATIONS FOR DESPERATE

MEASURES

D eclan stood with his back to the workers, taking his turn to stand watch while nursing arms as heavy as he could ever remember. Despite countless hours spent hammering at a forge, these lianas, despite being pliable and supple, were as tough as timber. Hacking through them was proving a challenge. The thinner ones broke after a half-dozen cuts, but with the thick ones it was like chopping down trees and they had no axes, just swords and daggers.

Declan knew that the edges would be as dull as kitchen spoons by the time they had finished and hoped he could find a decent stone to sharpen the blades before they set off. Tobias had quipped that they could use them for clubs should the need arise.

Benruf came to Declan and said, "How many more do we need?"

Declan replied, "Your guess is as good as mine. We'll need enough to tether all of us, as well as anything we manage to bring along, and perhaps have to haul some of us up a cliff face."

Benruf said, "Farther upslope is too hot and dry, and downslope is not hot enough. There are some more vines on the way back to camp, but I think perhaps we should start fashioning ropes with what we have."

Declan saw the afternoon was passing and the light was failing. "Finish up!" he shouted.

The men tasked with chopping loose the lianas needed no convincing to stop. Oscar gave out a loud exhalation to show his relief, and one man took another two strikes to cut through the last vine.

They loaded up their burden, wrapping vines around their shoulders, and Declan made sure no one was overladen. The trip back to the camp was arduous, but they traveled untroubled.

Once back in the village, Declan said, "Eat, sleep, and tomorrow we start making ropes."

Oscar said, "We should reset traps for the eaters before we start making ropes."

Declan glanced from Oscar to Tobias, an eyebrow raised in question.

"Every so often the eaters send somebody to sniff out our traps," Tobias answered. He pointed at Oscar and said, "He's a complainer, but he's got a nose for trouble."

"It's been too long," said Oscar.

"It has been a while," agreed Tobias.

"What do you mean by 'too long'?"

"It's not like a regular schedule," said Tobias, "but by now we'd expect to find one or two of them pinned to a tree, squashed by a deadfall, or in a pit." He thought about it, then said, "They're overdue for a visit."

Declan had a think. Losing a day chafed but getting attacked from the rear while climbing up that cliff wasn't a welcome thought. "How long would it take to go about making sure we're not hit from behind?"

Tobias said, "We could inspect the traps down to where the two trails meet. The pits we can't move; took a long time to dig them, but we reckon those who fall in aren't going to go back and tell anyone. If one of those evil bastards went back and told the others, and they have them marked, that has them walking into the deadfalls, spikes disguised under brush, and a couple of ankle-breaker snares. If you want to make certain, you drift a little down onto the sort of no man's land between those trails and where the eaters have their boundary."

"Where's that?"

"You'd have no trouble finding that border," said Oscar.

"Nope," agreed Tobias, "none. Heads, animal and human, weird signs painted on tree boles, rocks piled up and painted white. About half a day's creep south of there you might run into their hunters. They've got the whole of the Wound south of there to hunt—unless they have neighbors to the south nastier than they are, and I doubt that. I suspect they will come after us once in a while because we're close by and they think we may be easy pickings. Since the young bloods over there stumbled in here, we've scolded them eaters a few times when they tried. Now that you're here, unless they come in strength, we should run them off easily enough."

"And maybe someone gets wounded and can't keep up." Declan looked thoughtful for a moment, then let out a long sigh. "Bogartis told me once that when fighting certain enemies, wounding is better than killing, because if they care for their wounded, they slow down. Either they retreat slowly if you want to follow and pick them off or they follow slowly and you leave them behind."

Tobias tilted his head. "Can't argue that."

Declan weighed the pros and cons of an extra day and said, "First light." He glanced at Sebastian, who nodded agreement. Declan took a deep breath. "Tobias, first light," he repeated. "Me, Sebastian, and you two." To Benruf he said, "When we leave, start weaving those ropes, and if we don't run into trouble, we'll leave the day after." He stood up, and stretched a little. "We have a huge task ahead. Everyone, rest tonight, and we leave in two days."

No one voiced any objection.

HATUSHALY FLOATED IN HIS MIND, while actually sitting at the table in the library. His eyes were closed and he didn't move. Bodai and Nathan sat observing him.

"What's he doing?" asked Bodai.

"Learning," Nathan answered. "I'm going to join him, so don't interrupt me, please?"

Bodai was framing an answer when Nathan went rigid and his eyes closed. After a moment, Bodai softly said, "Very well."

In a floating void, Hatu was evaluating lines of force. He found that the less effort he put forth, the easier it was to recognize what he was observing.

There were countless lines, but he had quickly learned that they were tiered, the vast majority being trivial: a couple fighting, a flock of geese flying, two opponents in a contest, and other very normal human pastimes that caused links between opposing energies, or as Nathan called them, furies.

Then there was another layer, of those that resulted from the opposition of furies that impacted other lines of energy: a major conflict, celebration, or a large number of animals disturbed by earthquakes, storms, or fire.

He was on the edge of recognizing the next hierarchy when Nathan's voice came to him. "These are major movements caused by tremendous conflict between furies. This is toward the end of what you need to know for your challenges."

"Challenges?" asked Hatushaly, and abruptly he was back at the table in the library, blinking.

"That wasn't supposed to happen," said Nathan.

"What?" asked Bodai, looking first at Nathan, then at Hatu.

"He startled me!" said Hatu, rubbing his left eye with the palm of his hand. "Now I've got an ache in my left eye. What was that?"

"I was trying to evaluate your . . . lesson?"

"By barging into my mind unannounced?"

Nathan looked abashed. "Sorry. I thought your concentration was more disciplined than it apparently is."

"Maybe if you'd told me first you could do that, and then warned me you were going to," said Hatu, with a hint of anger. "Damn, that eye really hurts."

"It'll pass in a bit," said Nathan. "It's like a brain freeze."

"A what?" said Bodai.

"When you bite into something really cold and it shoots a pain up into your brain?"

"Why would anyone do that?" asked Bodai, his expression one of disbelief.

Nathan let out a sigh. "It's just an expression. Your brain doesn't really freeze. It just hurts."

"That still doesn't answer why would you do that?"

"Never mind. You don't have a lot of very cold things to eat or drink around here, anyway."

"Apparently not," agreed Bodai.

"Tell me what you were seeing, Hatu," said Nathan.

"Give me another minute," said Hatu, still obviously upset.

Nathan sat back in his chair. "Whenever you're ready."

Hatu blinked his left eye a few times, then said, "What I saw was what I told you last time. It starts the same way. Just a . . . what was that word?"

"Roiling?"

"Yes, that. A swirling, colors that aren't real colors, but seem

like colors. Behind the colors I sensed blackness, absolute blackness, like in a cave at night. Then the colors . . . settle down, start
to move into lines and grow brighter. The blackness, or sense
of it, fades until nothing remains but countless lines of color."

Nathan and Bodai had their eyes fixed on Hatu as he
spoke. This was their fifth time listening to his attempt to
examine the forces created by the furies surrounding them.
Each time he'd grown a bit more adept and able to decipher
the order of those energies. There seemed to be a pattern
and Nathan had been sparse in his instruction, claiming
that he was unsure what Hatu would encounter with this
exercise. There was a sense of progress, despite the ultimate
goal being vague.

"Then?" prodded Nathan.

Hatu shot him an angry look, but he kept his tone calm. "The
chaos of swirling colors and the blackness resolved much faster
this time; that part is getting easy." He waved his hand. "As I've
said, when I'm in that frame of mind, I have no sense of time
passing. Yet it feels as if it's going faster." He shrugged and the
last of the anger seemed to leave him. "Maybe I'm just used to
it, so it seems that way."

"About the same time passed as the last time," said Bodai, "so
if you feel you've got farther along in this exercise, then you are
going faster." His tone hinted at this being a question as much
as a statement.

"Indeed," offered Nathan. "Go on."

"This time I sensed that the lines I perceived were countless
ties between furies, energy moving . . ." He looked at Nathan
questioningly.

"As fast as light," supplied Nathan.

"Yes, like beams of light, but as slender as threads."

"Go on," said Nathan.

"They stretched out in every direction, but then . . . it's not as if I moved them, but rather they moved themselves as I needed . . ." He blew out a long breath, as if releasing tension, and shook his head in wonder. "I didn't feel as if I was controlling them, like you control a team of horses, or steal a boat." He collected his thoughts, then added, "It's as if they just did what I wanted them to do."

"Fascinating," said Bodai.

Nathan nodded. "It's a beginning. What else?"

"I saw . . . ordinary? Common flows along countless lines, then they faded . . ." He stopped. "I was beginning to sense . . . the origins, or endings?" He looked as if he was struggling to frame his words. "I think I was starting to understand what the pair of . . . furies . . . what they were. I think I'm beginning to see that they are endless, and only some are . . . important? No." He shook his head. "Important to me." Suddenly he sat upright and his eyes widened.

"What?" asked Bodai.

"People, animals . . . insects! Fish in the sea. Every living thing is connected through the furies!"

"Good," said Nathan. "Your apprehension of furies and energies, the very fabric and movement of the universe, is starting to come into focus for you." He slowly looked from Nathan to Bodai. "I've met only a handful of people who have that ability. Some have grown to be adepts, perhaps even masters of that knowledge. Some have learned how to manipulate the very stuff of the universe." He slapped his hand on the table. "What you call 'magic'!"

"What next?" asked Hatu, all his anger having fled.

Looking around, Nathan said, "I'm hungry and it's late. I think I spied a barrel of wine in the mess."

Suddenly Hatu was ravenous. "Have we finished?"

"For today. More tomorrow," said Nathan.

Rising from the table, Hatu waved a warning finger at him. "If you have some trick like popping into my head again, warn me first. I don't like tricks!"

Nathan laughed and said, "You're learning. They're all tricks."

BALVEN STOOD ON THE BEACH. A soldier behind him carried a small wooden chest. A wagon driver on the top of the hill turned his rig slowly to begin his return to the city.

The longboat pulled ashore and the crew made way for the soldier who loaded the trunk, then Balven waded out a little and awkwardly clambered over the gunwale and settled in the bow. The boat was quickly pushed back into the surf.

In a few short minutes the baron's brother climbed the rope ladder to the deck of the *Queen of Storms*. Hava stood there and when he was standing on the deck, said, "Welcome aboard."

"Thank you."

A rope was lowered and within a minute the wooden chest sat on the deck.

"Follow me," Hava instructed Balven, and he followed her to a doorway leading to three steps down to a short hall with three doors. She opened the centermost and waved him in.

Inside was a tidy cabin with a bed under a shelf below the stern windows, with just enough room for a chest of drawers and a map desk, illuminated by a single lantern hanging above the desk. There were candle sconces on either side of the door and Hava said, "At dusk one of the lads will bring in a taper from the galley to get the candles going. We keep a close eye on anything afire once we set out. If one goes out, don't try to light it yourself."

"I'll leave it to whoever you send," he replied. "Marquensas has never been a seafaring nation, so this is my third voyage in my lifetime, and the longest by far. I sailed from Ilcomen to Zindaros, a day and a bit, and back."

"Well, settle in. You're here for a good deal longer. This is my cabin, so you'll have to live out of your trunk, as the drawers are full of my rags."

"Where will you sleep?"

"I'll share my mate's bunk."

Balven's eyebrows rose at that.

Hava laughed. "I sleep while he commands the deck, and he sleeps when I do. Nothing else, though if something was going on with me and Sabien, I doubt Hatu would notice."

Her last remark was half humorous and half not. Balven's look was a questioning one, and Hava waved her hand. "It's just he's so caught up in his studies with Bodai, I only see him at night when I'm there."

"Oh," said Balven.

"Once we get underway, we'll set up the mess and you can eat here or on the deck."

"I'll eat where you do," he said.

"Fair enough."

She closed the door and left Balven sitting on the bunk, looking unsettled and a little confused.

DECLAN AND SEBASTIAN CREPT THROUGH the woods, trying to remain as silent as possible. First light in the Wound came long after sunrise above, as the steep canyon walls and thick tree canopy cut the light drastically. They were about a mile or so south of where the two game trails intersected, the boundary between the mercenaries' camp and "no man's land."

Declan tapped Sebastian on the shoulder and whispered, "We have to take the trail from here, I think."

As Sebastian was the more experienced hunter, he was in the lead, and over his shoulder he replied, "A little longer, I think, but yes, soon. You move quietly, but even so this brush ahead is thicker than behind us."

Declan said, "No words. Just turn and point where you want to go. I'll follow you."

Sebastian nodded, then turned and slowly took the lead. A few minutes later he stopped and pointed to a clearer area on the same side of the trail. Declan followed him.

They had left as soon as it was possible to move in the dim light of morning. Declan had put Sixto in charge of organizing the rope-weaving. Benruf had been correct that the strands of lianas were as tough as strong cord and with the thick ones at the center, only a few of the thin ones needed to be braided around them. They had discussed the way to organize the trek, and how much rope would be required. Declan allowed a little debate, but eventually just decided on what they would do. Long ropes would be burdensome, so shorter sections would be linked with interlocking loops, threaded one through the next, and after use, taken apart.

Declan knew he could trust Sixto to keep the men busy and had instructed the closest thing he had to a friend in this company what his idea was and how he should manage the attempt to escape from the Wound.

Declan was determined to escape as well: but if he was to die before avenging Gwen, Jusan, and Millie, at least he'd give his companions the chance to join Baron Dumarch in hunting down the murdering bastards.

Out of the woods, on the edge of the trail, Declan felt exposed. Sebastian turned and gestured to him that if he heard anything to dodge back into the trees as deep as he could. Declan nodded that he understood.

They crept along the verge of the trail for an hour, and Declan tried to keep the passage of time straight, so that he'd know when to turn back and reach the boundary before dark. He also had to take into account that they were descending deeper into the Wound, so the return trip would be uphill, and thus slower.

The canyon continued to widen rapidly, so they encountered a few clearings that to Declan appeared to have been harvested for timber but were now starting to regrow. He knew nothing about timber harvesting, save the bit here and there he had seen when delivering axes to lumber camps north of Oncon, and a few chats he'd had with those who harvested trees. For the most part he'd wanted to know why blades and saws needed to be fashioned in a certain way, and why steel wedges were needed to fell tall trees in a chosen direction.

Still, these areas looked as though they had been cleared many years before. The newer trees were still tall and had boles as big as two or three feet in diameter, and the big stumps were surrounded by undergrowth that would take years to sprout new trees.

A faint noise from ahead stopped Sebastian, and he held up a hand. The noise did not grow louder, so Declan assumed it wasn't a moving party getting close. Then it stopped.

Sebastian waited for a minute after quiet returned, then motioned for Declan to follow.

A few minutes later the sound resumed, and this time it was clearly that of voices, a loud chant or song. Again, it did not grow louder, and after a moment they continued.

They reached a large clearing, something of a choke point for those moving upward in the Wound, as the trail cut through the middle and the woods retreated on both sides. Sebastian turned and pantomimed a question: down the middle or to one side or the other? Declan paused and took stock of the terrain. Like the previous clearing, this had been harvested years before and there was some covering closer to the trail than the edges. He pointed to a small copse of younger trees, then made a motion of hunching over and scurrying from place to place. Sebastian nodded once and set off as quickly as he could to the first stand of trees.

By moving from one hiding spot to another, they reached the far side of the clearing and saw a gap between trees to the south. The odd chanting sound had again ceased, and Declan touched Sebastian on the shoulder and pointed. They set off to the south edge of the big clearing.

The woods close to the trail on both sides lasted for a hundred yards or so, then another massive clearing appeared. Both men stopped as they saw another hundred yards ahead a high wall, fashioned from the boles of big trees, the sort of defense construction that would have taken months to build. The timbers were covered in thick creepers, creating a massive green barrier.

There was a huge gate, open and showing signs of neglect, and around it were skulls, bones, and other items, clustered in such a way that Declan couldn't decide if they were trophies or some sort of warning. When they were within twenty yards of it, they crouched behind a small copse of trees and bushes to the east of the gate.

"Look," said Sebastian softly.

It took Declan a moment to understand what Sebastian was indicating, and then it struck him. Some of the skulls were not animal, but also human. And some of those that were animal appeared to be from beasts he had never seen before.

There was something like a crocodile skull from a distant swamp he'd seen hung over a tavern bar, but it was easily twice as large. Other skulls were almost familiar, but some were alien beyond his ability to identify them.

"What is that?" whispered Declan, pointing to something that looked roughly ape-like, but three times the size of a normal human skull, with long, almost knife-like canine teeth, and a band of pointed bone above the eye-ridges.

"I don't know," replied Sebastian, "and I hope to never find out. If that beast's skull is that size, it must stand . . ."

"Ten or twelve feet tall," finished Declan.

"Do we turn back?" whispered Sebastian, and Declan could tell which answer he would prefer.

"I'm not going through a gate that can be closed behind us," Declan whispered, "but I would like to know a little bit more."

He weighed curiosity against risk and was about to suggest they return when a sudden shout went up from some distance beyond the wall. Many voices sounded a low, growling sound that rose slowly to a shout. Then silence. A moment later the low chanting growl was repeated and again rose to a shout.

"Let's leave," said Sebastian.

"My thought exactly," said Declan, who turned and moved a short way farther from the gate and then took to the trail at a jog, Sebastian a few feet behind him.

As Declan had anticipated, the return journey took longer. Still, he felt that no eaters between their camp and the mercenaries' camp was a good sign. It meant that a journey to the escarpment should be relatively straightforward. Not fighting for their lives while trying to master the rocks that led to the foothills above the Wound was preferable.

He'd said nothing to anyone, not even Sixto, but not one man in camp was truly fit. His own men were still hurting from their time in the desert. Rest and meager food had helped, and at least there was abundant water from artesian springs nearby. The younger fighters were probably in roughly the same condition as Declan's men, but the older men like Oscar and Tobias? Declan knew that if trouble came, they'd give as good an account as possible, but doubted they'd survive any sort of stand-up fight.

Declan was also concerned that once out of the Wound, finding themselves on the wrong side of the low mountains separating them from the coast might be an insurmountable obstacle. Still, he'd rather die trying than any other choice available.

Near sundown they reached the mercenary camp and were greeted with clear expressions of relief. The stewpot was once again bubbling and Declan was so hungry that he didn't care if it was fresh, or yesterday's leftovers reheated.

Sixto handed him a platter. "What did you find?" he asked quietly.

"I found we owe Tobias and the others our lives. I never caught sight of a single eater, but what they've hung on the gateway to their territory tells me we would have all ended up hanging there, or parts of us at least."

Sebastian sat close enough to hear, and added, "And whatever they hunt on the other side of the camp, I'll be pleased to never see their like in this lifetime."

At that point the camp fell quiet and Declan realized all eyes were turned toward him. He took a deep breath and asked, "Ropes?"

Tobias said, "We finished what you asked for and even a bit more an hour ago."

"Good," replied Declan. "Eat as much as you can, and in the morning we'll finish off what's left. As soon as it's light enough that we can move without breaking legs, we start. We take whatever food we can carry and every water bag, the weapons and ropes. Leave everything else behind."

He glanced at all his own company, and said, "These men came down here the way we're going, so they know what I'm about to say. The escarpment will drain your legs. It's a gradual slope until the cliff, but it's still uphill all the way. It's certain we'll need to rest before we climb, and none of us were mountain fighters I suspect, so it's going to be slow going."

He sat down and continued to eat and heard Oscar mutter, "If we manage to survive this madness and get to a civilized land, I swear I'll never eat another stew for the rest of my life."

Declan found himself chuckling at that.

AN ESCAPE AND A MEETING OF MINDS

Declan sat eating the remains of last night's stew, which was cold and even less appetizing than normal, but needed for the tasks ahead. After the evening meal he and the others had organized as much as they could, ridding themselves of everything but food, water, weapons, and rope.

After sorting the supplies, Declan fell into an exhausted, but restless, doze. He had startled awake before anyone else, in the darkness, gripped by a terrifying uncertainty. Since Gwen's death and his own injury, he'd been haunted during his waking moments, filled with nameless forebodings.

As his injuries healed, pain would interrupt his sleep at first, and his mind would be seized with guilt and regret over why he couldn't have saved the people he loved. But as time passed his thoughts turned more often to whether he would be able to exact vengeance. Now his mind asked, could he save these men? Declan had given up on a good night's sleep.

He stood up and saw that everyone else was asleep, though Tobias was moving and in a moment he too sat up. In the half-dark as the world above them experienced first light, he got up and motioned to Declan to come away from the camp, so as not to wake the others.

Tobias said softly, "It's a good thing we're doing this."

"I don't know how you survived ten years here."

"Well, to start with, we were about three times the number when we got here, and ten years younger. We lost a lot of lads working out how to survive here."

Declan could only nod.

"Took a while to learn how to scrounge food, what we could eat and what killed us. Lost a couple who tried some lovely-smelling berries and died before they could bring a sackful back to us." Tobias looked away as if that memory was still painful.

He took a deep breath than tapped Declan on the chest with his finger. "If you save us, I'll follow you to the lowest hell, no questions asked. I've never been a leader, and I think the only reason the boys looked to me is I'm the biggest bastard in the company, and when the younger lads came tumbling down from above, well, they just took it for granted I knew what I was doing." He smiled. "You said you didn't choose to be a captain, but Bogartis knew what he was doing when he made you his deputy. You're a natural-born leader. You could command armies. And as I said, from this day forward, I'm your man."

Declan found himself moved. "I'll do everything I can to get us all out of here."

"And none too soon, from what you said about that chanting and howling down there," whispered Tobias.

"What do you mean?" asked Declan.

"I told you why we call them eaters."

Declan nodded.

"We know they're cannibals because the first time we tangled with them they killed maybe ten of us—it's hard to remember exactly—but the rest of us got away because a group of them stopped fighting and just started chewing on the bodies of the dead.

"They look like regular people, a little short and skinny, but though their skin is dark, as you'd expect in a hot land, some have white hair or strange yellow eyes. They're not skilled fighters as we'd usually reckon it, but they just don't stop coming. It's like they don't care who they lose. They'll just eat the fallen, I guess.

"But when they get all worked up, they just roll out of their village and kill and eat everything in sight." Tobias shrugged. "Remember how I said they left us alone after we gave them a beating? Well one time one of our scouts heard all the shouting and dancing, and came back to tell us, they hit us right after. Maybe they followed him, or maybe they were coming here anyway, but we lost another bunch of boys. The rest of us got away only because we bothered them with the traps, and we set fire to everything here so they wouldn't follow us.

"We hid for a few days up near those rocks we're going to be climbing. Took us weeks to rebuild the camp." Tobias fell silent at the memory. "After that, they went back to leaving us alone, and we kept clear of their hunting grounds. Like I showed you, everywhere but north of where those trails meet, and up the draw you came through." With a hopeful note, he added, "They might not be coming this way."

"But they might be, if they decide to ignore the traps," said Declan. He then glanced around and saw the sky above was lightening. "Time to get the men up."

Tobias nodded. "Good."

It took only a few minutes for the men to rise, eat what was left of the cold stew, and gather their remaining food, weapons and equipment. Declan did a quick look around the camp, ensuring that nothing had been forgotten, then moved to the head of the line where he just began walking.

Without orders, the others moved into a single file and followed their captain.

DONTE CHATTED WITH THE TWO Azhante prisoners, as each tried to gain a better understanding of the other's language. With Hava's departure, and Donte's need to fully heal, the baron had decided the time would be well spent if Donte could glean any more useful information from the prisoners.

"So, you get chosen to be Azhante, is that how it works?" Donte asked.

Sepi nodded, eating a grape. "They tell us it is an honor . . ." He looked at Firash, who also nodded. "An honor to take us to train when we are boys and girls."

"Same with us, sort of," replied Donte.

"But then," said Firash, "it is a harsh . . ." He turned to Sepi and asked something in a dialect Donte didn't recognize.

"Place to learn children?" Sepi asked. He had spent more time with Hava than Firash and had a better grasp of the difference between the two variant languages.

"School," Donte supplied.

"Harsh school." Firash nodded. "Bad lessons, many boys and girls hurt."

"Some die," Sepi added.

Donte nodded. "Ours, much the same, I think."

The door opened and Baron Daylon stood in the doorway, beckoning Donte to come outside.

Donte said farewell to the two prisoners and exited the room in which they were confined. A guard closed the door behind Donte, and he halted in front of Dumarch and gave a small lowering of his chin in what Daylon accepted as a bow.

"Learn anything useful?" asked the baron.

Donte gave a slight shrug. "Maybe. Interesting, but I don't know if it's useful."

"Explain."

Donte said, "To begin with, I think someone like my old master Bodai will be a big help if Hava and Balven can get him to come, because a lot of what we're talking about in there is . . . history. What I've pieced together is that Coaltachin was once a . . . clan? Or a big family. And we escaped, so the rest of the Azhante want to know how we did it."

"I got that much from Hava before she left," said Daylon. "Anything else?"

"As I said, I don't know if it's useful, but it seems like there are a lot of different nations on that continent and there are a lot of wars, and the Azhante are . . ." He looked frustrated as if fighting to frame a concept. "I don't know. They're commanded by the Pride Lords, and they sometimes stop wars, or jump in to win for one side, but the Azhante are not one people, but come from all the different nations. They're taken when young and sent to school, like my people are."

"Now, that may be useful to know."

Donte smiled, basking in that bit of praise. His status was uncertain—somewhere between prisoner and servant. For the moment, it appeared to be a bit of both.

"I have a task for you," said Daylon.

Donte said nothing.

"We're taking back the entire coast up to Port Calos and fortifying Copper Hills and building a new fortification for a garrison at Beran's Hill. Everything up there is in disarray, with people fleeing that way from the Wildlands to the Dangerous Passage."

Donte nodded, indicating that he understood. "You want me to keep an eye out for more like those two." He hiked his thumb over his shoulder at where the Azhante were quartered.

"Balven's right. You're a good bit cleverer than you let on. With the episkopos fleeing along that route all the way from Sandura, it must be total chaos from there across the Sea of Grass as well."

Donte laughed. "A carnival troupe of mummers, jugglers, jesters, and zanies could march through the Dangerous Passage in full costume playing instruments without attracting notice, so a few Azhante spies will be invisible."

"Pack whatever you have and be ready to leave within an hour. I'm putting Captain Baldasar in charge of the fortifications at Beran's Hill, so answer only to him."

"Then on to Port Calos?"

"No. Baron Rodrigo Bavangine of Copper Hills will assume control of Port Calos."

Donte gave one of his typical shrugs of indifference, but he smiled, so that he didn't quite look insolent. "Yes, m'lord," he said, offered his slight bow, then headed back toward the little room in the castle he'd recuperated in. He had decided, since getting to know the two Azhante agents, that he couldn't truly know which of them had stuck a dagger in him, so he had decided not to kill either of them. Besides, he was finding them quite likable, now that they had stopped trying to kill him.

HATUSHALY TOOK A DEEP BREATH, then asked, "So, where do we begin?"

"Where we left off yesterday," replied Nathan.

Bodai watched from the table, a large pot of coffee at his elbow. He'd carried it with him from the community mess, it having become a habit for the last week or so to consume it with the morning meal, and to bring it and his mug along. It had reached the point where this morning he had gone into the kitchen to inquire how the stock of coffee beans was holding up. He'd been gratified to learn that not many people besides himself and Hatushaly were drinking the dark brew, though they were running low on tea.

Hatu and Nathan stood facing each other, then both reached out and gripped the other's shoulders. Both lowered their heads and closed their eyes.

Bodai topped up his mug and settled in, knowing they might be locked in that pose for some time to come.

In the roiling void Hatu found himself alone with Nathan, and quickly Hatu used his emerging abilities to order the chaos. The swirls of color almost instantly became a myriad of threads, scintillating in every imaginable color and hue.

Hatu understood that his and Nathan's images were only a trick of the mind, that their actual bodies were standing motionless in the library. Yet he chose to imagine them as real, as that gave him a stronger hold on his identity. He had begun to realize a few days earlier that there existed a seductive aspect to this process, one he had discussed with Nathan, that the more power he commanded the less individual identity remained. It was addictive, Nathan had explained, and part of the risk of the training.

The most numerous and common of the threads fell away, a mental construct Hatu had fashioned, so that it appeared in his mind that he floated above the mass of energy threads between the furies. They were out of sight but he knew they were still there and that all this was an illusion he was manipulating, but as Nathan had instructed, anything he could do to preserve his sense of identity and place in the real world was welcome.

Then he let the second tier of lines fall, and then the third. The day before he had come to fully engage with what the fourth layer of these lines related to, flows of energy having their source in furies impacted by the actions of large groups, people, animals, fish, and creatures down to sizes so small that no unaided eye could see them. Intertwined with those forces were natural elements: wind, rain, tremors in the earth, tides, and currents.

He returned to where he had stopped the day before, studying the play of natural forces on groups, herds, pods of whales, flocks of birds. In his mind it was as if he reached out a hand and dipped it in water, feeling the flow of currents as countless schools of fish used them to move and find food.

"All movement, everywhere, is commanded by the tensions between positive and negative furies," came the voice of Nathan.

"I understand," said Hatu; that fact had been restated constantly since the lessons had started.

"The lesson for today is to sense which is life force and which is elemental force."

In his mind, Hatu put out his hand to touch the point where the forces intersected, then heard Nathan warn, "Be as gentle as you can, as if you were picking up the tiniest petal of the most delicate flower. The furies' lines are uncountable and massive in their abundance, but each line can be brittle. Should you break one, consequences might result, from the tiniest movement of a single fish in a school, to the collapse of a cliff face into the ocean. Until you completely master knowing which lines connect which furies, avoid interacting."

"How then do I do that?" asked Hatu.

"Get as close as you can in your mind, but not quite touching. Let the energy pulsing along that line reveal its nature to you. We are a long way from you actually interacting with all those forces. Think of this as learning to crawl before you attempt walking."

"I understand," said Hatu, though he wasn't sure he did.

Hatu returned his focus to the pod of whales he had sensed before and in his mind moved his hand to the very edge of where they swam. For a brief instant he attempted to judge where they were swimming relative to his physical location in the Sanctuary, but all he could tell was they were somewhere to the northeast.

He imagined that his hand was at the edge of the pod, moving in unison with them, as if he were some giant being standing knee-deep in the ocean, able to bend down and simply run his fingers through the ocean's swells.

Then he felt the sea moving in a different rhythm, almost a pulsing of energy rising and falling in a unity he could never have imagined before. It struck him like two songs sung by two different voices, one deep and mellow, a soft melody of relaxed power. That was the sea. The other was the energy from the whales, who swam in alternating counterpoint and harmony with the sea. He did as Nathan instructed, simply waited and let the energies reveal what they were to him.

Then he sensed a difference between the two and after pondering for a long time he said, "One is living . . ."

"Yes," said Nathan.

"The other is . . . something else."

"We need to leave now," said Nathan.

"Now?"

"You're succumbing to the lure" was all Nathan said.

Hatu was about to object, then realized that objecting was the trap of the lure of which Nathan spoke. He blinked and they were back in the library.

Bodai had slumped down in his chair, leaning to the right, his elbow on the table and his eyes shut. He was snoring.

Hatu laughed and Bodai's eyes opened. "Oh, I must have dozed off," said the one-time master from Coaltachin.

"Indeed," said Nathan.

"How long have we been gone?" asked Hatu.

Bodai looked around and muttered, "I need to get one of those water clocks or a sand clock." He blinked the sleep away and took note of the shadows from the high windows, and said, "Judging by the light and the hunger in my stomach, all morning."

"Let's say four hours," said Nathan.

"Inside it felt as if it was only a few minutes." Hatu rolled his shoulders and head to combat stiffness. "Now it feels like four hours."

"Time," Nathan said with a smile.

Hatu chuckled and shook his head. "Time," he repeated: it had become something of a joke between them.

Bodai said, "I think next time you go exploring in whatever that . . . void, or mind-space, or whatever you call it, I'm going to return to other tasks. This is not the best use of my time."

An expression crossed Nathan's face, a mix of recognition and humor. In a tone that could only be thought of as mischievous he said, "If Hatu is willing this afternoon we can bring you into his vision."

Nathan looked at Hatu, who nodded. Hatu said, "If you want?"

Bodai's eyes widened and he looked like a child to whom someone had handed a wonderful gift. "Can you?"

Hatu smiled. "After lunch, then."

"After lunch," said Bodai, now excited by the promise.

They filed out of the library to the community kitchen, and Bodai had a lift in his step.

* * *

Declan surveyed the company. They had kept a steady pace, jogging for a minute or more, then walking, a practice he had learned from Bogartis that ate up the miles.

He counted minutes in his head and tried to calculate how long until it would be too dark to travel. He was minutes away from ordering another march, when one of the younger mercenaries, Alex, stood up and pointed. "Look!"

Declan turned and looked in the direction indicated, and after a moment, saw what the sharp-eyed youngster had seen. Smoke was rising from behind them.

Tobias appeared at Declan's elbow. "They're burning our camp. Looks like they're coming."

Declan immediately calculated the distance they'd already covered and how much light was left. Then he shouted, "Everyone up! We have to move as fast as we can, as far as we can." He waved Tobias over.

"What?" asked the old fighter.

"We have to reach that first stone wall," said Declan, "and get up on top of it. If we can reach the higher ground, we may have a chance. If they stop following after dark, we might get high enough up the rocks after first light to get away from them."

Tobias whispered, "If they get here before we—"

Declan cut him off. "I know."

As the rest of the men also saw the smoke they began to ask questions, shout pleas, or, like Oscar, predict bloody doom.

Declan shouted, "Shut up! Get in line!"

Most fell quiet, but a few continued to yell out questions.

"We should have stayed and hidden!" cried Oscar.

"And we'd all be dead by now!" spat back Mick Sawyer. "Listen to the captain!"

"I said shut up, all of you!" Declan shouted even louder. "Now, if we're going to live through this, listen to me!"

The last men fell silent.

"We can't run. We run, we fall: we fall, we die. We have to get to the rocks before the eaters get to us. Keep your eyes sharp, watch your footing; break an ankle, you die. Understood?"

There was a murmur of assent.

"Now keep alert, but if you see anything we can quickly use for brands, a fallen branch, a shock of reeds, anything we can light, sing out!"

As he moved away, Tobias grabbed his arm. "You mean to climb in the dark?"

"If we reach a safe place and don't have to climb, we'll wait. If they keep coming and we need to climb in the dark, that's what we have to do, that's what we will do," Declan replied, pulling away from the man's grip and moving to the head of the line.

As he passed Sixto, Declan didn't look back to see if they were following: he knew they would be.

HATUSHALY STOOD READY, REFRESHED BY his midday meal, and saw that both Nathan and Bodai were ready.

Nathan spoke to Bodai. "You may feel disoriented for a while. It's hard to measure time in an illusion, so what feels like moments to one of us may feel much longer to another at first. Once we're all settled, time will seem to pass for all of us at the same rate and we can communicate. I suggest you remain silent, as that will aid your ability to relax and observe, and if you have questions, wait until we return to our consciousness here. Should anything go amiss to you, just return here."

"How?" Bodai asked.

"Just want to," said Nathan. "The moment you return just let go of my shoulder and Hatu's. Then sit and wait. You've seen how long we can be gone before. It may take moments or hours. Are you ready?"

"As much as I can be," said the old teacher.

The three men stood at equidistance, then each reached out and put his hand on the other men's shoulders. Bodai had seen Hatu and Nathan do this enough times not to need instructions. He leaned forward slightly, lowered his head and closed his eyes.

Instantly they were floating in the swirling chaos of colors Hatu thought of as the disorganized "face" of the furies. He quickly put the lines in order and then disposed of those he had ignored before, bringing all three of them back to where he and Nathan had left off before the midday meal.

Nathan said, "Now, let go of the forces of nature, leaving us only with living energy."

Hatu pushed away everything that echoed the slow rhythm, the rolling waves of nature's forces, and was stunned for a second at his recognition of life as a force apart from the bodies of living creatures. It felt as if an entirely new level had opened before him and he saw countless threads of vibrant life. The reverberations of the pulses varied from a frantic quiver that mimicked a high-pitched buzzing down to a deep rumble that cycled like a massive heartbeat.

Nathan said, "Life has one common note in that cacophony of noise. Seek it out."

Time passed as Hatu eased his mind into a relaxed state and in his imagination he didn't reach out his hand but rather leaned over to listen closely. He willed away the shrillest sounds and the lowest rumbles, and eventually he was left with what felt like the most perfect note of music. It was elegant and sublime, and recognizing it almost brought him to tears in this illusion of self.

Bodai had been instructed to stay silent, as Hatu's perceptions were shared, but the revelation of this profound energy caused him to whisper, "Exquisite!"

For what seemed a long time they simply watched the common pulse of life in the universe, then Nathan said, "You are accelerating your control. I am impressed. Now, find the common human rhythm."

"How?"

"You are touching Bodai. Sense his energy, then look for what is in common with other threads, beyond the fundamental of life."

Hatu hesitated and Bodai said, "It's all right."

Hatu let his senses enter Bodai for an instant, and in that moment he was almost overwhelmed with sensations and memories, flickering glimpses into Bodai's life. Hatu put up a barrier to that rush of another person's entire existence and created an illusion of distance from experience and thought. He then quickly moved his focus to the essence of the man, the energy that coursed through him.

Hatu had come to see his growing knowledge as listening to different types of music, played on pipes, lutes, a variety of drums, brass horns, and many other instruments. Each energy was distinguishing itself to him as if he felt a different note being played on a different instrument, and he was going to master them all.

There was a foundation within this magic harmony he knew to be what he was seeking. He shifted his attention to the maze of life energies around him, and suddenly all but one type vanished from view.

"Humans," he said calmly.

There were still countless threads tethered to different places, and just the sense of how much humanity existed nearly stunned him. He focused even more intensely and said, "Now what?"

"What you first sensed in Bodai, before you isolated the common thread of humanity," said Nathan. "That is what distinguishes him from every other living being; that is what makes him who he is."

"It nearly overwhelmed me."

"You've only lived one life so far, so being plunged into another without preparation can drown you, make you lose who you are. I was ready to end this but am gratified I didn't need to."

Bodai said, "I felt a . . . presence, but nothing more."

"One more step before we end this. Let the threads of humanity pass by but look for the familiar."

"What do you mean?"

"When you engaged with Bodai part of what sped through you was like a rushing wave, yet there were bits that would have felt familiar had you focused on them."

Hatu considered this then said, "I think I understand."

"So, the closest person in your life."

"That would be Hava, of course," Hatu replied.

"Then think of her, and simply wait to see if a thread echoes some familiar aspect of how she makes you feel, what being near her changes within you as opposed to when you're alone. That reflects the link that binds you and shows you where she is."

Hatu waited, and he had no sense of how long, but abruptly one thread stood out, as if it suddenly got larger and more vibrant, and it drew him. "Hava!"

"In time," said Nathan, "you may be able to talk to people over vast distances, or even travel instantly from place to place. We have no idea of the extent of your powers, Hatu. As Hava might say, we are in unknown waters."

Suddenly they were back in the library, and it was dark. What little light there was came in from the connecting hallway, and Bodai sat down as if exhausted. "That took the wind out of my sails," he said.

Nathan stretched and said, "The mind and body are still linked, and while we may have floated inside our minds, our bodies have been standing here for hours." He lifted one knee and reached to pull it up a little, then repeated the move with the other knee.

"It felt as if I could have reached out and touched Hava," Hatu said. "I have a sense of her being out there." He pointed to the northeast. "She's returning from Marquenet."

"That's good to know," said Bodai.

"You could have reached out and touched her," said Nathan, in a tone Hatu recognized. He was about to say something significant. "As I said in our shared thoughts, we do not know what you're capable of. The powers you possess are unique, and part of the reason I'm here is to prevent you from harming yourself or others."

"How?"

"As much as you're learning, so am I. You are unique and no one like you has lived on this world. As I said, unknown waters. If you were to touch those life energies with your mind . . ." He stopped, trying to organize his thoughts. "You are a child, holding your father's largest hunting knife. You may think you're ready to use it, but most likely you'll cut yourself or someone close to you. We will teach you how to use that knife without harming anyone by accident."

Hatu nodded. "I'm starving."

"You go on," said Bodai. "I have a few questions for Nathan. We'll be along shortly."

Hatu smiled and quickly left.

"What do you wish to know?" asked Nathan.

"A great many things about what I saw, and will probably never understand," answered Bodai. "But one thing first. Why was I invited in?"

"You were curious," replied Nathan.

Bodai nodded. "Indeed, but you could have asked, or Hatu could have asked before, yet it didn't come up until this afternoon."

"Why do you think?"

"I understand why you wanted me to believe in magic before you met Hatu, the logic of having me on your side as it were, but the thing that struck me today was you wanted me there for Hatu's examination of human energy."

"So?"

"So when you taught him to explore what made humans unique, you told him to examine me. Why bring me along and why not have him simply examine you?"

Nathan laughed, and narrowed his eyes. "Who said I was human?" He reached out a hand and Bodai took it. Nathan gently pulled him to his feet. "We need some food!" he said in a cheerful voice.

"Magic," said Bodai in a tone of wonder.

Nathan laughed loudly. "There is no magic. It's just tricks."

I 2

CONFLICTS, EVASIONS, AND A NEW

AWARENESS

Declan's company moved slowly through the dark. Each man made sure of his footing as often as possible as they were reaching the end of the escarpment, marked by thinning brush and no trees, and the ground below crunching as soil gave way to small rocks and pebbles.

They had some light courtesy of flaming brands they'd acquired along the way, slender tied branches and a few bunches of reeds and long willows they had quickly harvested from the last open water in this canyon. The men had cut them and refilled their water skins since there would probably be a long wait for more fresh water.

"Rocks ahead," said Sebastian, who again was breaking trail. Next to Declan was one of the younger members of the surviving mercenaries, the one called Mikola. He'd made a few trips back to the rocks since he and the rest of the younger company had fled down this way five years before.

Declan had asked Tobias how they'd come by that large cooking kettle. Tobias had explained that it had been in the trade wagon Mikola and the younger guards had been protecting, which had come crashing down from the flatlands above when they were being chased by nomads.

The wagon had provided the iron kettle and some other useful items which had been the prime reasons for Mikola and the other younger members of the company's return visits.

No useful part of the wagon remained: every scrap of metal and intact stave of wood had been carried down to the camp and used to construct their dwellings. The iron kettle they had simply rolled down the escarpment, for as Tobias had told Declan, it was pretty difficult to break such a thing. The one humorous moment in the tale was the man named Acke having to rush down and try to stop the kettle from sinking to the bottom of the pond they'd just left behind. That had left Acke soaked to the skin and with a broken arm, but the kettle had been saved.

"We stop here," said Declan. He turned to Tobias and asked, "Do those eaters come at night?"

"I don't know," the old man replied, breathing heavily. "I think I've told you all I know."

Despite Declan's concern over their lack of fitness, every man had managed to keep up. The need for a slow pace in the darkness was a significant part of the reason for this.

Tobias caught his breath and said, "The few times we had to face those murdering dogs was during the day . . ." He shrugged. "As slow as we're going, if they were following us, they'd be here by now."

Sixto spoke from behind them. "Maybe they burned the camp and went back."

"Maybe," Declan replied, "but if they camp at night, and start at first light tomorrow they will certainly be on us by noon if we're not up there." He pointed to the rocks before them.

"You can't be seriously thinking of starting a climb in the dark?" asked Toombs.

"No," said Declan. "Get the ropes organized, then everyone sit and rest as best you can, but the moment we can see our hands in front of our faces without a lit brand, we start climbing."

He had talked with every member of the company to discover who might have any climbing experience, and no one had more than he, so he decided he'd go first, with Sebastian last. The archer had only six arrows left and would climb behind Sixto. Declan wanted his two most reliable fighters at the rear, and would have liked to stay with them, but no one else could lead.

He started down the line as the ropes fashioned from vines were laid out, complete with looped handholds. The vine weaves were much heavier than hemp or coir fiber ropes. Declan knew that would take a toll, but it couldn't be avoided.

He finished his survey and said, "Make sure they're tied with a good knot so it doesn't slip down and trip you up, but not so tight that you're unable to freely move." He knew the makeshift rope was cumbersome, but it was strong and should save a man from falling. No drop from here, save straight back down the face, would prove fatal, but a fall to the side could cripple a man, or injure him enough that he would be unable to keep up.

Sixto came to him. "We're ready."

Declan said, "I certainly hope so."

They all sat, several facing down the escarpment in case trouble erupted behind them, the rest seeking to make themselves as comfortable as possible. Several fell to dozing quickly, but Declan found sleep slow in coming. He knew that once they got high enough up those rocks, repelling the eaters would be possible unless they came in huge numbers. Declan put off worrying about what might await them after they crawled out of the Wound. He was learning to keep his mind on the dangers of the moment, not those that might come. They had to survive this conflict before facing another.

At last he dozed, but as his head fell forward he'd jerk awake, having no sense of how much time had passed. He eventually fell into a short sleep and awoke with Sixto shaking his shoulder. "It's time."

Declan said nothing but shook himself fully awake and stood up before stretching and looking up at the sky. It was lightening, and he could see his hand, just, in front of his face. He gazed at the men around him, and in the gloom he could make out features here and there.

"I need whatever light we have on that rock," he said calmly.

A smoldering brand was blown alight by Sixto and another, bigger torch was lit with that. "This is what we have," said Sixto.

With mock humor, Declan said, "If I fall and splatter all over these rocks, you're in charge."

Sixto smiled and put his hand on Declan's shoulder. "I suggest you don't fall."

Declan smiled in return. "Get the light as close as you can without burning my arse."

Sixto chuckled. "We'll do our best."

Declan had spent a long time studying this rock face. He handed his sword to Sixto. At some point it would be hauled up to him.

With a long rope tied around his waist, the end trailing behind, Declan reached up and put his hand in a crevice about a foot above his head, placed his right toe atop a rock and pulled himself up.

It was an arduous climb up the first section of the face to a flat rock twenty feet above him. The light was still so dim that Declan had to depend on how well he had memorized the route from below. He felt his body tremble as he held his position and reached up with his right hand and felt around until he found another slight outcropping. He pulled up and blindly groped about until he felt a secure handhold and again pulled himself up, at the same time as he pushed with his left leg.

His shoulders and legs were afire and he was getting light-headed as he reached up and found his hand touching the lip of the shelf. He gripped it as hard as he could, forcing himself to remember where he had seen a tiny ledge for his left foot and sought it out. He finally found a place for his toe and pressed down on it.

His toe slipped and he felt a shock of a tiny fall and a bolt of fear, but he steadied himself. With a deep breath, he yanked himself upward, using his momentum to fall forward, until he was lying on the flat rock. He took another deep breath, then wriggled forward, moving his left leg until he could bring it up enough to crawl across the rock.

Declan rolled over and spent a minute luxuriating in the feeling of safety. He stared upward at the sky above growing lighter by the moment. He experienced a tiny sense of relief, and felt tears gathering in his eyes. He sat up and shook off the emotions of the moment, looking around for a place to make himself safe.

Seeing a ridge a few feet behind, he shouted down, "Give me a moment. When I'm set, I'll yank on the rope, and you can send the next man up!"

Sixto shouted, "We're ready!"

Declan looked for a crevice where he could jam his belt-knife, creating a makeshift belay. Finding one, he jammed home the blade, then after fastening the rope, he gave it a yank. Declan braced himself, feeling weight on the rope, and held his position as the next man climbed up, and when a figure appeared over the ledge, he felt a rush of relief. The figure resolved itself: it was Tobias Winters who stood up, untangled himself from the vines, and moved toward Declan. "The younger lads will be coming next, but I'm still the strongest bastard here even if my eyesight isn't what it once was."

Declan simply chuckled and together they held the rope for a third man.

It was Jack Sawyer, one of the brothers from Declan's company who was as fit as any man in this company. He grinned, while perspiration ran off his face, his dark skin glistening. He gave Declan a look of silent thanks.

Declan took a moment, and then surprised himself by clasping Jack in an embrace. "Let's get the rest of them up here."

The three of them quickly pulled Jack's brother Mick up, and as every man reached the wide ledge, they were able to contribute to the line. By the end, when Sebastian was brought up, it was a quick haul.

They waited a moment, mostly to let Declan rest. He took a look around and saw every man in the village was there, safe.

"That's a first step," Declan said, as he retied the end of the rope around his waist. The sky above was light enough that the few flickering brands could be tossed aside. "We should be able to get up a good way, but I'm going to test each rock before I climb, to make sure I've got solid footing, so follow exactly behind the man before you."

"What if it isn't solid?"

Declan recognized the plaintive tones of Oscar. "Then get the hell out of the way as fast as you can," he answered as he leaned against a large rock, and then shimmied up to stand on top of it.

He looked down for a moment and what he could see in the gloom of the morning revealed nothing but the dark tops of distant trees. He still couldn't trust that they were free of pursuit, so he quickly moved ahead, making room for the next man in line. This wide table rock would allow them to rest a little, as the farther up they pushed the more difficult the climb would be.

The party rested for a few minutes as the sky continued to lighten and then Declan heard something from the far end of the escarpment.

Tobias saw Declan's expression change, and said, "What?"

Declan held up his hand, as some other men started asking questions.

"Be quiet!" he said.

After a minute he realized that what he had heard was in counterpoint to what he wasn't hearing. The birds had stopped their calls, then the monkeys started to hoot warnings.

"We need to go now." The men looked from one to another, until Declan raised his voice enough to make it a command, not a request. "I said, now!"

HATUSHALY LAY IN BED, AWAKE early for no apparent reason. Early in his working with Nathan, he had learned the price of drinking too much at supper, before going to bed. The drink interfered with his sleep and he spent too many nights restless, and when he awoke he was still tired. So he had taken to having a single mug of wine or ale during dinner, and nothing after. He had no idea why he was suddenly awake in the dead of night.

As he moved to sit on the edge of his bed, he mused at his unexpected waking. Then he felt a sensation, as if a tiny breeze was tickling his cheek, or as though a single raindrop had struck his neck. He held his breath and waited to see if it came again, and as he was about to stand, there was another feeling of touching, like a feather brushing his face, or a draft through an open distant window.

He closed his eyes and rather than practice alone the routine Nathan had taught him, he waited as he had learned in the mind exercises, waiting for something to come to him.

Like distant music where the song cannot quite be made out, he knew something was touching him from far away. A flicker of recognition, and he realized he was again sensing Hava. As soon as he focused, the sensation vanished. He realized once more that as soon as he tried something, it failed. She must have been at quite a distance from here. He certainly couldn't have been spending any less effort to reach her. He had been sleeping.

He rubbed his face and hair, debating whether to return to sleep or to get up very early. He had no sense of what time it was, and suddenly agreed with Bodai. They needed some sort of timepiece. It might be hours to dawn, or the sun might rise moments after he returned to sleep.

He chose sleep, hoping there were hours of rest ahead.

When he awoke again, dawn was breaking and he felt more rested, so he assumed he'd guessed right. He dressed and went to the communal kitchen where he found the morning meal preparation was fully underway.

He sat at the usual table he and the others occupied, as a few workers entered and made their way to the table where the kitchen staff laid out the morning meal. A few chose to eat in this hall, but many just took plates to their work sites. This had started to become a point of contention between the staff and workers, since many workers never bothered to bring the plates and cups back, forcing the kitchen boys to have to visit every work site on

the island and collect them in large sacks, and then spend extra
time scrubbing dried-on food off them.

Bodai had observed at one point that it wasn't wise to anger
those who prepared your meals, and had convinced Catharian
that some sort of penalty needed to be imposed to let the workers
know that if they took dishes out in the morning, they needed
to return them in the evening. They were still trying to work
out what that should be.

Bodai and Nathan both wandered in a few minutes later and
Hatu said to Bodai, "I have a suggestion."

"What's that?" Bodai said as he loaded up his plate with
poached fish, a boiled egg, and a few local vegetables. Knowing
his penchant, a kitchen boy handed him a full pot of coffee,
which he took after tucking a mug into the crook of his elbow.

After the others had gathered their breakfast, they returned
to the table, and Hatu said, "The workers not returning plates?"

"Yes?"

"You were considering a penalty, right?"

"Hard to collect a fine when we're not paying them anything."
Nathan laughed.

"It's simple. As the kitchen boys know who the culprits are,
just have them tell you who, then make the workers wash the
dishes the boys bring back."

Bodai chuckled. "Some of those plates and cups get nasty out in
the sun for a day or more." He took a bite of fish. "I'll welcome
the day we can have a sausage or slice of ham." With a wave of
his fork, he added, "They're tired and they'll refuse to do so."

"Maybe if it's someone like Hava's mate, Sabien, who tells
them?"

Bodai emitted a low laugh. "He is a rather large fellow, it's true. Not a lot of men around here would try to stand up to him. I'll chat with Catharian. He was back from his journey to the Border Ports a few days ago; he'll show up soon."

They finished eating and carried their dishes to where the kitchen boys waited. Bodai hung on to his pot of coffee and mug and they started their short walk to the library.

"Hava woke me up last night," Hatu said offhandedly.

Nathan stopped, gripping Hatu's arm to stop him in his tracks. "How?" he said with concern in his eyes. "She's still at sea."

Hatu was surprised by the intensity of the question. He pulled his arm free of Nathan's grip. "I woke up in the middle of the night and didn't know why. After a moment I felt something. It was a . . . touch, a . . ." He furrowed his forehead as he thought. "I waited, as we did in the . . . mind exercise, waiting for it to return. When it did, I knew it was Hava. But as soon as I tried to find her, the sensation was gone."

Nathan nodded. He motioned for them to follow him into the library, where they sat down. "You sensed Hava when you were not looking for her, not in the mind-space we created." He paused as if framing his thoughts. "That's a level of sensitivity I would not have imagined possible in someone with your limited experience. It's a passive ability." He sat back, thinking, and then softly said, "I wish I understood better how power works in this world."

Both Bodai and Hatu exchanged glances, and Hatu said, "This world?"

Nathan ignored the question. "I'm changing the lesson for today. I think you've gone beyond where I thought you'd be at this stage. Are you ready?"

Hatushaly nodded, and they assumed their usual face-to-face position, while Bodai watched from the table.

As soon as the two men gripped each other's shoulders, Hatu plunged into the mind illusion.

Instantly they were standing upon the lines of force as before, and all the lines not connected to humans were gone.

"Impressive," said Nathan.

"Why?"

"You knew where you wanted to be within your own mind and didn't need to take steps to send away the lines of energy you did not care about."

Hatu sensed an almost-excited feeling from Nathan, and said, "Is that important?"

"I'll explain later. Push away all those lines of energy belonging to people you don't know," he instructed.

Hatu found it an easy task and suddenly felt a presence he had not expected. "Donte!"

"Who?" asked Nathan.

"A friend I thought was dead!"

Nathan said, "Your joy is an overwhelming wave!"

"What do I do?"

"Pull back and catch your breath."

Hatu understood that catching his breath was a metaphor for existence in the real world, that he needed to pause and sort out his thoughts, but it was instructive and gave him a perspective on what to do next. He moved his near-contact with Donte's energy line away a little more and waited to collect his thoughts for a moment.

Mentally, it was as if he took a deep breath. Hatu moved farther way until Donte was only a lingering presence on the edge of his awareness, then asked, "What now?"

"Find someone else, someone who is known well but not so tethered to your feelings."

Hatu took but a moment, then said, "Declan Smith. He's a good man. We bought our inn from his wife."

He sent out his consciousness as if he was spreading his mind over a large area, and suddenly he felt a familiar contact. He knew it was Declan, in some far-distant place, and the energy pulsed with a vibrancy he hardly recognized.

"I found him," he said to Nathan. "And there's something wrong."

"What?"

"I don't know."

"Get closer, but do not make contact."

Hatu moved his focus to what he knew was Declan Smith, a familiar pattern of energy, despite them not being close friends.

"Now look," instructed Nathan.

"Look how?"

"As I said before, we do not know what you're fully capable of, so this may not work, but try to imagine a distant window which looks out to where your friend is, then firmly grip that window and slowly pull it toward you, or move toward it, whichever feels more natural."

Hatu looked at the thread leading to Declan and put a window some distance away from him within his illusion. Then he willed it to move toward him. As it moved closer, an image emerged within it. It was darker where Declan was, so Hatu assumed he was still in Marquensas. As the image came closer, he felt that this was an incorrect assumption. Declan was farther south, and suddenly Hatu knew he was somewhere in South Tembria.

He drew the "window" closer until he could see a line of men scrambling up a cliff. They were filthy, ragged, and haggard. Hatu tried to extend his senses as close to Declan as he could without making any contact, aware of what Nathan said was grave danger.

"They're fleeing something," Hatu said.

"What are you seeing?"

"You can't see this?" asked Hatu.

Nathan replied, "This is your . . . space, from within your mind, and I have no control. I sense things, which is how I guide you, and I have enough experience to interpret much, but I literally don't—"

Hatu willed for Nathan to see the window, and his guide gasped. "How did you do that? I can see your window to Declan!"

"I don't know," Hatu replied. "I just did it."

Hatu felt a tiny echo of uncertainty coming from Nathan but he ignored it for the moment, and returned his attention to Declan.

The men were exhausted, almost dragging themselves up over boulders and ledges, helping each other with boosts and hands reaching down, but it was clear they were on the very brink of collapse.

"It looks as if they're in serious danger," Hatu said.

"You control that window. See what is following them but stay close to Declan or you'll lose that connection."

Hatu imagined his hands reaching out and moving the window so that it looked over Declan's shoulder. In the distance he could vaguely see figures. "They are far enough away that I can't see . . ."

"Bring them closer."

"How?" Hatu asked.

"What you 'see' is not real, but how your mind interprets what is out there. You control it. Will the image closer."

"Again, how?"

"As you do other things, by willing it without forcing yourself to try."

For a moment, Hatu struggled then realized exactly what

Nathan meant. Reading unknown languages, creating the fire on the ship, the display of blue energy when sailing through the Narrows, all had been done without thought, just by will.

Suddenly the image became clearer, and he saw the pursuers. He could make out details. They were all men, wearing clothing mostly made from animal skins, with some old and dirty cloth shirts and trousers.

All were lean and moved with surprising speed, given they were all barefoot, and they ran over rough and jagged rocks. They carried an assortment of axes and long knives, some made from metal, but others had been fashioned from branches and sharpened rocks. A few also carried crude spears.

Hatu had seen a few primitive people before in his travels, but nothing like these men. There was something profoundly wrong about them, as if normal men had somehow been corrupted, and from the odd bits of clothing scattered among the skins, they appeared to be scavengers. And he knew they had murder in their hearts.

"Declan and his men are lost," he said. "Can I help them?"

Nathan was silent for a minute and then said, "Possibly, but it will be dangerous."

"Tell me."

"Touch nothing living but seek out the quiet energy of the rocks and soil."

Hatu said nothing and began his search.

DECLAN UNTIED THE ROPE AROUND him and drew his sword. "Get down!" he commanded. "I see no bows, but some of them have spears."

He felt a cold sinking pit open inside him, for he knew his men could not best the eaters coming up from below. The men crouched and waited, and Declan judged they had two, three minutes at best, before the pursuers climbed up the last ledge face to where they waited.

The howls and screams from the eaters were almost animal in their tone and ferocity. Declan composed himself as he vowed to kill as many as possible before they were overtaken. Despite his own fear and exhaustion, he was gripped by a profound sense of failure, for he knew he would never avenge the killing of Gwen, Jusan, Millie, and the others who had died at Beran's Hill.

A spear was thrown, but it clattered harmlessly off the rock face below. Still, every man flinched at the sound.

Then Declan felt a vibration in the soles of his feet. A faint ripple of movement that grew until Sixto shouted, "Quake!"

Declan yelled, "To me!" as he moved to the center of the ledge.

The men scrambled to reach him, and once they were bunched together, the soil and rocks below them began to move. At first it was the loosest of the stones, which shook then rolled down, falling among the eaters. The movement seemed to last longer than any quake Declan had ever experienced.

Then came a massive jolt, and the entire rock face below them began to crumble. "Back!" shouted Declan, and everyone pressed themselves against the rock face, as far away as possible from the collapsing rocks, which were spewing dust and debris into the air, just below the edge of the flat stone ledge they occupied.

Large rocks and small boulders were dislodged as Declan and his men were thrown to the ground, some landing on top of one another. Cries of pain from below were followed by screams of terror as a flood of rocks came crashing down on the eaters.

Then, as suddenly as it started, the trembling stopped.

Thick clouds of dust filled the air and obscured their vision. Declan could hear the eaters that had survived the rockfall fleeing back down the rocks to the escarpment below, while those trapped by the rocks cried, whimpered, or screamed in pain.

His men got up slowly, coughing from the dust, and many with dirt in their eyes. After a few minutes those eaters trapped in the rocks fell silent, and the sound of the ones retreating faded away.

Toombs said, "What is that thing the Church of the One talks about?"

"A miracle," said Sixto.

"That was one of those," said Tobias.

As the dust started to blow away, Declan moved to the edge of the plateau and looked down. Sixto followed. They could see dozens of bodies strewn among a massive fall of rocks.

"No one's climbing up to here," said Sixto.

Below them a new, sheer face of rock rose more than fifty feet from the rubble below.

Tobias moved to stand next to Sixto. "At least this is now behind us."

"They didn't carry off their dead," Declan said to Tobias.

"The survivors just wanted to get as far away, as fast as possible. Even those bastards know you can't hold off a rockslide while you gather your dead," Tobias replied.

Declan turned and saw the lip of the flatlands up ahead. The rock above them did not appear to have shifted at all, and still looked climbable. He sat down, almost ready to weep with relief. Then he reminded himself that this was only the first leg. They still had to find a way past the mountains to the sea, but first they needed to find food.

"Let's rest a little, then we'll get out of here," he said.

He heard no objections.

* * *

HATU CAME OUT OF HIS mind state and staggered. Bodai was quick enough to leap to his aid and stop the younger man from falling.

He turned Hatu around and sat him in the chair he had just vacated and said to Nathan, "What happened?"

"Things I am not equipped to understand, let alone explain," Nathan replied, and his gaze held a touch of wonder as he looked at Hatu.

Hatu seemed disoriented and slowly his eyes came back into focus. At last he said, "I'm thirsty."

"There's water on that side table," replied Bodai. "I'll get you a cup."

He quickly fetched the drink and Hatu gulped it down.

"That was . . . amazing," said Hatu.

"What?" asked Bodai.

"I found Declan," said Hatushaly.

Bodai nodded.

"He was leading a company of men who were fleeing from . . ." Hatu took another sip of water, then cleared his throat. "Men who . . . they were evil, Bodai. And I'm not even sure they were men." Another swallow of water was followed by "So I saved Declan and his troop."

Bodai's eyes widened and he looked from Hatu to Nathan. Eventually he whispered, "How?"

"I caused a rockslide that drove off the men chasing Declan. His men looked as if they'd been through a lot—"

"You caused a rockslide?" interrupted Bodai.

Hatu nodded and finished off the water.

Bodai looked at Nathan with a questioning expression.

Nathan answered with raised eyebrows and a shrug.

Bodai said, "Hatu, are you even remotely aware of what you've done?"

"I just told you," Hatu replied.

Bodai again looked at Nathan who shrugged once more. Bodai muttered, "He's still so young."

Nathan studied Hatushaly for a moment, and said, "You do things no other man on this planet can do. You're the only man who can do any magic here. No woman comes close to your power."

Hatu weighed what Nathan had said, then smiled and asked, "What do we do next?"

Nathan said, "I have no idea."

13

REUNIONS, SPECULATIONS,

AND ADJUSTMENTS

Declan lay motionless as did the line of men behind him. They had been following a dry riverbed for a day and had seen no sign of others. Now they heard riders in the distance. Declan hoped they had managed to get out of sight in time below the tall dry grass that lined the bank. He knew from the fight outside Abala that if his company were fit and well, a band of riders would be difficult to deal with but could be beaten. With his company in their current condition, they stood no hope of survival.

They remained still, the sun beating down upon them mercilessly: there was scant shade. When they had crawled out of the northernmost canyon of the Wound, they had emerged near the border between the Burning Lands and the Range of the Border Tribes. Declan had no idea how long it would take to reach Abala or one of the villages just north of that port.

Still, they had found a well two days earlier, most likely dug by a band of nomads. Tobias and the others who'd served as guards on caravans crossing the grasslands said there were ponds and even a few small lakes to the north, but this far south one had to look for wells. Tobias also pointed out that they risked death by drinking out of any well without permission of the nomads who had dug it.

Declan was of the opinion they were dead even if they were spotted by any tribe out here. The attack on Abala indicated that whatever understanding might have existed between the nomads and those living along the coast had clearly come to an end.

Declan waited a few minutes more and heard no sound besides the breeze and some buzzing insects, so he crawled up the bank and hazarded a look over the top. No one was in sight, and he looked at the men behind him. With a nod, he stood up and the others followed.

"I think we need to pay more attention to dust," he said, realizing as he spoke that he was having a little trouble thinking clearly. He glanced skyward and judged it was still three hours or more before sundown. And they were marching westward, facing the blinding heat with every step.

He knew they needed to find shade and water soon, though a place to rest for a day would be even better.

Sebastian pointed westward and said, "Look."

Declan turned. "What? I see nothing."

"Birds," said the archer. "Not vultures."

"That means water," said Sixto.

"And maybe something to eat," added Tobias.

"Stay on the verge of the grass, and keep alert," said Declan, fighting off his lightheadedness.

Sixto noticed him struggling and thrust his water skin at Declan. "Here, you need it." When Declan started to speak, Sixto cut him off. "You need it! I'm not going to carry you, damn it."

Declan took it and lifted the skin. It was half-full and he took a long pull. The water still tasted of minerals, with a bitter tang, but he welcomed it, even if it was tepid.

He handed back the skin and took a moment, then turned and waved the men onward.

Soon Declan could also see specks circling above the distant horizon, and he marveled at how much better Sebastian's eyes were. As the sun began to lower, they saw what appeared to be trees dotting the landscape below.

"I hope that's an oasis," said Sixto.

"I wish I could see what the hell you're talking about," said Tobias, "but I hope you're right."

Less than an hour later they half-walked, half-staggered to the rim of what had been a gradual rise, and below saw a large pool, surrounded by trees and bushes.

Without Declan saying anything, the men broke from the line and hurried down a slope to the edge of the pool. Sixto took a quick look around, and said, "It's clear!"

Quickly all the men were lying on the bank, drinking and splashing water on their faces and necks, some draping their arms in up to the elbows.

"It's big enough to bathe in," said Toombs.

"Not until after I drink," complained Oscar. "You're filthy."

The water was fresh and cool, having been shaded from the sun for most of the day. Declan found himself reviving and sat up.

"Where does the water come from?" asked Mick Sawyer. His dark skin shone with reflected light, water dripping off, as he stuck his entire face into the pool to drink.

Declan took a deep breath as his head cleared and he sat back on his haunches. "There," he said, pointing. "It comes from there."

As the sun touched the topmost peak, the range of mountains above them was clearly revealed. They were not tall mountains, large hills mostly: he'd passed through taller ranges trailing from Beran's Hill to the Copper Hills, but that had been along well-cared-for roads. According to the South Tembria fighters, there was no safe passage over them. The Border Tribes used a short passage splitting off from a well-traveled route just to the north of the dry riverbed they'd followed.

Declan had debated with himself whether to risk the southernmost pass, the one most often used by the tribes when trading in Abala, or to push past to the foothills and mountains to the north. He had come to the conclusion that the men did not have the strength to force-march through open country to the hills to the north then find another passage through the mountains and loop back to Abala.

So far, they'd not encountered riders from the tribes, though once they had hidden after seeing a cloud of dust rising to the north. Declan assumed it was a company of horsemen moving parallel to them and decided it was time to come to a decision. His contemplation of the problem was interrupted by a voice.

"Dates!" shouted Acke, and he got to his feet and ran to a tree. "Give me a boost," he shouted, and Mikola and Jack Sawyer both hurried over to get him started shimmying up the tree.

Within a few minutes everyone was eating dates, and Declan leaned back against a bole as he savored the sweet fruit. He felt relief in the fact that so far he had managed to get every man out of the Wound. He also realized he had been in a far worse state than he'd admitted and only Sixto's insistence that he drink earlier in the day had kept him from succumbing to the heat. "I think we should rest here," he said.

Sixto came over. "No one may have visited here for a while, but that doesn't mean we are the only men on Garn to know about this place."

Declan nodded. "If you're up to it, take a walk around the perimeter and see how we are fixed?"

"I'll also see if we have a nearby place to hide if someone turns up unexpectedly. You rest."

Declan decided he wasn't about to argue. He'd never felt so beaten up and exhausted in his life. Even when he'd been recovering from his wounds after the sacking of Beran's Hill. He closed his eyes and within seconds was asleep.

HATUSHALY AND BODAI SAT IN the library, Hatu reading bits of books in strange languages, and Bodai writing down notes. "This is animal husbandry," said Hatu.

"That will be . . ." He checked a list, and said, "Number four hundred and sixteen."

Hatu stood up and carried the book to a large pile on the other side of a massive, now half-empty, bookcase. A pot of ink and a quill rested next to the pile. Hatu ripped off a small piece of paper, wrote the number, waving the paper about until the ink dried, then put the paper inside the cover of the book.

"That's about thirty books on farming and herding," he said to Bodai as he walked back. He stopped suddenly, cocking his head as if listening for something.

"What?" asked Bodai.

"Hava . . . should be here tomorrow." He smiled broadly.

Bodai was about to say something, when Nathan appeared from behind the same bookcase Hatu had just left.

Bodai said, "You just vanished!"

"I had to talk to someone" was all Nathan said as he pushed back a chair and sat opposite Bodai.

Suddenly, Hatu looked around, then at Nathan, and asked, "How did you get there?" He pointed to the bookshelf.

"And how did you leave?" asked Bodai. "You were gone, but no ship left port . . . for days!"

Nathan waved the question away. "I know a few tricks."

"Where have you been?" Hatu asked.

"Trying to get some answers," Nathan replied.

As Bodai was about to speak, Nathan cut him off. "You," he said, pointing his finger at Hatushaly, "are a problem."

Hatu sat down.

"You have abilities I have no idea how to help you control. Have you tried any more of your powers since I left?"

"No," said Hatu. "After your reaction to me helping Declan and sensing Hava while I was asleep . . ." He put his hands out as if in surrender. "I was afraid to try anything."

"You're smarter than you look," said Nathan.

"So, what did you learn?" asked Bodai.

"A few things," replied Nathan, "but I'll leave that for later." He paused for a moment, then said, "First you must understand the difference between knowledge and speculation."

"To what end?" asked Bodai.

"So Hatu doesn't end up as an agent of destruction."

Bodai and Hatu exchanged glances, and Bodai said, "I think we all agree on that."

"I cannot teach Hatu what I don't know," began Nathan. "It's hard to guide him in discovering things I know nothing about."

They were all silent for a few moments, then Nathan stood up and turned to face them. "I can listen to what you hear, see what you see, discuss what you experience, but at this point I have nothing I can teach you.

"Consider me as a pool of information, but it may not be the information you need. I can provide a context of sorts for what you're experiencing, but as long as you remain here, you will have to advance your knowledge by risking yourself and others."

"Remain here?" said Hatu. "Where else would I go?"

"That," said Nathan, "is a very good question. It's one I will answer, but not now. You are here for a reason, one that I probably do not fully understand, but for the time being, you will remain here. Once we discover why all this"—he spread his arms expansively, indicating all that had happened to Hatu so far—"has happened, then we can more fully understand what is needed. So, will you let me help you?"

Hatu was now slightly annoyed. "I never wanted you to leave in the first place!"

Nathan looked at Bodai.

Bodai said, "What I think is a moot point."

Nathan nodded. "Context. At this stage the best I can do to help you is to have you understand the context of your place in the larger scheme of things."

Hatu and Bodai both settled back in their chairs.

"Let's start with this," Nathan said. "You understand, to a point, that what exists between positive and negative furies is energy."

Hatu nodded.

"And that energy comes in different forms: heat, light, movement . . ." He paused as if to catch his breath. "And everything felt from the drop of rain on your arm to a massive earthquake is an expression of energy, right?"

Hatu again nodded.

"Forget for a moment the expression of energy as light, noise, vibrations, or anything else, and imagine energy as a thing unto itself. Energy is like water. It wants to run downhill."

Hatu said, "Water?"

"Positive energy is like being on top of a hill. Negative is like being at the bottom. Go see what I mean."

Hatu closed his eyes and instantly was floating in his mind-void. He saw endless strings of energy and picked one at random. Focusing his vision, he studied the pulsing. The rhythm was uniform, like a heartbeat, and when he pushed that perception aside, he saw that the pulse was heading in one direction, from the positive fury to the negative.

He opened his eyes and said, "I see what you mean, but then how does it not . . . fade when all of it is has passed into negative fury?"

"That's a mystery, but it doesn't. Somehow, the furies always stay in balance despite momentary imbalances. Certain facts are indisputable, and this is one. Energy is everlasting. It changes, but it never ends."

Bodai asked, "It's eternal?"

"As far as we can tell," answered Nathan. "Set fire to a piece of wood. Is the wood destroyed?"

"Of course," answered Hatu.

"No, it's not," Nathan replied. "It transforms into heat, light, and ash. Changes occur and we may not fully understand them, but in the end the wood is not destroyed, but transformed. Energy is constant, and eternal. Once you accept that, your understanding will begin.

"Hot descends to cold, fast to still, disorganized to ordered, it's all part of a system that . . . works." Nathan tried to find the right words. "So much of what we know is . . . incomplete." Then he shook his head and said, "No. Most of what we know is incomplete." He spread his hands in a gesture implying vastness. "Why do we get hot when the sun's light falls on us? We know it has to do with the nature of energy, but why?

"When we drop something it falls, but why? We say 'gravity,' but what is gravity? How does it work? We know the moon tugs at the tide, but why? Gravity from that far away or something else?" He pointed at Hatu. "We know you're becoming a master of . . . furies! But we don't know why. And especially we don't know how."

Hatu and Bodai exchanged glances, but both remained silent.

At last Nathan said, "And I have to piece together what I can in order to prevent you from setting fire to another ship, or starting another landslide by accident."

The three sat in silence for a long while.

DONTE WATCHED AS THE BARON's engineers laid out long lines of heavy twine from sticks a few feet away to another tall stick a hundred yards away. He had ridden up on the wagon filled with the engineers' equipment and was finding how they were planning the outline for the new garrison fascinating.

Beran's Hill was a burned-out shell of a town. Scouts reported that a few surrounding farms were again being worked and the nearby groves were tended, but the town itself had been abandoned. Streets were identifiable only by the burned sections of blackened walls and foundations here and there. Not one building stood completely intact, though a large warehouse where the final defense of the town had been fought was still standing, lacking one wall, with a roof that was half burned away.

The captain in charge, Baldasar, was planning on using the building as his temporary headquarters, so while the engineers laid out the lines for the garrison's foundations, he had workers shoring up supports and repairing the roof of the abandoned warehouse.

Donte had been given explicit instructions by the baron before he departed. His official role had been left vague, except that he was not part of the work gang, but a runner taking orders only from the captain.

That designation seemed to be especially annoying to one soldier, Jackson Deakin, with whom Donte had unfinished business.
A bully who had once tried to kill Donte, Deakin was a good
enough fighter that he'd been kept in Daylon's service, though
he had probably been tossed in the dungeon more times than
any man in the army.

He was currently with a detail checking anyone coming into
this part of the barony from the east. A few refugees were arriving but a large portion of those roaming that part of the
border with the Wildlands were bandits and scavengers. When
Donte was confident that no Azhante agents had already arrived
in Beran's Hill, he would be moved to that detail and inspect
wagons alongside the soldiers. At least Donte's status with the
baron would stop Deakin, if he was still there, from attacking
Donte. That, as well as a tough sergeant named Collin, formerly
the master-at-arms for the Baron of the Copper Hills. He was
a bear of a man, and from the Kes'tun, a mountain people who
brooked insult from no one. He'd come south after Copper Hills
fell and Baron Rodrigo's situation remained unknown and had
eagerly taken service with Baron Dumarch.

Donte hoped Deakin hadn't run afoul of Collin, angered the
former master-at-arms, and got himself killed already. Donte
wanted to experience that pleasure himself.

After a while he grew bored of watching twine being laid
out and chalk spilled to indicate where the foundation trenches
would be dug. He'd had enough mason work on the walls down
in Marquenet to last a lifetime and besides, he was supposed to
be looking for suspicious characters.

Donte thought about taking another wander through the
town, though he knew it was unlikely he'd find anything worth
reporting—the checkpoints inspected those slowly returning to

the town. But he knew Captain Baldasar had no particular use for him unless he found something. There was no surviving inn, so there wasn't even a place he could have a drink or pick a fight.

At last he decided that he'd done all he could, and went to find the captain. He wandered back toward the makeshift headquarters and realized that other than a few locals who had recently returned to find everything they owned gone, all the others were Baron Dumarch's men.

As he approached, he saw a pair of wagons moving toward the headquarters. The lead wagon was driven by a slender, dark-haired fellow, the sort who was all sinew and muscle. The second wagon was driven by a slim, sun-browned woman with grey-shot brown hair. As Donte came close the driver shouted, "Where's the captain?"

Donte pointed. "In there. Follow me."

The driver jumped off the wagon. As the man landed, Donte said, "Don't I know you?"

The driver said, "I don't think so. Name's Ratigan. Might have seen each other around. I've been driving back and forth for the baron since the raids."

"Well . . ." Donte halted, then said, "My memory was fuzzy after a head blow, so maybe I saw you when I was loading or something." His memory had been lost for a while, due to the magic of the Sisters of the Deep, not that he would share that story with anyone. "Anyway, the captain's inside."

They both entered and found the captain in an intact portion of the room in the otherwise empty warehouse. Baldasar was leaning over a table, looking at an old map of the area, surrounded by notes and short messages. He had a quill in his hand and was making changes in red ink. Donte and Ratigan stood silently until they were noticed.

"What?" said the captain.

Donte pointed to Ratigan. "Supplies."

"The baron sent tools for the new garrison," said Ratigan.

Baldasar said, "Donte, show him." Then he paused and said, "Is there anything else?"

"Been from one end of the town to the other a couple of times, Captain. Nothing here. I should probably head out to the border checkpoint."

"Then go," said the captain, apparently impatient to return to correcting the map.

"A horse, sir? It's a long walk."

"Remounts are out the back," Baldasar said.

"Sir," said Donte, gently taking Ratigan's arm and turning him. Ratigan yanked his arm out of Donte's grasp, but didn't say anything.

Once outside, Donte said, "Captain Baldasar has a lot on his mind."

Ratigan shot Donte a look that revealed he didn't like being manhandled, even slightly, but said nothing as he climbed back onto his wagon seat. "Where's the garrison site?"

"Down to that corner, right turn, then down two streets, then left and straight on. You'll see fellows with flags and that three-legged contraption they gaze over while they're pulling twine."

Ratigan turned and yelled to the second driver, "Follow me, Roz!" With a flick of the reins, he moved the wagon ahead, the second wagon moving a moment later.

Donte watched them pull away, then circled around the building to where a makeshift corral had been put up, and in which a small herd of horses waited. A series of braces topped by a long pole was near the gate and on it were saddles and blankets, and from dowels hammered into a tall plank behind hung bridles.

Two bored-looking guards were protecting the horses and gear and gave Donte a questioning look. The whole garrison had been instructed that Donte was the captain's runner, so they said nothing as he grabbed a bridle and opened the gate.

He selected a fit-looking brown gelding and approached slowly. The horse didn't shy and accepted the bridle without complaint. Once the headgear was fitted, Donte led the horse out of the corral.

He quickly saddled it up, mounted, and glanced around. From the angle of the sun, he reckoned he should arrive at the checkpoint a bit before sundown. He realized that he would miss the midday meal, but the food at the checkpoint was likely to be almost as good as that at the mess tent, so he decided that was a small loss.

As he rode through the town, he passed the two wagons beside the garrison and gave a small wave to Ratigan and the tall woman.

Donte had worked around enough horses to know how to rate his ride. He took the journey by turns at walk, trot, and canter, so that the animal would not need days of rest, and as he had anticipated, he arrived a little before sundown.

The guards were gathered around a newly fashioned barrier that would be swung aside to allow passage but would signal well in advance to anyone coming down the road to halt.

The twenty armed men next to it would be even more persuasive.

As he rode up, Donte saw the other horses tied in a picket line that lay on the ground. A chest-high line would allow faster untying of the animals, but Donte understood the relatively lax approach. Unless a company of cavalry rode down on them suddenly, the men were in a good position to defend this location.

The checkpoint was at the top of a long, gentle rise, so anyone coming toward them would be moving uphill, and there was makeshift breastwork behind which archers could loose arrows on anyone approaching. Donte rode toward a cook-fire and saw that most of the men were gathered around it, with two stationed a short distance down the road, as early warning.

The big sergeant, Collin, stood up and walked toward Donte as he reined in his mount. "Orders?" he asked.

"Nothing new," Donte replied. "Captain's done with me at Beran's Hill, so I'm here to sniff out any more of those eastern spies."

The exact nature of the Azhante prisoners had been kept secret from anyone not immediately involved with their interrogation or care. To the rest of the garrison, they were "spies from the east," and as Donte had predicted, the gossip had been rampant at the baron's castle. Most people assumed they were agents of Sandura.

"Well," said Collin, "see to your horse and come to the fire. Got some hot soup with bits of meat and some hard bread."

Donte dismounted and turned his horse, noticing that on the other side of the fire sat Jackson Deakin, who watched him with a narrow gaze. Donte indulged himself in a small smile and realized they both knew an accounting was due.

HATU WAS WAITING ON THE dock as the *Queen of Storms* pulled up close and was hauled by a dozen men on two hawsers, while a pair of boys dropped large fenders filled with sand between the dockside and the ship's hull.

Hava waved from the quarterdeck, and he returned the wave. He knew she would not depart until the ship was unloaded and made secure, so he moved out of the way and waited as a gang-way was run out.

First off were fifty people: Hatu's guess was craftsmen and

farmers, which would be welcome. One of Hava's sailors directed them to the main mess where they could grab a bit of food and listen to what was now a more or less standard welcome from Catharian and Bodai. Sabella and the other acolytes would help them. The leader of the Flame Guard was a man named Elmish, whom everyone addressed as "Prior," but he had retired to a small house atop a hill, looking down upon the Sanctuary. Apparently, with Hatu being found, their entire purpose was now being reevaluated. Hatu assumed that Catharian was now running the Sanctuary, as Bodai spent almost every waking minute with Nathan and himself, but no formal announcement had ever been made. To Hatu it appeared as if no one was really in charge.

After cargo started to be unloaded a man appeared at the top of the gangway and walked down and before Hatu fully recognized who it was, Balven, the baron's brother, was standing right in front of him.

"Hello, Sefan."

Hatu blinked for a moment, then laughed. "You're probably the only person alive who has called me that, Balven." With a wave of his hand, he said, "Welcome to the Sanctuary."

"Will you show me around?"

"I'm waiting for my wife," said Hatu.

"Ah, yes," replied Balven.

Hatu said, "She's going to be a while, so I can take you to someone who can show you around. Come with me."

If Balven was bothered by the lack of formal address, he didn't show it. Hatu led him to the common mess and saw that Catharian and Bodai had just finished their welcome talk, and many of the people were eating.

Escorting Balven to where the two men waited, he said, "Bodai,

Catharian, you may remember Balven, first adviser to Baron Dumarch."

Bodai said, "Hello. This is quite the surprise." To Catharian he said, "I met this worthy gentleman once, when returning Hatu's care to his brother, the baron."

"I recognize him," said Catharian with a smile and a slight bow.

"I don't believe I remember you, sir," said Balven.

"As I was playing the role of a mendicant monk at the time, you would have no reason to, m'lord. But I saw you several times when I was snooping around Marquenet looking for him." He indicated Hatushaly.

"You're the reason I'm here," Balven said to Bodai.

"Me? Why?"

"We captured two Azhante spies."

That statement seemed to hit Bodai like a blow. His face went pale and he said, "You took them alive?"

"Yes, and they told us many fascinating things."

"They're almost a legend in Coaltachin," said the old teacher. "They're greatly feared and to be avoided at any cost."

"Then we have much to discuss, and if you're willing, my brother would like you to return with me to Marquenet."

Hatu said, "I remember how you reacted when I saw them in Sandura." He looked at Balven. "I also would like to know—"

Balven cut him off. "Talk to Hava. She was the first to begin to unravel this knot of a mystery."

Hatu said, "Very well. She'll be off the ship soon, so I'm going back."

Bodai waved Balven to move away from the people eating and said, "We must talk."

"Absolutely."

Bodai looked at Catharian and said, "Why don't you keep an

eye on things here while I take Balven to the library." He glanced around and saw one of the kitchen boys and waved him over. Turning to Balven, he said, "Are you hungry, sir?"

"I can wait."

"Good." He said to the boy, "Fetch me a bottle of wine and two mugs."

Balven chuckled, then, noting Bodai's almost distraught state, said, "Better make that two bottles."

14

DECISIONS AND RISKS

D eclan rested the men for two days. They picked the date trees clean and found some sweet berries on the other side of the pool. Sebastian suggested he go and hunt, but Declan said no; he did not want to split the party for any reason.

The sun was rising in the east, and Declan was organizing the men, when Mikola came and said, "All the water skins are full again." When Declan just nodded, Mikola added, "Will we find more?"

"I don't know," Declan replied honestly. "But the farther northwest we march, the better the chances."

"Where did this water come from?" asked the young man.

"I told Mick Sawyer from those mountains we're heading toward."

"How?"

"Underground river."

"A river underground?"

"The water that gushed from the side of the cliff north of the camp in the Wound, that's also part of that underground river. Not all the rain that falls on those hills and mountains runs off. Some soaks in and runs that way." He waved in the general direction of the Wound. "It's why there are trees, bushes, and animals there. There's a place up near the Copper Hills where water springs out of the side of the hills. They told me it's an underground river. Now, let's get out of here before it gets too damned hot again."

Declan motioned for the men to gather, and said, "I've been content to lead, but this is one time I must ask you to take a vote."

"On what?" asked Sixto.

He pointed to the mercenaries from South Tembria, who'd been sheltering in the Wound when Declan's company arrived. "They said the mountains to the northeast of Abala are impassable, and they should know. We know the nomads came down to Abala through a pass between the mountains and the Burning Lands. So, the question is do we go north, and try to find a shorter way to Abala, or chance the passage the nomads use?"

Tobias said, "You decide, Captain."

Sixto followed. "What do you think is best, Declan?"

Declan was rested, but still felt nothing like his former self. Like every man there he was underweight, weakened by privation and the harsh trek out of the Wound. He took a deep breath, then said, "I promised Bogartis I'd get as many of you out of here alive as I could." He found moisture gathering in his eyes and felt a tickle of rage beginning to grow. "I will add those we found in the Wound to that promise, and I will do what I can to honor that pledge.

"But we do not have a chance in a stand-up fight against an equal number of rested warriors." He paused for a moment to allow for any dispute. When none came, he said, "If the raids are over, the nomads will have returned to their range on the grasslands. It's a two-, maybe three-day journey on foot through that passage. We will be exposed, in the open with nowhere to hide, should a band of those horsemen see us.

"Our other choice is to continue on past that passage, and hope we find another way over the mountains." Declan found himself on the verge of tears of frustration and anger and fought them down as he finished. "I want to get to Abala. I want to find us all safe passage away from this gods-forsaken land."

To Declan's surprise, it was Oscar who said, "We'll follow you anywhere, Captain."

Declan nodded. "We'll take the pass the nomads use, and if we have to fight our way through, we'll fight."

There was no cheer of approval, just a silent acceptance that this company was near the end of its rope. The oasis with its water and dates and berries had saved their lives, but the men were in no condition to fight a battle.

"Let's go," said Declan and he led them out of the deep depression that housed the oasis.

HATU LAY ON HIS BACK, staring at the ceiling after listening to Hava recount her encounter with the Azhante. They had shared a bath, made love, eaten, and made love a second time, and now the sun was starting to light up the eastern sky as she finished. "So, that's why Balven wants Bodai to go back to Marquenet. I reckoned no one is likely to know more about the history of things than Bodai."

"Probably," said Hatu, sitting up and swiveling round to put his feet on the floor.

"Where are you going?" asked Hava.

"I'm hungry."

"You ate!" she said, reaching over to pull him back into bed.

Laughing, he dodged her reach, and snagged his trousers off the floor. "That was hours ago," he said, pulling them up and tying the waist cord. "And you've worked up my appetite!" Pulling his tunic off the back of a chair, he slipped it over his head and asked, "Aren't you hungry?"

She thought for a second, then with a sigh said, "Yes, I am." Slipping out of bed, she donned her own shirt and trousers and then her boots, while he laced on sandals. She put on the black leather over-vest she wore aboard ship and tied a dark green bandana around her head.

Hatu smiled at Hava, who returned an expression he didn't quite understand, but he sensed that this might have been one of those moments he and Bodai had discussed where he had made a poor choice.

"Did I just do something wrong?" he asked.

"No. Everything is just fine," she said as she walked past him, opened the door to their quarters, and turned toward the community kitchen.

He hesitated for a moment, then followed, knowing with certainty everything was not fine. He opened his mouth to say something and realized that this was not the best time.

Reaching the kitchen, they found a few people already eating before going off to work, and quickly loaded up with plates of food and mugs of water. Hatu thought he might replace the water with coffee when Bodai arrived.

He was painfully aware of the awkward silence that now was like a wall between himself and his wife, and again weighed the value of trying to talk about it, but was saved from that decision by Nathan's arrival. He nodded at Hatu and then said, "You're Hava," and bowed slightly. "Hatu talks about you all the time."

She brightened at that and glanced at Hatu.

Hatu silently thanked Nathan as the mood instantly changed.

"And who are you?" she asked.

"I'm a traveler by the name of Nathan, and I've come to assist Bodai in Hatu's education."

"A preceptor, then."

"Of sorts," he replied. "Now, excuse me." He started moving to the long table and its food.

"You didn't mention him," said Hava to Hatu.

Hatu smiled. "Last night he was the last thing on my mind." She gave him a slightly narrow eye for a moment, then smiled.

Most of the conversation since Hava had returned had been about her voyage and the discovery of the Azhante spies, the astounding return of Donte and how he came to be in Marquenet, and Balven's conjectures. Hatu was both eager to know what she'd done, and also uncertain how to inform her about the extraordinary things he had discovered during the course of his training.

She'd witnessed the first manifestation of his power, when they'd traveled through the Narrows and he'd lit up with pulsing blue energy. Still, he hardly knew how to prepare her for all that he had discovered about himself in his recent training with Bodai and Nathan; his ability to sense her whereabouts, his discovery of Donte before she told him that their friend still lived, and his causing a rockslide to aid Declan half a world away, were things that were unimaginable when she left for Marquensas. He knew he would soon have to find a way to explain these changes to her, but he was desperate for a sense of the proper time and place.

He was saved from further worry by Bodai's appearance, as the teacher came from the direction of the library with a big coffee pot in his hand. He handed it to a kitchen boy, and Hatu realized that if he'd already gone through a pot, he'd been up for hours.

Hatu pointed at him, and Hava turned. "Finish up," he said, wolfing down what was left on his plate.

She seemed slightly annoyed by being told what to do, but her own curiosity was in play, so she also finished quickly and they took their dishes back to the table to be cleaned just as Bodai was getting his second pot.

Bodai smiled and said, "Good, you're here. You've eaten?" They both said yes, and Bodai waved them to follow him. "Good. Balven and I have pieced together some interesting ideas, and I was anxious to talk with you"—he pointed at Hava—"next, after you and your boy here had your reunion."

They entered the library a few moments later, to find Balven sitting at the table Hatu had been using for his lessons, a large piece of paper with a crudely drawn map spread before him. A quill and ink pot sat to one side of the map. Below the table, Hatu saw three empty wine bottles, and both Bodai and Balven looked fatigued, with dark circles under their eyes, drawn cheeks, and stubble showing both needed shaves, so he reckoned they must have been here all night.

Bodai filled mugs of coffee for Balven and himself, and waved Hatu and Hava to take the two empty chairs. Despite their haggard appearances, both men seemed pleased, even a bit excited. "We've come up with some interesting conjectures and a few conclusions," said Bodai.

Hatu and Hava exchanged a quick glance.

"Where to begin?" said Bodai.

"The beginning?" suggested Hatu, with a hint of humor.

"That's a guess," said Balven. "Partially because the two prisoners back in Marquenet are not what one might label well-educated." He glanced at Bodai.

"Then again," said the old teacher, "few are."

Balven nodded agreement. He turned to look over his shoulder back into the shadowy library and said, "I thought my brother's collection of books was impressive." He smiled ruefully. Pointing at a section of the massive shelves behind him he added, "All his books and manuscripts could easily be tucked into that corner."

"This was once a place of great learning," said Bodai, with a note of regret.

"As was the entire Kingdom of Ithrace," replied Balven, then he looked at Hatushaly. "Created by your ancestors."

Hatu had no inkling of what to say so he remained silent.

Bodai said, "What we know is that the Azhante prisoners appear not to be of very dangerous and high rank."

"Comparable to our Quelli Nascosti," said Hava.

Hatu turned to Balven. "That means 'Those Hidden,' or 'The Invisible,' Coaltachin's best spies and assassins."

Balven nodded.

Bodai continued, "Those are the ones you spotted at the cathedral the Church was building in Sandura. You can tell them by the emblem they wear."

"The black lacquer pendant!" said Hatu.

"Apparently they have the means to communicate by hand signs, so the pendant makes it clear to the lesser ranks who is in command."

"The two men we have in Marquenet did not have those pendants," said Balven.

"So," began Bodai, "ages ago, there was a family, or perhaps a clan, of some importance called the Coaltachin. They served the Pride Lords of Akena, the capital, or meeting place, of the Pride Lords. We now know the Azhante are . . . slaves? Or at least closely watched servants, whose families are held hostage against their good behavior and obedience.

"The Coaltachin family contrived a mass escape. Every Coaltachin leader in the Azhante, seven of them, and every relative fled Nytanny. We have no idea how, but we can assume they sailed to the east, perhaps even through the passage of Enast, as we know where they ended up."

"Coaltachin," said Hatu.

Bodai nodded. "My conjecture is they avoided the ports of Enast, Poberto, Fondrak, or any place with soldiers or warriors in number. The island we call Coaltachin probably had only a small population of farmers and fishermen—"

"And the seven leaders of the clan of Coaltachin moved in and took over," said Hava, her expression one of wonder and delight, but her tone thick with irony.

"So, the seven masters of the Council," added Hatu.

"Just so," said Bodai. "I know little of the history of Coaltachin, as most of it is lore handed down from father to son among the masters, and certainly it is not a subject dwelled upon in the schools."

Both Hava and Hatu nodded agreement to that.

"By how Coaltachin is today, Balven and I assume a clan of former spies and assassins organized themselves into a criminal enterprise to support themselves," said Bodai.

Hatushaly laughed. "So they started by taking over the home island, and then spread out from there."

Hava said, "And then they would take children with potential from families and send them to a school . . ." She shook her head slowly. "That's what the Azhante did."

Bodai nodded. "Obviously, without the Pride Lords controlling them, Coaltachin developed its own customs and organization.

"There are no ties between the Azhante and anyone else in the nations of Nytanny, while Coaltachin runs gangs and crews throughout the islands and the cities in the Twin Continents—or at least did until the sacking by the Pride Lords."

"Gangs and crews are pretty tough," said Hava. "I'm sure some are still around throughout the region."

"All very interesting," said Hatu, "but what do we do next?"

"We need more knowledge of the Pride Lords, and that means getting someone safely into Nytanny, preferably close to or in the city of Akena."

Hava and Hatu exchanged a glance, and Hatu said, "We'll go."

Bodai said to Hatu, "You can't. You have to stay here and master your powers."

Balven pointed at Hava and said, "And you can't. You've got to get Bodai and me back to Marquensas, with that treasure ship."

"You promised *Borzon's Black Wake* to the baron?" asked Bodai.

"Not all of it," said Hava. "But he has greater need and can put it to better use there than we can here."

Bodai started to say something, thought better of it, and fell silent.

Hava said to Balven, "We have crews for *Borzon's* and another ship to escort you, the *Sundown Raider*. Their captains are able enough to get to Marquensas without any difficulty. The Azhante ships are patrolling around the Border Ports, but we can provision well enough that we do not have to stop to resupply at Elsobas before making the long crossing."

To Bodai she said, "Unless you have any trained spies around here I don't know about, Hatu and I are the only two people who have any chance to get into Akena and get out again. I've spoken enough with the two Azhante that I can get by in their language. Because there are so many nations on that continent it's their trading tongue and there are many dialects of it."

Hatu said, "She can teach me about the differences."

"No," came a voice from behind them, as Nathan stepped out from behind a bookcase.

"How—?" Balven began, but Bodai simply put his hand on the other man's arm and shook his head slightly.

Nathan said, "Hava's right. You have no one else here trained the way these two have been . . ."

Hava nodded, then stopped when Nathan continued, "But Hatu cannot go. His time is limited and he must not be put at risk. He has a different role in this."

Balven finally asked, "Who are you?"

"I came to help that one"—he pointed at Hatu—"learn to master the powers his bloodline gave him, so that he can help save this world, not put it in greater danger."

Balven seemed taken aback, but he saw Bodai nodding and said nothing.

"I'm not letting Hava go alone!" Hatu said sharply, anger rising.

Nathan said, "You've only become aware of your potential; you have just barely glimpsed what is yet to come. There are even bigger threats awaiting than the Azhante and Pride Lords. There are things you must master before you can face them, and time grows short."

Hatu's voice rose, close to shouting. "I'm tired of all this avoidance and misdirection! It's the foundation of everything Hava and I learned in school, and practiced on the street, and I will have no more of it!"

Without moving, Nathan instantly seemed to stand taller, to become larger in everyone's eyes, and his expression changed to one of unalloyed resolve. He leaned forward the tiniest bit, yet Hatu found himself moving backward in his chair. Then Nathan spoke, and his voice was different, echoing with a tone of command they'd never heard before. "You will stay here!"

At that moment, Hatushaly knew he could not argue, as his anger drained away.

Then, abruptly, Nathan's bearing and manner reverted to what it had been before, easy and affable. To Hava he said, "Take Catharian. He's the sneakiest bastard working for the Flame Guard." He turned and walked away.

Silence gripped the four at the table, and then finally Balven asked, "Who is that man?"

Bodai paused for a moment, then said, "Someone we must listen to." He glanced at Hava. "Catharian?"

"Nathan's right," she replied. "He's the sneakiest bastard I've met who wasn't trained in Coaltachin."

Balven shook his head slowly. "I'm uncertain how you all arrive at these decisions, but I can only take back what I learn here, so, may I suggest that my return to Marquensas waits until you return from your explorations, Hava?"

Hava glanced at Hatu who just gave a little head shake and shrugged. "It's your decision," he said.

"No," she said at last.

Balven's face clouded over. He obviously was not used to people telling him no. "No?"

"You need to get information to your brother as soon as possible, and from what I saw, you need *Borzon's Black Wake* and its treasure"—she turned to Bodai—"less what we keep here." She resumed addressing Balven. "First, if I fail, you'll be delayed for no good purpose. Second, if I return with good information, I can take the *Queen* and travel as fast as possible to reach you."

Balven realized there was no point in arguing. "Very well," he said with a slightly amused smile. "I bow to your wisdom. There is another matter at home that needs my attention," he added, thinking that he should be there in the event Declan returned, to prevent him from haring off on another dangerous errand for Daylon. He sighed in resignation. "What are your plans?"

"It will take a week or more to get *Borzon's Black Wake* outfitted for the long voyage," Hava said. "She's a pig and the *Sundown Raider* will have to trim her sails not to run away from her.

"While that's being done, I'm going to visit Elsobas, and one or two other ports, and see if I can find anyone who truly knows what we should expect once we reach Nytanny. I know the city of Akena is somewhere on the northeast coast of Nytanny, so that cuts down the time of having to go looking for it."

"Let's get more specific, then," said Bodai.

She nodded agreement. "Let's begin by seeing what we can find anchored out in the harbor that won't look like something I stole from the Azhante.

"Then we'll schedule refitting . . ."

Hatu sat back and watched as his wife took over the meeting and realized that from her almost childlike desire to be a pirate to this day when she was counted as a vital part of governing the Sanctuary, she had grown magnificently. He had never loved her more than at that moment. He instantly felt a pang of doubt, despite his own rise in power: was he the man she needed?

DECLAN HUNKERED DOWN BEHIND SOME scrub brush which was just tall enough that he could crouch out of sight. The rest of the men were lying facedown in the dirt, for the third time since entering the passage to Abala.

It was clear that the raid had ended, but some bands of nomads had taken up residence in the city for a while. Those that passed by on their way back to the grasslands were leading horses and a few mules laden with whatever the raiders had pillaged.

Only twice before had they had to hide, so Declan's best guess was that these were the last nomads living in Abala. From his glimpses of them and their modest packs of loot, they were probably from smaller bands who had been forced to glean whatever remained after the larger tribes and bands had taken the best the city offered.

When the sound of the riders had faded, Declan chanced a glimpse over the top of the scrub and saw their backs moving away. He waited a few more moments, then signaled the men to rise slowly and resume their march.

Declan knew that every man shared his hope of a safe haven just a short trek away, resting on the sharp edge of terror at the chance of another conflict, a call they were unprepared to answer.

And all of which was buried under bone-numbing fatigue. Declan had never felt this tired in his life without a nearby bed to fall into. Even long hours in the forge on rushed work, for two or three days running, had never drained him of the ability to move and think coherently.

Yet he knew that after one more night they would be within sight of Abala. Forcing himself to put one foot in front of the other, he motioned for the men to follow as silently as possible. He prayed to whichever gods might listen that the setting sun would herald a trouble-free night, and a morrow without further deaths. He had promised Bogartis.

Donte watched as the wagon came to a halt. This was the fourth one so far today, and all had carried families seeking a safe haven as the world they knew crumbled around them. From the answers they gave to the guard's questions, a rough picture had formed that banditry and lawlessness had spread throughout North Tembria.

The Wildlands had for more than a generation roughly divided west and east. The west half had been somewhat tamed as it bordered on Marquensas and the Copper Hills. It had been underpopulated but was often used as a hideout for bands of bandits, and had a few small settlements, with nothing worth bothering about. Now all the areas from where Donte stood with the baron's soldiers eastward to the border of Sandura had descended into complete disarray. Passage Town, on the border between Ithrace and Sandura, had been raided and sacked three times and was effectively a ghost town. Sandura was now calm, but there had been a short, bloody conquest of Sandura's capital city by the Church of the One. Now it was garrisoned and patrolled by members of the Church Adamant, their military arm.

Donte considered himself fortunate that he had washed up on the shores of Marquensas when he . . . Was it fortune? He had asked himself that question before, and still had no answer. He knew the Sisters of the Deep wanted him to kill Hatu for some reason, and that desire to find him and kill him came and went, almost as if it was pulled along by the tide. He still had no clear memory of his time as a prisoner underwater, though flashes of images came and went.

Well, whatever the cause, Donte reasoned, there were many worse places he could have washed ashore.

Sergeant Collin nodded at him and Donte walked over to stand behind him, wishing the travelers a safe journey in the language of Coaltachin. It was a family, and the man driving the wagon looked at Donte with a confused expression. The woman next to him was leaning over, scolding two small children about something.

Donte shook his head and stepped aside as Collin waved them through.

"I didn't think so," said Donte. "Them being spies and all that. Just not likely."

"Most of the day is gone," said Collin, looking around as if expecting to see something that would break the monotony.

"I miss inns and taverns the most," said Donte.

"Well, except for young Bobby over there, who misses his young wife, I think every man here agrees with that sentiment."

As the sun lowered in the west, the two men continued chatting. Donte decided that come a brawl he wanted Collin on his side, not the other.

Suddenly a man over by the cooking fire shouted, "Look!"

The advance picket had shot a burning arrow into the sky, the alert that trouble was on its way.

Moments later the archer who had shot that flaming quarrel came galloping up the road with a company of horsemen mere yards behind. An arrow sped by his head, missing by inches, and he threw himself forward across the neck of his horse.

"Archers!" shouted Collin, and the men scrambled to their positions behind the breastwork. They had grown lax in their boredom, and it was long seconds before they were ready to let loose their own arrows.

Seeing a fortified defense, the raiders began to turn, and Collin shouted, "To horse!"

Donte stood closest to the picket line and grabbed the reins of the first mount in line. Half a dozen horses were left saddled against such need, while the others were left to rest without tack.

From what Donte saw, half a dozen armed soldiers should be able to chase that bunch all the way back to the Dangerous Passage. He would prefer it if the raiders turned and stood their ground, as he was bored, in a bad frame of mind spending days in the company of Deakin, and he just wanted a fight.

The reins were tied with a slip knot. With one tug, and a

half-jump into the saddle, Donte was away after the marauders. He didn't look back but could hear soldiers close behind him.

As he crested the ridge he suddenly realized he was in the vanguard, and that perhaps some of those raiders numbered skilled horse-archers who knew how to shoot behind them. Then it dawned on him they were riding toward darkness and he was outlined by the brighter sky.

As an arrow missed his right shoulder by scant inches, he realized he should have thought this through better. He pulled up slightly and dropped to the neck of his horse, waiting for the others to catch up.

They passed him, and Donte set his heels to his mount to stay even with them. A second, then a third arrow flew out of the gloom below and a soldier fell out of his saddle. The other four soldiers pressed on, but Donte realized within seconds, they'd only get more arrows as their reward or lose the marauders in the trees below. "Turn back!" he shouted, not knowing if he would be heard or heeded.

He turned his horse and found the wounded soldier on the ground, his horse wandering a short distance away. He went over to the man, and saw it was Jackson Deakin. "Well, isn't this a thing?" he muttered.

Jumping from his horse, he knelt next to Deakin. The soldier was in a great deal of pain. An arrow had taken him next to the breastbone, between the top two ribs. His breathing was labored. He looked at Donte and said, "Looks like you got what you wanted."

"You shouldn't wander around looking for strangers to kill, you stupid slug."

"Well, enjoy the moment," said Deakin between painful breaths.

"Oh, damn me," said Donte. "This is not fun." He reached over and grabbed the arrow, snapping it off, leaving the barbed head in the wound. Deakin cried out in pain. "All right, that *was* fun," Donte added.

Then he reached over and grabbed Deakin's right arm, yanking it forward. Deakin again cried out in pain, as Donte hauled him over his shoulder and stood up. As he moved toward Deakin's horse, the other soldiers returned and he shouted, "Keep that horse still and help me sling this bastard across the saddle."

One of the soldiers obliged and held Deakin's mount still while Donte hefted the man across the saddle.

Deakin was almost unconscious from the pain, but he managed to ask, "Why?"

Donte stood silent for a moment, then said, "I don't know. Maybe I'm a better man? Or maybe you'll bleed to death or fall off the saddle and break your neck." He took a deep breath and let it out slowly, as if feeling relief, and said, "But whatever happens, I'm done with you."

15

RETURN, DIVULGENCE,

AND UNCERTAINTIES

D eclan and his company walked through the southern gate of Abala dragging their feet and huffing for breath, but they were there, and they were alive. The sun was in the west and the day was fading. Declan stopped and surveyed the city from the southern gateway.

There had been no sign of any more nomads vacating the city and the emptiness reassured him that they'd reached their goal safely. Abala was still showing the ravages visited upon it, and here there was no sign of any other people. All the shops were empty and peering into an open doorway revealed debris and nothing of value.

Declan motioned for the men to follow him. They walked slowly past three empty storefronts, and at the first street, turned right. A long block away was a small plaza, one he had not seen the last time he was here, but one well known to Benruf. There was a public well, and if the raiders had not poisoned it out of spite, there they would drink for the first time in almost two days.

The well stood in the center of the empty plaza and after

drawing up a large bucket, they found the water untainted. Around the well were wrought-iron hooks bolted to the stones, from which copper ladles had once hung. Someone fleeing or a raider had taken them. Tobias Winters glanced around, and seeing nothing else to use to drink from, he picked up the large wooden bucket and poured it over his face, then opened his mouth and gulped.

He turned and poured the bucket over Mikola's face, then Mick Sawyer's. Eventually every man had gulped some water and the bucket had been lowered and refilled four times.

Near the well were stone benches, nicely carved and placed against the side of the shop that fronted onto the dock street. Declan walked slowly to one of the benches, finding a bit of shade, and sat down. Sixto joined him. "We should lie down and sleep. That's what the others will do."

Declan looked and saw men just lying down on the stones of the plaza, in the lengthening shade, and realized everyone was exhausted. They were soaking wet, filthy, and near starving, but they were alive.

"You?" asked Declan.

"I can keep my wits for a bit longer," Sixto answered. "Sleep."

Declan put his arms under his head as he lay down on the bench. Within seconds he fell into an exhausted sleep.

DECLAN AWOKE TO A SCENT of smoke in the air. It was dark and he felt only a little rested. Still, his head felt clearer than it had in days, and what had seemed a never-ending thirst was finally gone.

He saw that Sixto had positioned himself to the west of Declan's bench, where he would be the first to awaken if anyone approached from the dock side of the plaza. Everyone else was asleep, a few of them snoring loudly. Declan again sniffed the air and realized the smoke had to be coming from somewhere to the west, as there was a slight onshore breeze. He stood up and found every joint ached. He would rather have returned to sleep, but the source of the smoke intrigued him. That meant at least one other person was nearby in this city.

He moved past Sixto and ventured down the narrow street leading to the docks and felt a coolness in the air. Having lived his entire life on the edge of the sea, he knew it meant morning was still an hour or two away, as the previous day's heat was finally draining away and letting the moisture in the air turn to mist, perhaps even fog when the sun arose. Glancing upward, he saw the stars were fewer and dimmer than those he had seen inland, so he knew the weather was changing. If this had been Oncon, he'd have thought there might be a chance of rain.

He kept moving until he stood at the edge of an empty dock, and still the waft of air hinted at distant smoke. He peered into the darkness and saw nothing. He had paid no attention to the sea when entering the city, so perhaps he had missed a boat, or even a small ship at anchor. If it was shuttered or using a covered and vented brazier, that would explain the smoke but no light.

He felt as much as heard Sixto come up behind him. "Smoke?"

"Woke you up, too?"

"No, when you stepped past me. I sleep lightly."

"One way to stay alive," said Declan.

"I have found it so," Sixto replied.

"I took no notice of any ships or boats off the coast," Declan admitted.

"A ship could have been anchored a block north in the middle of the street and none of us would have noticed. My friend, you may not admit what a wonder you accomplished, but you took all the men from the Wound and kept them alive to this day."

"We got lucky," Declan said, thinking of the three days traversing the southern pass without being detected by any nomads.

"You were the luck, Captain," Sixto said with respect. "Bogartis knew what he saw in you, as did I when I trained you as you healed your wounds."

Declan was silent for a moment, then turned and said, "Standing here in the dark will not hasten dawn, and until the sun is up we won't know what's out there. When the men are awake we need to find out who is still around and where we can find food."

"Food will be precious."

Declan patted the side of his tattered shirt. "Bogartis told me to sew a small pocket here, and keep a few coins wrapped so they made no noise."

Sixto chuckled. He patted his own shirt and said, "Likewise. Between the two of us we may be able to bargain for some fish or bread. Though we may have to fight."

"If we have to fight, we fight," Declan said, leading the way back down the street to the market square.

HATU WAS FAR FROM HAPPY about the decision that he remain behind while Hava risked her life to gather information on the Pride Lords. Balven had left on the *Sundown Raider* with Captain George to inspect the Golden Pride's treasure ship, *Borzon's Black Wake*, and Hava was now sailing toward Elsobas in a slow trader's brig that she said waddled in a crosswind but was otherwise fit.

Hatu sat back and let out a low growl of frustration.

Nathan said, "What's on your mind? Because it's certainly not on the work before you."

"Hava" was Hatu's reply.

"Not your first time apart, so what is it?" Nathan asked.

"I don't know. When she was sent to school with the Powdered Women, I didn't know if I'd ever see her again. It's what happens when you're sent away after training. I went to a crew and ended up on that damned boat with Donte . . ." He fell silent for a moment. "They got me out of that deep-water cave, anyway . . . I didn't realize how much I missed her or was worried about her safety until I saw her again, and she was assigned to pretend to be my wife—"

"Pretend?" said Nathan. "I thought she was your wife?"

"At first she was assigned to keep an eye on me, by our friend Bodai. The other masters wanted her to kill me if the order came down, but Bodai was pretty sure she wouldn't do that. We bought an inn in Beran's Hill and actually did get married." His tone turned bitter. "We wed on the day the raids began."

"Things change," said Nathan. "We never know how long we'll be with other people." He looked out into nothing for a moment. "If you live long enough, you'll bury everyone you've ever known."

Hatu could hear the sadness in his voice. Then Nathan seemed to regain his composure.

"Live as if there's no worry, until life gives you something to worry about," Nathan said. "I've . . . been around, and I've seen more loss than I can remember, but in the end, each day brings an opportunity to start over.

"Your friend Declan, the one you saved, he's suffered great loss, you said?"

"Yes, his wife died on the day of that wedding festival, as well as his former apprentice Jusan and his wife. Unless someone else I don't know about is alive, I may be the closest thing he has to a friend."

"What I would say to him is what I'm saying now; what time

doesn't heal, it distances, and after a while the pain fades to a vague memory or is even forgotten. But even if remembered, it is no longer a sharp pain, a faint ache perhaps, but nothing crippling. Should anything befall Hava, you will recover, and if you vanish, she'll recover eventually."

"Is that supposed to reassure me?" asked Hatu.

"Only in the sense that whatever the future holds, you won't be shocked and overwhelmed by it. Prepare for the worst and hope for the best is a common proverb in many languages and places. If you want reassurance, consider that you may be a far better help to her in the future by being here now, than by being with her."

"How?"

"As you did with Declan, you may find a way to be of help in a critical situation . . ." Nathan paused for a moment, then added, "By mastering yourself and your powers."

Hatu considered that. "Sorry. I should have realized that myself."

"As I said, I cannot teach you any more, but I can act as a guide."

"So, guide me," Hatu said, his tone almost amused.

Nathan was quiet for a moment, then said, "I think context now might help."

"Context?"

"In everything, really. Ever talk to someone who in the middle of a discussion changes the subject and assumes you're following?"

Hatu broke out laughing. "I ran an inn. What you describe happened nightly!"

Nathan chuckled. "How did you deal with it?"

"Mostly by nodding my head and refilling their mugs."

Nathan smiled and said, "A good barman's answer."

"So, tell me about context."

"The powers you possess, what many people think of as magical abilities, exist in a state of energy they also think of as 'magic.' That often ends the entire discussion. For people who lack your abilities, or the abilities of other people, to manipulate the stuff of the universe, it is beyond their ability to comprehend. Contrast that with it being more familiar to you by the day.

"From what I could tell from the echo of what you saw, your mind has its own way of organizing the lines of energy between the furies. The glimmer I got was countless lines, like strings on a lute or threads on a loom."

"Threads on a loom," said Hatu. "Yes, that is an apt description, though the loom would be as big as the world."

"Other people organize things in their mind differently, each finding a unique perspective. Some might look at blocks piled one atop another, or countless balls the size of a child's marble, of differing colors, perhaps, or even light or sound. My talents allow me to do things you can't, or at least not yet, and there are things you can do that are impossible for me.

"But like all human behavior, you find people applying a hierarchy to 'magic' as they do to anything else you can imagine. This is greater than that, this is the province of holy wonder."

Hatu nodded that he understood.

"So, here is what we can say about the 'magic' you've encountered. The tale you told about being captured by the witches under the sea—"

"The Sisters of the Deep," Hatu supplied.

"If you could look at their powers, what would you see?"

Hatu shrugged. "I hadn't thought of that. For the most part, I try not to think of it."

"Often learning new things can be uncomfortable, even difficult, and sometimes impossible, so tightly do we hold on to certain beliefs and reject what doesn't fit our view of things."

Again, Hatu nodded.

"I can't tell you the countless times I saw people reject the truth before their eyes in order to hold tightly to beliefs that have been clearly proven wrong. It's the nature of people to find a comfortable place and remain there." He held up a finger. "Except for the ones who can't wait to find out what's over the horizon."

"I'd venture that most people don't care what's over the horizon."

Nathan bobbed his head in agreement, then said, "Let's talk about this organization of things.

"At the core, the stuff that makes up everything, an invisible arrangement of those energies you perceive in your mind, comes together in countless ways to form . . . everything.

"At the most fundamental level are the furies responsible for the four prime states: fire, air, earth, and water. You will discover within those fundamental states even more complex forms of energy, but those states are in constant flux. Without air, fire ceases, but too much fire, water turns to steam and flies away. Earth covers fire, and it dies, but hot enough fire, rocks turn liquid and erupt out of mountains.

"There are no perfect, static states; all is constantly in flux." He stopped.

Hatu weighed what he had heard and after a moment asked, "How is my lineage connected to fire?" He touched his head, now sporting a full copper-and-gold mane.

"You could use a cut," Nathan observed, then said, "We'll come to that later.

"Next below the elemental states are the natural states. Air, earth, water, and fire combine and create life. You have 'magic' in plants and people who worship the spirits in trees. It creates and permeates all animals, including humans, and some people worship animals, or people they see as special."

"Worship?"

"There are places where they believe all powers such as yours come from the gods, or a god, and you would be worshipped as a deity or an avatar of a divine being, or venerated as a messenger from some heaven or a prophet. And in other places you'd be put to death in one of several disagreeable ways as a walking blasphemy—reminding us of what I said about people hanging on to their beliefs."

Nathan shifted his weight in his chair and poured himself a mug of water. After drinking, he continued. "I will leave it to you to explore the things I've said, but to come back to your question on how you are connected to fire, we'll pause to say this about the Sisters of the Deep.

"They practice what we shall call 'blood magic,' which is almost always evil in design and intent. It takes the energies of life and corrupts them."

"Those fish-men," said Hatu. "Mermen, naga."

"Men died to create those servants of theirs. Not one of them is a natural being. It is that corruption of life force that allows them to live under the sea, against every natural aspect of their being." Nathan shrugged. "Once, perhaps, they were worshippers of some sea god or goddess, but whatever their time-lost origin, they are debased beyond redemption. There is only one source of 'magic' that is even more evil, and that is necromancy, eliciting energy from using death. Death magic, blood magic, and others are powerful and dangerous, but less so than elemental magic."

"So, again, how am I this unique vessel of elemental magic?"

"In some way I cannot begin to imagine, let alone explain. But I think that somehow your ancestors became linked to fire in a similar way to how the Sisters of the Deep became enmeshed in the blood magic of the sea.

"However that relationship came about, it drew others who added to that connection. So, ancient rulers of Ithrace formed alliances with families who were also connected to the elemental force, and from those marriages came children with an even greater affinity for the 'magic' of fire. Like all elements, fire can destroy, or it can burn brightly to chase away the darkness and keep you warm.

"Your ancestors were men and women of good heart, for they rose to power bringing light and warmth to others. The lore of the Firemanes is based on that fundamental truth. The legend of the curse is that should the last Firemane"—he pointed at Hatu—"perish, great calamity would descend on the world."

Hatu took a deep breath as he absorbed all this, and he finally said, "Well, I'm still here, but calamity descended on us all anyway."

"Well, prophecies of doom usually don't go the way people think. What happened was all the Firemane 'magic' was connected, over generations, most noticeably in the royal family, but through dozens of close cousins." He smiled. "From what I studied, your mother and father were distant cousins. That happens often in royalty."

Hatu said, "So you're saying that when my family was slaughtered, the magic had nowhere else to go but into me?"

Nathan grinned. "Exactly!"

"What now?"

Nathan said, "Within this library are books that account for how the Firemane children were raised, especially the girls, who could manifest the powers you're trying to master." He got up, motioned for Hatu to follow, and entered the main hall of the library. "We just need to find them and see what we can cobble together to continue your studies."

Hatu shrugged off the potential tedium, as it was what he and Bodai had been doing for weeks before Nathan appeared. "But we'll start that tomorrow. There is one other thing I'd like to try before we go and eat." He walked back toward the table.

Hatu followed him and sat once more. "What?"

"You demonstrated that you could find someone familiar to you."

"Yes," said Hatu, not sure if that was a question or just a statement.

"I'd like to see if you can return your senses to where you saw Declan, in that canyon."

Hatu said, "What for? He's no longer there, I'm certain."

"Humor me," said Nathan.

Hatu stood and Nathan faced him, and they gripped each other's shoulders.

Immediately Hatu felt the organization of the energy lines take place at what he now considered the speed of thought. He merely located a thread, and within seconds he could see the location of where he had caused the rockfall.

"Fascinating," said Nathan. "You didn't even think about allowing me to see through your eyes, and now I'm seeing what you're seeing."

"I assumed you wanted to."

"You were correct in that assumption."

"What now?"

"Turn your attention to the farthest point you can see down into the canyon."

Hatu did and cast his gaze beyond the rockslide. The fallen

dead below the boulders and rocks had succumbed to scavengers, so that only bones and a few shreds of flesh could be seen. He panned across to a large outcropping of rock in the right wall of the canyon, one that was noticeable as it was almost white in color. "I see something in the distance."

"See if you can move there, reposition your perspective from that point."

Hatu paused, considering how he'd "moved' his perspective before, then just willed his vision over to the rock outcropping.

"Well done," said Nathan. "We may not know all there is to know about what you can do, but it's clear that once you've mastered a trick, it becomes effortless."

"Not entirely," replied Hatu. "I can feel the beginning of a headache."

"Then let us continue. How far down the canyon can you see?"

Hatushaly focused his attention to the limit of what he had seen previously when aiding Declan, then looked farther down the escarpment, and after a moment said, "There is a trail, and it intersects a clearing."

"Move there," instructed Nathan.

Instantly, Hatu complied and they found themselves at a place near where the two game trails connected, the boundary of the mercenary camp. "Can you keep moving ahead?" asked Nathan.

"Yes," said Hatu and he picked a feature and moved his mind there. He repeated this several times then saw the wall of the eaters' compound.

Both Hatu and Nathan paused, and finally Hatu said, "What are those . . . things on the wall?"

"Bones of no creature natural to this world," said Nathan, his tone revealing concern. "Move past it."

Hatu ignored the tone lacking any hint of request, but rather being an order, and did as he was asked. Quickly they moved through what appeared to be a large camp, or small village, and then past crude gardens, where whatever was grown was hardly tended.

Then they came to the center of this settlement, and against the southwest-facing cliff face, from deep within the Wound, they could see a massive pit. Without much thought, Hatu moved his vision to the precipice of the pit.

"Stop!" Nathan commanded.

Hatu froze his position in his mind, his anger rising at being commanded. "What?" he said in his mind and it sounded like a shout.

"Do not gaze into that pit."

"Why? What's down there?"

"Something I fear more than simple death itself."

"You don't want me to see it?"

"No," said Nathan, "I don't want it to see you."

Suddenly they were back in the library, and Hatu released his grip on Nathan's shoulders. As he stepped back, he saw an expression on Nathan's face he could never have imagined before: terror.

HAVA HAD ALWAYS ANCHORED THE *Queen of Storms* on the other side of the island when visiting Elsobas, but as the trading ship she commanded was so nondescript and had no name painted on the bow or stern, it was hardly likely to be noticed should any Azhante be around. She had a small gig lowered and two of her crew rowed her the short distance from the ship's anchorage to the dockside. She quickly climbed the ladder and walked toward the small building closest to the landing.

Catharian sat before the cantina, sipping a mug of fruit-flavored wine as Hava returned.

"Any joy?"

"Shechal," she said.

Catharian closed his eyes as if in pain, slowly shook his head, and said, "That pesthole?"

She nodded.

"You're playing find the criminals, aren't you?"

"You have a good bit of skill in being a spy, Catharian," Hava said, "but you have absolutely no idea how to be a criminal.

"If you want to go somewhere the people living there don't want you to go, you find smugglers."

"Smugglers?" His eyebrows rose slightly as his expression turned appreciative.

Hava chuckled. "I don't care where you look, if there are profits to be made, someone will work out how to sneak past the authorities."

"At the risk of death?"

Hava took his mug and drank it down, then put it back in front of him. "Nobody ever said criminals were the smartest people around. Go get us another round of wine and we'll talk about the next leg of this journey."

Catharian scowled, then rose and took the now-empty mug to the open window where orders were taken. He returned a moment later with two full mugs of fruit-infused wine.

After taking another deep drink, Hava wiped her face with the back of her sleeve, and said, "I could get used to this sweet wine, Catharian."

He laughed. "It is a lovely choice on a hot day if you don't mind being unconscious under a tree by sundown."

"Like all vices, if a little is good, a lot may not be your best choice."

Catharian again laughed and said, "When did you get so smart, youngster?"

She gave him a scowl. "Where I grew up, lessons were harsh and failure to learn could mean death."

He nodded. "So, next?"

"Two things: first we travel to Shechal, learn as much as we can about how to reach the city of Akena, and along the way I need to teach you as much of the language used by the Azhante as possible."

He sat motionless for a moment and said, "I think more wine is needed."

16

MORE DISCOVERIES AND

REDEMPTION

———✦———

Declan and Sixto stood on the docks, in the same position as in the dark the night before, and a faint glint appeared slightly above the water. "There," said Sixto, pointing.

"I saw it," Declan replied. "What would I give for one of those spyglass tube devices."

"Don't waste time wishing for toys," said Sixto. "I'm wishing for a full stomach."

"We'll see what Tobias and Benruf turn up. Right now, I'm curious about that ship. Last night, none of us had the wits to think, let alone scan the harbor for ships that might have crew aboard." Declan nodded his appreciation.

The ship was lying low in the water, apparently because it held a heavy cargo. But the crew had taken down the masts and used the sails to block light from reaching the shore. It was far enough offshore that it would have been difficult to see any details even if the sails hadn't been used as a cloak.

"What do you think she is?" he asked.

"Two masts, seventy, eighty feet maybe," Sixto surmised. "Hard to judge with nothing around her and she's far enough away to make judging distance difficult."

"I think we might have to go out and pay her a visit," Declan said.

"Why is she just sitting there?" wondered Sixto. "Someone's aboard, going by the smoke we smelled last night, but they're trying to hide."

"My guess," said Declan, "is that during the raid some of the crew got caught ashore, and there were enough men left to hide her, but not enough to sail her."

"Probably," agreed Sixto. "Can't see the horsemen from the grasslands bothering to send boats out if a bunch of them are already raising anchor and dropping sails."

Turning away from the view of the sea, Declan said, "We need to find food."

Sixto pointed up the street. "There's Tobias and Benruf."

When Tobias and Benruf drew near, Declan called, "Any luck?"

"A little," Tobias replied, lifting a large sack off his shoulder. Coming closer, he put the sack down. "Found a market a few streets up where some traders were haggling. Men with knives and gold were persuading them to not drive too hard a bargain."

"You didn't rob them, did you?" asked Declan, trying not to laugh.

"Hell, no!" said Tobias. "It was your gold."

Sixto laughed at that. "Let's see what you have."

Tobias opened the sack, and they peered in to see a cooking pot and some kitchen tools as well as a few vegetables.

"We passed an abandoned inn back that way," said Benruf. "It may have a working kitchen."

"Go get the others," Declan said to Sixto, "and fetch them to the inn." Benruf quickly told Sixto its location and Sixto headed back to the plaza where the men were resting. Declan followed Benruf and Tobias as they returned the way they had come.

Five doors past the next street, they came to the abandoned inn, and Declan turned and said to Benruf, "Stay out here to show the others where we are in case Sixto gets lost."

Declan followed Tobias into the abandoned inn. A few chairs and tables were still intact, though they had been overturned and damaged. Shattered wood littered the floor, and Declan said, "At least we have fuel for a stove if there is one."

"Through that door," Declan instructed, pointing to the door to the right of a long bar.

Going through, they saw before them a respectable kitchen: a stone stove with an open oven for roasting, a grill top, and above, a large spit.

"My mouth is watering thinking of a haunch of beef or mutton on that spit," said Tobias. He put down the sack with a sigh.

Declan inspected the kitchen and as he had expected almost every implement used for cooking—skewers, pots, long forks, and especially knives—had long since been carried off. "We can get a fire going easily enough," he said, "but without more implements, cooking will proved difficult." He motioned for Tobias to open his sack. "Let me see that pot."

Tobias opened the bag. He held up a good-sized iron pot and handed it to Declan.

The former smith inspected it and nodded. "Good. No cracks, but we'll be handing out soup a mug at a time . . . if we had mugs."

A few minutes later Benruf entered, with Sixto and the others following him. Hearing Declan's last remark as he entered, Benruf said, "Tell me what you need, and I'll take some lads and we'll go scavenging."

"Use your imagination," said Declan. "We have thirty-eight mouths to feed, so cups, bowls, forks, knives, spoons, mugs, whatever else you can find." Then he turned to Tobias. "What else did that tinker have?"

"Some more of what you're looking for, but I spent all the gold you gave me."

"You're going to make that tinker rich," said Declan. He reached into a pocket and pulled out another pair of gold coins, and a half-dozen silver coins.

"Pots, pans, cups, and the rest," said Tobias.

"Go with him," Declan said to Tobias. "Cooking gear first, like tongs and long forks. You're far less likely to find those than bowls and mugs."

Tobias handed the bag to Sixto and he and Benruf left together.

Sixto removed the rest of the contents from the bag. "Real onions, not those tiny bites they've been eating for years, and real carrots."

Declan nodded his approval.

"Turnips, and peppers!" Sixto held up a pair of large peppers, and sniffed. "And they're fresh!"

Declan poked around in the cabinet near the stove and said, "Gods! Spices! Real spices. Whoever stripped this place didn't carry off everything." Then a thought struck him and he said to Sixto, "Come with me."

Sixto followed Declan to the far end of the kitchen where a door hung half-open with one hinge broken. Declan pushed it aside and looked around. The rear yard, which was used to unload supply wagons, had a well directly behind the kitchen, to the right of where Declan stood. Hurrying over, he found that where there should have been a bucket hanging, the rope had been cut.

"Let's get that bucket from the well in the square and get

down there to see if this water is any good. We'll have water either way, but here will be a lot easier."

Sixto said, "You've gotten good at this giving-orders business, Declan."

"If it wasn't me, it'd be you," Declan answered.

"Maybe, but you have a knack I don't think I have, and I don't mind. Bogartis trusted me with many things, but I don't think he ever considered me his second."

"Either way, this is what it is, right?"

"Right."

Declan looked around. A heroic amount of rubbish filled the delivery yard. He pointed to the farthest corner on the left and said, "What's left of the privy will be under all that. It's as far from the well as they could dig."

"I'll have some of the boys clear the debris away," said Sixto.

Declan nodded, and said, "If we can't find anything like a bath house or even a big tub we can haul here, at least we can wash a little in the harbor, then rinse the salt off."

Sixto chuckled. "We're getting seriously civilized."

Declan glanced about the yard once more then moved to the area to the left of the door. He pushed some of the debris around.

"What are you looking for?" Sixto asked.

"A door, maybe flat in the ground, or slanted with a couple of steps." Declan continued to move things around. "An inn or tavern in a land this hot either gets a new delivery every other day, or it has a cold cellar."

Sixto joined in the search. After a few minutes, they found a cellar door between the kitchen and the well and moved broken boxes, bits of furniture, tree palms, and many rocks out of the way. Once the debris had been cleared, Declan could try the door, but it was warped and stuck firmly.

He and Sixto found some rags and cobbled them together to form a small rope which they tied to the door's sturdy-looking wooden handle. Declan pulled it just enough that Sixto was able to stick a rock under it to wedge it open. Then the two men caught their breath, stood side by side, and heaved the door open. A stench from within rose and caused both men to gag.

"What died?" Sixto asked.

"How long were we gone?" asked Declan.

"I lost track," said Sixto.

"Whatever meat was stored in here is long turned. Hold your breath and let's find whatever is still good."

"We'll need a light," said Sixto.

Declan said, "Let's start a fire in the stove."

A small box of flint still stood behind a corner of the stove, so it was brightly burning with flaming kindling within a few minutes. Once it was going, Declan lit a broken chair leg and carried the makeshift brand out to the steps leading down to the cold cellar. Sixto and the boy Billy Jay followed.

The reek had subsided somewhat, but the stench still made the three men cover their faces by pulling up the fronts of their tunics. By the light of the brand, Declan could see the barrel of fish from which the worst of the stink was emanating. Sixto and Billy Jay both grabbed the barrel, lugged it up and out of the cellar and dumped it in the farthest corner of the yard.

Returning to the cellar, Sixto said, "Between a hot sun and scavenger birds, that'll be gone by sundown."

A small haunch of beef hung from a hook, and Declan said, "This doesn't look rotten but it's halfway to being jerky. Maybe if we slice it and let it go all the way?"

"We're going to need salt."

Declan said, "If we can't find a bag here, we can use brine.

It won't taste like much, but some of us haven't had beef in years."

Declan opened the lid of the barrel in front of him. "Dried fruit," he said, pleased, then he quickly inspected the other barrel. He made a sweeping hand gesture. "That's a good supply of rice, beans . . ." He opened the tie on a large sack and exclaimed, ". . . and best of all, nuts!"

The sack in the corner contained pounds of salted almonds, and Sixto smiled.

"They won't last long," he said.

"This will keep us going two, maybe three days," said Declan.

Billy Jay asked, "Why salted almonds?"

"Some inns put bowls of them out at the bar," answered Sixto.

"Or other types—pecans, peanuts—but always salted," Declan added. "Makes you thirsty, so you drink more."

"Oh," Billy Jay said.

"Most of this is still good." Declan pointed to a stack of flour bags. "We can make flatbreads and if we can find a little salt and with those spices in the kitchen, even make them tasty."

Sixto nodded and before Billy Jay could ask, Declan said, "My wife grew up in an inn, and I helped out a lot while courting her." Thinking about Gwen turned his mind to a dark place where he didn't want to go, so he pushed that thought away. To Sixto he said, "We have a few coins left, but we need more, so unless we turn to banditry, we have to find whatever we can to trade."

"A pair of horses would be welcome so that we could head up the coast a bit and see whatever else is left," said Sixto.

"Take some men and work your way through the city, and then head up the coast. If there are loose animals, they're going to be near grazing and water, places they are more likely to know."

Sixto nodded and left the cellar. Declan said to Billy Jay, "Let's start hauling some of this up and into the kitchen."

The boy agreed and shouldered a big flour sack. Watching him exit, Declan remembered when he was that age, still mastering the smith's craft. He had saved these men and now they were scrambling to get organized enough to head back to Marquenet, and for a brief moment Declan felt a sense of accomplishment. Then that vanished almost instantly as he acknowledged they still had a very long way to go.

BODAI AND HATU SAT REVIEWING their list of books, manuscripts, and the other contents of the library and Hatu said, "This list is getting very long, and the piles are getting very high."

Bodai put down the book he was examining. "We could bring in a couple of lads and get them started stacking the books in some sort of order, using the numbers we give them. I can number each shelf, and we have already numbered the books, so a list should be straightforward enough to compile."

"I was thinking," said Hatu, "we could also bring in one of the acolytes. They're often free now they're no longer spending their lives looking for me," he added with a note of dark humor. "While you do the listing of books by location, she could write down subjects and then we'd have a list we could combine so no matter where the book was, you could easily find it."

"Clever," said Bodai. "Sabella writes well. She or one of the others would be just the answer."

Hatu sat back and gave out a long sigh. "This work is necessary, but hardly vital."

"You've always been plagued by curiosity ever since you were a child," said Bodai. "The frustration of not knowing leading to those outbursts of anger—"

Hatu interrupted. "At least I have my anger largely under control these days."

"To the relief of us all," added Bodai. He leaned forward, elbows on the table. "You want to know what it was Nathan warned you away from, what you said absolutely terrified him."

"I want to go back—"

"No!" Bodai pushed back and slapped the table for emphasis. "Nathan can divert a conversation more adroitly than any confidence trickster in any crew from Coaltachin, misdirect attention like a pickpocket, but there are things about him that are absolutely trustworthy and in the main he has done nothing but help you, far more than I ever could. If he says sending that mind-sight of yours anywhere near that pit puts you at risk, believe him!"

"Damn it," was all Hatu could say. "When do you think he'll return? I have questions."

"You heard him the same as I did," Bodai responded. "It's a long walk, whatever that means."

"We're on an island! It's big, yes, but how far can he walk?" Hatu's manner showed that he was edging back to his childhood pattern of mounting frustration leading quickly to anger.

Bodai said, "I'm inclined to think he was speaking figuratively." He was silent and thoughtful for a moment. "I'm sure you notice how he appears at odd times from behind that bookcase over there."

Instantly Hatu was on his feet heading for the indicated location. Bodai was slow to follow and when he caught up, he found Hatushaly standing at the corner of a long bookcase and the stone wall. He had his eyes closed and was holding his hands up and palms forward, as if feeling for something in the air.

"What?" asked Bodai.

Hatu didn't answer but slowly moved his hand until he suddenly froze, then dropped his arms and turned, opening his eyes. "There's something here. I don't know, the energy . . . is different."

"I wish I understood half of what you've experienced."

"It's a door," said Hatu. "Or a passage."

"Behind the wall?" Bodai stepped past him and started running his fingertips over the stones. "I've seen secret entrances before . . ." Then he stopped, looked around, and said, "This wall . . . on the other side is what used to be a garden. We enjoyed it when I was a boy training here. It's a big patch of earth now."

"Could there be a false wall here?"

Bodai shrugged. He motioned for Hatu to follow him and they walked beside a long bookcase till they reached an opening where an old window still emitted daylight. Bodai craned his neck and got his face as close to the glass as possible, then said, "I don't think there's enough room."

"Then what am I feeling?" Hatu asked.

"Another question to ask Nathan, when he returns," suggested Bodai.

Hatu shook his head in resignation and said, "Books."

Chuckling, Bodai patted Hatu's shoulder as he passed him, to return to their work. "Yes, books."

CATHARIAN SAID, "ARE YOU CERTAIN?"

Hava said, "How many knife fights have you been in?"

Catharian's expression became sour. "Very well. You go first."

The sailor they had met up with in Elsobas, Makenny by name, had agreed to travel with them from there to the port of Shechal on the island of the same name. It had taken a day and a half of sailing with favorable winds, and during the trip Hava and Makenny had many long conversations, half of which were beyond Catharian's understanding because of his lack of knowledge of smuggling and other criminal undertakings.

Now they had reached a long, rickety-looking pier, its appearance suggesting it might topple into the sea at any moment. They had to shimmy up a frayed rope that seemed on the edge of breaking. Makenny was staying aboard and when Catharian had asked about that, all Hava said was, "Someone's got to get word back that we're dead."

Catharian had decided not to voice his concern about the boat still being there when they did return, as even to him it did not seem a prize worth stealing.

They entered South House, a very large building, especially for such an out-of-the-way place as Shechal. Catharian had traveled widely enough to know it was big because not only was it an inn, but also a smugglers' clearinghouse. A large portion of this two-story building would probably comprise a warehouse, with a bar room at the front, a kitchen to one side, and the sleeping rooms all on the upper floor, no doubt containing any number of whores, depending on the level of traffic.

Hava led the way and pushed through two swinging doors with latticework panels, letting fresh air in. The room was filled with smoke, some from an indifferently vented kitchen, and the rest from a few men smoking pipes. Tobacco wasn't cultivated on the Twin Continents, though it did grow in the south of Enast, so smoking wasn't widespread. As Catharian's eyes began to sting a little he thanked the gods that it wasn't.

He'd had that reaction before, and knew it would soon pass, but as on every occasion that he entered a place like this, he wondered what the appeal could be. Some hints of other combusted plants were also in that smoke, and he realized he needed to limit his time in this room to avoid becoming intoxicated.

Hava went to the bar, beckoned to the barman, and leaned over to ask him a question. He nodded and pointed to a table in the far corner.

Hava nodded, then moved purposefully to the table, ignoring the men who were staring, some muttering remarks. One very drunken man rose from his chair to block her path only to be backed down into his chair as Hava held her dagger to his throat. "That's the smarter choice."

The man she headed toward chuckled at the exchange as Hava motioned for Catharian to come join them.

When they were seated, she said, "I asked the barman for Red Sweeney. Did he lie?"

Now genuinely amused, the man replied, "No, he did not." He was of late middle years, balding, and the fringe above his ears was grey. He had large shoulders, and from what they could see of him above the table, a lot of his muscle was slowly turning to fat. His huge fingers were decorated with gold rings inlaid with gems, and a large emerald was set in his left earlobe. "Who sent you?" he asked.

"Makenny," Hava replied.

"No one's killed that dock rat yet?"

"Not as of today," she said.

"So he sent you here alone?" He laughed. "Wise choice on his part. We have unfinished business. Not so wise on yours."

"I can take care of myself," Hava said without bravado.

"So I saw," Red Sweeney replied. "Now, if you have business, state it."

"I need to find a safe place to land a boat on Nytanny."

"Do you wish to die?"

"Not particularly," Hava answered.

"If an Azhante patrol doesn't discover you, the locals are just as likely to cut your throat for your clothes as to listen to what you might have to say." He paused, then added, "Actually, more likely if you don't speak their tongue."

"I speak Azhante."

For the first time, Red Sweeney's mask of indifference dropped, and his eyes widened. "How'd you manage that?"

"My business. I have been told versions of the tongue have become a common trading language."

"This is true, but you're not from any part of Nytanny I know, and I'm one of the few men who've seen most of the continent and lived to leave. I settled here"—he gestured, indicating the building—"because it's the closest thing I've had to a home for thirty years."

"Makenny said you were the best smuggler around."

"Retired smuggler. The rest of the good ones are dead or staying out of sight. You heard about the massive fleet that—"

"I was there," she interrupted.

"Oh?" said Red Sweeney, his eyebrows raised, now clearly intrigued.

"I also have unfinished business."

"Well, if you plan on single-handedly opposing the Pride Lords and the Azhante, far be it from me to stop you."

"Can you get me ashore on Nytanny?"

"I could, but as I said, I am retired. But I can tell you where to go ashore, and who to look for. If he's not dead, he'll be able to get you where you want to go. It's a small port town, not too far from Akena by boat, one week's sailing at the most."

"By foot?" she asked.

"That's trickier. There are three different Pride holdings between the town of Jadamish and Akena, and you have to get damn close to the Curb."

"What's the Curb?"

Red Sweeney sat back, drummed his fingers on the table, and said, "So you know nothing about Nytanny and want to go there?"

She reached into a small pouch under her vest and took out a pair of gold coins. "That's why I'm here."

He picked them up and smiled. "Marquensas mint? Haven't seen those for years." He put them in a pocket in his trousers, then said, "We need drinks."

Catharian stood up. "I'll get them. What would you like?"

"What do they have?" asked Hava.

"Bad wine and worse ale," answered Red Sweeney. "They have a local type of whisky, but it's made from cane molasses, called rum."

"What should I pay?" Catharian asked.

"For the good stuff, five coppers each. Any more, he's robbing you. Make certain he's pouring from the black bottle, not the green or blue, else he's cheating." With a chuckle he said, "Just tell him it's for me.

"So," he continued to Hava, "this is getting more intriguing by the moment."

"Can you get us ashore safely?"

"I can get you ashore, yes. Safely? That depends."

"On what?"

"How good a sailor you have getting you there. Nothing particularly tricky, but if you get lost and land in the wrong place, as I said, the locals are not particularly hospitable."

Catharian returned with three mugs and put them on the table. Hava picked up hers and took a sip, and grimaced. "Damn me, that's sweet!"

"You get used to it," said Red Sweeney, taking a good swallow from his mug. Wiping his mouth with the back of his hand, he said, "I can draw you a rough map if you'd like."

"Unless you have a chart, don't bother. I have a good memory."

Sweeney sat back in his chair and looked Hava up and down, as if trying to see something he missed the first time. "Chart? So, you're the sailor, too?"

Modestly, Hava said, "I've probably sailed more deep water than most around here."

Red Sweeney gave out a small laugh. Looking at Catharian, he asked, "Really?"

"If she says she's done a thing, it's going to be the truth."

"So, just course and distance?"

"Tell me where to start, what bearing we should take and what I'll see at landfall if I've gone too far or not far enough."

"Very well," Red Sweeney said. "Think of Nytanny as a big pie."

"Pie?" asked Catharian.

"It's not really pie-shaped, just roughly a bit round, with places that stick out here and there. The first thing you'll find is that Akena sits a bit to the north of dead center on the eastern coast. It's a small sort of a peninsula so if you were hugging the coast you'd sail right on into it.

"So, a pie. In the center is this big hole. Around the hole is the Curb. It's a place . . ." He shrugged. "I don't know if I can describe it. I've never been, and I've never met anyone who has. The truth is, no one who has been there is alive to talk about it. All we know is if you try to pass the Curb, you never come back."

"Why is it called the Curb?" asked Catharian.

"I don't know," said Red Sweeney. "It could be called a lot of things, the wall, the barrier, maybe because it's there to curb your curiosity?

"Whatever the reason, it's about a mile around this clump of mountains." He made a circle on the table with his fingers. "The rest of Nytanny is like most places, hills, mountains, rivers, flat land, all of it, no deserts though." His finger stabbed the table in the center of the imaginary circle he'd drawn. "These mountains are different, magical they say."

"Who's 'they'?" asked Catharian, while Hava shot him a black look for interrupting.

"People. People have stories. But the fact is, there's no living man who's ventured past the Curb and returned to tell of it, and those who say they have are liars."

"So," said Hava, tapping the table with her finger. "We don't go there."

"Yes," said Red Sweeney.

"Wasn't planning to, anyway," she said, again throwing a look at Catharian that suggested he put a lid on his curiosity.

Red Sweeney continued. "Now, the pie. Every so often there's a border that runs from the Curb to the coast, and in that 'slice' is a nation, or even two. Once in a while the line isn't straight as it meanders along a river course, or a line drawn along the peaks of mountains, but imagine lines."

Hava nodded.

"There may be a hundred, two hundred nations scattered across the continent. Some of those nations are in federations, and others are alone. They all have their own language, and warfare is constant as alliances shift and change seemingly at random. And you want to go there?"

Hava nodded once. "You seem to have managed to go there repeatedly over the years, and here you are."

"First because I know a few places that are safe to visit."

"Which is why we sought you out," said Hava.

"And because I spent a lot of years avoiding . . . let's say it took me a long time discovering that not all Azhante are strictly obedient to their masters, the Pride Lords."

"How did you discover which they were?"

"There are some incorruptible Azhante who you just avoid at all costs. They're fanatics who think of the Pride Lords as saviors."

Hava reached into her waistcoat pocket and said, "They wear these?" She put one of the black lacquer badges on the table.

Immediately, Red Sweeney shot halfway out of his chair, moving backward at speed as if the emblem was cursed. "Where did you get that?"

"Off a dead Azhante," she said calmly.

Catharian produced another, on a chain, and put that on the table as well.

Red Sweeney sat back down. "You too?"

"No," said Catharian. "She gave it to me."

Red Sweeney sat motionless and silent for a long minute, then exploded into laughter loud enough that other customers looked over at them. After his mirth faded, he took a deep breath. Looking at Hava, he said, "There's a story, more, several stories, going around. There's this mad woman who stole the Azhante's best ship, the *Queen of Storms*, from them without any trouble. She stole the Golden Pride's treasure ship and has captured two or three other Azhante ships." He gazed at her with wide-eyed wonder. "That was you?"

"Perhaps," she answered.

"So, you're the Sea Demon."

"Sea Demon?" Hava's eyes narrowed. "I don't know if I like that."

Red Sweeney laughed again. "How many of those badges do you have?"

"As many as I need," answered Hava.

Red Sweeney regarded her silently, then said, "What do you plan to do?"

Hava said, "First, to explore and see how things are there.

Then, I plan on helping bring whoever ravaged my home to their knees."

Red Sweeney grinned. "If I were forty years younger, I'd marry you, Sea Demon."

"I think we need to change that name," said Hava.

"What should I call you, then?" asked Red Sweeney.

Hava could feel the rum starting to hit her and realized she was one more drink from being drunk. "I like Queen of Storms, a lot, but that's the name of my ship." She looked at Red Sweeney and said, "Captain Hava will have to do."

"Captain Hava, it is," said Red Sweeney, sticking out his hand. She shook it.

Catharian said, "My name—"

With a wave of his hand, Red Sweeney said, "I don't care."

Catharian sat back, with an expression that suggested he had just been slapped.

Red Sweeney put his hand out and gently gripped Hava's wrist for a moment, then as he released it, said, "I'm coming with you."

"I thought you were retired," said Hava.

"I'm an old man, but I have a fight or two left in me, and no man knows when and how the end comes, but I will happily die before my time to see what mayhem you have planned for the Pride Lords."

Hava smiled, glanced at Catharian, and said, "Good. We can never have enough sneaky bastards."

17

RETURN AND RECOVERY

Declan had let the men set their own pace. A few of the older ones slept a great deal, recovering from the ordeal of escaping the Wound. Declan admired them the most, as they were the hardest pressed to carry on, yet somehow they did. Many would probably never have the strength to fight again, no matter how willing they might be, but Declan silently vowed to Bogartis's memory that no man with him would ever be cast out of this company as long as he led it. There were many tasks a former fighter could provide with honor for a mercenary company. Should any of them wish not to continue, he would seek to provide for them in Marquensas.

In the three days since occupying this abandoned inn, the members of Declan's company had scavenged enough items to make the kitchen functional, including a small bag of salt that had been claimed from an empty farm, to add to the spices already in the kitchen.

Some bartering for fresh fish, and freshly churned butter from a farm half a day's walk north, and the men were finally eating well enough for the younger fighters to seem fit to travel.

Sixto appeared at the door, motioning for Declan to come out of the inn. He had been on a systematic search of the city and had a large sack over his shoulder. He put it down, and when the bag touched the stones, Declan heard glass clinking.

He asked, "More success?"

"Far more than I expected, or we deserve," Sixto answered with a smile. He opened the bag and Declan saw three large bottles.

"Wine?"

"In a corner of the cellar of some rich merchant's home. And there's also this." He opened the bag wider and Declan saw a plain wooden box. "Open it," said Sixto.

Declan reached in, lifted back a hinged lid, and saw beneath it, coins. "Gold!"

"Whoever once occupied that nice home fled before he could take his hidden wealth," said Sixto. "I judge it to be more than a hundred pieces."

Declan realized he now had enough to hire a ship back to Marquensas, with enough left over to do more equipping here in Abala. The people of the city were slowly returning and some were bringing goods to trade or sell.

Declan said, "Wine tonight. It will do the older men some good and there's not enough for anyone to get drunk and do something stupid." He glanced back at the box and motioned for Sixto to close the bag. "Whoever that merchant was, he's either dead or miles away, or that gold would not have been there to find." He threw Sixto a questioning look. "Just how did you come to find it?"

"It was a cold cellar, a good one I think, as I still felt some coolness lingering there. The floor was covered in glass from broken bottles, and the place reeked of spilled wine. Those three bottles had rolled into the corner and had been ignored by whoever looted the cellar, but the small cask sat alone atop a smaller rack, and I wondered why it had been left. I turned a spigot and nothing came out. So I yanked hard, and the false front came off and therein sat that box."

Declan laughed. "You have the makings of a thief yet."

"I think not. If the raiders hadn't drunk themselves stupid, they might have found the box."

"Well, some good fortune at last. Find a quiet corner when you can and count it out."

"What are you going to do?"

"I'm nagged by that boat floating out there and am going to see if I can find a dory to row over there."

Sixto nodded. "I'm curious as well. Let me give the bag to Tobias to watch, and I'll come with you."

Declan nodded and in a few minutes they were both walking northward along the quay. "Before we got run out of the city," Declan began, "I recall the small boatyards were farther up that way." He pointed ahead of them.

"Nothing near the south gate, as I recall," said Sixto.

"How far north did you go with your scavenging?"

"About halfway, moving from the docks, traveling northeast, then back. Just about everywhere south of the big market square leads to the central city gate, the one the raiders came through. I was planning on starting on the other side of the square next."

Declan walked to the edge of the quay and peered down.

"What are you looking for?"

"It's possible a longboat overturned and sank, without being holed."

Sixto came over and peered in. "I see only mud."

Declan nodded. "If it's more than six feet down, we'll see nothing." He abandoned the edge of the quay to continue on with Sixto.

Nearing the center of the city, he noticed more people hovering in doorways and moving along the streets. There was nothing resembling order yet, so people were wary of the sight of two armed fighters, and vanished around corners, closed doors, or shuttered windows as they approached.

A few more adventurous or avaricious souls had set up makeshift shops in abandoned stores, or were selling out of carts, or under hastily erected stands comprising little more than four poles supporting a large piece of cloth.

"Life returns, if slowly," observed Sixto.

They saw more people the farther northwest they walked.

Declan stopped, and looked around, getting his bearings. "We docked up there, right?" he asked, pointing off to the northwest end of the quay.

"Yes," Sixto replied.

"Then we came toward here . . ." Declan said. He looked around once more. "And we were running past here . . ." He pointed. "That boat-seller is up ahead."

"The frantic one?"

"He was the only one we talked to," Declan replied with a mock scowl.

The dockside was returning to business, and Declan and Sixto found the boat-seller in the same place he had been when everyone fled south. He was a little more haggard-looking, but his clothes were cleaner, and where jewelry had left white bands on his fingers, several gaudy rings now rested.

"My friends!" he said with a seller's enthusiasm. "You survived! How wonderful! You seek a boat, yes?"

Declan scanned the area, noting that where low trestles had stood before, supporting each boat, now only empty ground was evident. "We were, but you seem to be lacking boats."

"They are all safe," said the merchant. "Garange knows when trouble comes, to swiftly hide the boats." He beckoned them to follow. "Come, I'll show you."

"You're Garange?" asked Declan.

"It is so," replied their guide.

He led them through a street adjacent to the store and then down a winding narrow alley to a warehouse. "This is not an easy place to find," Garange said. He produced a large iron key and fitted it into the largest lock Declan had ever seen, and with a bit of trouble got the lock to turn. It released a bolt which passed through two huge rings, one in the wall, the other matched to it on a big wooden door. "Besides," he said as he pushed the door open, rolling it into a pocket on the other side, "what do horsemen want with boats? I hide them here so they don't break them out of spite."

Declan saw half a dozen dories and skiffs of various sizes resting on wooden trestles. He pointed to one and said, "That's the crab claw you were going to sell us before the raid."

"Yes! Most excellent choice."

Declan considered something for a moment, then turned to Sixto. "Most of the men could use a few days' more rest, so we can still complete our task."

Sixto nodded, knowing that Declan meant the three or so days it would take to go fetch the precious forging sand.

"Besides, what we really need is a ship."

Garange's eyes widened and his expression became one of genuine happiness. "You have need of a ship? I can arrange that! I am also a broker!"

Declan's gaze narrowed. "A broker?"

"Garange has all things necessary to travel to and from Abala! I am a seller of boats, camels, horses, wagons, and carts, and a provisioner as well." His demeanor became a little less enthusiastic as he added, "Though, to be honest, my store of provisions is somewhat lacking. I've sent word up the coast, so more fresh food should be arriving soon."

"Where is the ship?" asked Declan.

"When the raiders come, sails drop and anchors are raised, but many of those crews are ashore, so some ships sail short-handed and hide."

"Anchored off the westward islands!" Declan exclaimed.

"It is so," said Garange. "I only need to send a message, and have a ship here in a few days, then avail myself of sufficient crew for a full voyage. Where do you wish to travel?"

"Marquensas," answered Declan.

Garange nodded, considering for a moment before saying, "That is a long voyage, and needs a goodly ship and crew. And many provisions." He looked at Sixto and Declan. "Besides yourselves, the crew must eat."

"And thirty-six more," said Declan.

"Ah, that is a lot of food."

"The cost?" asked Sixto.

"These are hard times as you know, my friends." Garange looked calculating as he inspected them closely, trying to ascertain just how much he might get from two bedraggled-looking fighters. "And so, perhaps more than—"

"Name a price," Declan said calmly.

"For the longboat, three gold."

"Done," said Declan. "Now, to the ship?"

"First, I must find a captain willing to take that voyage, and many will say no. And then I need to negotiate—"

"Price?"

"For my services, five more gold, but the price for the voyage will be between you and the captain."

Declan glanced at Sixto and said, "We will be back in an hour's time. You'll have your gold. And whatever provisions you have coming into the city, you'll hold for us and not sell off to others first, agreed?"

The merchant cocked his head, then realized he had a selling advantage, so smiled and nodded.

As Declan and Sixto began retracing their steps back to the inn, Garange closed the door and refitted the lock.

HAVA HELPED REEF IN THE sails, while Catharian held the helm steady, and Red Sweeney dropped anchor. Hava knew it was almost useless unless it hooked something on the bottom, but the drag would at least stop the boat from drifting too far off course with the current.

Sweeney's ship was anchored just off a small island a morning's sail away, and the three of them were now heading toward the mainland in a dinghy powered by oars and a single sail.

"What do we do now?" Catharian asked when the boat came to a halt.

"We wait," answered Red Sweeney.

"For what?" Catharian looked impatient.

"To be seen," said Red Sweeney. Looking at Hava he asked, "Is he always this full of questions?"

Hava gave a small chuckle. "You have no idea. He was a spy for years."

"Oh!" said Red Sweeney. "That explains a lot." He gave Catharian another up-and-down once-over, and said, "Brilliant! You don't look in the least bit dangerous."

Hava realized Red Sweeney took the word to mean a spy in the Azhante context. She thought it best not to disabuse him of the idea: it might gain Catharian some respect. So far, Red Sweeney had been treating Catharian as if he was Hava's servant.

Hava said, "Explain 'to be seen.'"

"If we sail right in before they know who we are we may not live long enough to be recognized. As soon as the light fades, either they'll have figured out it's me, or I'll use a shuttered lantern to signal. Once it's safe, we'll go ashore."

"So we just sit until then?"

"That's the plan," said Red Sweeney.

"So," began Hava, "while we wait, let's talk about Nytanny over there, the pie?"

Red Sweeney shrugged. "What do you want to know?"

"At one point you said that the Azhante sometimes stop wars or sometimes help one side to win, and what I want to know is, is there a pattern to those decisions?"

"The only pattern I can see is to keep the nations under control." Red Sweeney thought about the question some more, then added, "There are legends."

Hava nodded.

"Time was, they say, when whatever is inside the Curb . . . some call them 'Dark Masters' . . . took people, to keep a balance here, maybe over all of Garn.

"Then something happened, no one knows exactly what. Stories of great tears in the sky, through which magical beasts entered the world. Legends of wars between people and the Dark Masters. Then, many more stories and legends. It was a time lost to any history, then there was another change. Again, no one knows the truth, just speculation. After whatever that change was, the Pride Lords rose. They were traders, clans of some sort, not by blood, but by association."

Red Sweeney stopped for a moment, concentrating hard as if trying to unravel a complex knot.

"To begin with the Dark Masters lived within the Curb, so the stories go, and left the people of Nytanny alone, except at times of feast or celebration, though that is hardly the word. A rite of some sort? Sacrifices were demanded. I don't know exactly, but whatever it was, a time came when people had to send . . . had to be sent, to the land inside the Curb. That was the only time people outside the Curb were allowed to enter without being destroyed."

"Go on," said Hava.

Red Sweeney slowly shook his head. "I don't know what's true, and what's a story made up by madmen or drunks, but it's said that when the Dark Masters stopped culling the nations, the nations grew and became more contentious.

"Look," he added, "there are always people who will seek to take advantage, even in the worst of times. The Pride Lords were just better at it than everyone else." He rubbed his chin. "I never once in my life set out to commit murder, but I've killed a fair share and more along the way. Sometimes you find you have no choice."

Hava nodded.

"Some people like killing," Red Sweeney continued, "but not me. I'll cut a man's throat in a heartbeat if I must, but I take no pleasure in it. Mainly because it's bad for business."

Hava grinned.

"Now, maybe someone up in Akena knows truth from legend," Red Sweeney said, "but whatever happened, here is what we know today. According to the Pride Lords these so-called Dark Masters are rumored to be about to return any moment, so we all must behave. They probably told the same thing to my grandfather, and maybe his as well, for all I know." He shrugged. "Apparently, some people got impatient with the Prides telling them how they should behave when there was no sign of the Dark Masters, so the Prides created the Azhante in order to maintain control.

"They'd take children from different families, train them up as an army. Made their whole family behave. Shared punishment, you see? They kill you for some misdeed, but they'll also kill your family. Even so, rebellions erupted, and the Azhante put the rebellions down, with the help of any other nation that wanted to stay on the Prides' good side.

"Now, these Prides," Red Sweeney continued, "they don't fight each other direct, but their respective fortunes rise and fall within their big city up there. Akena." He pointed in the general direction. "Since I was a little boy, the Golden Pride has been the big power."

"Why 'Pride'?" asked Catharian.

"I don't know, like maybe after lions or something? Big cats roam the grasslands here. It's just a name. But they all are this Pride or that Pride. Some are named after animals, like Tigers and Jaguars—more big cats."

Hava nodded that she knew what they were.

Red Sweeney continued. "Others after gems like Opal or Onyx, or . . . whatever some founder thought was bold, Thunder, Storm, anything. The Golden Pride was something else to start with, I forget what, but the grandfather of the current Pride Lord got really powerful, renamed his lot the Golden Pride, and they've hung on to control of everything for a long time, three generations or more, and his Pride has more control of the Azhante than any other. Those tough bastards you seem to have no trouble killing"—he pointed at Hava—"are his father's creation, the special spies and assassins."

Hava was silent for a minute as she considered what she had heard. "Seems to me there may be a lot of people here who might want to see the reign of the Pride Lords ended."

"Want to? Absolutely," said Red Sweeney. "Willing to help, probably none. Not while a party of Azhante assassins might show up in the dead of night and slaughter your entire town or village."

Hava glanced at Catharian, then looked back at Red Sweeney. "I may have an answer for that."

Red Sweeney smiled. "That's why I'm here with you. That's an answer I want explained."

"In time," said Hava.

"There," said Red Sweeney, pointing ashore. Hava and Catharian saw a lantern being swung from the beach. The sun was now behind high bluffs to their west.

"Switch with me," he said to Catharian, "and pull up the anchor." To Hava he said, "Take the tiller." He reached down and pulled up a pair of oars, and when the anchor was up, he handed one to Catharian. Catharian sat next to Red Sweeney, who said, "And . . . pull!" They easily got into a rowing rhythm and Red Sweeney said, "Just steer toward the light. There's a deep shelf, so she'll anchor to sand and we can go ashore."

Hava did as instructed and within minutes they were out of the longboat, wading ashore. Three men approached in the twilight, one barely more than a boy, holding the lantern. He had now shuttered it as it was no longer necessary.

The other two appeared to be father and son, perhaps all three from a family. The oldest man said, "Red Sweeney, you dog robber! I thought you said you had quit the game."

"Dog robber?" replied Red Sweeney with a smile. "If there's a thieving bastard anywhere around here, I'm looking at him!"

Both men laughed and embraced.

"Who are your friends?" asked the oldest man.

"Let's get inside before we do introductions," said Red Sweeney and he led the way up the beach.

As night fell, they reached a pathway through a stand of trees above the verge of sand, and continuing on they came to a few ramshackle buildings. All had their windows facing the ocean shuttered, but when they climbed a wooden set of steps up to a porch, and the door was opened, light flooded out.

It looked something like an inn, but the shabbiest inn Hava had ever seen. A pair of tables were on each side of the door, and a bar, comprised of two planks atop two barrels, stood against the wall opposite bearing jugs and bottles and empty pottery mugs.

"Help yourself," said the old man, pointing at the make-shift bar.

Catharian went to examine the choices.

Their host, as Hava thought of the old man, said, "It's all free. A bit of unofficial tariff on what passes through here from time to time. We have one fellow up in the city of Wandasan has a yen for that dreadful whisky made up in North Tembria. I personally can't abide it, but some folk like it. There's a couple of bottles, and the rest is wine and rum.

"We don't drink the water around here unless we cut it with something, or you can get a miserable case of the runs." He turned to Red Sweeney. "So, what's the plan?"

Sweeney grinned. "We're going to overthrow the Pride Lords."

"Ha!" barked the old man. "No, seriously, you wouldn't be here without a plan."

"Not my plan, but hers," Red Sweeney said, indicating Hava. "Hers?"

Indicating the older man, Red Sweeney said, "This old thief

is Anton Macaulish. That's his son, Ranuf, and the good-looking lad over there is his grandson, Michael. Gents," he said, turning slightly in the chair, "this is Captain Hava, and she has a plan."

"Truth?" asked Anton.

"Truth," said Red Sweeney.

"Have you lost your wits? Not that you ever had that many to begin with, but this girl and this . . . fellow, are going to over-throw the Pride Lords?"

"You might know Hava by another name . . . Sea Demon."

Everyone fell silent for a long moment, then Anton said, "Truth?"

"Truth," replied Red Sweeney.

"So you're the woman who goes around killing Azhante as-sassins and stealing their ships?"

"Only when I have to," Hava replied.

"Michael," said Anton, "run to the house and fetch that jug of special rum. This is a tale I want to listen to."

"Absolutely," said Red Sweeney.

Catharian returned from the bar and sat down.

Hava looked from face to face and said, "Let's wait for the rum."

DECLAN AND FIVE MEN CARRIED the longboat to the quayside and down a small wooden jetty that sloped gently down to the water. When they were knee-deep, they set the longboat afloat. As the boat settled and began to bob, Declan said, "The rest of you head back to the inn and wait."

The others turned, leaving Sixto and Declan alone to row the boat. Besides wanting to test it and get its feel, Declan was curious about the vessel he and Sixto had spotted floating just outside the harbor.

They easily got into a rowing rhythm and headed toward

where Declan had last seen their target. He checked over his shoulder from time to time, until at last he saw something bobbing above the waves.

"Over there," he said, and Sixto looked. They corrected their course and after a few more minutes rowing, Declan saw it was a small ship, perhaps sixty feet, the bow tilted down slightly and listing a bit to starboard.

They rowed to the starboard side and tied off their longboat to a cleat next to an opening in the railing. The deck was three feet above the water, so Declan assumed the ship was slowly taking on water.

Both men climbed aboard and saw and heard no one. From what Declan could see, this was a coaster built for speed, but able to carry a fair-sized cargo.

They trod carefully along the slippery deck toward the stern.

"Ever see the like?" asked Declan.

"Never," answered Sixto.

At the stern on the starboard side was a tall, raised section, atop which stood the wheel that controlled the rudder, and beside it a tall wooden structure that extended to the port rail. "Guess the wheel doesn't have to be in the middle," said Sixto.

"I guess," replied Declan.

Declan opened the door to the rear structure, and both men instantly stepped back as a wave of stench swept over them. It was the smell of death mixed with an acrid note Declan knew well. "Damn," he said.

They waited for a moment, then pulled their tunics up over their noses, and stepped in. It was dark in this cabin, but the light from the door revealed what had happened.

Three men lay sprawled around a brazier that was no longer alight, their faces already starting to bloat.

"Idiots," said Declan. "They closed up the doors and window and burned charcoal."

"That is bad?" asked Sixto.

"Lots of things burn, and I've used most in the forge at one time or another, but with charcoal you need fresh air. There's something about it that can put a man to sleep and then kill him. They probably thought this would burn through the night and not have to have wood added to it. They did it to keep warm." Declan shook his head in pity. "Let's get them over the side."

They made quick work of tossing the corpses over the rail, and by the time they returned to the cabin, the open windows and the door had helped, but the stench still lingered.

They looked through the litter on the floor and found nothing of significance. "Let's check below," said Declan. "They stayed aboard for a reason."

"Maybe they had nowhere else to go," said Sixto. "Remember what Garange said about crews being ashore when the raid started."

"Yes, that's true," Declan conceded.

They stepped back outside and Declan noticed that the masts had been unbolted at the base and the sails taken down in order to lower the ship's profile against the sunset. He motioned to Sixto and said, "Easy to take down, but almost impossible to put back without a shipyard, I think. It needs a hoist."

"They were hiding," said Sixto.

"Apparently. Probably going to wait another day or two then somehow get to shore." He looked around and then pointed behind the rear "shack" as he thought of the odd deck structure. "In that," he said, pointing to where the bow of a longboat protruded from behind it.

"From that smell, they must have died the night we saw them light up that brazier."

Declan nodded. "Now, how do we get belowdecks?" he asked.

"Over there," said Sixto, pointing to a small hatch just ahead of the foremast. A covered main hatch lay between the two masts. The smaller hatch was on a hinge and lifted by a rope loop. Declan pulled it up and looked down. "Not much light down there."

"Nothing to make a brand with, either," said Sixto.

"Ah well . . ." Declan saw the first step of a ladder nailed to a bulkhead and stepped down. He climbed down carefully and waited until Sixto joined him.

Declan tried to see into the gloom, but the contrast with the daylight meant that his eyes were slow to adjust. He knelt and felt the deck and said, "No water."

"Not sinking?" Sixto asked.

"Big cargo shifting might have canted her toward the bow and starboard," Declan said. He looked around. "There are two holds."

They were in the smaller, forehold, he reckoned, and he could make out a door that must lead to the main hold. Declan opened it and found a large set of crates all straining at retaining ropes because of the angle of the ship.

"Dark as a cave," said Sixto.

"What's over here?" asked Declan as they turned toward the bow.

A number of crates and boxes had slid forward and to the right and were now jammed together. At the edge of the cargo, Declan could hear his feet splashing. He knelt and felt around in the darkness and said, "There's a leak."

"How long?" asked Sixto.

"Until she sinks?" Declan asked as he moved back toward the ladder topside. He considered how long it had been since he had spied the boat. "Days," he reckoned. "It's a slow leak." Once up on the deck, he said, "One of those big crates might have cracked a board in the hull, or maybe just sprung some caulking. Either way, some of the lads can muscle those crates back, haul them up here if needed, and we can have a look. That bit of water would bail out in less than a day."

"What are you thinking?"

"I don't know what's in that cargo, but it may be useful. Even if we end up throwing it overboard, we can haul this beauty into the harbor and do some trading with our friend Garange. No need to spend gold if we can keep it, right?"

Sixto laughed. "Right."

"So, let's organize the lads, get some rope and lamps, and while that's underway, see about finally getting that damned sand."

For a moment Declan felt almost cheerful, but then his dark desire returned: to get on with forging swords and use them on those who had killed his wife.

18

AN EXPANDED PERSPECTIVE AND

AN EXPEDITION

Hatu stood in the center of the library, which was now brightly lit by a restored massive chandelier. Workers had finally repaired the chain-and-pulley assembly, so that it could be lowered and the glass-encased oil lamps lit, then hauled back into place. This would make working at night far less tedious.

Hatu nodded his approval and the workers lowered the chandelier and began extinguishing the lamps ready for them to be lit again for night work. The next task would be replacing all the empty sconces along the walls, so that the perimeter of the room would come alight. The windows were being repaired by carpenters who'd arrived with Hava's ship, and some day in the future they might even be painted to improve the look.

Hatu waved his thanks to the workers and returned to the usual table at which he, Bodai, and Nathan used to study, and found Bodai sitting with Sabella and the other acolytes.

Sabella smiled at him, but the other young women seemed a little self-conscious. Despite Hatu having lived at the Sanctuary for some time now, he was still a source of curiosity and wonder to those who had been here before he was found, those who had been tasked to find him. The five young women had spent so many hours in meditation and mental search for him. Now that the hunt was over, finding new positions for them was the order of business.

Hatu knew the other four young women only by name: Annisa, Farah, Bairavi, and Kole. He nodded a greeting and said, "The chandelier is restored."

"We noticed," said Bodai. "And we are making progress with cataloging the books."

Smiling at the young women, Hatu said, "I've noticed. Thank you, all of you. Your work has been amazing."

They all returned his smile.

Bodai said, "We have a lot to do."

Hatu understood Bodai was referring to all the issues that had been put aside until Nathan returned, and the longer he wasn't around, the more concerned Hatu and Bodai became about what they should do next. More than that, Hatu was deeply worried about what he should do regarding Nathan's warning about the thing in the pit. Should he just forget about that encounter, or take things in hand and begin his own investigation?

Still, Hatu had found since Nathan's departure that turning his mind away from those questions and focusing on more immediate concerns was refreshing.

Bodai said, "I think I know what we should do." He smiled at the young women, then at Hatu.

"When you do that, you look downright devious," Hatu chuckled.

Sabella ignored the banter and said, "I like this cataloging and organizing, so I will become a . . ." She looked at Bodai.

"Librarian," he supplied.

"Oh?" said Hatu, and after a moment's consideration, he said, "Oh! Indeed, yes. You have a wonderful knack."

"Farah will also be doing that work," said Bodai. "And with all the new children running around with little to do besides running errands and helping here and there, Annisa, Bairavi, and Kole are to become teachers, what you would have termed preceptors. So, I will leave the book organization to Sabella and Farah, and until Nathan returns, I shall start teaching the teachers." He seemed positively beside himself with delight.

Hatu smiled and gave Bodai's shoulder a quick squeeze. "Full circle, then. Back to what you were before fate turned you into a spy."

"Indeed." Hatu had never seen Bodai this happy in all the years he had known him and it pleased him, though a dark thought crept in, which he kept to himself: *What do I do if Nathan never returns?*

DECLAN HELPED PUSH THE FINAL crate up and Sixto and two other men quickly tied it off and cleared the way for a local shipfitter Garange had recommended to inspect where the water was coming in. After less than a moment, he said, "I can fix this in a few hours. It's just a misaligned hull plank." He indicated the large crate they had just removed. "As you thought, something caused that crate to break loose, it slid over here, hitting hard enough to cause a tiny leak, and as water came in, the ship rode lower, and . . ." He shrugged. "I can patch it here. If you can get the ship righted by bailing out the water so that the bent boards are a few feet higher, I can hit the other side with a big soft mallet I have back at the shop and get the overlap back in place. Some fresh caulking and she's seaworthy again.

"Now, getting those masts back in place will take a bit of work, but you've got a lot of men, and mostly it's down to muscle."

"Good," said Declan. "One of the boys will row you ashore and bring you back. When you return, tell us how many men you need to work with you."

The fitter nodded and climbed the ladder to the main deck.

Declan waved Sixto over. "Looks like we have a ship to trade with Garange."

"Why trade?" asked Sixto.

"Looks a bit strange," was Declan's immediate reply, which as he said it he realized was hardly a good reason. Just because it had a pulpit helm, as the shipfitter called it, and an offset cabin on the main deck, it was still a worthy ship. "All right, so that's a stupid reason. Let's see what the other compartment holds."

They entered the split between fore and aft holds and saw that Tobias had overseen a pretty organized investigation of the crates. Several had already been opened, inspected, and re-closed. Declan came to stand next to the old fighter and said, "So, what have you discovered so far?"

"Blankets," Tobias said, pointing to a crate in the corner behind them. "Those two there are full of pots, pans, kitchen tools. That big one over there, more blankets."

"How many?" Declan asked.

"Rough guess is a few hundred."

"Trade goods," said Sixto.

Nodding, Tobias said, "My guess, too. Both parties that got run into the Wound were guarding traders who tried to go into the Border Tribes' territory uninvited. Whoever brokered this shipment knew that it's only when the tribes come here that serious trading gets done.

"So, they trade directly with the tribes when they come through, or maybe go to local merchants so they can handle the trade, and then it all goes whopper-jaw. The tribes show up, but not to trade, and whoever the poor sod is who owns this cargo is either dead, or ran away, and lost his ship and cargo."

"What else?"

Billy Jay came forward, hiking a thumb over his shoulder. "You should see this."

Tobias grabbed the closest lantern and they followed the younger fighter. He had prized the top of a crate loose and yanked it up. Packed in fabric, large hunting knives were visible.

Declan picked one up and inspected it in the lantern light. "Pretty good work. Very useful."

Tobias pulled his own knife from his belt and put it next to the other. "Hunting or fighting, not a lot of difference, is there?"

"What else?" Declan said to Billy Jay.

"Bows."

"Where?"

"That crate over there. Short bows, like for horsemen."

"How many?" asked Sixto.

"I don't know, must be hundreds." He pointed in another direction. "And arrows."

"How many?" asked Sixto again.

"Looks like a dozen crates, so probably . . ."

"Thousands," said Declan.

Sixto's face broke into a broad grin, and Declan turned and said, "You're right. Why trade this ship?"

HAVA NODDED THAT SHE UNDERSTOOD as Catharian quickly transcribed as much as he could. He had already scrounged every piece of paper, parchment, and even some scraps of pale wood, and was now using the last bit of charcoal he could find.

The small smugglers' port was situated close to several towns, and between two good-sized cities, but it became clear that while the Macaulish family might have a fairly sophisticated appreciation of the world beyond Nytanny, they were woefully ignorant of how things worked in this continent.

To remedy that, the grandson, Michael, had been bringing people, one at a time, to the smugglers' village to tell Hava what they knew about the surrounding nation. Hava thanked the old woman, by the name of Ahana, for telling what she knew, and watched Michael escort her out.

"The Pride Lords don't like people traveling much, do they?" said Hava to Catharian and Red Sweeney.

Catharian nodded, then put down the stubby piece of charcoal he was trying to write with. His fingers were completely blackened and he had smudges on his face where he had absently scratched it. "It keeps them from forming friendships or alliances." He pushed away from the table and stretched. "As best I can tell, the Pride Lords are barely in control, and they use setting neighbor against neighbor as a means of keeping that control."

"It's the Azhante," said Red Sweeney. "People are angry at each other as a rule, but they're terrified of the Azhante. And it's not just having them kick down the door and dragging you out because you got drunk and mouthy, but because they'd drag off your whole family, too."

"And the Azhante, for the most part, seem just as fearful as everyone else of having their families dragged off, so they do what the Pride Lords tell them to do," added Hava.

"So, what have you worked out so far?" asked Red Sweeney. "We need a plan fast!"

Hava scowled. "Fast?"

"We're almost out of rum!" Red Sweeney laughed and slapped his hand on the table.

Catharian gave him a narrow gaze and said, "You're a smuggler. Go smuggle!"

"Joking," replied Red Sweeney. "That's where Anton and his son are off to, to resupply. Anyway, what have you figured out so far?"

"I'd like to get a look at how people are getting in and out of Akena. What my old teacher Bodai calls strategy, I call a plan, but what he calls tactics, the fine bits, well, I have no idea how to do that."

Catharian asked Red Sweeney, "Have I learned the Azhante tongue enough to pass as a visitor from some distant place?"

Red Sweeney shrugged. "You don't sound much more ignorant than a lot of folks, but as you've seen, there's not a lot of travel done here, especially the closer to Akena you get."

"We need some Azhante," said Hava.

"What?" asked Red Sweeney.

"Seems to me," Hava continued, "if Baron Dumarch sails a fleet across the sea the way the Pride Lords did, he's going to find a lot of angry people who will just start fighting because that's what the Pride Lords have had them doing for a long time. He might not even get his army to Akena if, as you said, there's no good place to land close by.

"But if the people here are ready to join up and overthrow the Pride Lords, that's a different story. And the key to that lock is the Azhante. Get them on our side, and it's pretty much over, right?"

Red Sweeney nodded. "Except for those fanatics, it would just be a matter of chopping through people who get in the way. Chaos would follow, as everyone would run amok and we'd as certain as sundown have more war, but it wouldn't be the Pride Lords having their way."

"Well, I never thought of that," said Hava. "Which is why I need to find out more and get back to the baron." She looked at Red Sweeney. "So, how do I get a couple of Azhante to talk to without bringing a company of them down on my head?"

"Braci," he replied. "It's a town two days on foot to the south.

There's a tavern where the Azhante visit between patrols. They're not supposed to, according to the Pride Lords' rules, but some of the younger Azhante visit there for drinks and women. You won't find any of the hard-bitten ones there, or even the more obedient youngsters. They think they're far enough away from Akena to get away with disobedience. For the most part they're right. Even when a few get caught out and punished, there are still others who think they're a bit cleverer. I remember being young and thinking with my cock, so there's your place. But how to do it?"

Hava remembered her failed training with the Powdered Women, and said, "I'll think of something. How long could one of them go missing before they start looking for him?"

"A day, maybe two, at most."

"This should work," said Hava.

"What?" asked Catharian.

Hava asked Red Sweeney, "Can you get me some clothes a whore would wear?"

He laughed. "That's easy enough. Probably some sitting in a trunk around here."

"Good, then I'm going to need two men to go with me who can handle a brawl without killing anyone or getting themselves killed."

"Again, easy enough."

"Good, then we're going to catch ourselves a stupid young Azhante."

DECLAN WATCHED FROM THE POOP deck as the small ship was towed into place next to a makeshift hoist at the quayside. It was going to be completely refitted once the masts were replaced. Every foot of rope, from sheets to shrouds, would be refitted where needed, and the oddly designed wheelhouse would be closely examined for any flaws.

Declan had made a full inventory, and besides bows, arrows, and knives, a large crate of leather chest-armor had been found. Not everything for trading with the nomads would prove useful to Baron Daylon, but enough would be that Declan felt this journey would be fruitful despite the appallingly high cost. In the forehold, they found what must be trade goods for the people of Abala, and what appeared to be enough to equip two full kitchens had been ferried to the docks.

Tobias had told Declan that he, Oscar, and a few more of the older survivors wanted to stay here to operate the inn. They even decided to name it the Old Guard. Declan agreed with relief, as he knew most of them would be of little use once the baron started his campaign against the raiders.

The shipfitter told Declan he could have the vessel completely seaworthy within a week, which gave Declan the time he needed to find the legendary sand Edvalt required for King's Steel.

He turned to Sixto and said, "Get the others. It's time."

Sixto waved to four of his men: Billy Jay, Toombs, and the Sawyer brothers, who returned the wave. By the time he and Declan reached them, he saw that four wooden boxes had been stored in the bow of the longboat he had purchased from Garange. He had also procured enough food for a three-day journey. Following Edvalt's instructions, they should be back well before the refitting of the ship was finished.

Getting in last, Declan took the tiller. The four rowers got into an easy rhythm. Declan steered them out of the harbor and they turned south. They quickly raised the sail and caught the wind. Declan knew exactly which prominence of land to look out for. He also hoped that the trees Edvalt had described were still there. His original instructions expected him to ride a horse, and swim, but he was going to carry back a hundred times the amount of sand that Edvalt had originally planned. The secret that Edvalt had taught Declan was for forging swords of the highest value, made only for the richest nobles. At that time Edvalt and Declan might have expected to make half a dozen or so in their lifetime. Now they planned to make a thousand such swords.

By sundown they were reaching the point along the Scorched Coast where the bluffs began to rise, and Declan turned the boat into shore. They should reach the island early the next morning.

Once they beached the boat, Declan unpacked food and a bottle of wine.

"No fire?" asked Sixto.

"Do we need one?" joked Mick Sawyer. The heat of the day was lingering: the Scorched Coast was a well-earned name.

The wine was uncorked and the bottle passed around. Toombs said, "I thank whatever gods thought of these hats." He took off a broad-brimmed hat woven from straw. "It provides good shade and the breeze sort of drifts through it. I'm taking this one back to Marquensas with me."

Jack Sawyer laughed. "It doesn't get that hot up there."

Toombs pointed a finger at Jack and in mock-accusatory tone said, "Listen, youngster, I've had enough sunburn to last me the rest of my life, and I plan on living a long time now that we're out of that hell." He glanced at Declan with an expression of silent gratitude. Turning to Sixto, he said, "Where'd that wine bottle go?"

Sixto chuckled and handed it over. Toombs took a good swallow, then passed the bottle to Mick. Declan lay back, arm behind his head, and wondered if the fight would ever end for him. Still, although the ocean breeze didn't bring much coolness, it did cut the dryness out of the air, and he had eaten well for weeks. As far as he was able to, he relaxed, and soon was asleep.

DECLAN WOKE AS THE HEAT of the sun seemed to wash over him, and he realized he was still in the shadow of the bluffs. He quickly roused the others and they pushed the boat back into the waves, raised the sail, and got underway.

In less than an hour the promontory he sought appeared in the distance, with the three ancient trees still dominating the skyline. He kept clear of the beach, but steered a course toward them, and an hour later they were close enough to where he would have been standing had he followed Edvalt's instructions to the letter. He brought the boat around and faced due south.

As Edvalt had promised, on the distant horizon he saw the island. A strong man could swim there in an hour, Edvalt had avowed, not that he could swim back again with the sand; but it took Declan and the others only minutes once they caught the wind. About a mile from the shore, Declan dropped the sail, and they secured the mast, then rowed.

They pulled into a small inlet, a sandy cove, rising to a grass-covered hillock. They got out and placed an anchor deeply in the sand against a possible rise in the tide.

"The north side," said Declan, pointing to the edge of the grass.

The Sawyers, Sixto, and Toombs each grabbed an empty box. "Why the north side, Declan?" asked Mick Sawyer. "Why not here?"

Declan said, "Look down and tell me what you see?"

"I see sand," Mick replied.

"It's not the right sand," said Declan.

Toombs and Jack Sawyer both laughed.

They marched for about ten minutes to reach a bend in the

island and were now on the north side. Declan led them a short distance, knelt, and picked up a handful of sand, letting it sift through his fingers. "Here."

Mick unstrapped a small spade he carried across his back like a bow. As he started filling a box, he asked, "All right, why *this* sand?"

"I'll tell you something few besides master smiths know, Mick," Declan replied. "The secret of turning iron to steel, the smelting, is to add something to the molten iron that adds to it, so it's stronger."

"Sand?" asked Mick as he quickly filled the first box.

"Sometimes," answered Declan. "Coal dust, limestone dust, other things. Do you know what's in sand?"

Mick paused for a moment and said, "In sand?" He looked down. "It's sand!"

The others laughed. Declan shook his head. "Sand is many things, often different things in different places. Silt and stones wash down from the mountains, waves wear down rocks of quartz or limestone to powder. The sea grinds the shells of crabs, fish, and other rocks like a mill grinding down wheat. It's different everywhere, so, look down. What do you see?"

Now Mick laughed. "Sand!"

"What is it like compared to the sand where we landed the boat?"

Mick stopped shoveling and knelt, duplicating what he had seen Declan do, grabbing a handful and inspecting it. After a moment he said, "It's . . . whiter, finer, less coarse?"

"There are legends among sword makers which are half myth, half true remembering, of great swordsmiths who had secrets that created what we call 'King's Steel.' Those secrets were lost," Declan said. "But how they were made is not lost. There are a

few ways to forge fine steel, but what was lost? The magic in-
gredient those masters used to create their steel." He pointed to
the sand at their feet. "What makes this sand the way it is, only
the gods know, but it will forge a blade that can cut through a
lesser blade like an axe through kindling. If it comes to pass that
I die, one of you can tell another master smith where this beach
of sand lies. And that secret will be passed on."

"You're not going to die soon," said Sixto, "unless I kill you
for making us lug these boxes back to the boat. Next time, how
about we put in over there!" With a lift of his chin, he indicated
a lovely little beach that would have been easy to land on.

Declan shrugged. "Take it up with Edvalt when we get back."

"Gladly," said Sixto, and everyone knew the prospect of returning to Marquensas was now looming on the horizon.

They hauled the boxes back to the boat. Once the boxes
were secured and the longboat shoved off, they turned north.
The day passed quickly and the night was uneventful, and by
noon on the next day they tacked back in and were greeted
by the sight of their ship with two newly installed masts.

They came into the harbor and when the sail was dropped,
Sixto looked at the ship and said, "We should name her."

Declan realized there was no name visible on either the stern
or bow. "I never thought of that. What do you think?"

Sixto laughed and Declan could see a strong emotion hidden
just below the surface as he said, "I think *Change of Luck* would
be appropriate."

Declan found his eyes welling and he wiped away the moisture
before it could fall as tears. "Find a painter and get it done."

When they reached the quay, they tied off the boat, where
Declan had the others carry the boxes aboard the newly named
Change of Luck, and he hurried back to the Old Guard.

At the door he saw men milling about outside, and when he pushed past to get inside, he saw Tobias frantically pouring mugs of ale.

Tobias handed the mugs to a very pretty girl, who smiled at Declan as she sashayed past him to take the mugs to a table of four men.

"What is this?" Declan asked.

Tobias pointed to Oscar and beckoned him over, then ushered Declan out of the back door. "Apparently, we're the first provisioned inn in Abala. So, with ale comes many customers."

"Where did you get the ale?"

"Garange, the provisioner, he said you bought everything coming in, so he delivered it here."

"Did you pay him?" Declan asked, half-infuriated, half-amused.

"Of course," said Tobias. "You left me in charge of the gold."

"Do I want to know what you paid?"

"Probably not," said the old fighter, "but a great deal of haggling was involved."

"Tell me we have enough provisions to sail back to Marquensas."

"You do," replied Tobias, "and more are coming soon. Did you get what you came for?"

"Yes," said Declan with a hint of relief. He looked around the inn, taking stock of the number of men inside and outside. "All of these are customers?"

"We have a thriving business, but no, most of these men want to join you."

"Join me?"

"For Baron Daylon's army. We spread the word and you know how fighters get when they're drinking and swapping lies. There's little future here for a mercenary with the nomads on a rampage.

Everyone who can afford guards hired them, and the rest are broke, hungry, and looking for work."

"How many?" Declan asked.

"What you see."

Declan did a quick estimate and said, "Looks like a hundred men."

"And there are more camped outside the gate and scattered through the rest of Abala."

"How many?" asked Declan again.

"I'm guessing," said Tobias, "but a thousand swords or more."

Declan looked stunned and put out his hand to steady himself at the door. "A thousand?"

"I'm guessing," Tobias repeated.

"We're going to need more provisions," said Declan. Then he took a deep breath. "And we're going to need more ships."

"Garange will want you to marry his daughter, if he has one, before you get away," Tobias said with a chuckle.

19

SHARING KNOWLEDGE,

PREPARATIONS, AND CHOICES

———+———

Hava watched from across the street, while men and women stumbled in and out of the inn. It was where Red Sweeney had told her she had the best chance of finding her mark. She hid herself in the shadows between two buildings opposite an alley where Red Sweeney said men would go to piss if they didn't want to wait for the two outhouses in the back to be available. Even from here, Hava knew she had the right inn and alley. In this warm weather, the ammonia-like reek was noticeable.

She had begun to think of the Azhante as two distinct and different units, comprising a leadership class, like Coaltachin's Quelli Nascosti, formed of master spies and assassins, and those below, more common soldiers, though these were also well trained and deadly. Her plan to single out a suitable Azhante would depend on finding one who was like Sepisolema and Firash, eager to cast off the Pride Lords' control.

At last she saw an Azhante come out of the inn, look around, and move toward the alley across from her position. He didn't stagger, but instead moved with that carefully purposeful walk of someone working hard not to appear drunk.

She had positioned two of Red Sweeney's young smugglers behind the building, just out of view of the alley, who wouldn't move until Hava signaled. She was garbed like a street prostitute in a red blouse with a low neck and a tight, mid-calf black skirt. She missed her boots, for she now wore woven sandals, but the disguise was necessary in case anyone questioned why she was lingering around the inn. Since she had arrived at dusk, no one even spared her a glance.

A moment after her target disappeared, she scurried across the street and peered down the alley. In the deep gloom, she could barely make out the silhouette of the man swaying slightly as he pissed against the wall. The reek of urine made Hava's eyes water. She wondered if these people had ever heard of slit trenches next to their outhouses.

When the young Azhante was finished, and tying up his trousers, she said in a clear voice, "Looking for fun?" Given the mix of accents on Nytanny, she had practiced speaking clearly, without hesitation.

She got the desired reaction: the young man turned and saw her outlined against the light from the inn's streetlamp. He smiled. "Fun?"

"What do you need, handsome?"

He started to move toward her and said, "How much?" just as Red Sweeney's two burly lads came up on quiet feet from behind. One struck him hard enough to stun him without breaking anything, hopefully, and the other grabbed him to prevent him from falling facedown into the very nasty mud.

In less than a minute they were gone from the street, down another alley to a waiting cart and on their way back to the smugglers' warehouse in Braci.

The warehouse was currently empty as all smuggling had more

or less come to an end during the attack on North Tembria and was now also slowed due to Hava's predations of Azhante shipping. Red Sweeney waited with two other men while Macaulish's grandson Michael waited with horses.

The plan was simple: to get what information they could from this captive, and if it was what Hava hoped to hear, let him return to the inn, and if it wasn't what she hoped to hear, leave him dead in the piss-pooled alley, the victim of a simple robbery. Red Sweeney was of the opinion the Azhante would make a show of questioning people but wouldn't be too offended by one of their own being stupid enough to get himself killed outside an inn.

They tied the young man down in a heavy chair, then one of the men threw a pail of water at him. He revived, slowly and still drunk, and confused by the blow to the head.

When his wits returned, he realized he was a prisoner in a room lit by a single lamp, the shutter opened in his direction with everyone else in darkness. He said something in what Hava assumed was the local language, not the Azhante tongue.

As she had instructed, no one spoke.

The captured Azhante spoke again, his tone threatening as he tried to see through the gloom to make out who had captured him. Again, his demands were met by silence.

As he started to raise his voice even more, Hava stepped forward where he could see her and put her fingers to his lips, while holding up her right index finger before her own, making a shushing sound.

His eyes widened and he was on the verge of saying something else, when she put more pressure on his face, forcing his head backward in a manner that was uncomfortable but not yet painful.

He fell silent.

In her own native version of the local dialect she said, "Azhante."

In the Azhante dialect he said, "Let me go!"

She said nothing but smiled at him.

"What do you want?"

Again, silence.

After a few moments of demanding to be released, his tone changed and he said, "Let me go and I will stay silent. No one needs to know you've assaulted an Azhante."

Hava stayed silent but kept smiling.

He promised again to stay silent, but his tone became slightly more frantic.

Hava realized at this point that whatever else was different between the Azhante schools and Coaltachin's, this young man had no training in questioning a captive or resisting interrogation if captured. All students in Coaltachin were thus trained, as how well you performed was an important part of advancing to further training in the Quelli Nascosti. She had seen many students sent away from school to work as street criminals for crews because they had failed the early tests. She was now certain that the Pride Lords only wanted their most loyal servants to be more than disposable soldiers, what she heard characterized as "fodder for the wall."

After more pleading and threatening, the prisoner fell silent. Hava let a few moments pass, then looked past the captive at Red Sweeney, and asked, "Local boy?"

Red Sweeney nodded. Hava had given strict instructions that she be the only one to speak. If this small adventure went askew, she wanted to be the only person the captive could identify. She had made sure they knew it was her first priority that no one else be identified, one way or another.

Softly she said, "Local boy, what is your name?"

He swallowed hard and licked his lips, then said, "Dahod."

She turned and walked out of his field of view, paused a moment, then returned with a large cup of water.

"Thirsty?"

He nodded, and Hava lifted the cup to his lips and let him drink.

When he had finished, she again returned to a table out of his line of sight and paused. One of her early lessons in interrogation had been to avoid patterns: routines become reassuring, predictable, and that was dangerous. She waited long enough that he might think she had left and then she returned.

She saw what she had hoped to see, a flicker of relief at her coming back into his field of view. As she had been taught, the unknown is far more frightening than possibilities of harm. A runaway imagination was far more effective than threats if there was enough time. Anticipation was more terrifying than a beating. She had let him learn that if they were talking, he was not being tortured.

"Do you serve with joy?" she asked softly. As she had expected, his expression revealed he had no idea as to the context of the question.

He said nothing, lost in confusion.

"Do you serve the Pride Lords with joy in your heart?" she said, expanding the context. "Would you die to serve them?"

His eyes widened and Hava suspected he was wondering if this was some sort of test. Without any conviction in his words, he said, "If I am to die . . ." He looked to be on the verge of tears. He swallowed hard. "I die willingly."

Hava paused, then again stepped beyond his vision. She let that answer hang in the air but came back into his sight far more quickly than before, to break the pattern.

Kneeling once more, she asked, "Do you serve with joy?"

The color seemed to be draining from his face by the second, and she knew the answer without him speaking. Yet she understood this had to run its course.

"Do you serve with joy?"

As she had hoped, his confusion grew and he glanced around as if trying again to see who was lurking in the dark. His expression had now gone from fearful confusion to terror.

Dahod's eyes watered. "I serve! I . . . I'm sorry, I should not have gone to the inn. I will never do it again. Please, don't hurt my family. I'll serve with joy! I will do whatever—" His voice broke and he began to sob.

Hava took a deep breath then nodded to Red Sweeney and the others to step outside with her. She looked from face to face and said, "I'd hardly call this boy a fanatic."

Sweeney said, "He became an Azhante to save his family from slaughter." He looked genuinely disgusted. "I hated the Pride Lords before, but seeing that lad pissing himself and trying not to fall apart because he loves his parents, brothers, sisters . . . it's poisonous."

Hava took a deep breath. "I have no problem with killing a man who deserves it, and take no joy from that, but this?" She pointed through the door to the warehouse. "If there's anyone who deserves a slow, agonizing death, it's the Pride Lords."

She beckoned the others to follow her back inside, took a deep breath and then returned to where Dahod could see her.

She leaned close to the now-terrified Azhante. Looking into his face, she realized she was probably a bit younger than he was, yet she thought of him as still a boy. She gave his shoulder a gentle squeeze and said, "No one will harm you or your family."

He looked at her face in the dim light as if fearing this was another trick.

She just stared at him for a long moment, then added, "We are coming to help you."

"Who?" he asked, trying to regain some composure.

"We are coming to free you."

"Who is?" he asked.

"We are."

He again looked around the room in vain.

At last he caught his breath and in a calmer voice softly asked, "Who are you?"

"We are Coaltachin," she replied quietly.

His eyes widened and an expression of doubt and wonder crossed his face, then he closed his eyes and suddenly began to cry like a baby, his body racked with sobs.

Hava nodded, and the men began slowly moving to where the horses waited outside. Red Sweeney stayed behind, while Hava let Dahod cry himself out, and when he regained his wits, she said, "We will now let you go. Speak to no one of this but know there are others like yourself who have been told of our coming. We mean to free our lost brothers and end the Pride Lords. I will send someone here in a week's time. Will you serve us?"

Overwhelmed by emotions, he could barely speak. He nodded and whispered, "Yes, on my life."

Red Sweeney came from behind and put a blindfold over his eyes and began untying the ropes that bound Dahod. Hava helped the young man to stand. He was no longer intoxicated, but he was still shaky.

She said, "Say nothing, but when I leave you, wait until you hear horses ride off, and then remove the blindfold. Can you return in a week?"

"Yes," he said, his voice barely above a whisper.

"Then return to the inn, but do not go inside. Across from

the inn is an alley. Someone will be waiting for you there. Say nothing more."

She led him out of the warehouse and down the long avenue, then to the right up another, and doubled back, and then led him around the block. She patted his shoulder and slipped away.

Reaching the warehouse, she passed through a red door. There she found Red Sweeney and the others waiting with the horses.

Red Sweeney said, "That was a bit of work. I'd have just beaten it out of him."

As she swung up into the saddle, Hava vividly recalled when she had first come to her school. "They take them from their mothers when they're still children. Some grow up hard, unbreakable. Those are the tough ones. The rest? Some become men, and some stay children. A woman's soft touch reminds them of their mothers."

"Are there others like him?"

Hava took a deep breath as she sat back in the saddle. "There will be. We have to start somewhere."

"If it didn't work?"

"I'd have cut his throat," said Hava calmly.

Red Sweeney said, "It worked."

"Throat-cutting or beatings are hard ways to make friends," she replied, turning her mount.

As they rode off in the direction that would lead them back to the smugglers' village she said, "And before we're through, we're going to need a lot of friends."

HATU WAS LEANING BACK IN a chair, half-dozing, when Bodai entered the library. He pulled out another chair and the scraping sound brought Hatu back from the edge of sleep.

"Need a nap?" asked Bodai with a jocular note. It was less than an hour after they had had their morning meal.

"No, it was this book," Hatu replied, pointing to a volume bound in leather.

"That boring?"

"Quite the opposite." Hatu sat up and shook himself alert. He held up the book, and Bodai could see it was tall and wide, but slim. "It's all handwritten by a scribe or perhaps some user of 'magic' by the name of . . ." He opened the cover to look at the thin vellum, and said, "Kondroc, whoever he may be. The language is Direl, and I have no idea where people who speak that tongue reside." He sat back and for a moment thought hard, then burst out, "I'm an idiot!"

"No doubt," joked Bodai. "What?"

"Where are we?"

"The Sanctuary," replied Bodai. "You know, these questions you know the answers to get annoying."

Hatu laughed. "And where do you think Hava and I and every other student learned that annoying trick?"

Bodai sat back, his expression slightly crestfallen, and quietly said, "Oh."

Hatu swept his hand in a theatrical gesture. "And what massive piece of land lies over there?"

"Nytanny," answered Bodai.

"And how many nations . . . ?"

"Hundreds," said Bodai, now laughing. "Of course, before the relocation of the Flame Guard to Ithrace, we would have come across books and papers written by the scholars of Nytanny."

"Yes," agreed Hatu.

"So, what is special about this one?"

"As I read, at first nothing made sense. In fact, I thought this might be a book of codes, for most of the words here are nonsense in any language I have read and, as you know, at this point that is a lot of languages."

"True."

"At first I thought it was gibberish. And then I thought perhaps if I read it aloud, it might make sense. As soon as I started on this page . . . I felt something, a sensation I only experience when working with Nathan, when trying to understand how I interact with the furies.

"So, I tried reading at the same time as letting my mind slip into the state I use when training and I saw . . ." He closed the book and put it on the table. "I don't know what I saw."

Bodai said, "I wish I could understand, but I don't."

"All those lines of energy I see, between opposing furies, from small creatures to aspects of nature, there are more!" said Hatu, excitedly. "There are things out there that are . . . invisible! Things I can't name, but I can sense them. When I caused the rockslide that saved Declan, I was using a massive hammer." He waved his hand. "That's not what it was, but how it felt. When I sensed the presence of life force, Nathan warned me not to touch it, for I could cause harm by the slightest contact. That tickled like a tiny hair falling from a child's head to land on your arm." He shook his head. "Less than that. But this . . ." He paused and looked intently at Bodai. "This is so much finer. It is the tiniest grain of dust beside a mountain!" Hatu took a deep breath. "But the number of them . . . they're countless. They are everywhere."

"Fascinating," said Bodai. "I saw a little of what you saw when I joined you and Nathan. I don't pretend to understand what you're seeing, feeling, able to do, but just from what you said I am coming to believe that we understand very little of what there is to know."

Hatu smiled. "That's only part of it. There are lines of

combined forces, like twisted fibers of a massive rope, and they are countless, entire collections, spanning distances I can't imagine!"

"And the book?" asked Bodai.

"As I read aloud, I could feel powers rise up and begin to cause the lines to . . . vibrate differently, to . . . hum?"

"I wonder," said Bodai. "Could it be some missing part of discovering your powers?"

"Maybe," said Hatu.

A voice from behind the long bookcase said, "It's a book of magic spells."

Both Hatu and Bodai turned in their chairs as Nathan returned to the library. He looked tired, and he sported what appeared to be several recent bruises on his face.

"Nathan!" Hatu exclaimed, standing up. "Are you all right?"

"I've been better. It's a long walk getting back," Nathan replied, then sat heavily in the seat Hatu had just vacated. He looked bone-tired. "I could use a drink."

"What?"

"Wine, ale, whisky if you have it."

"We have some, I'm sure," said Hatu, and he headed toward the kitchen.

Bodai looked at Nathan. "Do I even ask?"

With a wave of his hand, Nathan said, "There is much to discuss, but wait until Hatu gets back."

Hatu returned, a large black bottle in one hand, three mugs held by the handles in the other. He set them down and said, "I found this whisky from I don't know where."

"Thank you," said Nathan. He poured a tall measure, took a long swallow, then squinched his eyes tightly and shook his head. "Ohh, that's a nasty batch."

"Something wrong?" asked Hatushaly.

"How that was made, yes. Otherwise, pour me another," said Nathan.

Hatu obliged, and Nathan took another drink, but didn't quite empty the mug.

"Where have you been?" asked Bodai.

"Traveling to meet with people who know a lot more than I do, seeking help with what you are facing."

"Facing?" Hatu looked uncertain.

"One thing at a time," suggested Nathan. He motioned for Hatu to hand him the book. Hatu complied and Nathan opened it, looked at a page, then flipped to another. "This page you were reading, it's a simple spell, to start a fire."

"A spell to start a fire?" echoed Hatushaly.

"I went to visit some very old acquaintances who understand this 'magic' business far better than I. To me, what you've discovered as a function of your nature is somehow tied together in intricate ways to everything else." He took a sip of whisky.

Hatu looked lost. "So, what I'm doing is magic? True magic?"

"Powers, skills, whatever you want to call it. Manipulating the very stuff of the universe." Nathan leaned forward, and before Hatu could ask about the bruises, continued, "People have a way of looking at things, and they love putting names to everything, to organize and . . ." He took a breath, then another sip. "How things are related, one to another, it's very human to do that. How living things are related one to another, what is called a taxonomy. So how close are sheep to goats, oxen to cattle, big fish to tiny fish—there are people who spend their lives organizing that type of information.

"Magic is what people have organized from observing things like you do, or at least they think it's organized. This book," he said, handing back the volume to Hatu, "shows a set of sounds, nonsense words, that trigger the ability of someone with power to start a fire. I suggest you try it outside, if you must. There are systems of magic that need constructions, devices, mixtures of various ingredients into potions, trinkets fashioned as charms."

He exhaled slowly and seemed to relax a bit as the whisky took hold.

"Remember what I told you about elemental magic, natural magic, blood magic, and the rest?"

Hatu nodded.

"There's a person I've known a long time who would call what's in that spell book 'Greater Magic.'"

"Greater?" echoed Bodai.

Nathan nodded. "You memorize that spell, as you might a recipe, and once you have it firmly in mind, at any time thereafter, you simple mutter those words, with perhaps a gesture or two to focus what you're thinking, and *poof*, a flame appears where you want it."

Hatu smiled. "That would prove handy when traveling and having to sleep outside for the night."

"Undoubtedly," said Nathan. "Though I suspect you do not need to memorize it."

"Really?"

"After what I saw you do to save Declan? I'm almost certain." Nathan was silent for a moment, then said, "Put out your right hand, palm up."

Hatu did as he was asked.

"Close your eyes."

Hatu closed his eyes.

"Now, imagine there's a thin covering of invisible armor coating your palm. And on that protected palm a little flame, the size of my thumb, comes into existence."

Nathan sat back and finished off the whisky in his mug. He motioned for the bottle, and Bodai handed it to him. As Nathan poured another drink, they both saw Hatu's body shift in position and suddenly a tiny flame began dancing on the palm of his hand.

Bodai opened his mouth, but a cautionary gesture from Nathan kept him from speaking.

Nathan said quietly, "Now, stay relaxed and open your eyes."

Hatu did and his eyes widened, and suddenly the flame began to get larger, and Nathan said, "Close your hand and put the flame out."

Hatu did and the flame was gone. Then his entire manner changed, and he laughed. "That was wonderful!" he said.

Bodai could only silently nod.

"So, some people use spells, or devices," began Hatu, "but if I just clear my mind, I can make things happen. What do the people who can do this call this type of magic?"

Nathan sat back, took another deep drink, and said, "I have no idea."

"Really?" asked Hatu. "Why?"

"Because you're the only person I've ever met who could do that."

"READY?" ASKED DECLAN.

Sixto turned and waved to the ship behind *Change of Luck*, the *Brigida*, which had sheltered in the islands after the raid. That captain was more than happy to return to North Tembria and had accepted the payment to carry back as many fighters as he could pack aboard. Three other ships had also been procured, to Garange's utter delight. Between the found gold and bartered goods from *Change of Luck* he was probably now the wealthiest merchant in Abala.

Declan heard Sixto say, "All ready." He looked at the ship's captain and nodded.

The captain began barking orders and the anchor was lifted, the sails lowered, and the makeshift fleet was underway.

"It'll be good to go back," said Sixto.

"I never took you to be a man attached to a place," said Declan.

"Not since I was old enough to shave," admitted Sixto. "But I've had enough of this place."

Declan walked over to the rear railing, gripping it as Abala receded, while the ships moved away from the harbor, seeking fair winds. "One stop for water, and then back to Marquensas," he said.

"We said farewell to some good men," said Sixto as he came to stand at Declan's side.

"Brothers," Declan said softly.

"So I name them," agreed Sixto.

After a few moments of silence, Sixto went on, "One day you'll come to understand what you've done, Captain. There are men on these ships who will gladly die for you, because they owe you their lives, and every moment from then to now is a gift of life they otherwise would not know."

Declan stood quietly, then said, "I only did what Bogartis asked, save as many as I could."

"As I said," Sixto replied. "One day you'll understand."

20

INFORMATION EXCHANGED,

PLANNING, AND DECISIONS

—✦—

"Twenty-five days," said Hava. "*Queen of Storms* is the fastest ship anyone has seen, and with a few extra hands, I can make it in twenty-five days to Marquensas if the wind's fair. If it's against us, thirty, maybe forty. A week or so to refit, have a talk with the baron and Balven, find out what the next step is, and then come back."

"So, three, maybe four months?" asked Hatu. He found himself feeling at cross purposes. He hadn't realized how much he had missed Hava until she'd appeared, so distracted had he been by his studies. Nathan's return and the discovery that he could do things unknown to Nathan further amplified his eagerness to continue exploring his powers. So Hava talking about leaving again bothered him a great deal more than he would have anticipated.

"We have a limited opportunity," she said. "We don't know how long it will last."

"I understand," said Hatu. He sat on their bed as she got dressed, ready for another day of overseeing the refitting of her ships for the next voyages.

"I am impressed with how much work has been done here,"

she said in a cheerful tone. "The library looks amazing, and the restoration of the outer buildings is . . . surprising."

She had sailed in at sunset the night before, and between bathing, eating, making love, and sleep, there hadn't been a great deal of time to share their plans. Hatu recognized that she'd made up her mind what she needed to do next in this campaign to overthrow the Pride Lords and avenge the destruction of everything they prized back in Beran's Hill.

Hava glanced at Hatu as she finished dressing and said, "You coming?"

He realized he'd just been sitting on the edge of the bed, thinking, and nodded. Putting on his tunic and trousers, he said, "What about Catharian? He didn't come back with you?"

"He's staying with the smugglers." She had given Hatu a brief summation of what she'd accomplished so far.

"Why?"

"He's learning as much of what passes for Azhante as possible." She waited while Hatu put on his sandals, then as they left their quarters, added, "One thing Catharian knows is how to infiltrate and blend in. The Coaltachin language is probably the only one in the Twins he doesn't speak, major language, anyway."

Hatu had to agree. When he had first met Catharian, the false monk had shown no discernible accent to betray his origins.

"If that boy Dahod honors his pledge, sometime tomorrow Catharian should be getting the information he needs to wend his way toward the Pride Lords' city, Akena. I'm going to bring those other two Azhante back with me, unless the baron objects." She shrugged. "Not sure why he would."

They reached the dining hall, which was also benefiting from repairs and a cleanup. The long makeshift table had been replaced by a well-carpentered, massive buffet table immediately adjacent to a cleared passage to the kitchen, making it easier for the kitchen crew to provide food, and another passage was being cleaned that led to a terrace overlooking the sea, which would provide a wonderful place to dine outside when the weather permitted.

"What about Donte?" asked Hatu as they carried their food to a free table. "Think he'll want to come?"

Hava laughed. "Probably, but I don't know if the baron would permit that."

"Why?"

"Let's say his status is hovering somewhere between guest and prisoner."

Hatu laughed. "That's Donte. Still, another person from Coaltachin could be very helpful."

They sat down and Hatu said, "Back to Catharian. Is he going to be able to get you the information you need?"

"He's well trained in spycraft," said Hava as she started to eat. "As I said, he's the sneakiest bastard not trained in Coaltachin I've ever met."

Hatu nodded in agreement.

Hava asked, "What about you? This training you've been doing. Is it getting you anywhere?"

Hatu held up his right hand and pointed his index finger upward. Abruptly a flame was dancing on the tip. Hava froze, a spoonful of boiled grain meal halfway to her mouth. She stared for a moment, then Hatu let the flame go out.

"Oh," she said. "I see."

Hatu could tell she was surprised and maybe even a little put off by the display. "Sorry," he said, "I couldn't resist showing off."

"No, it's all right," she said. "I was just surprised." After a moment, she asked, "What else can you do?"

He suddenly realized that in the scant time they had had

together since he had come to the Sanctuary he had never fully discussed what he was learning. He put down his spoon and said, "It's hard to explain. The fire trick is one of the few things I can do to show other people. Most of it is studying things . . . that are hard to explain." He could see she was genuinely interested, so he continued. "Let me try to put it this way, everything"—he made a sweeping motion with his right hand—"I mean *everything* is connected to everything else in ways that almost no one can see. Think of it as tiny threads, in a gigantic loom . . ." And he tried to help her understand.

For almost an hour he explained and answered her questions, though he still avoided disclosing the help he had given Declan. For some reason he was uncomfortable revealing even to Hava that level of his power. After he had answered her last question, she said, "This is hard to understand, though I thank you for taking the time. I remember that blue light we saw during our first passage through the Narrows, and I always thought that it was . . . part of something bigger." She stood up and started gathering up her dishes. "I think whatever you have in store is maybe not the same thing I face in aiding the overthrow of this powerful gang."

Hatu smiled as he also rose and gathered dishes. Only a child of Coaltachin would look at a ruling class like the Pride Lords and think of them as a "gang."

"I think there's a relationship between our different tasks," Hatu said. "I just don't know what it is, yet."

"Well, if you find out let me know," she said, kissing his cheek. "I have a ship to refit, and you have your studies. I'll try to be finished by supper."

He watched her walk off. For a moment he was again gripped by uncertainty about where all this was leading them, but he decided to push away that worry and turn his attention to matters closer to hand. Leaving the dining hall, he headed for the library.

DECLAN GLANCED UP AT THE lookout. Then he left the poop deck, crossed the main deck, and climbed to the forecastle deck from where he could see three ships sitting at anchor.

Earlier that day his squadron had rounded the westernmost point of South Tembria and was now sailing eastward along the coast, looking for a place to fill their water barrels. They would also buy provisions if they could find some. Declan estimated they could reach Marquensas with what they had, but it would be nice to add fresh food to the stores.

"Any signal?" he shouted now to the lookout.

"I see a parley flag being waved from the bow!" came the reply.

Declan turned to the ship's captain. While the original crews had been culled by the raiders, there were enough surviving sailors and mercenaries with shipboard experience that Declan had managed to crew all five ships. Declan shouted, "Bring her alongside!"

The ship's captain shouted back, "There are five of us, three of them, and we have enough swords in hand that I don't think they intend to board us. I can anchor alongside."

He started shouting orders and the sails were reefed, and the other ships behind bore to port in order to pass by slowly.

When Declan's ship was as close as was comfortable, the captain had the anchor dropped.

Declan shouted, "You seek parley?"

From the closest ship came a reply: "Where are you bound?"

"To Marquensas to join the baron's fleet. Where are you bound?"

"Can I come aboard?"

Declan shouted back, "Come aboard!"

A longboat was lowered from the other ship, and by the time it had arrived alongside the *Change of Luck* they had lowered a rope ladder over the side. Declan saw a youngish man top the ladder, then hop over the railing. He was dressed in a simple white tunic and blue trousers, and his feet were bare.

"You the captain?" asked Declan.

"Yes," said the young man. "Name's Kean. I was the mate, but the captain got killed when some pirates tried to ambush us."

"I'm Declan and the man up there's the captain, but I command this squadron."

"So you're bound for Marquensas?"

"Yes, we have a commission from the baron."

"We got trapped between the pirates and the fleet from Zindaros." Kean pointed to the other two ships. "We're traders, but we have no port. We put in here for food and water, and we have nowhere else to go." He appeared to be at the end of his wits, and he looked at Declan as if expecting an answer.

"What cargo do you carry?"

"I don't know, but it must be worth defending, as our owner put extra guards aboard."

"On all three ships?"

"No, just this one; the other two are from different owners and I have no idea what cargo they're carrying. We're just trying to stay out of harm's way and been too busy to look at what we carry."

Sixto was at Declan's side, and nudged him. "Bring them along, what harm can it do?"

Declan turned to Kean, "Is there water there?" he asked, pointing toward the port.

"Yes," Kean said.

To Sixto, Declan said, "Get the water barrels ashore and see what stores we can buy."

To Kean, Sixto said, "I'm taking your gig. I'll be back soon." It wasn't a request. He shouted for some sailors to bring the empty water barrels to the rail and others to rig a sling to lower them to Kean's longboat.

Kean nodded. "I have cargo and nowhere to land it."

"You'll do well to come with us. Whatever you have, I dare say the baron will buy it."

Kean shrugged his acceptance. His expression revealed that he was both relieved and already curious about the cargo, as the crew would be splitting whatever was paid for it.

Sixto returned after less than an hour, and the fresh water was brought aboard. Kean went back to his ship. He assured Declan that all three ships would join his flotilla and follow them to Marquensas. Whatever cargo they might be carrying was immaterial because Declan knew the baron would need ships for his planned invasion.

It was a beautiful day, clear blue skies, a light breeze, not too hot or humid: the sort of day that made him want to give up all conflict and strife. It would be wonderful to just find a quiet place to live with fishing and hunting nearby, watching sunsets from a beach, a life without worry.

He let that dream go and turned his attention to the matters at hand. Soon, water barrels were being ferried to the shore and in a while, they would again be underway.

Declan examined the shoreline again, taking in the ships at anchor and the rest of his own small flotilla changing course to idle while they waited. He let the breeze caress his face and the sun warm his back and shoulders, while he fixed this moment in his memory. He knew he would have few moments like this in the future, so he would savor this one now.

HAVA ENTERED HER AND HATU's quarters to find him sitting on the bed, apparently lost in thought. "There you are," she said. "I thought I'd find you still in the library when I didn't see you in the kitchen."

"Not hungry," he said, then turned to look at her. "How's the refitting?"

"We'll be ready to sail tomorrow, so I'll be leaving the day after."

He shifted and sat on the edge of the bed. "I wonder if we're getting too used to being apart," he said.

"What's that supposed to mean?" she asked, sitting down next to him. "We've had times apart before, but at least this time I'm not worried if you're still alive." She put her arms around his shoulders and said, "When Catharian, Denbe, and Sabella took you, I had no idea if you were dead or on a slave ship."

He reached up and gently touched her face.

"I looked for you, and I found you." Then she kissed him.

He put his arms around her and hugged her tight. "It's easy for me to forget all you went through, because I was just here, looking at books. I suppose I thought you'd be with the baron, so you'd be safe." Then he smiled. "I had no idea you'd do such a foolish thing as to come after me in the middle of an invasion!"

"It all worked out," she said. "Neither of us can change the past."

"Still, I worry about the future," said Hatu. "Neither of us has to leave here unless we want to."

"I feel obliged," said Hava. "You were taken before you saw

the worst of it. Only Molly Bowman and Declan Smith survived among our friends."

"Speaking of Molly, she's been gone a long time," said Hatu.

"There's a lot of game on some of these islands and we have a lot of mouths to feed," replied Hava. "Besides, I think she's finally taken a lover."

"Finally?" Then his eyes widened. "You mean . . . ?"

"She never had time, looking after her da," said Hava, nodding.

"Who?"

"Big burly fellow, who does remind me a bit of her father, and he's a hunter, too. He just took to her the moment he saw her, and finally wore her down, I guess. His name is Luke."

"Well, good for Molly," Hatu said. "I wonder how Declan fares?" He felt a little awkward saying this, knowing what he knew.

"I dare say I'll find out when I get to Marquensas," she answered. Then she looked at him with a concerned expression. "I wonder how *you* are faring? You look worried."

He tried to shrug it off. "It's my habit to worry."

"No, this is something else, what?"

He sighed. "One of the things I've learned from Nathan is how to follow those lines of force I've spoken of, and apparently there's something at the end of one that's a danger."

"How do you mean?" she asked.

"I'm not sure. I was hoping Nathan might help me discover what it is, but he keeps angling me away from the subject to concentrate on the other abilities he thinks I have . . ." He saw her expression change and said, "What?"

"You speak of these abilities . . ." Her demeanor altered and she seemed to slump a bit. "It's just I really don't comprehend any of it. You've been to sea, you know how to crew a ship, so when I tell you what I've been doing, you understand. But when you tell me what you and Bodai and that fellow Nathan are doing . . ." Her expression turned to one of resignation. "I will never understand."

Hatu was silent for a long moment, looking into her eyes, then he said softly, "I can show you."

"Show me what?" It came out as almost a whisper.

"What I see, what I . . . do."

After a pause, she said, "All right."

"Close your eyes," he said, and he put his arms around her. "Relax and know nothing bad will happen."

She hesitated for a moment, then closed her eyes and laid her head on Hatu's shoulder.

Suddenly it was as if they were both together in a void, floating with nothing in sight but each other; then a thrumming vibration seemed to run through their bodies, and brightly colored scintillating lines resembling a massive loom appeared at their feet.

"What is that?" Hava asked.

"Those are some of the lines of energy that lie between positive and negative furies."

"Furies?"

"Little . . . points of . . . something. I don't know what. But the tension between them, positive and negative, creates these lines. This is a tiny part of the fabric of everything, a little piece of the universe laid bare."

"Why so many colors?"

"I think it's how my mind is beginning to see the differences between forces: animals, plants, the very rocks themselves."

"Rocks have energy?"

"Everything does, Hava. Everything, and one day I will know what all of this means."

He let some lines fall away and brought others into her perception and let her feel what he felt at that moment, that somehow there was a harmony to the entire universe, but it was just too vast for even the most accomplished mind to comprehend.

"Now let me show you something I discovered recently."

Instantly they seemed to be floating in the night sky. Below was the roof of their quarters a short distance from the dome of the library. "How—?" Hava began.

"It's an illusion," said Hatu. "I can do it, but I can't truly explain how I do it. Some lines of energy are connected to things I can . . . not control, but take advantage of, especially when they're close to where we really are, which is below, on the bed."

"But it feels so real!" Hava's tone showed that she was clearly more excited than she had been by the view of the energy threads.

"Look up!"

She did so and abruptly it felt as if they were flying upward at a dizzying speed. "Oh!" she exclaimed.

"Remember, this isn't real." He paused then said, "Rather it is real, but we're still sitting on the bed. It's our minds that are free to fly up like this. Now, look."

Hava again looked up, and Hatu could feel her awe. Alone at sea, at night, the stars were a blanket of lights, and to the north if she sailed far enough, lights danced in the sky. But nothing she had seen before compared to this. A thousand times more stars than she had ever seen blazed across the arc of the sky and sprinkled between them were iridescent clouds of bright gas, of copper and blue, or pulsing with light of their own.

"It's wonderful," she said.

Suddenly they were back on the bed and for a moment she held him tight. Then she pulled back and said, "Thank you. I may never truly understand what it is you are doing, but I see the . . . beauty of it."

"Now you see why I want to know more."

She smiled broadly. "You've *always* wanted to know more, ever since you were a child."

They both laughed.

"One more day," he said with a hint of regret.

"Still not hungry?" Hava said teasingly as she began unbuttoning his shirt.

He laughed and jumped up to close the door.

"SAILS AHEAD!" SHOUTED THE LOOKOUT and Declan left the captain's side and hurried to the bow. They had been sailing along the northern coast of the Marquensas peninsula and had noticed a lot more activity than when they had left, months before. At least a dozen ships were anchored off the coast as they neared the port of Toranda.

Declan saw no sign of any conflict and yet experienced an unexpected jolt of worry. He realized that so much of how he looked at things now was the residue of what seemed like endless conflict, and the way he had felt before losing Gwen was a fading memory.

A flicker of blue caught his eye and as they neared the city they saw a newly erected tor, atop which flew a banner.

Sixto came up beside him. "The baron's been busy."

"Apparently so," agreed Declan. "Looks like Marquensas has a banner."

"I thought only kingdoms flew those," said Sixto.

Declan chuckled ruefully. "Are there any kingdoms left?"

"At least one, it seems."

A white parley flag was being waved, so Declan had Sixto send word to the captain that they needed to stop. As they dropped anchor, Sixto returned and Declan said, "Have the others heave to, until we find out what is happening."

As the other ships came up, one of the sailors half-hung over the *Change of Luck*'s rear railing and shouted instructions, which were passed along in turn.

The last ship was slowing as a boat was rowed from the tor to the ship. As there was no rope ladder, the messenger had to shimmy up a dropped line, but he did so with no difficulty.

"Who's in charge?" he asked as he climbed up onto the deck. He was a young man dressed in common work clothes. The stone dust on them suggested that the tor wouldn't be finished for quite some time.

"I am," said Declan.

Seeing that there were several fighters coming up on deck, the messenger said, "Is your name Bogartis?"

"He's dead, I'm captain now," said Declan.

"Is your name Declan?"

"Yes."

A look of relief came over the youngster's face. "I am glad to hear that. This is perhaps the tenth ship I've had to row out looking for you."

"Why?"

"You're not to put in here. There's a new port being built up at North Point, and the king wants you there."

"King? The baron's now a king?" asked Sixto.

"A week and some days since. The proclamation went out, and Baron Bavangine is sworn in as his oathman, and has been put in charge of Port Calos. Some of the nobles from Ilcomen have become his oathmen, too. Lots of things changing since the raid."

"Anything else?"

"No, just you're to go to North Point as soon as you can."

"Very well."

The messenger stood awkwardly for a moment, then gave a clumsy salute, turned, and shimmied back down to the waiting rowing boat.

"So, we're serving a king now," said Sixto.

"Other than a title and a whole lot more land to govern, I don't expect much else will have changed. When we get back, we'll get the new men settled, and then I'll return to doing what I do best: making swords."

Sixto said, "If you make swords better than you fight, my friend, they must be exquisite blades."

"They will be," Declan said quietly.

His mind turned once more to the fact that the precious sand he needed had been bought with precious blood.

21

UPHEAVALS, OBVIOUS AND SUBTLE,

AND HIDDEN CHANGES

As the morning sun rose above the eastern foothills, Declan saw a signalman furiously waving a flag from the top of the tor. From his gestures, Declan assumed he was being instructed to berth his ships in this wide new harbor they were still dredging. He waved back and hurried to the captain. "We're putting in here, apparently."

He could see North Point in the distance. Major construction had been going on. By the look of it, the workers who were still dredging the small bay would eventually double the size of the harbor. North Point tor was the lookout for a fortress that was being built overlooking the harbor. In the distance Declan could see buildings had sprouted up nearby, and he imagined in years to come that this would be Marquenet's closest major port. One day North Point would be a city.

If this new kingdom survived.

The captain had the orders passed back to the other ships. A distant figure waved from a newly erected dock on the other side of the harbor, just as Sixto arrived and said, "Looks like someone wants you there."

"You have better eyes than anyone other than Sebastian, can you tell who it is?"

"I'm not sure, but I think it may be the man who's always with the baron."

Declan chuckled. "You mean Balven, his brother?"

"That would be him."

"Get a boat ready," said Declan.

Soon he was approaching the dock while the other ships in his flotilla were dropping anchor and getting ready to disembark the men and unload the cargo.

The man waiting was indeed Balven, who came forward and said, "We got word by swift pigeon it was you down at Toranda, so I left the city as soon as I could. The messages said you were now captain."

"Bogartis is dead, yes," confirmed Declan.

"Did you get what you were sent to get?"

"Yes, enough for a thousand or more swords if we can get the iron."

"The iron trail is clear now, so we have miners up there, and we'll send more if we must." Balven looked at the ships. "These are all with you?"

"Your brother said get more men, so we did," answered Declan. "Eight ships and a thousand men."

"I'm impressed." Balven glanced around. "I'm not sure where we'll put a thousand men though, so if they can march to the city, that's probably the best option. We have new barracks there and have been training hundreds since you've been gone."

Sixto said, "I'll go tell them to start the unloading." He gave a casual bow to Balven, turned, and started to jog along the harbor's edge.

"Sorry about your man Bogartis," said Balven. "I didn't

know him, but even the castellans spoke well of him. I respect that."

"He was a good man" was all Declan said.

A soldier rode up to where they stood and handed a tiny scroll to Balven. "Message, sir."

Balven took the message and unrolled it as the messenger turned and rode off again.

"We have word that the *Queen of Storms* is a half-day behind you."

"The *Queen of Storms*?"

"A friend from Beran's Hill, Hava, yes?"

"She and her husband bought my wife's inn," said Declan. "Yes, she's a friend."

"Come," said Balven. "There's a poor inn here now, little more than a barn, but the food is better than what we can get at the soldiers' mess. I'll send a message to your man—"

"Sixto," supplied Declan.

"Sixto, and he can oversee your men as they march to the city. I hope they have provisions, for we have none to spare."

"We don't have much, but enough to last a few more days," said Declan.

"Come, Hava's ship should arrive before midday, and I have a coach waiting to carry us to the city. And I would very much like to discuss something with you alone before then."

DECLAN PUSHED AWAY THE EMPTY plate, having discovered he had been far hungrier than he had imagined. It was simple fare, but the fruit was fresh, the bread baked that morning and still warm, and the cheese was just down from an alpine meadow that had escaped the raiding. He had taken water instead of ale, feeling the need to keep his wits about him.

He had heard Balven lay out an incredible story and had listened silently while they ate. Balven had stopped talking a few minutes earlier, fixing a questioning gaze on Declan, but saying nothing.

At last Declan said, "We're brothers?"

"I saw it the first day we met, when you came to Daylon to fulfil Edvalt's promise. I told Daylon then, and more than once since, that you look more like our father than either of us. Moreover, you have his manner, his toughness, and determination to finish things once started, much like Daylon."

The meal had started with Declan telling Balven about his trials and finally getting the sand needed for forging the weapons, and Balven had commented on his commitment. Then Balven had told Declan of what he had discovered about his true birth and coming into Edvalt's care, not the fable fashioned to hide the truth.

Now, Declan took a deep breath, and said, "Well, it's nice to know, but Daylon is now a king, and you may be a bastard like me . . ."

"But things are not that simple," said Balven. He stood up and said, "Come, walk with me."

They left the ramshackle inn and started up the road that would eventually take them to Marquenet. "You're how old, Declan?"

"From what Edvalt said, maybe twenty-three, twenty-four. I'm not certain."

"Actually, twenty-six, I think," replied Balven. He glanced around, making sure they were not overheard.

Declan nodded slowly.

"Father had been dead less than a full year when we were called to the Betrayal. That was during the first few months of Hatu's life, and I don't even know if Hava had been born. So, do you fully understand when I say it was a long time ago?"

"A lifetime," said Declan dryly, "at least to us three."

"Daylon is past sixty, as am I," said Balven sadly. "He was deeply in love with his first wife, but she died early and left him heartbroken. Our father"—he gestured to include Declan in this plural—"married him off to a woman of rank, in the hope of having heirs. Father died and Daylon became baron and less than a year later we were murdering a dynasty, and somewhere along the way, you were born. We probably have a few more unknown brothers and sisters out there since bedding young women was one of Father's proclivities when he drank.

"But you're the only bastard with a noble mother."

"Noble?"

Balven told him what he had discovered, then added, "There is even a possibility you're not a bastard, as Father may have secretly married your mother, but that is actually far less important than some people think."

Declan found himself completely unprepared for any of this. At last, he asked, "What, then, is important?"

"Our brother came to care for his second wife, if not with the deep passion of his first, but he adored his children. He doted on them, and when his entire family was butchered, he changed. He lost . . . let's say a lot of good things inside him died along with his children.

"He won't wed again, even though he could still give this new kingdom an heir, but I know him. He's about to embark on as dangerous an undertaking as can be imagined and I fear this new kingdom, this barony that has been in our family for generations, may be a kingdom without a king before too long."

Declan said nothing, finally coming to realize that Balven was telling him something far more important than just Declan's personal future. He was speaking of a nation's future.

Balven stopped talking and looked at Declan. "I know everything you loved was taken as well, and you two are enough like Father that I will never persuade either of you not to visit personal vengeance on these Pride Lords. So, I won't ask, but listen carefully. At least one of you must come back alive." He pointed his finger at Declan and added, "And if it's you who comes back from this war alone, then you, my brother, will be King of Marquensas."

HAVA COULD SEE THE NUMBER of ships that were clustered along the coast for days. She first saw them as she approached Toranda and then as she continued up the coast. She stopped counting once she passed one hundred, and that was the day before. She was also surprised to see a kingdom banner flying from various fortifications along the way.

Still, politics was not her main concern. She had vital information for the baron . . . or rather, king, she corrected herself, and then as soon as possible she needed to return to the Sanctuary and then head for Nytanny.

She knew Hatu had held back some secrets about his studies despite his letting her experience a bit of what he was doing, but she had also held back part of her work in Nytanny, with Red Sweeney and the smugglers.

Even now Catharian would be sowing rumors of Coaltachin returning to save the nations. She hoped he was achieving enough to start the Pride Lords worrying. And the most critical thing she needed to tell Daylon—whether he be baron or king—was that there was a deadline coming.

In the distance she could see *Borzon's Black Wake* at anchor. The ship was probably deserted but battened down against the need to transport a great many troops. Hava estimated a thousand foot or four hundred cavalry and horses could be crammed aboard that former treasure- and slave-ship.

She got as close as possible to the new dock but kept out of the way should any other ships need to unload. When the ship was secure, she gave instructions to Sabien to allow the crew to visit whatever amenities the new town had to offer, certain that at least one of those buildings would be an inn. She lowered herself into a longboat and was rowed to shore.

To her surprise Balven and Declan were waiting for her on the new dock. Balven waved as she approached and gave her a steadying hand as she came ashore.

She embraced Declan. "I heard what happened to Beran's Hill. Gwen?"

Declan's expression darkened.

"I'm so sorry," she said softly.

He said, "Jusan and Millie, also. You, Hatu, and I are the only ones I know who have survived."

"And Molly Bowman," said Hava. "She and a few others from Beran's Hill are safe. Not many."

Declan seemed relieved that a few others had escaped safely.

Hava looked at Balven. "Big changes. Your brother is a king now?"

"Marquensas is now a kingdom," he declared, somewhat wryly. "We had a ceremony, with that fraud Bernardo offering a blessing. Word reached us that the Church has thrown him out, so I don't know how much that blessing counts, or even if it would have had the Church kept him." Balven sighed. "Now that the Church controls Sandura—they killed Lodavico as a heretic—they control both the continent of Enast and a large piece of North Tembria. War is inevitable if they try to expand, but let's hope we can stave off that crisis for a while."

Hava knew that given Balven was waiting for her at North Point, a signal had no doubt been sent from Toranda to

Marquenet, by messenger pigeon most likely. Which meant there would be a carriage waiting to hurry them to the capital. "You seem less than enthusiastic about being brother to a king," she observed.

He laughed. "My estimation of you grows each time we meet, Hava." He shook his head slowly. "It began almost as a joke, and my brother thought so at first. Then we realized that we had become complacent for too many years, only to be caught off balance by Sandura's plan to destroy Ithrace."

At this moment a carriage pulled up and Hava was impressed to see a smaller, wider vehicle drawn by a team of six. "This one goes faster?" she asked, her tone slightly tinged with sarcasm.

"You have no idea," Balven replied.

He opened the door, then stood aside and allowed her to enter first, despite his own rank; then Declan after her. Once they were all seated, Balven said, "Our newly ensconced monarch, my brother, is a man of vision. We now have a waystation between here and the capital, and a widened road, half a dozen hills having been excavated so that the route is flatter. I think we'll arrive six hours faster than the last time but sleeping is maybe no longer an option."

"I'm a ship's captain," Hava replied. "I can sleep anywhere, through anything."

Declan laughed. "If you'd seen the places I've been sleeping since I left, you'd understand why I envy you a cabin even in a big storm."

Balven grinned. "Do you need to sleep?"

"Frequently," she replied, with a touch of mirth.

"I'm fine," said Declan, "and the day is not over."

"That's good," Balven said, "because I'm opening wine."

"Good," Hava said, "because I need it. There's a great deal to share with the . . . king. We've begun to glean much of what is happening down in Nytanny."

Balven was silent for a while, staring out of the window as the coach started moving. He opened the wine, and then said, "I'll wait for your report to Daylon. No need for you to have to repeat everything twice. So, why don't you two catch up, and I'll listen, then if you need to, you can sleep until we reach the waystation—probably around midnight." He looked at Declan and said, "We built it at the crossroads where this route reaches the highway to Beran's Hill, and we're building a garrison at Beran's. We will rebuild the town."

Declan remained still for a long moment, and Balven realized he knew what Declan was thinking: if Daylon had not used Beran's Hill to set a trap for Lodavico of Sandura, and had fortified those two locations, the town might have survived.

Hava could feel the tension in the coach, but then Declan simply said, "Good."

Hava looked at Balven and said, "So, king?"

"My brother has never been a man of ambition, much like our father. He saw himself as a . . . caretaker, a preserver of what our father left us until the Betrayal.

"You were a baby or maybe even not born when the Betrayal occurred. Do you know the history?" he asked, handing her a mug of wine, then giving one to Declan.

Hava nodded. "Some of it," she replied, "and now a bit more as I see the hands of the Pride Lords and their Azhante servants manipulating the Church of the One. I may not know how the Church convinced the kings and barons to attack one of their own, ending the Covenant, just that they did."

Balven glanced out of the window for a moment, and sighed. "Daylon loved Steveren Langene like a brother. I never had a jealous nature, but at times I was envious because they had so much in common. Daylon was new to his rank, as our father had passed but a year before. He'd already lost his wife unexpectedly, and was married to a woman for political advantage, whom it was hoped would bear him an heir.

"He loved the King of Ithrace, but he loved his own people more. It was the night after that battle when we found Sefan, your Hatu. I think the bitterness of betraying someone he loved was why he sought to hide Hatushaly. Many of the barons and their oathmen would have delivered the baby to Lodavico of Sandura in order to curry favor. He had me seek out an agent of the Hidden Kingdom, and I did. That decision was a small bid for redemption."

"Hardly small from where I sit," said Hava. "That baby is my husband, and I'll tell more in detail when we see the king, but he's becoming someone who is powerful in ways I can barely describe, let alone understand."

Declan raised an eyebrow at that remark.

"Interesting," said Balven. "With Lodavico dead and Sandura now controlled by the Church, the existence of a Firemane baby is hardly of interest to anyone. Lodavico's hatred for Steveren was madness, unmitigated envy, and jealousy. The Church seems to care only for power, and now they have it."

Hava glanced out of the window past Balven as they crested a rise and in the distance saw a tall construction. "Quite a lot of building going on. I noticed several new fortifications along the coast when I sailed in."

"As did I," said Declan.

"What is that?" Hava indicated the project that had caught her attention.

Balven said, "That is where the river is going to be."

"You're moving a river?" Declan's expression was one of incredulity.

Balven nodded. "That's a dredger. The king is altering the course of that pleasant little stream that runs past Marquenet. New fields are being cultivated and new orchards farther away from the traditional ones. New pastures are being cleared in the hills ready for herds. In a few years, according to the newly named Royal Engineers, Hava and you will be able to sail your ships from that big harbor down at North Point right up to the large lake being dug north of Marquenet, or have them towed if the winds are right. In any event, it has a lot to do with dams and locks and a great deal of faith in knowing what they're doing will work as planned.

"I blame you," he said lightly, pointing at Hava.

"Me, why?" said Hava, finishing her wine.

"That treasure ship, whoever's *Black Wake.*"

"*Borzon's,*" Hava replied.

"As a result of the treasure she carried we can pay workers, and even feed most of them. We finished the new fortifications and now that we're a kingdom, Daylon's decided that Marquenet needs direct access to the sea."

"Wouldn't it be easier just to move the castle?" she asked, half-joking.

"To build a new one near the ocean, probably, but we have tradition, an ancestral home, and all that. Part of Daylon's plan is raising ourselves to be the new Ithrace. Now, Daylon sees this new kingdom as preserving what is left of Ithrace's glory. He even dreams of restoring the Covenant."

With a mix of humor and a hint of bitterness, Declan said, "Well, if they ever make me king, I'll keep that suggestion in mind." He held out his mug and Balven refilled it. Declan muttered, "Expanding Toranda would be cheaper."

Hava considered what Balven had said, then replied, "The flaw with the Covenant was assuming it was a rational agreement between men of good faith, and that alone was why it would endure."

Balven nodded. "You rise continually in my regard. I'm not the marrying type, but had I met someone like you a few decades ago?" He turned away from the window. "I admire intelligence more than any other quality, except perhaps a good heart. It's rare."

"So I have found," she agreed.

Softly, Declan said, "As have I. I've bidden farewell to many good hearts, and good minds, since I last saw you." He looked pointedly at Balven.

Balven saw the pain in Declan's face and for a brief moment his expression revealed concern. Then his well-practiced mask returned and he said, "The Covenant did endure for years, but you are correct in thinking that it required principled men to keep honoring it. Our ancestors never anticipated a murderous lunatic like Lodavico being a king.

"You must be tired, and we only stop once to replace the horses, so if you can, get some sleep. As you can imagine, I have a great many things to consider, even before hearing what news you bring."

Hava yawned. "Sleep is always a good thing."

Balven rose from sitting next to her and took a seat on the cushions opposite, next to Declan.

Closing her eyes, Hava nestled down into the corner of the carriage and after a minute, fell asleep.

Declan followed suit, crossing his arms and settling into the opposite corner.

Balven watched Hava a moment, thinking how fate had at least brought interesting people into his life, and then he set to considering the future of this new kingdom. Glancing at his newly revealed brother, he wondered if Declan really did represent the future.

DONTE SAW THE CARRIAGE ROLL into the main courtyard of the castle. Turning to the two former prisoners, Sepisolema and Firash, he said, "There she is!"

Balven had sent for Donte when word reached him via carrier pigeon that Hava's ship had been sighted off Toranda, and Donte had ridden the day and a half from Beran's Hill, which was now being called the Beran Garrison. Balven had been on his way to North Point, to meet Hava, when Donte had been given the simple task of staying with the prisoners in Balven's absence.

Donte found both the young Azhante men affable company, now that they were fully recovered from the beatings they had received at the hands of the king's interrogator. They were apt students of the local language, and what used to be the "Covenant Tongue," the de facto trading language spoken all over the Twin Continents.

Donte turned to the two Azhante and said, "If you go back to your rooms, I'll send for you when Hava has time to see you."

The two men waved and left for the castle. Donte watched them enter through a side door then noticed again the brand-new banner flapping in the breeze from a tall pole above the highest tower. He thought the entire king thing was amusing, though a great many people around him seemed to think it had some greater importance that he failed to see. Still, he did enjoy telling guards at the checkpoints that he was on a mission for the king, which earned him a great deal more deference than he had ever experienced before in his life.

The carriage rolled up to the main entrance to the castle and a guard quickly opened the door. Balven and Declan climbed out and Donte was standing next to them by the time Hava exited the carriage.

They hugged and Hava said, "So, they haven't hanged you yet?"

"Not so far." He laughed.

Balven said, "He's actually been behaving himself and has been useful. Helped chase off bandits a while back."

Hava gave Donte an appraising look. "Trying to be a hero?"

"Hardly. I just don't like people shooting arrows at me."

Balven turned to Declan and said, "I think you'd best go see Edvalt, and let him know what is coming. If I or the king need you, we'll send for you."

Declan's face was an inscrutable mask as he said, "I'll be at the smithy," and he left.

Balven gestured for Donte and Hava to follow him. "When you meet the king, bow like you did before. Daylon dislikes the bending the knee business. Reminds him too much of Lodavico, I think. Address him as highness, sire, or majesty. He doesn't seem to care which, but it's a matter of court dignity."

Hava asked, "Did you get a new title as well?"

" 'Sir' works just as it always did," Balven said, "but my new title is 'First Minister to the King' and my old one is still 'Daylon's bastard brother.' "

Donte laughed and Hava smiled.

"It's all theater," said Balven.

"But important theater," said Hava.

He raised an eyebrow approvingly. "You are a bright one."

Hava saw that the hallways had been recently scrubbed, the stones stripped of the years of soot from the candle sconces, and the wooden chandeliers all stained back to their original color, with the brass fittings polished to a shine. Banners had been cleaned and rehung, so everything looked brighter, and there was indeed a feeling of freshness throughout the castle.

They passed through what was now the king's throne room, which had previously been the baron's meeting hall. It was still being used as before, a place to hold court and, should the occasion arise, to entertain guests and host banquets. Hava doubted there would be any of that for some time to come. Guards wearing new tabards stood at each door leading into the large hall. The old symbol of Marquensas, a sword crossed with a branch of orange blossoms, now boasted the addition of a three-pointed crown above it. Hava thought the white and gold on a field of light blue was regal-looking indeed.

They reached the door to the king's private study, a room both Hava and Donte had previously visited. Balven held up his hand, signaling the need to wait. He knocked and when he heard "Come in," he pushed open the door.

Daylon's private study was unchanged. Whatever alterations he had instigated in order to emphasize the newfound grandeur of Marquensas's elevation to a kingdom, he apparently felt no need to change this one room.

Hava and Donte both bowed, and Daylon waved away any further need for ceremony. "Sit," he instructed, and both Hava and Donte took chairs, with Balven remaining standing, as was his habit.

"We—" Daylon began, then he looked at Balven and pointed at Donte. "Does he need to be here?"

Donte started to rise, but Balven took a step and put a hand on Donte's shoulder, gently pushing him back into the seat. "I thought he might prove useful," he answered, and the newly invested king seemed to consider that a good enough answer.

Focusing on Hava, he said, "We need to hear what you've discovered."

Hava began with her exploration of the Border Ports, including what she'd uncovered about the Azhante ship patrols, then she went on to detail what she'd arranged with Red Sweeney, and Catharian's mission to sow dissension and ensure that King Daylon's forces were not opposed by local fighters if possible.

The conversation dragged on, and Daylon sent for a meal as the sun lowered in the west. The discussion, questions and answers continued throughout the meal and into the night.

At last, Daylon said, "So, to sum it all up, these murderous bastards are planning another attack here? Soon?"

"We'll be coming up to midsummer in only a few months," said Hava. "From what I've cobbled together from the pieces of information I received, there were these sacrifices—"

"Yes, to the Dark Masters," said Daylon. "And warfare between . . . tribes? Nations?"

"I only saw one tiny bit of Nytanny and it reminded me of a whole lot of island towns where I grew up. But the people I talked with told me of big cities, and thousands of towns and villages . . ." She put her hands up and shrugged. "It's a very crowded place, from what is said. Part of the reason behind the attack here was simply to get rid of a lot of fighters."

"On their own side?" Balven asked, frowning.

"Since these Dark Masters have . . . vanished, apparently, the Pride Lords have had to put down rebellion after rebellion, and one tactic is to turn nations and tribes against each other. Another was this attack here."

King Daylon put his hands on the desk and made to rise. "It's been a long meeting and I am still trying to unravel what you've told me. We'll continue tomorrow when I've had time to ponder it all."

Hava rose and said, "Highness, the single most important thing is that you now have a deadline, and a choice. The deadline is how long we have until they move again to destroy what's left—in other words this kingdom—and the choice is if you want to launch a preemptive strike there, or wait to defend against them here."

Daylon stood motionless for a moment, then said, "I understand. Get some rest: we'll pick this up tomorrow."

They bowed and departed and once outside the private chamber, Hava looked at Donte and said, "That is absolutely the longest I've ever seen you sit in one place and say nothing."

Donte smiled. "No one asked me to say anything, and I've learned it's not wise to interrupt a king."

"How long were you in the dungeon?"

"Only a week. Let's get something to eat."

Hava laughed. "You are always hungry."

PLANNING AND CHOICE

E dvalt faced the other smiths in the newly constructed foundry. He put his hand on Declan's shoulder and said, "A few of you know me, or have heard of me, and this is Declan Smith."

Declan was pleased to see Gildy and a few other familiar faces mixed in with a host of strangers. Marquenet had been spared from the raids, so a dozen local smiths, masters, and journeymen, and their apprentices, lived close enough to the foundry to walk home every night. Another score had arrived among the refugees, so now the king had nearly forty sword makers. Other men who were familiar with metal-working—tinkers, coppersmiths, jewelers, and foundry men—were busy preparing to equip the king's army to carry the fight back to Nytanny.

Edvalt said, "Declan traveled to the Burning Lands and returned with the rare sand I used to finish my blades, to create King's Steel. Those of you who know the secret of King's Steel, come and stand beside us."

Only six master smiths crossed the room.

"That means there are eight of us to show the rest of you how to make King's Steel. The hoarding of that secret is over!" Edvalt shouted as a few smiths began to object.

Declan held up his hands for quiet and after some muttering the room fell silent. "When I created this," he said, lifting the scabbard in which his masterpiece rested, "it was to be for a wealthy nobleman, but he was killed in the war. He was old and fat and wanted it as a trophy unearned. He was not going to strike a single blow with it, while brave men fought and died because their blades failed them."

A few of the smiths nodded, understanding and agreeing.

Declan continued. "Edvalt and I know that not every blade we make will match this one. We do not have the time to take three or four days to forge each blade, but we can show you how to finish one in two days, or less perhaps. These will not properly be 'King's Steel,' but they will be far better, stronger blades than you've made before."

Edvalt said, "Declan has brought back sand from down near the Scorched Coast, a source passed down to me from my master, from his before him. Declan, please show the blade."

Declan removed his belt and took the sword from out of the scabbard and passed it to the nearest smith. Several, like Gildy, had seen it before, but even those who had took a moment to relish holding it once more. The quality was so apparent that even the youngest journeymen could see it when they held the blade.

"That is what we strive for," said Edvalt. "Many of the swords we make will not be equal to that blade, but most will come close, and perhaps a few will match it. But the swords we make here, after today, will break many of the blades you forged in the past, and few we make will fail those who wield them."

Declan took back the sword and returned it to the scabbard, then fastened it around his waist once more. Edvalt took to setting up eight teams of masters and journeymen, so they could all learn how best to work using the rare sand.

A court page arrived and approached him. "You're Declan Smith?"

Declan nodded.

"The king wishes you to come at once."

Edvalt overheard and raised his eyebrows in silent question. Declan shrugged, indicating he had no idea why he was being summoned. Edvalt signaled he'd start with two groups and Declan again nodded.

He followed the page to the king's private chamber, where Daylon sat with Balven and Hava. Glancing at Balven, Declan bowed to King Daylon, who said, "Sit down."

"How many swords can you make in a month?" asked Daylon.

Declan considered the smiths he had just been with and said, "If we work in shifts, twelve crews to a shift, I think we can produce close to a thousand in a month, no less than eight hundred. I'll safely say nine hundred."

"We need eighteen hundred swords of the highest quality," said Balven.

Declan glanced at Hava and then asked the king, "We have only two months, sire?"

"Yes, we must depart within two months."

Declan sat back and waited. He had many questions, but he would save them for later.

"Hava brings us news, but we need more, so she has agreed to act as a messenger between those at a place known as the Sanctuary and here."

"Remember Catharian, the monk who would tell tales at the Inn of the Three Stars?" Hava said.

Declan replied bitterly, "I remember. He wed all of us . . . that day."

No one needed to be reminded of what day that was. Married and widowed on the same day, Midsummer's Day.

"He was not truly a monk, but an agent for a group known as the Flame Guard." Hava quickly recounted the events from Hatu's capture and being brought to the Sanctuary, as well as her own captivity and escape, finishing with her seizing the *Queen of Storms*. "It's the fastest ship afloat and I know the course." She added a few details about Nytanny, but a glance from Balven made it clear that he or the king would provide Declan with whatever information they felt he needed.

Declan nodded. "Not an easy time, by any measure." Turning to the king, he said, "Sire, I answered your question regarding swords, so why else am I here?"

Daylon nodded to Balven, who said, "Another attack is coming next midsummer, according to Hava."

Hava looked at Declan, and said, "I can explain at length, but the Pride Lords needed to cull some of their own more rebellious nations by sending them raiding here, but then they needed to get them back to deal with their crops and herds. After that, they plan to return here again with colonists, to finish what they started last year."

Daylon spoke. "They expect Marquensas to be a pit of disease, the disorganized remnants of the population left fighting over scraps. They have no idea I am building an army and ensuring that this nation is well defended should another fight come here. So far, we've only encountered the two spies we found in Delnocio's retinue, and we're being as alert as we can be for others."

Declan glanced at Hava and said, "When you have time, I'd like to know more. Why would they imagine we'd turn on ourselves?"

It was Balven who answered. "From what I've learned from the Azhante we captured, as well as what Hava has learned from her voyage to Nytanny, I surmise it's for two reasons, the first being that it is in their nature. These Pride Lords are not monarchs or nobles as we think of rulers. They feel no concern for the welfare of the people they govern. Even a madman like Lodavico understood his power rested on the well-being of his nation. These Pride Lords see the inhabitants of the various nations as . . . property, and since the departure of the so-called Dark Masters, they are exploiting them to the fullest."

"They're not rulers. They're landlords," said King Daylon. "They're brokers, and if I understand what Hava has told me, they have competing motives, differing interests."

He looked at Hava and with a gesture indicated she should clarify. Hava said, "They're not even landlords, sire. They're crime lords, gang bosses. Each Pride numbers a group of people who oversee different . . . interests in various places, so they have no sense of a . . . home." She paused, trying to organize her own thoughts. "Even my people, who are descended from the Azhante, we think of ourselves as Coaltachin. Ignore the legends and rumors—most of which we started about ourselves in order to look far more powerful than we are. We still think of ourselves as a single people. Just as the people of all the other nations think of themselves as one people, for the most part."

Declan nodded his understanding as Hava addressed the king.

"You rule this nation, sire, but you are also part of this nation. The Pride Lords have no nations: they are what anyone from Coaltachin would think of as masters, clan bosses. They control vastly powerful groups of gangs able to field dangerous men, but they have no sense of shared character and no sense of shared history. As a child of Coaltachin, this is easy enough for me to understand."

Declan nodded.

"I planned to assemble the largest army in the history of the Five Kingdoms," said Daylon, referencing the long history of the Five Kingdoms that had created the Covenant. "But I think with your thousand men, Declan, along with the core I've created, and those I'm currently having trained, we should be able to bring four thousand, perhaps more, trained soldiers to attack this city of—" He looked at Hava.

"Akena," she supplied.

"Akena. From what Hava has said, that's where the Pride Lords will be most vulnerable . . ." He looked to Hava. "You finish."

"In Coaltachin, we have a group of deadly people we call the Hidden Ones, the Quelli Nascosti. Think spies and assassins: you've heard the legends."

"They move invisibly, fly over fortress walls, kill from a distance," said Declan. "Even as a child in the Covenant I heard the tales of the Hidden Kingdom's magic warriors."

"Our rumormongers are among the best," said Hava, with pride, "and the price paid to secure the services of any among the Hidden Ones is very costly."

Daylon nodded.

"Below the *Quelli Nascosti* you have the more common fighters, those we call the sicari, which basically means 'knife-man,' someone who carries messages, does specific tasks for masters, and often is the person who oversees the gangs. They are wicked fighters alone, but they are not trained soldiers able to coordinate as a group.

"What Coaltachin has that the Pride Lords lack is a criminal organization that runs much of the crime in the Twin Continents and most of the surrounding islands, one that is trying to gain control of the other half."

"Why is that important?" asked Balven.

"It means," answered Hava, "that the Pride Lords do not have thousands of eyes and ears in every city, town, and village. Inns and brothels, marketplaces, merchants to travel, all are potential sources of intelligence. The one thing that makes Coaltachin so powerful, so effective, is that if a gang boss or crew chief sees anything that he or she thinks could prove of interest to the masters, that information is sent through a network of couriers and messengers as quickly as possible.

"The Azhante have become guardsmen or police, and they depend on informants from within the very people they're terrifying."

"So some of the information may be useless," Declan observed, "because people tell them whatever they think they want to hear."

Hava nodded. "That's my guess. And given the constant fighting in one part of the continent or another, just enough accurate information trickles through, that they think what they're doing is effective."

"How is this going to aid us?" asked Declan.

"Because when we attack," said King Daylon, "most of the most loyal Azhante will be out of the city of Akena, and a great many of the less loyal will be fighting with us."

Smiling, Hava said, "I'm starting a revolution."

Declan stared at her. He was silent for a moment as he digested what he was being told. Then he smiled.

HATU LAY FLAT ON HIS back, eyes fixed on the night stars.

Bodai climbed up the small hill and said, "Still trying to get a closer look at the stars?"

"There must be a way," Hatu answered, "to follow the force lines."

"I thought you said there had to be some sort of connection, like your link to Hava and Declan, or to a place you know well."

"That's what Nathan said." Hatu got up, dusting himself off a bit. "One day . . ."

"Then let me know what you find. I'm interested, too."

"Turning in for the night?" asked Hatu.

"Yes, as interesting as the discoveries are that we've made in the library, and the brilliant reorganization Sabella has conducted, my old eyes need some rest."

They walked down to the library and approached the walkway around the perimeter which had a roof extending over a line of pillars.

A voice said, "Rest will have to wait."

Nathan stepped out from behind a pillar and said, "There is something we must do now."

Sounding tired, Bodai said, "Your use of the word *now* suggests that this has nothing to do with casual research."

"Hardly," Nathan said, coming closer. He stood in front of Hatu. "I need you to do something dangerous."

"What?" Hatu asked.

"I need you to return to the pit."

"The pit? Oh! The pit in Garn's Wound!"

"Yes," Nathan affirmed.

"I thought you said not to look into that pit."

"I did," said Nathan.

"What's changed?" asked Hatu.

"Come inside, and I'll explain," Nathan said, turning toward the entrance to the library.

They made their way around the building, to a door which Nathan opened, then down the short hall that connected the rear of the building to the library and entered. Most of the candles in the sconces and all the lamps had been extinguished, so when they got to their usual table, Hatu used his ability to create a flame on his finger to light a pair of candles.

Nathan said, "Can you get your remote vision back to that pit?"

"I think so," Hatu answered, making to sit down.

"Don't sit down. I need to see what you see."

Bodai sat down. "Do you really need me?"

Nathan paused for a moment, then said, "If anything occurs whereby I suddenly do not seem to be myself, either hit me with a chair as hard as you can, or run."

Bodai's eyes widened.

Hatu placed his hands on Nathan's shoulders, and felt Nathan's hands on his own, and closed his eyes. A cascade of lights passed in an instant as Hatu ignored the lines of energy springing up all around them, and abruptly there was nothing but darkness.

"You're doing this?" asked Nathan.

"Who else?" asked Hatu.

"Just being sure," replied Nathan. "You usually enjoy exploring the colored threads."

"This seemed urgent."

"It is," Nathan replied.

Abruptly, the darkness was replaced by a swirl of light and colors which began to resolve itself into the place where Hatu had caused the rockslide in the Wound. "This is my most vivid memory of a location," Hatu said.

"Understandable," Nathan replied.

"I should be able to reach our last point faster this time."

As soon as he said this, the entire landscape sped by on both sides, as if they were flying down the Wound to the wall embedded with skulls and bones.

"That was impressive," said Nathan.

"I've been toying with that ability while you've been taking your 'long walks,'" said Hatu. "I've been trying to look closer at the stars, but that's not working so far."

"Give it time," said Nathan. "Now no matter what happens, none of the people we encounter from here to the pit will have any inkling of what we're doing. Get as close to the edge of that pit as you can, without looking directly into it."

Hatu said nothing but began retracing his route to the center of the village and the edge of the pit. This time he paid more attention to the people living here and realized there was something profoundly wrong with them. In his travels he'd heard stories on the islands east of the Twin Continents of cannibals, most of which were highly exaggerated by seafarers telling tales in exchange for drinks.

There was no need to exaggerate with these people. To Hatu it appeared that they had lost most of their humanity. They lived in filth, with dogs and vermin infesting piles of garbage. There seemed no organization to this large village that Hatu could discern, no central lodge or hall, no obvious place of worship. Except around the pit, where some care had been given to keeping it free of debris. The pit was shaped like a half-moon, the flat side hard against a low, flat rock face, as if a hill had been cut in half by a giant sword. A railing had been constructed, running from one stone face to the other on the other side, and in the center, a platform had been built to overhang the pit.

A child, covered in dirt, was standing on that platform now, held by a woman Hatu assumed was her mother. Both were silent, but when the mother picked the child up and held her aloft Hatu's concentration was shaken. For a brief moment he felt the urge to somehow intervene in what he saw coming, but Nathan's voice rang out in his head, "Don't!"

Feeling horror rise up like bile, Hatu watched the mother fling the child into the pit, then turn away. The child's expression never changed and it fell in silence.

"How is that possible?"

"The thing in the pit has warped these people into something barely human. They sacrifice to their 'god,' with no idea what they face," Nathan said. "Now, slowly move your perception to the edge and see what you can make out in the pit."

Hatu slowly moved his perspective to the pit, then angled it downward. It was dark, and by will alone he changed his perception to see in the darkness.

The child's broken body stared up at him with lifeless eyes, as her blood ran over rocks and pooled around . . . a massive black creature.

At least Hatu assumed it was a creature, for it was nothing like any living thing he had seen or imagined. It defied every expectation. There were no evident lines of force associated with it. It was as if it existed in spite of the energies created by the furies, rather than as part of them.

And it seemed amorphous. It must have some sort of shape—arms, legs, a head—yet he could not make them out. All he could do was try to make sense of a void within the lines of energy, and he sensed he might not actually be seeing anything, and that the amorphous shape was just his own mind trying to make sense of something incomprehensible.

Abruptly, Nathan released his grip on Hatu's shoulders and they were back in the library. Nathan moved to an empty chair and sat down.

Bodai looked at his pale expression and then glanced at Hatu, who was visibly shaken, and said to Nathan, "What is it?"

"Something I can barely comprehend," said Nathan. "Something that by any measure should not exist here. I must leave."

"Another long walk?" suggested Hatu. His face was devoid of color, with a sheen of perspiration, and his question echoed a sense of forced humor to fend off terror.

"I don't have the time," said Nathan. He had left his rucksack on the floor and he picked it up. Rummaging around in it, he said, "Where is that damn thing?"

After a moment he pulled out an orb, which appeared to be made of gold.

Hatu said, "What is that?"

"Something I haven't used in this lifetime," Nathan answered. "Be quiet for a moment," he instructed, then he closed his eyes. "I think I remember," he said to himself, then he held down a section of the outer casing of the orb.

Hatu noticed that the orb was formed by interlocking pentagons. He heard a faint click.

"That should return me here," Nathan said, then he touched a different pentagon and was gone. There was a noise of inrushing air to fill the void he had created.

"Now I've seen everything," said Bodai.

Hatushaly shook his head and said, "Probably not."

"Do we wait?"

"I think we should go to bed," suggested Hatu. "I suspect if he comes back soon, we'll know."

"What did you see, where he took you?"

"Nothing I understand," said Hatu, standing up. "And I'm not certain I want to."

Bodai put his hand on Hatu's shoulder, then said, "I have a feeling you're right."

Silently they left the library and headed to their quarters.

DECLAN HAD FINISHED INSTRUCTING THE newer smiths and other metalworkers and went to find Edvalt. Edvalt had become something of a leader of all the metalworkers in Marquenet. Declan didn't find that a surprise, as he recognized that no matter what Edvalt might claim about Declan's skills, the older man was still the finest smith in Marquensas, perhaps the best on all of Garn.

Portions of the foundry had been partitioned off so that the final phase of regarding the color of the steel and deciding when to temper it would be untroubled by daylight. Edvalt was leaving such an area when he spied Declan.

"How are they doing?" Declan asked.

Edvalt gave a lopsided smile. "Well enough, I guess. Some are better than others at this part. I had one lad I sent to work at the foundry casting blanks."

Blanks were the rods of steel yet to be fashioned into blades. Declan's expression was curious. "Only one?"

Edvalt laughed. "Only one. And it turns out I found a young journeyman, barely a year out of his apprenticeship, who may be as good as you one day."

"One day," echoed Declan with a laugh.

"Look at this," said Edvalt, handing a newly minted blade to Declan.

Declan took the sword and hefted it, then he stepped back and executed a few sword strokes and flipped it to his left hand and repeated the moves.

"Two hands now?" asked Edvalt.

Declan nodded, flipped the sword into the air with his left and caught it with his right. "That's a damn fine blade," he said. "A year out of apprenticeship?"

Edvalt nodded.

"He may end up being better than both of us," said Declan with a chuckle. "I was thinking of getting some food. Our shift is nearly over, and we rarely get to spend any time together anymore."

Edvalt said, "Some other time, I think." He pointed past Declan, who turned to see a court page heading toward him. "I doubt the king wants to see *me*."

Declan slowly shook his head and said, "Maybe tomorrow."

"Maybe," Edvalt replied.

As he had predicted, it was a summons for Declan to go to the king's chamber.

Declan followed the youth, and once he reached the door of Daylon's private chamber, he knocked.

"Enter," said the king.

Inside he found Daylon at his usual place behind his large but simple desk, with Balven standing at his shoulder in his usual position. Declan gave a quick bow.

"Sit down," commanded the king and Declan did as instructed.

"Balven tells me he's been digging around in . . . family history."

Declan was silent, then after a moment said, "Is that a question, sire?"

"No," said the king. "Whatever he's turned up, we'll put that aside. My immediate concern is this coming war, and ensuring we fully avenge the injuries done to us." He paused for a moment, locked eyes with Declan, and said, "All of us."

Declan gave a slight nod. "Making them pay is all I wish for." Both brothers had lost their wives, and Declan understood that the king had also lost all his children, a loss he could only imagine.

"We'll revisit the family question after we've crushed these Pride Lords."

Again, Declan said nothing but gave a slight nod of agreement.

"I've considered different contingencies," said the king. "Your second, Sixto?"

Declan said, "Yes, sire."

"I want him to lead your forces. I want you to remain here and make swords and other weapons, against the possibility we shall have to retreat and defend here."

Declan sat motionless, locking eyes with the king. After a long pause, he said, "No."

Daylon's eyes narrowed and his expression darkened. "No?"

"No, sire."

Balven moved slightly, putting himself between the two men.

"You would say no to your king?" asked Daylon, his voice rising.

Declan said, "I took your service, m'lord, but I swore no oath. Unless you mean to end all the traditions we held to, unless I'm deserting in battle, without a contract, I am free to leave your service at any time." He shifted his weight forward in his chair. "It's the mercenary's code. I will serve with you in killing those who took my family, and yours, from us, or I will get my own ships and I will find my way to them, and end them!" He kept his voice even, but the rage within his words was barely contained.

"I can put you in a dungeon for this!" yelled Daylon, surging to his feet.

Balven held up a cautioning hand to his brother. "No, not this way."

Declan stood up. "I have a thousand men camped not a mile from this castle."

"You would raise arms against me?" Daylon shouted, and

Balven again moved his hands in a calming gesture, trying to get his brother to sit back down.

"No," said Declan. "I have no cause to raise arms against you. My men will stay where they are and I will order Sixto to ready them to leave Marquensas." He took a breath, and Balven and the king could see it was taking all of Declan's determination to keep from shouting. Through clenched teeth, Declan said, "I will pay my men with what's left of our plunder and they will be free to serve whoever they wish to serve but, again, I took no oath, and neither did my men, and they follow me, King Daylon Dumarch of Marquensas, not you." He lowered his voice. "Without them, you do not have a large enough force to act within the time left to you."

The two brothers faced one another, Daylon leaning so hard on his desk that his knuckles were white.

Declan said, "I will kill everyone who took my wife and friends from me, somehow, or die in the attempt, but no one on this side of death will keep me from trying." Without waiting for a dismissal, he got up and left the chamber, not quite slamming the door behind him.

King Daylon grabbed a quill from its inkwell and threw it hard against the wall. Then he walked to the door that led to his quarters.

Balven found himself alone in the chamber. He closed his eyes and took a slow, deep breath. To himself he muttered, "That was predictable."

He stood silently for another moment, breathing deeply. He was about to leave the chamber through the door to the throne room when he realized he wasn't sure which brother to speak with first.

23

THE BEGINNING OF RETRIBUTION,

AND HORRORS UNIMAGINED

‡

Hava sat across the table from Red Sweeney in a corner of South House. She had arrived two days before and had waited until he received word that she was on Shechal, waiting for him.

Two mugs of rum sat between them, and Red Sweeney took one, drank, and said, "Ah, you remembered the black bottle."

"I just said it was for you," she replied lightly.

Red Sweeney was silent for a long moment, then looked at Hava and said, "That man, Catharian, he is completely mad."

"I could have told you that," she replied, trying to hide her amusement. "Why, what has he done?"

"He started small, chatting up that Azhante boy you didn't kill."

"So, Dahod came back," said Hava.

"I'm not sure what he was more afraid of, more Azhante being there or you not being there." Red Sweeney took another drink. "But Catharian is as adroit a spy as you said he was. Never saw anyone pick up a language as fast as he did with the Azhante tongue, and even though that boy was very disappointed at not seeing you again, despite you saying he would be your agent, well, Catharian had the boy convinced in less time than I'm taking to tell the story that you were the agent of some distant and powerful nation that was coming to save all the Azhante. He took what you told the boy, embellished it, and expanded it . . ." Red Sweeney took another drink, wiped the back of his hand across his mouth, and slowly shook his head. "An army is going to swoop in and end the Pride Lords."

"Not that far from the truth," Hava said, "though saving the Azhante would be an unforeseen benefit to them, not any goal of my people."

"You rid us of the Pride Lords, and it's the same thing, though it will get messy for a while after."

"I was born just after a major upheaval in the order of things across the sea, so I know how brutal power struggles can be after a big change."

"I'm old enough to remember hearing about that . . . the Betrayal, they called it, right?"

She nodded.

"Never got to the Twin Continents, myself," Red Sweeney said, "but I've made it to the Southern Islands below the Clearing a few times, when I was young and foolish."

She laughed. "Actually, you weren't that far from the Kingdom of Night if you knew but where to look."

"That a fact?" He chuckled and finished off his rum. "Anyway, your boy Catharian has managed to start at least half a dozen brawls in inns between Azhante regulars and local town thugs, has spread rumors about a coming revolution, almost had the entire Azhante garrison at Jadamish turned out to repel an attack that never happened a day's ride away." Red Sweeney laughed. "He's what we used to call a 'right mixer,' the sort of chap who gets everyone drunk, starts flinging insults around, then says, 'why don't you fight him,' and sits back and watches the dustup. I can't see why the Azhante haven't rounded him up by now."

"He's hard to catch," said Hava. "He can change his look as fast as any thief I've known. Comes in one door and he's a tall man in a black tunic, and a minute later he's skulking out of another door in a blue shirt, hunched over so that he's shorter, hair messed up or even a different color. It's impressive to watch if you're not in the brawl."

"Anyway, he's out there stirring up trouble like you wanted. So, what news?"

"There's an island. The Sanctuary."

"I've heard of it, long time ago. Reckoned it was a story."

"It's real. That's where Catharian and I are based when we're down here."

Red Sweeney said nothing, just nodding once.

"It's hard to find," said Hava, "which is why it's become a story."

"There's a place around the northeast of the islands, lots of shoals, fog, mist, tricky to navigate," said Red Sweeney.

Hava smiled. "It's in there. You never went looking?"

"No reason," he replied. "I let others go off chasing legends and lost treasure. I never had time."

"But you know the islands?"

"More than most men, but not all of them. There's a lot of empty up there."

"Which is why a fleet of ten ships is heading there."

"When?"

"They should be underway within days," said Hava.

"Where are they headed?"

"If the maps I've seen are accurate, there's a pretty big empty island less than a day's sailing to the northeast of Akena. I don't know the currents and winds well."

"I do," said Red Sweeney. "I know that island. If there are no storms, you have a good chance of a wind at your back. You leave there halfway between sundown and midnight, you sail right into Akena's main harbor at dawn." He laughed. "Ten warships would wake them up."

"Especially if their fleet is somewhere else."

"So, you need a really big dustup a day or two's sail away." He thought about it for a moment, then said, "A big northern port, say Wandasan or Tobilo . . . let me work backward." He held up a finger. "Can't travel by horse in numbers because of some nasty mountain roads. So, ships. Major uprising, that's three, maybe four Azhante ships, the big ones carrying fifty or more men each. Three, maybe four, days to send word to Akena that they're in dire need and to send help . . ." After a pause, he said, "Tobilo. We get Catharian to start his rebellion there."

"What does that leave us with in Akena?"

"It's a strange city, and you only go there if you absolutely must. Unlike the rest of Nytanny, that city is . . . it's almost like a religious place. Everything is a ritual. They have a man whose only duty is to wake everyone up at dawn and keep track of the hours.

"They treat their servants differently there. The Azhante families are held hostage against good behavior, but the city servants' families are treated like nobility. They live in something close to luxury. Some of the servants who are privy to Pride Lord secrets know they will be put to death when their service is no longer needed, but they do so willingly, because their families will continue to be well treated after their death."

"Will they fight?" asked Hava.

Red Sweeney shrugged. "Some, perhaps. Others will simply get out of the way. Despite the reward, they're still as much prisoners as the Azhante."

"So, what King Daylon—"

"King?" interrupted Red Sweeney. "I thought he was a baron last time we spoke."

"Things change," she replied.

"Apparently. Go on."

"King Daylon is bringing four thousand of his hardest, best-trained fighters. He'll need a few days to stage things, get the horses ready."

"He's bringing horse soldiers?"

"About four hundred heavy cavalry."

Red Sweeney said, "That should prove entertaining. There are no big clear areas for any major battle, but a lot of them running around the streets will create confusion and havoc." He drummed his fingers on the table while he thought. After a moment, he said, "Tell your king it's going to be ambushes around every corner if he doesn't get up to the central palace where the Pride Lords live when they're in the city. If there's enough trouble in the other cities, some will leave their distant estates thinking Akena is the safest place to be."

"So Pride Lords into the city, Azhante fanatics out." She nodded. "Seems like a good plan."

"You say you have a good memory and don't need a map?"

"Why?"

"Because I don't have anything to draw with."

Hava laughed.

"First thing, there are no defenses facing the sea, and only old walls, easily breached, around the central enclave of the Pride Lords. When the Dark Masters ruled, they had no fear of any attack. So, the king can sail in easily and in force, with no need to sail in a file, and land his ships almost at the same time.

"When his fleet enters the harbor, they'll be looking at a

wide series of docks and quays. They may be clear and that's where he needs to land as quickly as possible. If there are vessels tied up there, he's going to need to just lash his ships to them, cross the decks and get to the quayside as fast as he can." Red Sweeney was lost in thought a moment. "Tell him there's a shallow beach at the southwest edge of the docks, and that's where the horses should be offloaded, so that ship must be on the far left!" He began to become excited at the idea of invading Akena. "There's not much of value there, and no guards at night to speak of, so if he unloads his horse soldiers there, then rides them up the quay to the second—not the first, but the second—major street on his left, that's a straight route right up the hillside."

"Go on," said Hava as she fixed every detail he spoke in her mind. She knew the king would have his best-trained soldiers with the best swords and armor in that unit.

BALVEN STOOD ON THE DOCKS at the new harbor in North Point, which was still shrouded in predawn gloom, though the sky to the east was brightening. Beside him stood the king, and down below he could see Declan taking charge of his mercenaries. It had taken days, but he had finally brokered a peace of sorts between the two brothers. If he had held a sliver of doubt as to Declan being blood kin, that had all vanished when the conflict arose between them. They were two of a kind, and when they were angered the resemblance was obvious. They even sounded alike when they raised their voices.

Declan resembled a much younger version of Daylon, but even though he lacked the years of education and training there was an eager mind there, albeit one blunted and beaten down by events that had crushed his spirit. Balven thought he saw that spirit slowly beginning to return now that the harrowing mission to find that special sand was far behind him. He stood on the verge of meeting those he needed to punish, and that was fueling a growing anticipation and readiness. In that, Balven conceded silently, the two brothers were twins. Both hungered for vengeance.

"What are you thinking?" asked Daylon.

Balven said, "After more than sixty years together, I assumed you could read my mind."

"You're thinking that you might end up king if both of us get ourselves killed."

"Hardly," said Balven with a bitter chuckle. "I'm not a ruler."

"And Declan is?" Daylon's tone revealed he still retained some anger over the young man's defiance.

"He could be, with help." Balven put his hand on his brother's shoulder. "I'd rather not have to do that if you don't mind."

"I don't plan to die anytime soon," said the king, "if that makes you feel any better."

A large man hiked up the hill and bowed. He said, "We're ready to load the horses, then the men," then added after a pause, "Majesty."

"Sabien, isn't it?" asked Balven.

"Yes, sir."

"How long until you're ready to depart?"

Hava's former first mate turned and surveyed the loading barges lining up, and the men, equipment, and horses being readied. He looked back at Balven and said, "The rest of today: we should be ready by the evening tide."

"How long to reach this island?" asked the king. "Hava was uncertain because she didn't know how many ships there would be and which would be making the journey."

Sabien pointed to the northernmost part of the harbor. "That's the longest ferry, from that end of the docks out to *Borzon's Black Wake*, and we have readied the lowest deck for the horses. We have a hoist set up and just getting them aboard will take most of the day. The soldiers will embark quickly after that.

"The other ships will start loading soon. Once we're underway we'll move as swiftly as the slowest ship and that's *Borzon's Black Wake*. With fair weather, we should reach the island in forty days. With good weather, a few days earlier."

Balven said, "Good. That gets us there just before they begin to organize for coming here. Signal when it's time for the king to board."

"Yes, sir," said Sabien, then he bowed to Daylon. "Sire."

"You shouldn't wait around," said the king. "I hardly need to see you waving from the top of the tor as I sail away. We still have a kingdom to build."

Balven said, "I thought as much. The coach is ready."

He glanced down to where Declan was still organizing his men, and Daylon said, "Go on, and say whatever you wish to."

Balven said, "Whatever else, he is our younger brother. We would both do well to remember that."

"Trust me, I will never forget that." Daylon shook his head, then suddenly laughed softly. "Damn, but when he shouts he sounds so very much like Father."

Balven shared the humor. "You both do."

"You know, if we both come back, we're going to have to do something."

"What did you have in mind?"

There was a long silence, then Daylon said, "Name him as my heir."

Balven was surprised and it showed. "But—"

"I know, you thought you'd have to talk me into it." Daylon let out a breath that bordered on a sigh. "I'm never going to wed again, and you, dear brother, have steadfastly refused to. We have some cousins out there, still, no doubt, who avoided being murdered during the raids. If I die without naming him heir, every distant kinsman will suddenly appear, and we'll have factions fighting for power.

"In my desk, I signed the papers, in case I don't return."

"Did you?"

"Well, I thought I'd better tell you as you'll no doubt be rummaging through my desk as soon as you get back to the castle."

Balven laughed. "As any competent first minister to a king should."

"So, what evil scheme have you concocted to avow that our brother is legitimate?"

"Simple, really. We know his mother was Abigale Lennox, who is, or rather was, a cousin to both the royal families in Ilcomen and Ithrace, and her father claimed the title of court baron. I just happened to have stumbled across a witness who said a dying priest of some temple or another secretly wed her and Father."

Daylon nodded. "Who can dispute it?"

"Who indeed?"

"Well, go and say goodbye and get back and keep our kingdom intact."

"Should I tell Declan he's officially a prince?"

Daylon actually burst out laughing. "Good gods, no! He's got enough on his mind. Just tell him we both insist he not get himself killed."

The brothers embraced and Daylon headed over to where his castellans would board their ship, and Balven jogged down the hillside to where Declan waited.

Declan saw him coming and moved away from Sixto, to whom he was giving last-minute instructions.

As he approached, Balven said, "I came to bid you farewell." He extended his hand and Declan took it.

Then with a completely unanticipated impulse, Balven wrapped his arms around his younger brother in a hug, saying, "You stay alive, Declan."

Sixto looked on with thinly masked amusement as Declan froze in place from the unexpected embrace.

Declan let out a long-held breath when Balven released him and said quietly, "That is my intent." He looked past Balven toward Daylon, who was watching his horse being led away to join the rest of the mounts to be loaded onto *Borzon's Black Wake* before walking toward the landing where his personal retinue would board the lead ship. "The king?" he asked.

Affecting a casual tone, Balven said, "He's coming around to having a little brother . . . slowly." He gripped Declan by the shoulder. "Neither of you has given much thought to what happens after this war. So I've had to do it for both of you. You must come back, both of you."

Declan was as surprised by the intensity of that demand as he had been unprepared for the hug. He nodded slowly and said, "I'll keep him safe, if I can."

"Keep yourself safe, too," said Balven, unexpectedly showing rising emotion. He tried to shake off those feelings and after clearing his throat said, "I'm off back to Marquenet. Farewell!"

He quickly turned and marched up the hill.

Sixto approached, watching Balven's retreating back, and said to Declan, "We're ready to board."

Declan also watched as Balven continued up the hillside to where the carriage awaited. After a moment, he said, "Send a message to the captain of the ship, and when he signals, launch the first boat."

By the time Declan turned around to face the waiting ships he had purged his mind of whatever confusion Balven had caused, returning his focus to one thing: the destruction of the Pride Lords.

HATUSHALY STOOD ON THE HILLOCK behind the library as the sun was setting. He marveled at how the stars would appear as the light to the west faded, and slowly sweep across the vault of the sky. He had realized at last that it was a sort of illusion, as the world was turning and they were now beginning to face away from the sun, so in a sense he was moving in Garn's shadow. For some reason that concept both delighted and fascinated him.

"Trying to see stars up close again?" Bodai asked from behind him, coming out of the library door.

"No," said Hatushaly. "I just thought I'd get a bit of air, and watch the sunset and the stars come out." Then he laughed. "Stars come out, but they are always there, right?" Bodai nodded. "We just can't see them because the sun's light obscures theirs."

"That, apparently, is the case," said Bodai. "Eating this evening?"

"Yes," said Hatu. "Shall we?"

They went and got their food and sat down, and Bodai said, "We should have heard something from Hava by now, I think."

Hatu inclined his head slightly, as if agreeing, then said, "But I try to not think of that, or I start to worry."

"Your wife," said Bodai, pointing at Hatu with a spoonful of soup, "is perhaps the most competent person I've ever met, so if anyone's going to survive this madness, it is she."

"Agreed," said Hatu, "which is why I can avoid worry . . . most of the time. I can't keep checking on her with my . . . powers, because then I'd be doing nothing else."

Bodai laughed. "I understand."

"You worry, too, I know."

"Since you were brought to Coaltachin, and since the two of you became a pair, yes, always." He cast a glance toward the door, as if expecting Hava to walk through it at any moment. "Yes, I worry, but that doesn't change the fact she is more than capable of taking care of herself."

"I have discovered something interesting," said Hatu. He glanced at the entrance to the hall leading to the library. "With Nathan gone, I do try to poke around the edges of what I know, sort of extending my understanding."

Bodai chuckled. "Understandable."

Hatu scowled slightly. "Let me show you." He picked up a small piece of carrot that had fallen off his spoon and tossed it in the air. Suddenly it froze as it began to fall.

Bodai said, "I've seen you levitate objects before, Hatu."

Hatu grinned. "Look around the kitchen."

Bodai did and his eyes widened as he realized everyone in the kitchen area was frozen motionless, even in mid-step, but nobody was falling over. "What . . . ?"

Abruptly, everybody began moving again as if nothing had interrupted their movement, and the bit of carrot fell to the table.

Hatu shook his head slightly, as if clearing it. "I think I can stop time." Bodai's eyes grew even wider and he appeared speechless. "At least in a small area around me."

"How . . . ?"

"I don't know. It's another of those things I did by accident, or maybe it's not stopping time, but . . . freezing everything around me . . . but not me?"

Bodai said, "Will wonders never cease?"

A sudden surge of energy washed over Hatu and he dropped his spoon on the table.

"What?" asked Bodai.

"Did you feel that?"

"I had a sudden touch of gooseflesh, as if a cold draft came and went."

"Library," said Hatu.

They hurried into the dark library and halted. A strange shimmering ball of green energy hovered between the stacks of books near one shelf, and as they watched, both felt the hair on their arms and heads rise.

The orb was of scintillating green light, then it drew itself upward, like a curtain rapidly disappearing into a spot in the air, to wink away in an instant, leaving Nathan standing there holding the golden orb he'd shown them days before, and next to him was a slightly older man in a dark robe, holding a wooden staff. The older man had dark curly hair dusted with grey, and a lightly lined face, yet his bearing was upright and he seemed to emit energy as if he were still a young, vigorous man.

"Nathan!" said Hatushaly.

Nathan guided the other man toward Hatushaly and Bodai. He seemed slightly disoriented by whatever it was they had just been through.

Bodai said, "How did . . . ?"

Nathan indicated the orb, then replaced it in his rucksack. "It's very old . . ." He shrugged. "I inherited it." He guided the older man to the table and said, "Sit down." He looked over to Hatu and Bodai. "I thought it best to seek out someone who might know exactly what that thing in the pit truly is, and I hope I'm wrong about my conjecture."

The stranger's eyes came into focus and he smiled. "Hello," he said.

Nathan said, "The younger fellow is the one I told you about, by the name of Hatushaly. That is Bodai," he added, indicating the teacher.

The older man nodded. "Pleased to make your acquaintance. My name is Ruffio."

SINCE LEAVING RED SWEENEY AT Shechal, Hava had made a few stops and tracked down Catharian. It had taken more than a week to find him from his last known location, and she was as impressed by his espionage skills as she was annoyed by the effort it had taken to find him.

Catharian was now in the city of Tobilo with Dahod and two other rebellious Azhante ready to ride swift horses to the nearest large command between there and Akena. She and Catharian had refined Red Sweeney's suggested plan and now had a firm timetable in mind.

Hava stood on the beach on the big empty island Red Sweeney had told her about where King Daylon would stage his attack, watching the sails appearing on the horizon, and felt a surge of relief. She had complete trust in Sabien, but he was still sailing through treacherous waters, and if those who followed were sloppy in following his instructions, there were shoals and reefs waiting to rip out a ship's bottom.

She turned to Billy, who was acting as her mate while Sabien commanded the king's fleet. "Send the message. Be ready to cast off as soon as I'm back aboard."

Billy picked up a long pole with a piece of green cloth tied to it and waved it back and forth. A minute later another green flag was waved from the poop deck of the *Queen of Storms*.

Hava could hardly wait to get back on her ship after having captained the slug of a freighter that had carried her here.

A small company of workers from the Sanctuary had labored for the last few days to prepare a staging area for the king and his army. Canvas lean-tos had been erected against the prevailing winds, which were mild during the early summer in any event, and firepits were ready for cooking. There was also a somewhat nicer tent for the king's use.

Hava felt impatient, which was not her usual nature, but the coming fight was putting her on edge, and she was determined to make sure that everything within her power was done right.

Eventually, the lead ship changed course to enter the sheltered bay directly below the camp. Billy signed with the pole and flag, a long sweeping motion, indicating that the first ship should sail as close to the *Queen of Storms* as was safe, then the others anchor in a line stretching to where Hava stood now.

The instructions were followed and within an hour the king's ship was made fast and a boat lowered. When the king's launch reached the sand, Hava saw Daylon and Declan sitting in the stern.

They both waded ashore and Hava gave Daylon a slight bow, then embraced Declan. "I thought you'd be with your own men," she said.

It was the king who answered. "We put in at whatever island your man Sabien chose for water and I had Declan come aboard my ship." He thew a look at Declan and said, "We had some things to discuss."

Declan inclined his head in a gesture that indicated that this was all they would be saying on the matter.

"I've got a fire going and they're cooking you a supper," Hava said, moving aside to let the king pass, but he waved her ahead and said, "Lead on." Then he looked at his half-brother and said, "As long as it's not that monkey stew you told me about."

Declan chuckled. "Something a bit more appetizing, I hope."

They reached the tent, which contained a small table and two chairs, one of which Daylon occupied, while Hava and Declan stood. At last the king said, "Will one of you just sit down, so I don't feel like a complete idiot? I got enough of the protocols of court from Lodavico of Sandura."

Hava said, "You've been cooped up for days and I've eaten."

Declan hesitated, then took the chair. One of Hava's crew appeared holding two bowls of savory soup, a vegetable mixture seasoned with dried beef. "I have fowl on the spit, Majesty," he said, "and we've got a field oven baking bread."

"Fresh bread!" Daylon was nearly giddy. "You surpass every expectation, Hava."

"If all goes according to plan, you have four thousand or more men who will come ashore in the next few hours, and all of them will be hungry after weeks at sea on dried rations." She indicated the view out of the back entrance to the tent, a flap held aside by a tie loop, and Daylon and Declan could see dozens of workers scurrying around lighting cooking fires and carrying beef carcasses on massive iron spits. "I had every cooking device we could spare from the Sanctuary sent here, and they outdid themselves."

"I approve," said Daylon.

Hava asked, "How long before you're ready to fight?"

"How long from here to the enemy?" asked the king.

"Nine hours if the wind's right. You leave three hours after sunset and you sail into Akena at dawn."

Daylon put down his spoon as a roast chicken and vegetables were brought in. He looked at Hava and said, "Why don't you tell me what you need?"

Hava said, "The call is going out across all Nytanny for the armies to gather, for another raid on North Tembria. They plan to strike Marquensas this time." She paused. "Every ship capable of making that voyage will be reaching harbor in three weeks or so, to make the voyage in time for midsummer."

"We need a week to graze the horses," said Daylon, "to get them fit for battle; we were lucky and only had to put down one that got colic. And we must rest the men. After that, what is our best choice?"

Hava calculated for a silent minute, then said, "Eleven days, from tonight. I have a signal fire set up on one of the bluffs south of here. I need to see if Sabien's got one of those long tube spyglass things."

"He has," said Daylon. "I saw him using it to scan the horizon for raiders."

"Good. In eleven days at sundown, if there is nothing amiss, a fire will be lit that maybe could be seen by a sharp-eyed man, but by anyone with one of those spyglasses, and that's the signal that at three hours past sundown, you set sail. Board your horses that day, and all the support equipment, then wait for me."

"You're joining us?" asked the king.

"I'm leading you," said Hava. "Catharian thinks the Azhante fleet will pass you by heading north, a day or so before, looking to quell the rebellion in Tobilo. I'm leading this fleet in case there are Azhante ships trying to block the harbor." She smiled. "Besides, I've never gotten to use that nasty ballista that fits in the bow. And there's one more reason," she added, almost joyfully.

"What's that?" asked Declan.

"Catharian said the Azhante are so angry with me that they've put a price on my head. Moreover, they've built a bigger, faster ship that should be finished soon, called *King of Breakers*."

Her smile broadened. "I've got to steal that ship."

24

ASSAULTS, PUNISHMENT,

AND REVELATIONS

———✦———

Toachipe watched for the first sign of light, his eyes scanning the eastern horizon as the brightening sky hinted at the coming dawn. Today would be a clear day: the sky had been brilliant with stars all night.

His duty always had him searching the east for the false dawn, when the sky lightens slowly before the disc of the sun appears over the eastern sea. Save for days of inclement weather, he found this time to be his favorite, for it was a time of calm and silence in a city of noise and tension once he had awoken the Pride Lords and begun another morning in the realm.

Movement to the northeast caught his eye as the sky lightened. At first he saw flickers of grey against a darker grey, but in a few minutes, the images resolved themselves.

Ships! He quickly counted nine of them. At full sail and approaching the open harbor swiftly! Within moments he knew that these were not Azhante ships or local trade ships, but something alien and unwelcome.

Just before the sun rose, a knock at his door preceded the arrival of the first runner. He called, "Enter!" and seconds later a young man stood ready for Toachipe's announcement of a new day to the runners assembled in the hall, so that each might dash to the apartments of the Pride Lords slumbering in their chambers.

The runner came to Toachipe's side and looked out to see the ships nearing the almost-empty quays. Only one ship remained in harbor after the Azhante fleet had been dispatched to quell a rebellion in Tobilo.

"What is that?" asked the runner.

The sun peeped over the eastern sea and Toachipe saw a ship moving to the southernmost end of the quays. It was a ship he recognized, one he had seen enter and leave this harbor many times. *Borzon's Black Wake*, the treasure ship of the Golden Pride.

"The sun has risen!" said the runner, alarm in his tone. "And whose ships are those?"

Toachipe held up his hand and for an instant was fascinated by looking at the back of it as if for the first time. It was the hand of a strong man, one who had served the Pride Lords for years, in order to provide for his family. In his other hand he gripped a heavy oaken ceremonial staff. And then he realized that it could serve well as a battle staff.

His view returned to the familiar ship.

Men shimmied down ropes as the captain turned the big treasure ship sideways and let it slip onto the beach. Then as if by some sorcery, a large door fell from the side of the ship and he could hear a loud pop, as caulk and canvas was ripped from wood, and ramps were run from the lowest deck to the sand. Horses led by armed men came quickly down that ramp.

"Look," said the runner, pointing to the other end of this flotilla and there Toachipe saw another familiar ship, the *Queen of Storms.* Instantly he knew exactly who these newcomers were. And he knew that the Pride Lords were about to face vengeance.

"Dawn has come. We must awaken our masters!" insisted the young runner.

Toachipe turned to him. "Not today."

"To fail in our duty is death!" the youngster protested, now in a state of panic.

Toachipe looked back over his shoulder at the soldiers now swarming off the ships and organizing on the quay, then returned his gaze to the young runner.

"Death?" He smiled. "Eventually, but perhaps not today."

DECLAN'S MEN ASSEMBLED. HE AND Sixto had instructed them to wait until the cavalry had advanced ahead of them. Declan saw them organizing and that Sixto was scanning the streets leading to the quays for defenders. But the only sounds in this harbor were coming from the ships unloading.

Sixto said, "I expected we'd be dodging arrows at least by now."

"No sentries?"

"Apparently not."

"Too many years of absolute security," said Declan. "It simply didn't occur to them they might be attacked here."

A few local residents began to appear in the streets, but most took one look at the assembled army and raced back inside their homes and slammed their doors.

"We've got a few more minutes, then I think it's going to turn nasty here," said Sixto.

Declan nodded and turned to face his men. Half his force was still aboard the ship, ready to fall into line behind those already on the quay.

"Get ready!" he commanded, and swords were drawn, and bows nocked with arrows.

Declan glanced to where the king was organizing his forces and saw that almost every mount was off the ship and had a rider in the saddle.

A squad of Azhante guards appeared, running toward them from the street Declan had been told was the main approach to the Pride Lords' palace.

Hava had stressed many times that the first thing he needed to do when facing Azhante was to shout. So in his loudest voice he cried, "Coaltachin!"

Two of the Azhante drew their swords and died before they reached the first line of soldiers from a fusillade of arrows shot from the deck of the ship. The other four stood paralyzed by uncertainty. The next phrase he and the others had been drilled in was, "Join us or get out of the way!"

The four Azhante exchanged glances, and one ran off, but the others stripped off their black tunics and head covers and moved to where Declan pointed with his sword. He saw immediately that these three young men were more than ready to fight.

"If it all goes this well, we can have our midday meal from up there," said Sixto, pointing at the hilltop that was their destination.

"I wouldn't count on that," said Declan.

Suddenly, the king rode up to him, pointed up the main street, and shouted, "Follow us!"

The sound of four hundred horses' iron-shod hooves pounding the cobbles shattered the early morning calm and echoed through the lower city. Doors and windows were opened then quickly shut as the cavalry passed by.

As soon as the last horse turned, Declan shouted, "Ready!"

Not only his men but the king's specially trained soldiers stood poised to move. Working from Red Sweeney's memory of this city, passed on by Hava, Daylon split his forces into two flanking groups, as he and Declan had agreed that the mercenaries would serve better if they were unburdened by too many instructions. The flanking units would come up two other large streets, one on each side of the main street, then if they were blocked they were to move in behind Declan's forces.

Declan waved his sword in a circular motion and shouted, "Forward!"

He and Sixto set out at a quick jog, since charging uphill was not a practical decision over a long distance and given that the balance of Declan's forces was still on the ship, he did not want to leave them strung out behind in a long line. That plan had been developed because they had expected resistance from the docks, but so far only the one squad of Azhante had appeared.

That changed quickly once they reached the first cross street. Arrows came flying down from above, and Declan leapt close to the wall on his left. He glanced upward but saw nothing.

The buildings this close to the harbor were all shops and residences, with warehouses sprinkled in between, but there were larger buildings farther up the hill. Declan shouted to Sixto, who was hunkered down across the street, "Can you see where they're coming from?"

Sixto raised his sword and pointed up and back. "Somewhere over there."

A few more arrows arced down, and Declan saw that Sixto was right. Archers on a rooftop the next street over were blindly shooting in the hope of hitting one of the invaders. He judged it more of a nuisance than a serious threat. Still, a lucky arrow could kill a man just as dead as a targeted one.

"The king's men need to get someone up on the roof!" shouted

Declan. He glanced back and saw that his forces were piling up behind him.

"Maybe nobody is shooting at them?"

Declan found this almost amusing. He waited and then another flight of five arrows came down, one striking the wooden shutter of the window under which he crouched. He motioned for the men nearest him to race across the street and wait on the other side. He counted and held up his hand, stopping the men, and more arrows landed. He heard one of his men shout in pain, then curse loudly. From that he judged at least the man wasn't dead.

After the next flight of arrows, more men crossed the intersection and Declan sprinted to Sixto's side. "Help me up," said Declan.

"Onto the roof?"

Declan nodded.

"Are you mad?"

"Probably. Wait for the next volley."

As soon as the arrows struck, Declan stood and signaled for the men to charge up the street after the cavalry. With only five or six archers above them, most of the men would make it past this intersection safely, but Declan wasn't going to leave them behind his forces. Half a dozen archers standing on rooftops with quivers full of shafts could kill a fair number of men.

Declan heard arrows striking and a couple of curses, then he nodded to Sixto who gave him a boost up to where Declan could grab the eaves and pull himself up onto the roof. He rolled flat, looking to see if he could spot the archers, saw nothing, then turned and dropped his hand to Sixto.

As he had expected, his second in command was ready to jump and grab his arm. In a few seconds, Sixto lay on the roof next to him. Declan asked, "Spot them?"

"Over there," said Sixto, pointing.

"Crawl, then jump and charge," said Declan.

"You know, we are terrible leaders."

"What?"

"A proper leader would send other men up here to be shot with arrows while he stayed below telling the rest of the men where to go next."

Declan said, "You picked a wonderful time to bring that up."

Sixto said, "Would you have listened?"

"Probably not, now crawl."

The two men crawled on their stomachs till they reached a narrow alley. The archers were on the next building over, and now they were shooting at both Declan's men and the king's men coming down the next broad street.

Sixto looked down, and said, "That's only seven or eight feet," in a sarcastic tone.

"Easy as falling off a chair," said Declan.

"You could have put that a little differently."

"When I say go, back up three steps, then a run and a hop and we're across."

Sixto nodded.

"Ready . . . go!"

Both men stood up, took their three steps back, and then leapt across the alley. On the other side were five archers, and one was restringing his bow. The other four were now shooting straight down into the king's forces below.

By the time the first archer saw them and shouted a warning, Declan and Sixto were almost upon them. One bowman turned and let fly, the arrow missing Sixto's neck by a scant measure, before he even had time to react.

With only bows, the archers were almost defenseless, but they tried to use their bows as clubs. Declan carried a sword, and Sixto a sword and belt-knife. Within seconds all five Azhante bowmen were dead.

Declan and Sixto ran and jumped back on the building overlooking their company and by the time they returned every man was up the road in front of them. Declan put his hands onto the roof tiles, then turned to lower himself and dropped to the ground. Sixto jumped and landed with a roll.

"You could break your neck doing that," Declan said.

"Or I could land safely," said Sixto.

They both turned to follow the company of mercenaries and were nearly out of breath when suddenly they encountered a wall of bodies.

"What's the problem?" Declan asked.

"Damn me if I know," said the man in front of Declan. "Nothing but men standing ahead."

"Let me through," Declan commanded, and when the fighter turned to see who was giving the orders, he said, "Sorry, Captain. I thought you were up ahead."

Sixto smiled and said, "A proper leader, right?"

Declan's dark look revealed that he didn't appreciate the humor.

They forced their way forward, earning some curses and a few attempts at backhand blows until someone decided they should shout, "Make way for the captain!"

By the time Declan reached the front of the column, he saw that a huge conflict was raging as Daylon's cavalry was attempting to force their way past a hastily erected barricade at the bottom of the road that led steeply up to the top of the Pride Lords' hill.

Daylon was pulling his horse soldiers back as the barrier was preventing the riders from getting behind the barricade, while the defenders were using spears to jab at both horses and riders. Two horses, with arrows protruding from them, lay at the foot of the barricade as Declan surveyed the fight.

Within seconds he shouted, "Archers to the fore!"

Word was passed and in less than a minute half a dozen archers were answering his call.

"They've got three of their own archers up there. I saw them a bit ago." Declan pointed to a rooftop on the corner of the street diagonally across from him, where three archers were standing. "If you can't hit them, at least keep their heads down."

He turned to the men behind him and said, "You lot, get across there and get those horses out of the way. If they're still alive, cut their throats so they don't kick anyone to death."

He stepped back and waved them on, then turned and saw Daylon sitting a short distance away, watching. Declan ran over to him and said, "We'll clear a way: I'll signal when it's done."

Daylon ignored the lack of formal address and just nodded. "Get that barricade down."

Declan ran back. His men were already climbing the barricade. He saw half a dozen get up on the roof where the archers had been shooting from and quickly bring them down.

Declan shouted, "Clear this street for the cavalry! Search every house for Azhante." He had given strict orders that only Azhante be killed. Any murder, looting, or rape would get a man hanged. He had promised them enough gold after this war that he hoped it would prevent wanton destruction. Not only had he no taste for it after the pillaging and plundering of Beran's Hill, but it was a waste of time: he might need every fighting man when they reached the Pride Lords.

His men cleared away the barricade that had been made from

furniture ripped out of nearby houses, crates from warehouses, and anything else these Azhante could find. Not one of them asked for quarter, but kept fighting until they were overwhelmed.

Declan moved to the center of the street, turned, and pointed to each side of it, splitting his force in two, the men going door to door.

Sixto came up and said, "We let the men do the hard work?"

Declan let out a long breath and just nodded.

"As a proper leader should," said Sixto.

Declan feigned striking him in the face with a balled fist, then turned to walk down the middle of the street, glancing upward to keep watch for more archers but seeing none.

The men proceeded cautiously, at a walk, wary of ambush. As doors were kicked open, Declan heard screams from inside, but his men were back out on the street quickly so his message of no looting or assault of the common people seemed to have gotten through.

"We have another barricade, Captain!" someone shouted up ahead, and Declan and Sixto hurried to the next cross street.

There they saw a few dozen black-clad Azhante fighters rapidly building a blockade out of debris and an overturned wagon, and Declan didn't hesitate. "Charge!" he shouted, and he turned to run at the defenders.

He jumped onto a crate, which slipped backward. He brought a crushing blow down onto the neck and shoulder of the closest defender as he fell, landing facedown on the cobbles, the breath knocked out of him. His head swam until a strong hand gripped him under the armpit and hauled him to his feet.

"That was stupid," Sixto said, pulling him away.

"Agreed," said Declan, shaking his head at the ringing in his ears.

By the time he had regained his wits, the fight was over.

"This is too easy," said Sixto. "Where is their army?"

Then it struck Declan. "They don't have one."

"Then how did they ravage North Tembria?"

"It wasn't their army! It was all the nations that are currently riding in rebellion, the ones they wanted to cull!"

Declan took a quick look around in a complete circle, trying not to feel dizzy. He shouted to the men behind him, "Pass the word back to the king to bring the horses up! Clear the road!"

He waited for word to be passed, and men on both sides pressed themselves back against the buildings so that they wouldn't be trampled.

Declan shouted, "Pass the word! Leave the houses and follow the cavalry!"

Sixto said, "What do you have in mind?"

"They've been delaying us, trying to buy time for those up at that palace. That's where they will defend with everything they have!"

Sixto looked up toward the massive structure at the top of the hill and said, "I told you this was too easy."

"I hate it when you're right," said Declan, clapping Sixto's shoulder.

A short time later the king and his cavalry rode past. When the last horse had gone through, Declan waved his men to follow and started running.

Hava made her way to the bow where two archers waited. "Nothing?"

"Nothing," answered one of the men. He pointed high up past the lower buildings. "The noises are coming from up there, somewhere, but anyone living down here is probably hiding under their bed, and we're not seeing anyone with a weapon."

Hava turned to Billy and said, "Is Sabien ready?"

"The straw and oil are in place. His crew is aboard."

Hava said, "Send word that we're a long way from knowing what's up there, but if he's the last man, burn her!"

"I'll send word."

Hava turned and looked at the far south end of the harbor where *Borzon's Black Wake* was beached. The king's engineers had cut a huge door into the side of the ship Sabien had swung into the beach, and then caulked it with heavy canvas. They had cut it just above the waterline, to keep leaking to a minimum, and that had facilitated the quick unloading of the horses and riders.

But the ship was now useless, and the plan was for the king and the others to return here and board *Queen of Storms* if she was still docked, or whichever ship had room if she was engaged with an Azhante ship. Two of the king's ten ships had been left back at the island base, and Hava had led the eight ships attacking.

The grim decision had been made to abandon the horses, and likely enough men would be killed that there would be room on the ships for them to return to the island. If one or two of these ships didn't return, well, they still had two others to get them back to Marquensas.

A few minutes later, she saw flames spring from within *Borzon's Black Wake* and Sabien jogged into sight. The big, ugly treasure ship had been useful, but she felt no regret at all seeing it in flames, remembering all too well the misery of those who had been chained within.

Sabien reached the deck and came to her. "It's done, Captain."

Hava nodded. "So, we wait."

* * *

Hatu nervously sat at the table in the library, his worry clearly visible, and at last he said, "I could look."

Nathan said, "Don't. Not until we know more about the thing in the pit—"

"No, I meant at the battle," said Hatu. "Hava is there, so I can find her easily and see how it goes."

"I worry, too, but if you're constantly checking on how she's doing, we get nothing done here."

Since Ruffio had arrived with Nathan, he had methodically questioned Hatu on every aspect of his powers. His approach was different to Nathan's: it was as if he were creating a catalog of his abilities, as Sabella had with the books.

"You can distance-see?" asked Ruffio, who still expressed surprise at many of the things Hatu achieved.

"Not everywhere," Hatu answered. "It has to be somewhere I've been and remember, or if I can find someone I know well, then I can see them, and that's when I see where they are, and that I can remember." He shrugged. "I'm not explaining it well."

"No, that's fine," said Ruffio. He looked at Nathan. "Still, no spellcraft or devices?"

It was Hatu who answered, "No. I just do it." He scowled at Ruffio and said, "You keep asking the same question. I don't know any spellcraft, if you mean something like that book over there Nathan showed you, and the only device I've used was a compass, a long time ago . . . Oh, and one of those long-distance looking-tubes, a spyglass. I looked through one of those, once."

Ruffio said, "Let's leave this discussion for some other time." He looked at Bodai. "That's the longest distance I've ever traveled. When I finished my studies ages ago, I took a little time off to wander for a while."

"Twenty years is a little time?" Nathan asked in a mocking tone.

Ruffio fixed him with a dark look. "You more than anyone know the answer to that."

Nathan shrugged. "I told you there are many things I don't remember."

Ruffio waved that comment away and said to Hatu, "So, can you take me to this pit and show me what's in there?"

"Easily, but first I'd like to see how my wife is doing."

Hatu sat back, closed his eyes, and after a minute he said, "She's on her ship in a harbor and the battle is at a distance from her." He opened his eyes, a look of relief on his face. "So, it will be dark soon. If you want to look at that place, we should do this now."

Ruffio said, "Very well. What do I do?"

"Get up," said Hatu, and placing his hands on Ruffio's shoulders he said, "Put your hands on my shoulders, then close your eyes."

Ruffio did as Hatu told him and suddenly he seemed to be floating in a void with Hatu. "Where are we?"

"I don't really know," said Hatu. "I think of it as 'my place' and from here I can do many things."

The latticework of energy lines appeared and Ruffio said, "What?"

"I'll explain later. This is where we want to go."

Suddenly they were hovering near the rim of the pit. It was night in the Wound and Ruffio gasped, which Hatu assumed was a mental mimicking of what he was doing in his physical body.

"Nothing here can hurt you," said Hatu. "Now look."

He ushered Ruffio to the edge of the pit and changed the light so he could see down inside. The broken body of the child had been joined by a dog's corpse and what appeared to be a severed ear.

Beneath the corpses, the massive creature lay motionless. But Ruffio said, "Gods above! No!"

The connection was broken and Hatu found himself back in the library. Ruffio was reeling as if he had been physically struck.

"What is it?" asked Nathan.

"It's what you feared."

Nathan's face drained of color and he moved to a chair and sat down.

Bodai said, "What is it? What has shaken you so?"

Ruffio glanced at Nathan, who said, "They won't understand."

"You haven't warned them?" Ruffio sounded angry.

"I saw no reason to worry them in case it was something else."

"Something else!" Ruffio's voice rose to a shout. His face became a mask of outrage and his tone was accusatory. "You as much as any being in this universe know what this is."

For the first time, Hatu and Bodai saw Nathan angry. His eyes welled with tears of frustration and with thick emotion he shouted, "I didn't ask to be here! I was sent here with most of my memory gone! I don't know what you think I should know, but I am as ignorant as these two"—he waved at Hatu and Bodai—"about many things!"

Hatu took a tentative step, ready to get between the two men. "Wait!" He held up his hands in a placating gesture. "What are we doing here?"

Ruffio nodded and regained his composure. "That thing in the pit . . . it's an agent of the Void. It is the single most powerful creature of the Void."

Hatu said, "The Void?" He looked at Nathan with an unspoken question.

Biting back anger, Nathan said, "Before this!" He waved his

hand in a large arc. "Before everything, this universe . . . other universes, *everything!* There was this . . ." He winced as if struck by a sudden pain. "I need to remember!" he shouted, as if addressing some unseen agent.

Hatu could see Nathan was battling his mounting frustration and accompanying fury.

Nathan winced again as if another pain struck, and then he let out a long breath, seeming of relief, and he lowered his voice. "Thank you," he said, again as if speaking to someone or something invisible.

Hatu used his power to see if another entity might be in the room, but he sensed nothing.

"Before the beginning," Nathan said in calmer tones. "All, everything existed in a . . . perfect instant." He leaned over and tapped the table. "Matter, energy, time, all bound up in a . . . ball, let's say. Something happened," he continued. "In a sudden moment, everything changed. Time unraveled, spooling out to become what we experience. Massive bursts of energy also, with matter forming, dust, then gravity turned them into rocks, planets, and stars, air and water, anything material. No one knows how long. Billions of years, or longer. Stars were born and died, life arose and went extinct. The best explanation anyone can come up with is pure speculation. I fear we may never know, or perhaps we are incapable of understanding, how this could be. Imagine two fundamental forces, primal furies let us say, in a harmonious balance in that single moment, that perfect instant.

"Suddenly it was not perfect, out of balance, and everything flew apart."

Hatu, Ruffio, and Bodai were rapt and remained perfectly silent.

"One of the forces tore that perfect instant asunder. I choose to think of that as the chaotic force, the demand for change, evolution, uncertainty.

"The other force was supreme contentment. I think of it as the ordered force, and now it's seeking to return everything to that perfect instant. I have no reason to claim knowledge, but it seems fit to say that ordered force is frustrated and angry."

Hatu softly said, "You mean that thing in the pit is an agent of a fundamental fury that wants to return everything to . . . one instant of bliss?"

Nathan had a tear running down his cheek. "Yes, that's what it is."

Ruffio said, "The thing in the pit is a Dreadlord. It has the power to consume all life on this planet and destroy everything right down to the smallest grains of dust, and expand out from here, and eventually destroy . . . everything."

Hatu tried to absorb this. He found himself shaking. "Why is it here?" he asked at last.

Ruffio said, "That, my friend, is an excellent question, and one for which I have no answer. Because until this moment, I thought I knew for certain that this thing was trapped somewhere else, locked there in an eternal battle with another being far beyond your imagining."

Nathan said, "What do we do?"

"I go back, as quickly as possible."

"Do you need the orb?"

"No. Now that I've been here, I can return without that cursed device. I won't need the protection shell in case we accidentally appear inside a mountain." He took a breath. "That device is not entirely accurate, and occasionaly it misses the target destination. That protective shell makes me woozy."

Hatu said, "What are you saying about that Dreadlord?"

"All that you love is at risk," answered Ruffio, "because all that exists is at risk. There are people I need to speak to, and things I need to learn. Attend to the battle and your wife, for while that is important to you, it's trivial compared to the true risk."

Hatu found his childhood annoyance at not comprehending returning rapidly and his temper rose. "I don't understand! What does it all mean?"

Bodai put a reassuring hand on his shoulder, while Ruffio turned and looked at Hatu. "The universe is complex beyond understanding. What we call 'the Void' is . . . the space between all those particles you call furies. The Void is . . . this utterly empty, grey nothingness, a perfect balance between pure white and absolute blackness. The Dread are the single most effective creatures of the Void. The thing slumbering in that pit can, at full power, devour a star. I'm going to have to go and talk to people who know more about this than even I do." He looked at Nathan and said, "I'm sorry. I do not know what you've been through, what you've forgotten. I ask for your forgiveness."

Nathan nodded.

Ruffio closed his eyes and moved his hands slightly, and a tall oval appeared next to him. It had a scintillating silver sheen, wavering like pond water, and he stepped through and into it. In a few seconds, it collapsed into nothing and there was a slight sound of inflowing air where he had stood.

Hatu asked, "Where did he go?"

"To get help," Nathan answered.

DECLAN SWUNG HIS SWORD, TAKING the man opposite him in the shoulder. Blood arced upward and bone was exposed as he cried out in pain and fell out of Declan's way.

Daylon's forces had battled to the very gates of the Pride Lords' palace grounds, finding a large wooden gate partially closed. It had been open for so long that it had sagged and warped the hinges, so it wouldn't fully close.

Declan's men needed once again to clear the way for the king's cavalry and the bloody struggle had been at a critical point of balance for almost an hour.

As Declan's men fought their way to the small opening, the defenders would push back at them to stop the attackers from opening the gate any wider. Declan, Sixto, and the most experienced soldiers in his company rotated in and out of the vanguard as often as possible, resting for a few minutes between fights.

The attackers would gain an advantage for a minute or two, and the gate would swing slightly wider by inches, but for every two inches gained, the defenders gained back one. Still, the swords Declan, Edvalt, and the other smiths had fashioned were breaking blades, cleaving armor, and allowing the attackers the ability to hew their way through the defenses.

At last, the gate moved more than a few inches, and with the loud screech of wood on stone, the right-hand gate was pushed back, and the attackers flooded in.

There was a handful of Azhante, and from the way they fought, these were the most loyal of the fanatics. With them were many men dressed in ornate costumes, looking more like ceremonial sentries and guards than true soldiers.

After an hour of fighting at the gate, the battle in the massive courtyard was over in minutes. Many of the men in robes and decorative armor threw down their weapons and cried quarter. Declan shouted, "Take prisoners!" But he knew those surrendering would be lucky if his men heard the order.

They swarmed into a large plaza that served as the entrance to this massive palace complex.

Declan had his men fan out and soon there were no defenders left outside. The entrance to the palace complex comprised two massive wooden doors. They were shut, and almost certainly barred from inside.

Daylon rode into the plaza and dismounted. He looked back and shouted, "Get the horses out of here!"

One rider in three would dismount and lead away his horse and two others, so that two out of three could fight on foot.

Daylon was short of breath and looked his age. When he removed his helm, his grey hair was matted to his skull, his eyes were sunken with dark circles below, and his cheeks flushed red.

"Are you all right?" Declan asked.

"I will be when we finish this." Daylon glanced skyward as the sun rose higher. The day was getting hotter. "Water!" the king shouted and shortly after a man brought a water skin. Daylon took a long drink, then handed the skin to Declan.

Declan took a long swallow, then handed the remaining water to Sixto. Sixto finished the skin and tossed it aside.

Daylon motioned for the company to follow him and moved toward the main doors. Declan scanned the dozens of windows, topped by open terraces, that went up and up for half a dozen stories.

"You fear archers?" asked the king.

"They have few," answered Declan, "but it only takes one."

"Truth," agreed Daylon. "Where are they?"

"They have no army," said Declan. "Don't you see?" He repeated the insight he had shared with Sixto and finished by saying, "They're jailers, and the Azhante are constables, sheriffs, tax collectors, spies, but not soldiers." He took a deep breath and added, "They may be assassins, but they're useless in a stand-up fight. What did Hava call them? Crime lords?"

Daylon was confused for a moment, then his eyes widened. "Of course!" For the first time since this campaign had been conceived, the King of Marquensas looked almost happy. "Getting in is the problem." He studied the edifice before him. "This . . . warren is four or five times bigger than my castle, but so far we've seen nothing that resembles a defensive fortification. Unless we run into killing rooms, traps, and squads of soldiers waiting for us, it's just a matter of finding our way to wherever these Pride Lords have barricaded themselves in, get in, and kill them all. Once we've done that, it should be over quickly." He glanced up at the sky and saw that it wasn't yet noon.

It was Sixto who pointed at the massive doors they faced, twelve feet tall or even higher, each one ten feet wide, carved out of ancient wood that was probably as hard as steel, and said, "I hope you are right, my king, but first we must get through those!"

25

RESOLUTION, DISCOVERIES, AND

TRANSFORMATIONS

———†———

D onte waved at Hava from under the bowsprit of the ship next to *Queen of Storms*. She was watching from the poop deck as a longboat tethered to the bow of her ship was rowing out, turning the ship in case they needed to defend themselves against any unexpected visitors. The other ships would likewise be turned once the king and his army reboarded.

She waved and he hustled over and dived into the water. Her eyes widened as he came to the surface and swam over to a rope ladder that was now twenty or so feet from the quay.

In a moment a dripping Donte stood next to her and said, "Did I need to ask to come aboard or something like that?"

"It's the custom," she answered, trying not to laugh. Mirth seemed inappropriate in the midst of an attack.

"I never remember those things," he said.

"I thought you were in Marquensas, with Balven."

"I am supposed to be, but I just thought this would be more interesting. So, I sneaked aboard the king's ship. People at the castle have got used to seeing me running errands, and the 'on the king's business' thing worked well enough on the ship. I grabbed a bit of food here and there, usually with the ship's crew, not the soldiers."

"Why didn't I see you on the island?"

"You were spending a lot of time with the king and other important people," he said as he tried to squeeze water out of his shirt sleeves. "If the king saw me, he'd probably put me under guard." He glanced back up at the Pride Lords' palace. "How's the fight going?"

"I have no idea," she answered. "We're getting ready to leave whatever happens, but I expected we might be attacked." She pointed to the main deck, where a squad of twenty of the king's top soldiers were lined up, ready to defend, alongside the ship's crew. "People in the city are staying inside, and I've only seen a few dead Azhante over there." She turned to the far end of the quay where the ships were beginning to be towed into position for departure.

Donte shook more water off his clothing. "The best part about being friends with you and Hatu is all the amazing things I get to see."

She kissed him on the cheek, then said, "Shut up and get out of the way."

Donte laughed.

Hava watched carefully as the longboat pulled the bow of the *Queen of Storms*, swinging her away from the quay, then glanced over her shoulder. As the ship aligned in the desired direction, she said to Donte, "I wish I knew what was happening up there." With a nod of her head, she indicated the battle on the other side of the city.

"We'll find out soon enough, I suspect," said Donte. He looked toward the bow as the line turning the ship was cast off and men began disconnecting the sheets that ran from the bowsprit to the foremast. "What are they doing?" he asked.

"This beauty has a ballista that replaces the bowsprit. Slows her down a bit, but it's got a nasty bite. And despite it, she's still faster than most." She smiled. *"Queen of Storms* is an ambush predator and I wouldn't mind someone turning up so I could finally use that giant spear."

Donte's expression was dubious, as the best option was nobody showing up in a warship. He pushed aside that observation and asked, "What'll it do? Kill a lot of people at the same time?" He grinned.

Hava laughed. "Only if they get in the way." She pointed to where the bowsprit was being removed. "You just point your ship at the enemy ship and if you're breaching troughs or crashing breakers, when the ship lifts at the bow, you shoot that big nasty bolt, and if you aim it right, it'll completely ruin the other ship's rigging and sails. Get lucky and one shot will quickly have the other ship dead in the water. You swing alongside and swarm the deck and capture the ship without sinking it."

"Sounds like fun," said Donte. He stood motionless for a moment, then said, "Something is changing."

"What?" asked Hava.

"Remember what I told you about the Sisters of the Deep, and . . . well, I came back to kill Hatu."

Her eyes narrowed as she said, "I thought that was a very bad jest."

"No," said Donte. "They put something in my head . . ." He looked as if he was fighting for words. "But whatever they did, it's fading."

"This was all serious?"

"As serious as I ever get," he replied. "They sent one of those sea creatures to command me . . . so I killed it. You know I don't like to be told what to do."

She was caught halfway between disbelief and fear. "Do you want to kill Hatu?"

Donte took a deep breath. "No . . . but maybe beat him up a little."

She stared at him wide-eyed, then hit him hard on the arm. "You bastard! Some things you don't joke about!"

"Ow!" he cried out. "You hit hard!"

Tears were welling up in her eyes. "You deserved it."

"Probably," he conceded, then he turned and looked out over the aft rail. "I wonder how the king is doing up there."

"WE NEED A BATTERING RAM," said the king, "but the engineers are back on the island."

Sixto, standing behind Declan, said, "Doors that big need a rolling ram with cover, better if it's pushed by oxen. Nothing we can cobble together here will serve. Biggest damn doors I've ever seen."

Declan asked, "Is this the only way in for a place this big?"

"I'm waiting for scouts who're riding the perimeter, but however many other doors they find, they're all going to be locked and barricaded," said Daylon.

"If there's a smaller door," said Sixto, "we could chop down a tree and a few dozen men could use that as a ram."

Daylon said, "We have some four-man log-rams ready, but they're effective only for smaller interior doors."

Declan said, "Making a bigger ram will take too long, even if we find what we need in the city, and I've spotted archers up on that first open terrace.

"Given how weak the defense has been, I'll bet gold that as soon as they saw us coming, they pulled everyone with a weapon back into this palace complex. As big as it looks, it's got to be a warren in there. Expect room-to-room fighting, and even if we get through a smaller door, that'll just be a choke point."

Suddenly Daylon said, "I'm a fool."

"What?" asked Declan.

"Those doors, they're wood. Ancient, polished, massive wood. Oak, hickory, whatever, planks glued and bolted together, but still wood."

"And wood burns," said Declan. Without waiting for Daylon's order, he turned to Sixto. "Get a squad, search the shops, find anything that'll burn."

Sixto nodded and ran back to where Declan's company waited, half a block away. "You're going to need shields," he said to the king.

Daylon nodded and waved over a runner. "Get Collin here. He's over on the right flank."

The soldier said, "Yes, sire," and sprinted off.

In less than five minutes he came running back, a very large man following him, wearing heavy chain armor but despite this keeping pace with little effort.

The big sergeant inclined his head in a bow. "Yes, highness?"

"I've got a nasty task that needs doing."

"That's the kind I like, sire." Seeing Declan, he nodded, and patted the hilt of his sword.

Declan took that as a compliment.

"I need shieldmen to carry as much as they can to that door. We're going to build a huge rubbish pile, then set it alight."

"Sure to be archers up there who will object, highness. I see the need." He turned to survey which companies stood where, and then said, "I think we can do this, sire." He gave another short bow and then started shouting instructions to men standing off to the king's right.

"He's got one of the good ones, right?" asked the king.

"One of the first," said Declan, knowing that Daylon meant the King's Steel blades. "Collin recognized my blade the moment he saw it and had me make a blade for himself and Baron Rodrigo."

"Knew he was smart when he first turned up," said Daylon.

"Kept Copper Hills in good order until they were overrun," observed Declan as the first of his men appeared with arms full of flammable materials.

Collin returned with a company of men carrying long kite shields, made to deal with the possibility of facing cavalry. The pointed bottom could be jammed into the ground and still cover a man holding a long spear. In the hands of a well-disciplined company, they could break a cavalry charge. Until this moment, Declan thought they'd be useless, but Collin instructed his men to run to the massive doors, and they formed up with the shields held high overhead.

The archers above began firing as soon as Daylon's men came into range. Two men were struck, one obviously killed. The wounded man dropped his shield and hobbled out of arrow range, but the rest reached the massive doors. Slowly, the line of men with shields snaked its way back beyond the range of the archers. The noise of steel-tipped arrows striking the shields was like a deafening rainfall.

Daylon said, "Good thing those archers don't have any of those wicked bows the hillmen north of Marquenet use. Those hunters can hit a target at a ridiculous distance. Even with elevation, those bastards up there are missing far more than they're hitting."

"What's Collin doing now?" Declan wondered.

A second line of shield-bearers ran quickly to stand beside the first, and as the men reached their position, they turned to face one another. Then they raised their shields in such a way that the tips jutted between each other, almost interlocking.

"He's making a damn tunnel!" shouted Daylon.

"Well, he was Baron Rodrigo's master-at-arms," Declan said. "He worked with engineers as much as with soldiers."

"Marquensas never had a master-at-arms. Grandfather and Father always oversaw the army personally. Well, he's mine now, so I'll take care of that oversight as soon as this fight is over."

Archers carried their large rectangular shields they could shoot over. They dashed along each side of the first lines and knelt down, forming walls so that arrows from above couldn't strike legs or ricochet off the stones and injure the men that way.

Declan motioned for his men to move out, shouting, "Form a line and pass the rubbish from hand to hand!" He grinned at his older brother. "I think I know exactly what Collin is doing and we can't have men tripping over each other, so a passing line is the best way to pile litter up against that doorway."

Sixto returned. "How much more do you need?"

"Everything you can find," said Daylon.

"Oil!" Declan shouted as Sixto turned to instruct more men to scavenge. "Get lamp oil, and tallow if you find it."

The line of men carrying the rubbish reached the doors, then stopped and began passing items forward. After a sizable pile had risen on the left-hand side of the doors, the booming voice of Collin rang out: "Halt! On my command, three strides to the right! Now!"

As if they had done this before the four lines of men moved slowly to the right without falling over each other.

Daylon said, "I watched him from time to time drilling these men, but this is remarkable."

"If I'd had him with me down in Abala," Declan said, "more men would surely have returned."

Daylon stared at Declan for a moment before saying, "You're battle-hardened, yet you will always carry the death of every man you commanded with you. Time will distance that, but you'll never forget."

Declan looked at the man who had surprisingly turned out to be blood family, and said, "Thank you."

With almost perfect precision, the movement along the front of the doors continued. When the rubbish reached the right side of the doors, men came running up to the back of the lines with lamp oil in large skins, boxes of tallow candles, and glass lamps, all of which were passed along to the men in the formation. Collin started the men moving across to the left, drenching as much of the debris in flammable liquid as they could.

In less than an hour the preparation to fire the doors was finished. Declan's men came out of the makeshift tunnel first. Collin had a torch brought out, lit it, and said, "Time to get the lads out of harm's way, highness."

He shouted orders and the men retreated from the door, almost in lockstep, but as soon as they were out of the archers' range, they ran.

Collin signaled and a young soldier hurried over, carrying the largest bow Declan had ever seen. His moustached face split into a grin as he took the bow and said, "Now let's light that pile of rubbish."

The soldier who had brought the bow and a quiver of arrows almost as tall as the grizzled former master-at-arms handed the quiver to Collin. Collin said, "Hilda will get an arrow where it will do some good."

"You named your bow Hilda?" asked Declan.

"All Kes'tun lads learn to hunt about the time they start walking. When your da thinks you're ready, he has a longbow made as a manhood gift. It's tradition to name your bow after your ma."

He pulled out an arrow and nocked it. The soldier who had carried the quiver wrapped the head of the arrow in cloth, then poured some lamp oil over it. Another held the flaming torch and lit the tip of the arrow from it. Once it was alight Collin turned and raised the bow to a high angle, then drew the bowstring and let loose.

The arrow sped through the air and even at this distance, Declan could hear the shouts of the archers atop the palace compound.

The flaming arrow fell just short of the rubbish pile but slid across the stones and plunged into it. Within a few seconds flames began to appear.

"That was not good shooting," said Collin, in a sour tone. He nocked another arrow and held still while it was wrapped and lit. He adjusted his angle and let fly again. That bolt landed directly in the middle of the pile. "One more should do it," said Collin.

The first arrow had skidded to the right, so he planted the third shaft on the left, and in a few seconds three large blazes had begun to grow. As the fire spread, Daylon said, "Unless they have the means to pour a lake from above, those doors should be burning shortly."

Smoke began to roil above the flames and Declan judged that Daylon's prediction was likely, especially as, set back under the first terrace, the massive doorway had none of the defenses of other castles Declan had seen. A castle would have archer holes in any overhang, through which bowmen could shoot down and defenders would pour sand or water to extinguish the flames.

"Now we wait," said Daylon.

HATU HEARD THE FAINT BUZZING sound and felt a twinge of energy flowing. He got out of bed, dressed quickly, and hurried to the library.

Ruffio stood at the spot from which he had vanished days before, accompanied by another man. The second man had greying black hair, a mustache, and goatee beard.

Ruffio looked untroubled by the journey, unlike the last time when he had appeared in that odd green bubble of energy. He said, "Hatushaly, this is Zaakara."

Zaakara spoke a word in a foreign language, closed his eyes, and for a moment Hatu felt a ripple of energy flow around the man, who then opened his eyes and said, "Greetings." He glanced at Ruffio who nodded. Zaakara extended his hand and Hatu took it.

"It's hard to know greeting customs," said the newcomer. "In some places gripping a man's hand is an insult, while in others it's a courtship opening."

Hatu looked at Ruffio. "What are we doing?"

"We need another look in that pit, and . . . let's sit down."

When the three men were seated, Ruffio resumed. "That thing in the pit is a Dreadlord, frozen in an instant, stuck in a moment of time. There are only four men besides me who have any experience with such a phenomenon."

"And you are one of them?"

"Not exactly," said Zaakara. "My father is too old to come, or you'd be talking to him, but he has taught me my entire life."

"What?" asked Hatu. "Taught you what?"

Ruffio answered. "Zaakara is what is known as a warlock among his people, as was his father. They are experts in a specific type of magic."

"Demons," Zaakara interjected. "I'm one of the few men in my world who is knowledgeable about demons. I can summon them, control them—sometimes—and banish them." He shrugged.

My world. Hatu had suspected that Nathan and Ruffio were not of Garn, but it had never been confirmed, and when he had raised any sort of question regarding their origin Nathan had deflected the conversation and avoided answering.

"So that Dreadlord is a demon?" asked Hatu.

"No," said Ruffio.

"I'm confused," said Hatu. "If the Dreadlord isn't a demon . . ." He flipped his hand outward, toward Zaakara. "And where is Nathan?"

"Consulting with some other people on this very matter," said Zaakara. "Including my father."

"Because my father faced the Dread, as did Ruffio," said Zaakara. "But the one thing a warlock knows more than almost anyone who practices any form of magic is how to bind powerful creatures."

"The Dreadlord I faced," said Ruffio, "was the ultimate mani-festation of the Void, and to imprison it required a warrior of exalted power and dropping a mountain range on top of it."

Hatu was speechless. "That's what's in the pit?"

"No," said Ruffio. "That was on another world. The one you found should not exist, not here, or anywhere else. So, we must investigate more and discover what it truly is and why it's here."

"When?"

"We should rest," said Ruffio, looking at Zaakara. "Neither

of us is a youngster like you." He glanced around the library. "What time is it anyway?"

"It's the middle of the night," said Hatu.

"Hence the candles," said Ruffio.

"We'll go in the morning," said Hatu. "Follow me to the room you and Nathan used before."

He guided them to the room, then wandered back to his quarters where he lay awake, staring at the ceiling. His worried thoughts drifted to Hava, wishing she were here.

Without a moment's hesitation he sought her out. He had rigorously avoided doing this for a long time, as it felt like spying on his wife, as well as diverting his attention, but he felt she was the anchor in his life, and he needed just a glimpse of her. It would be day where she was.

It took him scant seconds to sense her and send his vision there. He almost lost the view in delighted shock as he saw Donte standing next to her. Both of them were on the poop deck of her ship, looking up the street behind the quay.

He could see smoke in the distance and after lingering for a moment watching Hava, he sent his vision up the street. A mass of Marquensas soldiers and mercenaries jammed the street leading to a massive structure, bigger than anything Hatu had ever seen built by the hand of man.

He judged that it must have a thousand rooms or gigantic halls and galleries. Up there, he sensed Declan and sought him out easily. Declan was standing next to a man he recognized as the former Baron of Marquensas, now the self-proclaimed king.

Both were staring across a huge open plaza where a fire was burning before enormous wooden doors. The wood was darkened and smoldering, but not in a way that would burn through quickly.

Hatu used his vision to glance back at Declan and the king, and realized they were also considering how to fan the flames.

The fire was waning, with the flames receding. It was old wood, hard and close-grained, laminated so that it was as strong as steel and resistant to fire. Hatu realized it was the entrance to the heart of the Pride Lords' bastion. He also realized that King Daylon, Declan, and the invading host needed to breach that entrance.

Hatu reached out as he had before when he had helped Declan with the rockslide, only this time he had no issue with identifying the flames of that fire. More than any energy he'd ever encountered, the flames sang to him. He knew that energy precisely and understood exactly what to do.

"MORE OIL?" ASKED DECLAN.

"I think so," answered Daylon. "The door is only smoldering. If it's laminated planking, we'll need more heat. If we can burn it enough, perhaps a ram will splinter it. And more—" He stopped and said, "Look!" pointing at the door.

The flames rose, suddenly and evenly, and in a moment all the men facing that way could feel a wave of heat roll over them.

"It's as if someone opened the door to a forge!" Declan exclaimed.

Instinctively, the men recoiled.

The fire grew brighter. Declan and the king saw the wood of the door begin to glow, like fired coals. A groaning sound came as the wood, twisted by the heat, slowly began to warp, straining at the massive hinges that held them in place. Then the center of the flames started to turn white hot and the wood cracked and split. The iron hinges and bolts began to glow red, with flames sprinting up around them as they grew hotter.

"How is this possible?" asked Declan.

"I have no idea, but if it gets any hotter, we'll have to move back."

As the flames ate away at the doors, the men surrounding Daylon and Declan began to cheer.

"Get ready!" shouted Collin.

"I think he just assumed he was still a master-at-arms," said Declan. "Even your captains are obeying him."

"I never claimed to be the smartest man in Marquensas," said Daylon. "That would be our brother. I'm just the most powerful, but I do manage to learn something new every now and again."

Declan smiled and nodded.

"Ready!" shouted Daylon as he ignored the waves of heat and moved to stand next to Collin.

With a loud tearing sound, the doors collapsed off their hinges in an explosion of sparks, ash, and flaming splinters falling onto the stones. The heat washed over Declan and the other attackers, then the flames subsided.

"Don't burn your feet going in!" shouted Collin, sounding amused.

"Charge!" shouted Daylon and he ran toward the doors.

Abruptly, the flames they would have had to dash through vanished, as if all the heat had been sucked out of them. Even the smoke thinned to a faint cloud, heavy with the stench of char.

The doorway opened into an immense hall, three stories high, and Daylon and Declan both edged around the now-ruined doors, waiting for an attack.

Declan glanced at the rubble-strewn entrance and said to the king, "That's nothing natural."

"We'll puzzle it out later."

Daylon moved into the entrance, looking around and up. "No arrow loops or murder holes, just a balcony and a long flight of stairs, and those doors," he said, pointing to four doors that lined the opposite wall a good thirty yards away.

"Room by room, then," said Declan.

He turned to see Collin standing at the king's side, listening to instructions. Then Collin moved to the center of the entrance and bellowed, "By squad, inside!"

He came over to Declan and said, "This was easy."

"We had help," said Declan.

"That's for certain," agreed the taller man.

"Kite shields?"

"Might have faced cavalry."

"Pavise shields for the archers?"

"Seemed like a good idea."

"Can't deny that," said Declan. He pointed to the distant doors.

"The lads have half a dozen four-man rams they're bringing up from the back," said Collin.

"Did the king order all that?"

"He was a wee bit distracted, so I assumed he'd want some things he wasn't thinking about at the time."

"Did he tell you he's planning to name you Marquensas's master-at-arms?"

"It was inevitable," said Collin with a smile, then he turned and shouted, "You lot, over there!" He pointed to the farthest door and ran across to direct the incoming squads.

"Inevitable, indeed," said Declan to himself.

Sixto arrived and said, "All the men are under the overhang."

"Keep them ready but tell them we're letting Collin and his door-crasher open up some routes for us." He pointed upward. "From what we know, we can expect whatever the Pride Lords have to be waiting for us up there."

Sixto nodded and turned to pass the word.

Declan looked down at the now-cool burned wood and wondered what magic had been employed.

HATU OPENED HIS EYES. HE felt oddly exhilarated. Using his power to control fire had been profoundly invigorating. It was only the second time he had done it, and the only time he had done so by design. The first time he'd almost burned a ship down to the waterline by accident.

It was still night and morning was hours away. He knew he couldn't sleep so he got off the bed, slipped on his sandals, and returned to the library.

There he found Nathan sitting, as if waiting for him.

"You're back!"

Nathan said, "That was foolish. Foolish and dangerous, too."

"What?"

"Intervening in that battle."

"I did it before, when I helped Declan with the rockslide."

Nathan pointed to a chair, and Hatushaly sat down.

Nathan said sternly, "That was before we knew there was a Dreadlord slumbering in that pit!" He took a breath. "Had I even a hint back then that you might do this, I would have forbidden you even to try to help Declan."

"You'd have let him and the other men be killed by those—" He paused, because he could no longer think of the denizens of that village as people. "Those things?"

"Rather than risk calling attention to you? Absolutely." Nathan leaned forward, elbows on the table. "Now that we know what is in there, there is no question about it." His temper seemed to settle. "And we still don't quite know what to think about you."

"What does that mean?"

"Ruffio and Zaakara will help sort that out. My time here is almost at an end."

"Why?"

Nathan gave a small shrug. "I don't know. I just feel the end coming. I've been through this before."

"But you've shown me so much . . . so many amazing things!"

Nathan smiled. "I was just a guide. Those two"—he nodded toward where Ruffio and Zaakara were sleeping in their chairs in the library—"they are your teachers now and can show you tricks I can only imagine."

"So, what do we do now?"

"We wait, and in the morning we will seek out something terrible."

THE FIGHTING ON THE LOWER floor was over in minutes. Barricaded doors were broken down, and a few Azhante with swords put up a fight, only to be quickly disposed of by Daylon's trained troops. Long halls were spread like the spokes of a wheel, and companies of Marquensas soldiers methodically worked their way down each of them, smashing doors into rooms that were empty, or held stored goods. People who appeared to be servants would cower, scream, and cry. They were shocked when they realized they were not going to be killed but instead herded toward the main hall. A few had to be grabbed, dragged, and shown the way, or harried along by soldiers yelling at them to get moving.

Once the captives were gathered in the hall, they were shown out into the street. The "join us or get out of the way" phrase was repeated often, and many of the servants lingered behind the army under the protective overhang.

Some ran toward the city and a few arrows were shot at them

from the terrace above. Most missed the fleeing servants. A pair died, and Sixto said, "They're killing the helpless out of spite."

"We need to finish these people," Declan replied.

Soldiers returned to report that the halls had been cleared. Daylon turned to Declan and said, "My men will flood those halls to the back of this palace. You split your force into two squads and take the stairs." He pointed with his sword to the far right- and left-hand ends of the hall. "We'll find whatever stairs are back there and meet you somewhere in the middle."

Declan nodded, "Yes, sire."

After the king had led his men away, Declan asked Sixto, "What are we likely to find up there?"

"A great many arrows," Sixto answered.

"There are a great many shields strewn around outside, and some of the men have bucklers, but they're pretty useless against archers."

"Pavises?" asked Sixto.

Declan nodded. "Fetch as many as the men can get in here without getting killed."

"King's still got a company of archers out there," said Sixto. "If I ask nicely, I'm sure they'll try to give us cover from those archers on the terrace."

He ran outside, calling for men to follow. Sixto pointed as he shouted instructions to the bowmen still on the outskirts of the plaza. A few immediately ran forward, shooting upward to keep the defenders hunkered down.

In a few minutes, as more of the king's soldiers flooded down the long halls, men returned with the pavise shields, which were large enough for one man to crouch behind while another shot over the top.

"How many archers do we have?" Declan asked.

"None were hurt, so all of them."

"That's welcome news." He knew his almost a thousand men included more than a hundred archers. "How many shields?"

Sixto did a quick count. "Twenty."

Declan made a rough estimate of the width of the staircases. "I want ten men in front, with two or three bowmen lined up behind. Any man who runs out of arrows drops to the back." He saw a familiar face and waved Toombs over. "Can you dodge arrows?"

"Never tried," Toombs said. "What do you need, Captain?"

"Get to the rear." Declan pointed at the door. "Find the baggage train. Ask the master of baggage how many arrows he has in his wagons and bring back as many as you can."

"It's the king's baggage, and he may be reluctant to part with them for a group of mercenaries," said Toombs. "I've run into that little problem with nobles' men before. I may have to persuade him," he added with an evil smile.

"This battle is going swiftly enough, but we don't need a brawl back in the baggage train."

"Tell him it's for the king. He won't know," said Sixto.

Toombs laughed. "I think I'll drive the whole damn baggage wagon with the arrows in it up here, and if he objects, then I'll persuade him."

After Toombs had called over a few of Declan's old friends— Billy Jay, the Sawyer brothers, Acke, and Mikola—they all ran as fast as possible across the plaza. Sixto lifted his chin in the direction of Collin, who was still directing a column of tools into various hallways, and said, "Master-at-arms? Think Captain Baldasar will object?"

"I would pay to see that fight," said Declan. "But the king's the king, and besides, Daylon can always make Baldasar a general or give him a title. Now, let's get organized and get up those stairs. I'll take the company on the left, you go over there on the right."

Sixto had the shields brought up and laid on the floor, ten to the left and ten to the right. Then he organized the forces as Declan had instructed, a swordsman to carry the big shield, and two or three archers behind him. The rest of the men split into two groups, one behind each wall of shields.

With a sweeping wave of his sword, Declan signaled to Sixto that it was time to get up the stairs and seriously join in this fight.

26

RETRIBUTION, TRIUMPH,

AND TERROR

"Remember when we thought this would be easy?" Sixto asked, catching his breath, as perspiration ran off his face.

Waiting for them at the edge of a garden terrace were five large men with huge axes.

"On the count of three!" Declan shouted, then he counted loudly, "One, two, three!"

Declan and Sixto charged. Declan knew that a dozen more men would flood through that door after them, even as he raced toward the five axmen.

Declan's men tried to swarm the defenders and two fell to blows from the massive axes. Declan ducked under one huge blade and thrust his sword into the man's side.

Once the first wave struck, the defenders were down.

Declan got to his feet and realized he'd hurt his leg, but it felt like a muscle bruise, not a significant injury.

Sixto came to his side. "Are you all right?"

"Banged a muscle," said Declan. "I'll be fine."

Looking down at the dead axmen, Sixto said, "That is not serious armor."

The dead men wore leather harnesses which attached to ornate shoulder pauldrons, matching wide, ornate leather belts, loincloths, bare legs, and cross-gartered sandals. They were large men with dramatic muscles, who would appear imposing as guards, but in the reality of warfare were extremely poorly equipped.

"This is ceremonial wear," said Sixto. "Nothing a warrior would wear into battle."

Declan nodded. "Yes."

"But those were damn big axes," added Sixto.

Watching the injured and dead being carried away, Declan said, "I think the higher we climb, the worse it will get."

Sixto nodded.

AN HOUR LATER, DECLAN LOOKED around the room he had just charged into and saw a dozen men in black trousers with no shirts, others wearing tunics whose badges had been torn off. He turned to Sixto and said, "How many Azhante have come over to us?"

"I don't have a count, but many."

"Before we go charging upstairs, let's find out what's waiting on the next level."

It had taken hours to clear the first floor, and their fatigue was mostly due to kicking down doors with no idea of what lay behind them. The archers had proven relatively simple to deal with, and Declan lost only a few men clearing the terrace above the ground floor that overlooked the courtyard. After their first volley of arrows, Declan's swordsmen made short work of them. After that, though, it had taken hours.

Most of the rooms were empty, but some of them had contained enough Azhante ready to die for the Pride Lords that fighting had erupted and slowed them down. Daylon had said to "meet in the middle," but still they hadn't found the king's company, and the sun was lowering in the west.

As Sixto hurried over to the Azhante who had changed sides, Declan sat down, signaling with his hand to indicate it was time to rest.

A few minutes passed and Sixto returned. "I don't know if I understand all of what I heard from that Azhante over there, but I think we don't try to clear the floors above, but just loop to the next flight of stairs and keep going until we get to the top floor. There we will find the Pride Lords."

Declan considered this, then said, "So we don't clear the floors above but climb as high as possible, as fast as possible."

"What about the king?" Sixto asked.

"I have no idea where he is or what he's facing," answered Declan. He was silent for a minute as he thought.

Glancing out of the windows that opened on the plaza, he said, "It's getting dark, and we have carved our way to this end of the third floor." He stared past Sixto, as if he could see something in the distance. "Let's go to the top. If we get hit from behind, I'll be surprised."

"Seems to be the pattern," said Sixto. "They hide until we find them."

"So, we ignore the floors above until we reach serious opposition," said Declan. "Pass the word." He saw Billy Jay and waved him over. "I want you to go back down a floor, then through a hall to the back of this building, to find the king. Get word to him that our company has stopped trying to clear every floor. Got that?"

"We're not clearing any more floors," said Billy Jay.

"Tell him we're going to the top, to where the Pride Lords are, and he'll find us there."

"You're going to the top where the Pride Lords are," said Billy Jay.

"Take a squad with you in case you run into trouble. Now go find the king!"

Billy hurried off and Declan looked at Sixto. "Fighting since dawn, and we're only now getting to the third floor?"

"There are a *lot* of rooms here, my friend." Sixto let out a breath that was almost a sigh of exhaustion, then smiled and added wryly, "And we only have maybe nine or ten more floors to go, right?"

Declan took a deep breath and said, "If I'd wanted to live here, I wouldn't have done so much damage to the place."

Sixto laughed as they split their force again, and each led their group up the next stairway. The stairs switched back halfway between floors, with a square landing at midpoint, so that each level was smaller than the one below, a bit like a layered cake Declan had once seen at a festival as a youngster, when he was traveling with Edvalt.

When he reached the next floor, he halted and saw Sixto come into view. He waved then started up the next flight.

Eventually, they all reached the topmost floor.

Sixto's mercenaries looked around in awe. This single room was a gigantic anteroom with polished marble floors. For a moment he was struck by the work required to build with this much stone this high, as well as by the army of workers needed to carry out the task. The wall facing the city was windowed, the glass as clear as any he'd ever seen, without any hint of distortion or flaws.

During daylight the view must be amazing, he thought as he gazed out over the city, which lay in darkness as frightened residents stayed hidden in their homes. The opposite wall was equally impressive, with a pair of large doors in the center that were twelve feet in height. The entire wall was faced with hand-carved wood, a majestic bas-relief mural showing incredible creatures seemingly locked in a battle with men in armor.

"Make way for the king!" sounded the call from behind them and men flooded out of the stairway behind Declan.

Daylon walked up the last few stairs. "What is this?" he asked Declan.

"I don't know," answered Declan. "But if the Pride Lords are anywhere, it'll be behind those two big doors there."

"If they're not," said the king, "we'll just start kicking in all the doors on the way down."

Soldiers in the king's tabards appeared carrying water skins. "There are kitchens on every floor at the back," said Daylon. "I thought your men might be thirsty."

"They are," said Declan, taking a skin from a soldier and drinking from it. He handed it back to the soldier who joined others passing around the water skins to the mercenaries.

Daylon and Declan walked together beside the mural, which showed warriors in oddly ornate armor fighting creatures of strange proportions, with pointed bodies, thin arms, and round heads with bulging eyes.

Toward the big doors in the center of the wall, the mural depicted the bizarre creatures defeating the humans, with huge monstrous beings apparently devouring some dead people, while other humans were on their knees, prostrated before them, as if praying.

"What was it Hava told us about the legend of the Dark Masters?" asked Daylon.

"I don't remember all of it, but thousands of people were apparently sacrificed to them, and the Pride Lords rose to control who was sent to die and who was spared. Then for some reason the Dark Masters . . . vanished. And the populations grew until the Pride Lords had to set them against each other in order to keep the numbers down. Something like that."

"If this mural is in any way historical, these 'Dark Masters' were not human," said the king.

"Perhaps these murals just show monsters out of legend?" suggested Declan.

"We've had monsters in our stories as far back as we've had storytellers. Creatures, spirits, things that lurk in the forest, or swim under the sea. They can't all be imagined," said Daylon.

Soldiers took their ease for a few minutes, then teams arrived carrying the battering rams from the rear of the king's forces.

Declan and Daylon stepped aside as the king pointed at the heavy wooden doors and said, "Break them down."

A ram was positioned opposite each door, and the men stood in wait. If it was a long process, the first teams would take their rest as others stepped in to take their place.

On Daylon's signal, the rhythmic pounding began.

HATU AND BODAI ATE BREAKFAST with Ruffio and Zaakara. The food was still simple but becoming more abundant and varied now that a population had grown up around the Sanctuary on the surrounding islands. Bodai was close to ecstatic that a sausage maker had turned up and a long, spiced pork sausage was added to his selection of oatmeal gruel, boiled eggs, and fruit. He also offered his coffee to the guests.

Zaakara waved it off, but Ruffio took a cup. After sipping it, he said in an approving tone, "At home, I take a drop of sugar, but this is fine. Interesting blend."

"Sugar?" said Bodai. "I never thought to try that."

"Some other time," suggested Hatushaly. "I doubt our guests traveled across the universe to sample breakfast drinks." His

tone was a mix of irritation, concern, and a hint of fear after
the strict talking-to he'd received from Nathan. "Has anyone
seen Nathan?"

Ruffio shook his head and Zaakara said, "He'll turn up when
he needs to. He always does."

"So you've known him a long time?" asked Bodai.

Ruffio and Zaakara exchanged glances, then Ruffio said, "In
a manner of speaking." He sat back as if considering what to say
next. "I have no idea what he has told you and I would like to
respect his personal choices in what he shares." He again glanced
at Zaakara, who nodded once.

"Nathan isn't like us," said Ruffio. "That is, he looks like us,
but he's . . ." He shrugged then looked again at Zaakara.

Zaakara said, "He's a demon."

Bodai's expression was one of incredulity. Hatu sat there
wide-eyed.

At last, Hatushaly said, "A demon? You can't be serious."

Zaakara said, "You've been around him long enough to know
that he means you or anyone else here no harm. And 'demon'
may not be entirely accurate." He leaned forward, pushing his
plate aside. "You"—he pointed at Hatu—"have seen the universe
in ways no one else I know can even begin to imagine. These
'furies' as you call them, these energy nodes, are the fundamental
stuff of everything. That is critical, as Nathan would not have
discovered you if some higher power hadn't become aware of
your abilities."

"Higher power?" said Hatu. "Like gods?"

"It's complicated," began Ruffio, then stopped himself. "It's
always complicated," he amended. "Compare what you see, what
you've learned, to what ordinary people know. They're oblivious
to things you can see with ease, can't even imagine the things

you can do." He paused. "I've known only one other person who could simply summon up power and employ it without a complex spell or a device, and he . . . left us." He seemed saddened by that reference he had just made, but then continued, "The battle with the Dreadlord and other agents of the Void changed my world.

"Magic, or what you think of as the powers of the furies, was unleashed at an unimaginable scale. A scale at which mountains fell and rivers changed their course. Entirely new species of animals and plants sprang into existence, and half the magic-users and priests with magic powers who were involved in the battle died or went mad." He sat back and swallowed hard. "It was a very long time ago, but I remember it as if it were yesterday."

Hatu could see that Ruffio was genuinely troubled by the memory. He looked at Zaakara and said, "And you?"

"I wasn't even born," he said.

Hatu's eyes widened and Bodai said, "How long ago was that?"

"More than a century," said Ruffio.

"How is that possible?" Bodai asked. "You don't appear—"

Ruffio interrupted. "That's a subject for another time." He looked at Hatu.

Then he and Zaakara stood up.

"It's time, and I expect Nathan will be waiting in the library."

They took the empty dishes to the kitchen boys then headed to the library. Nathan was waiting for them there.

THE BATTERING RAMS SLAMMED REPEATEDLY against the doors and they started to splinter. The way they were buckling, Declan assumed there wasn't a massive bar on the other side, but most likely just a lock or latch.

"Should we axe it at the hinges?" Daylon asked.

Declan didn't answer but looked to Master-at-Arms Collin

who stood on the king's right. "Shouldn't need to, Majesty, unless the hinges warp and the doors block the way. That lock should spring . . ."

The doors suddenly swung open.

". . . now," finished Collin.

Azhante fanatics rushed out of the door and the fighting commenced. As Declan's men had experienced before, these men would die before they surrendered, but they were not highly trained and fell like wheat cut by a scythe. The superior King's Steel blades shattered the Azhante blades and cut through arms and legs. The few Azhante wearing armor found it useless. The slaughter took less than ten minutes, then a powerful-looking man in decorative armor trimmed with gold came forward, followed by four others in similarly fashioned armor.

The man was huge, easily two inches taller than Collin. He was broad-shouldered with a narrow waist, a physically imposing man under any circumstances, but standing virtually alone facing an army, he was daunting in appearance. His skin was dark, and his glare was one of pure hatred. The gold trim on his armor reflected the light from a massive chandelier hanging from the ceiling.

Declan glanced at the nearby Azhante and saw that they looked terrified. He said to Daylon, "I think we've found the Pride Lords."

"That big brute at the front is mine," said Daylon and he charged.

The men hesitated, seeing their king running at the Pride Lords, with no order given. Declan was a second behind his brother and he took the closest Pride Lord, an older man whose armor was adorned with onyx. As the men moved forward, Collin shouted, "Easy! I have orders. No one moves until I say."

Declan realized Daylon must have told him that when they found the Pride Lords, the king would take his revenge. Declan dodged one thrust by the older Pride Lord, easily cutting his throat.

Then Declan turned to see if his brother needed aid. Two other Pride Lords were attempting to join the first and come at Daylon from his left side. Declan intercepted them easily as they circled behind the impressive Pride Lord in the gold-trimmed armor.

These were younger men, one with an embossed tiger on his breastplate, and the other an eagle. The two of them were proving a challenge, even if they weren't particularly skilled. Declan knew that whether killed by a skilled expert or a lucky blow from a novice, you were still dead.

He parried while trying to keep an eye on Daylon, who was holding his own against the bigger man, despite the king's advancing years. Daylon parried with skill, while the bigger man flailed away. They were punishing strikes, but the king deftly avoided them. Unless someone intervened, it would be a case of who became most fatigued more quickly.

An opening presented itself and Declan slid his blade in between two pieces of chain armor worn by the Eagle Pride Lord as he thought of him, impaling the man in the side. His enemy's eyes opened as if he was about to scream, but blood flowed from his mouth and he fell forward.

Declan yanked his blade free and made quick work of the second Pride Lord, the Tiger. Glancing for a moment over at the king's struggle, he saw the fifth Pride Lord, bearing another type of cat on his armor, standing and looking uncertain. The man saw Declan turn and threw down his weapon, holding up his hands in surrender.

Declan walked over to him calmly, then raised his sword and drove it into the man's throat. "That's for my Gwen," he said

as the man's eyes rolled up into his head and the Lord of the
Jaguar Pride died.

Declan circled around the king and his opponent. Declan
assumed this figure must be the Lord of the Golden Pride. He
said loudly, "All the others are dead."

Nearly out of breath, Daylon tried to jump back, and stumbled. Falling backward, he barely avoided a powerful blow that
likely would have decapitated him. The powerful Pride Lord
raised his sword to finish the fight, but like a cat striking Declan
took two steps forward and thrust his sword point up into the
man's armpit.

While the king scrambled to his feet with Collin's aid, Tarquen,
Lord of the Golden Pride, teetered. Then his left knee gave way
and he fell sideways onto the marble floor. He groaned and tried
to move, but before he could even try to stand again, Daylon
took a step and, with a powerful swing, cut the man's head from
his shoulders.

The room erupted with shouts and cheers. The battle was
finally over.

Declan moved to his brother's side and help him to stand.
"Are you hurt?"

"Only my pride," Daylon answered. He took a step and winced.
"I might have cracked a hip, truth to tell."

The two men stood close, Declan with his arm around Daylon's
shoulders, and they looked in each other's eyes. Eventually, Daylon
said, "Now, we can start thinking about the future."

"Can you walk, sire?" asked Collin.

"If not, you can carry me," Daylon answered as he took another
step. "Nothing broken. Just sore as hell."

Daylon, followed by Declan, Collin, Sixto, and the others
walked past the dead Pride Lords into a big circular room with

a circular dais upon which sat five ornate chairs, or thrones, and at their feet were cushions and writing tables.

A voice from the farthest point in the room said, "This is the Camera where the Pride Lords passed down edicts." The speaker stepped forward. He was a man with a tall staff.

"You speak our language," said the king.

The man bowed. "I am Toachipe, the Keeper of Hours. I have had years to study, including the 'traveler's' language, as we call it."

Daylon nodded: the man was speaking the common trading language of the Five Kingdoms. Now one kingdom, he thought bitterly to himself.

"What is a camera?" asked Declan.

"Simply, a round building, or room."

"This is where the Pride Lords ruled, then," said Daylon.

"Not quite. This is where the Pride Lords settled disputes by vote among the rulers of the five most powerful prides."

"How many more Pride Lords are there? Where do we find them?" demanded Daylon. "I am King of Marquensas and I mean to have revenge on all of them!"

Toachipe waved across the room and another man came out of the shadows. "This is Nestor, the First Speaker, who is the only man not of a Pride to be allowed in this room."

"How did you get in, then?" asked Sixto, oblivious to protocol for the moment. Then he glanced at Daylon and said, "Sorry, Majesty."

Daylon waved away the apology.

Toachipe showed them the ceremonial staff he carried. "The guard behind the dais had little time to argue once the big doors were breached. Nestor can tell you more about the Prides than anyone here, but I will have to translate for him. But to answer your questions there are dozens of Prides, including the five biggest, whom you have already destroyed. Without leaders, they will fall apart. As for the others, word is spreading now that the Pride Lords are falling, and the nations will turn on them. Without fear of the Dark Masters, the armies will rise up against any force of Azhante that try to restrain them.

"The rule of the Prides is over."

"Well, then," said Daylon, "what of this place?" He gestured to indicate the massive palace. "Should we leave it or burn it to the ground?"

The two men exchanged glances, Toachipe speaking to Nestor, and Nestor quickly replying. "Burn it," said Toachipe.

"Collin," said the king.

"Majesty?"

"Let the men rest a bit, then start marching them back to the docks. No rape, looting, or killing. Any man who troubles the locals along the way will be hanged. These people have suffered for a very long time."

"Sire."

"If the men encounter any Pride Lords skulking about, no prisoners."

Collin nodded.

Daylon continued, "The last squad to leave will start fires along the way. When clearing those rooms below I saw many places that are filled with fodder for a blaze. A dozen on each floor, from back to front, should do it."

Daylon settled down on one of the cushioned niches created for the recorders who sat at the Pride Lords' feet. "While I'm waiting, can you tell us something more about these Dark Masters?"

The Keeper of Hours spoke to Nestor, who nodded and began speaking. Toachipe translated. "Once, when the sky was rent, darkness flowed through. A host of evil was the Darkness, and they began a great battle with men."

Declan and the others settled in to listen to the story.

HATU CARRIED THE OTHER TWO with him in his mind. Zaakara had already been astonished by that art. Now they hovered over the image of the pit in the village and Zaakara said, "How do I see what I need to see?"

"Tell me what it is?" said Hatu.

"There are strands of . . . time?" Hatu sensed the uncertainty. "When my father and Ruffio were back at our school, other magicians from around the world participated in banishing the Dreadlord from our realm of existence. The forces were unimaginable, but as I understand it, the final blow halted time?"

It was Ruffio who said, "Nathan, what do you know?"

"At the moment the rift to the Void was shut, a great warrior almost the equal of the Dreadlord was locked in combat with it, and then the entire world changed. The Dread are of the Void, so for them time is just now as it always has been and always will be, so the Void and the Dread still exist, but everywhere and in no single place."

Hatu pondered that, then extended his senses closer to the motionless Dreadlord in the pit and said, "I showed Bodai something I learned of the strands of time."

"What did you do?" asked Nathan.

"A trick of making time pause for a moment, while I could still move through the moment."

In his mind Hatu heard both Zaakara and Ruffio gasp.

"Making time stop!" said Zaakara. "Is it possible?"

Ruffio replied, "I think with Hatushaly, anything is possible. He carries a world's magic within him."

Nathan said, "We can discuss that later. What do you see here, Hatu?"

Hatu paused as if considering, then said, "This is what you seek, I think."

Instantly, there were lines of force surrounding the Dreadlord, entangled and woven around him like a web or net, but then Hatu said, "This is strange."

"What?" asked Nathan.

"Those are lines of time, like the ones I halted for a moment, but unlike every other energy line I've encountered, they're . . . dead."

"Dead?" asked Ruffio.

"No, that's wrong. They're motionless. All lines of energy between furies are living things, pulsating with unique rhythm and color, or at least that's how I see them, but these . . . it's as if they're . . . waiting."

"For what?" asked Ruffio.

Hatu hesitated then said, "I'm just guessing, but from what I've seen, maybe this net of time is about to start moving again."

"As bad as I feared," said Ruffio. "It's trying to wake."

"We don't know that," said Zaakara.

"I think I can do something," said Hatu.

"What?" asked Ruffio.

"Give me a moment," said Hatushaly, sending his awareness to the finest perspective as he had ever tried before. He honed his newfound perception of time and gently approached the nearest strand, getting as close as he could in his mind, envisioning his hand hovering over it but not quite touching it. He felt a surging presence he had to defend against, dark . . . empty. It was the

Void personified, and in all his life he had never encountered anything that simply was empty of everything. Just being near this mockery of a creature using his mind was chilling and he fought back as every fiber of his being demanded he flee from its presence. He studied the threads and focused on what he saw was a slow awakening.

After long moments of examining the tension in those strands, he said, "I can do something."

"What?" they all asked.

"The best way I can explain it is that these strands of time want to wake up. Perhaps I can calm them down and put them back to sleep.

"You might wish to leave me and get comfortable. This will take a while."

Nathan first, then Ruffio and Zaakara found themselves back in the library and let go of one another's shoulders, leaving Hatu alone, his arms reaching out.

"Is he all right to be left like this?" asked Zaakara, looking at the still figure.

Bodai sat in the chair he had occupied since they started. "He'll be fine. Though I don't know if I will be."

The other three sat down and Zaakara said, "Neither do I."

NESTOR HAD FINISHED HIS STORY, and Daylon said, "I would have said it was a fable had I not seen this place and that mural." He stood up and called for Collin, who was just outside the door to the Camera, giving instructions and receiving reports.

"Sire!" said the large soldier, coming in.

"Are the ships ready for boarding?"

"They are, sire."

"The men?"

"The first companies should be arriving at the docks now." Collin looked at Declan. "Along with most of your lads."

"Then let's get out of here," said Daylon. To Declan he said, "Sail back with me. I have more things to discuss with you."

Declan nodded and waved to Sixto. "You're now in charge, Captain."

Sixto laughed. "I told you, I'm not cut out to lead."

Declan's eyes grew moist. "You greatly underestimate yourself, my friend." He took a deep breath to regain his composure. "We'll speak of this more when we get home."

In an unexpected gesture, Sixto embraced Declan. "Until the day I die, I am your man." He turned and hurried out to oversee the mercenaries.

Declan went to stand next to his brother and waited. Deep inside he still ached for Gwen, but he truly hoped Daylon was correct, and that time would distance that wound.

HATU MOVED AND SAID, "I need to sit down."

Ruffio got out of his chair, and Hatushaly sat down heavily, obviously fatigued.

"What did you do?" asked Zaakara.

"I don't know how best to explain it, but I told the binding on the Dreadlord to sleep and wait."

"Wait for what?" asked Nathan.

"Words are hard, and I think you three"—he indicated Nathan, Ruffio, and Zaakara—"know what I mean. What is the sound of red? How bright is the noise of wind in the trees? What does moonlight feel like?"

All of them nodded.

"The time energy is motionless. That is something I've never seen. All lines between the furies . . . move." He took a deep breath. "The time-lines want to move, vibrate. All other time-lines not confining the Dreadlord are moving." He shrugged. "I can't explain it any better. Maybe if I knew more."

Ruffio said, "We must talk about that."

"Later," Hatu said. "My wife is on the edge of a battle and I want to see how she fares."

Nathan seemed on the edge of objecting but thought better of it and sat back in his chair.

Suddenly Hatu was looking down on Hava and saw that the king's army was returning, and that the men were walking casually, with no evidence of strife. He was tempted to try to speak to her, but suddenly Nathan was in his mind. "Don't!"

Hatu opened his eyes and saw Nathan standing over him, gripping his shoulders. "You could kill her," he said.

Hatu said, "How do you know?"

"Because you miss her so much, and you are so very young." Nathan stepped back. "These men are far more experienced, yet they have nothing like your power."

"We have to understand the way power works here," said Ruffio. "This link to the furies, how your bloodline is a key to your power, and what about the other elemental furies?"

"What elemental furies?" asked Hatu.

Nathan looked at Bodai, and said, "He's been given so much, some of it will be forgotten."

Bodai said, "The earth, air, and water elemental magic."

Suddenly, Hatu said, "Water magic!"

"What?" asked Ruffio.

"I have a debt to settle."

Hatu closed his eyes and within seconds found himself in the underwater warren of the Sisters of the Deep. It was dark without the phosphorescence that had illuminated it when Hatu had last been there. A few bodies floated facedown in the water, the half-man, half-fish creatures the Sisters of the Deep had created with their dark magic. The two oldest women, Hadona and Madda, sat in the dark, clutching one another, while the younger woman, Sabina, lay nearby on the rocks, dead eyes staring upward.

For a moment, Hatu was severely tempted to do something to punish them, when again Nathan intruded. "If you act, you may endanger those you love. But the last shred of water magic is fading. They will die within hours."

"Soon?"

"Very soon. With their passing, you will be the only being of power, the only wielder of magic on Garn. You are the Master of Furies. But you are young, you need training."

"Then I'll leave them to the slow death they've earned."

Hatu let his consciousness rise effortlessly to the surface, but rather than snap back to the library immediately he lingered for a moment as if he was floating, simply drinking in the energy of this world.

Suddenly he felt a tingle. He returned his vision to Hava and saw a bright light in the distance. He moved to view it more closely and realized that the mammoth building he had seen earlier was now ablaze. People were still fleeing from the lowest entrance, smoke billowing out behind them.

He assumed that Hava had become excited about a safe trip home, and for a moment he savored the profound relief of knowing she was all right. Donte was at her side and Hatu felt a wonderful sense of completion, seeing Donte alive and the Sisters of the Deep dead and dying.

Then he felt a strange sensation, a distant vibration that tickled his curiosity. He gave up watching Hava at the quay and moved toward the far-off hum.

It took seconds for him to reach the source, and suddenly he stopped to examine the origin of that vibration.

Hatushaly returned to the library and looked at Zaakara, Ruffio, and Nathan. "There's something you should see."

The other three men joined him in a square, and he returned to his vision.

"There's a barrier," said Hatu.

The others waited, then Nathan said, "Share your sense."

Hatu fumbled for a moment then said, "I think this will do it."

Suddenly the other three felt the itch, the buzz at the end of perception, and Hatu said, "This is the barrier, around this huge plateau."

He pulled back his perception as if he were miles away, and Zaakara said, "Whoa! You're making me dizzy."

Nathan said, "You'll get over it."

"What is that?" asked Ruffio.

Hatu adjusted his sight and saw a massive structure, something like a maze of stone, with mounds pierced by tunnels. It was a dark, desolate, lifeless place, covered by a dome of energy.

"Get closer!" said Zaakara.

"This may be painful," said Hatu.

They passed through the barrier and a snap of pain ran through them all.

Nathan said, "That's a death barrier. Any living creature should have perished the instant they crossed."

"I felt a touch of the Void in it," said Hatu, "so I sheltered us all."

"How did you do that?" asked Ruffio.

"I don't know," said Hatushaly. "I just didn't want you to get hurt."

"What is this place?" asked Zaakara.

Hatu swooped his perception downward and began moving over the maze of stone.

After a moment, Nathan said, "Oh, gods!"

"What?" asked Hatu.

"Leave!" said Nathan. "Get out of here!"

"What is it?" asked Hatu.

"That's a warren of the Children of the Void," said Nathan.

"Who are the Children of the Void?" asked Hatu.

"They go by many names, wraiths, specters, wights, ghosts, bodach, and others. No matter what name they go by, they are destroyers of life."

"How are they linked to the thing in the pit?" asked Hatu.

"We don't know," said Nathan.

Suddenly they were back in the library.

Ruffio shook his head to clear it.

Hatu said, "What was that?"

"It'll be a long explanation," said Nathan.

Hatu said, "My wife is returning, and will be at the staging island in less than a day, and I want to be there to greet her. But if I am to do so, I must leave shortly."

Ruffio said to Hatu, "I think if you show me where that island is, I can take us there in moments."

Hatu was briefly silent, then nodded. Nathan tossed his head slightly, in a gesture he wished to speak to Hatu away from the others.

Hatu nodded he understood and got out of his chair. He and Nathan went to a quiet corner of the library, and Hatu asked, "What did you mean when you said your time here was almost over?"

Nathan seemed uncomfortable. "I can't explain. My existence is . . . limited and not mine to control." He smiled. "You ask many questions, and I don't know if I ever would have the time to answer them all.

"The Children of the Void are . . . creatures is not an accurate label, but think of them as lesser beings from the same place that spawned the Dread, the Void. Why they are here and what they have to do with you must be investigated."

"I gathered that much," said Hatu, "but what was that place?"

"I do not know," said Nathan.

"Then who does?" asked Hatu.

"There are two here who have studied the Void and others who know even more. If you're willing, they will continue . . . teaching you may not be the right expression." He stared off for a moment, then said, "Assisting you in learning, perhaps, is a better way to put it. There are men and women of great talent and powers who can prevent you from harming yourself or others while you master your powers. It is your choice."

Hatu looked conflicted. "What should I do?"

Nathan was about to answer when a thrumming filled the air.

He smiled and reached out to grip Hatushaly by the neck, pulling him forward so their foreheads were touching. "My time here is over."

"Where are you going?" Hatu asked, feeling a rising alarm.

Nathan smiled and softly said, "Many places . . . many times . . ." Seeing the look of confusion and concern on Hatu's face, he went on, "You may be the only person who can understand . . . one day. Ruffio and Zaakara will take you to the next place, if you are ready."

Eyes closed, Hatu asked, "What are you?"

In reply, he heard a soft whisper with a note of humor. "Once, a man, now I don't know."

Hatu opened his eyes and stepped back. Nathan began to

shed tiny flakes of glowing energy, pieces of him that peeled off and floated away like the seeds of a dandelion blown by the wind. The tiny flakes, pinpoints of light, swirled in a circular cloud, spinning rapidly, climbing into the air, and then all trace of Nathan was gone.

Hatu looked around and saw Ruffio and Zaakara staring at the spot where Nathan had been. He could see from their expressions that they were as disturbed by Nathan's fading from existence as he was. Bodai's eyes were wide and blood had drained from his face.

There was a profound sense of loss in the library, an echo of a note ringing in a vast hall, that finally faded to nothing.

HATU STOOD OUTSIDE THE LIBRARY and felt conflicting emotions. He was ecstatic that Hava was returning and would be at the staging island in less than nine hours. He could hardly wait to see her. He knew his sense of loss would fade, and some day he might understand more about Nathan, but for the time being he was content to put that behind him, while anticipating Hava's arrival.

Ruffio had followed him outside. "I must speak to you."

Hatu looked at the star-strewn vault of the sky and said, "There's so much out there I don't understand, but I need to know."

Ruffio said, "You are a being of unique ability and incredible power. I can't begin to explain how uncommon you are. I can only say it would be your best choice to leave here and come with Zaakara and me."

"Where?"

"To the place where the best minds I know will aid you in coming to terms with who you are. As I heard Nathan say, there are many who can help you learn. Nathan said no one can teach you, but there may be one. I'm uncertain, but you should come and learn who you truly are."

"And who am I?" asked Hatushaly. "The child of parents I never knew?"

"More, much more," said Ruffio. "Magic on this world is almost finished. Why that is, and what part the Firemane line has in this, and why there are elements of the Void here—all are intertwined mysteries. All that is fundamental in that art now resides in you. The energy that you control—the 'stuff,' as Nathan called it—will always be here, but no one else will be able to manipulate it the way you did, the 'tricks' as Nathan loved to call magic.

"If you come with us, the thing that allows the creature in the pit and the Children of the Void to exist in Nytanny may stay at rest, from what you did with the restraints of time."

Hatu was motionless as he considered this. "So, this world would be safe?"

Ruffio said, "Safer. Until we have fully learned what the foundation of this Void and its creatures rests on, we cannot be assured of Garn's lasting safety. This war between the Void and the . . . existence we take for granted has been waged across time. It may never end." Ruffio paused and then said, "All we can do is fight in the moment, take our best course to stem the end."

"I don't know what to do."

"Come with Zaakara and me to where many talented people can help you master all the power you have within you."

Hatu frowned deeply. Then he said, "What about Hava?"

"Your wife?" Ruffio said. "She would be welcome, but you must understand something. When I told you that I witnessed a conflict more than a century ago, that was truth. The power that resides in you will keep you alive for more time than most mortals can imagine. It is a burden of the gods, or fate, that demands commitment to a higher good, and the price you must pay for it is that you will live long enough to see those you love die. Everyone you know now, from this life, will die before you. It is a terrible price."

Hatu said nothing for a very long time, then looked at Ruffio. "And if I don't go?"

"I suspect you'll suffer the same fate, and end up a vigorous and powerful man, years from now, be it in the Sanctuary or in Marquensas, alone after seeing those you love die of old age."

Again, Hatu paused before replying. "I will talk to Hava."

"I will wait," said Ruffio.

ON THE BEACH WHERE THE armies of Marquensas had gathered in preparation for their attack, Daylon Dumarch, King of Marquensas, stood on a hastily erected platform. In front of him the entire army he had assembled stood waiting and he surveyed his soldiers slowly. Eventually he said, "We have triumphed!"

The men roared their approval and cheered for a long minute.

Daylon held up his hands, and when the troops fell silent, he said, "Tomorrow we return home!"

Again, the bay echoed with the soldiers' cries and applause.

"When we reach Marquensas I will host a celebration. Each of you here will be gifted with enough wealth to secure your families' futures." He grinned. "And if you have no family, enough to get you drunk for the rest of your life!"

Again, cheers rang out.

"Every man here is my man. My brothers in blood and arms, and you"—he indicated the mercenaries who stood behind Declan—"are my men as well. Each one of you who wishes to serve will be given a place of honor, and those of you who choose to do otherwise will always be welcome in my kingdom."

Declan felt strong emotions rising up in him for the first time since the loss of his wife and friends, a hint that there might be hope in the future.

The king dismounted from the dais and beckoned Declan to join him.

When they were alone, Daylon pointed to the setting sun and said, "Tomorrow is the first day."

"First day of what?"

"The first day of our future." Tears formed in Daylon's eyes and he wiped them away. "When my family was destroyed I lost all hope for a future, little brother. But now I have you." He grabbed Declan, hugged him, and when they separated, tears were running down his face.

"You may not have been what I wished for in an heir," Daylon continued, "but you are what the gods have given me. I've seen you. I saw how you led, and how you cared for your men. You are the best man to follow me."

"We've talked about this," said Declan. "For hours."

"I know, and you are wrong, Declan Smith. You are the next King of Marquensas, and I will announce that when we are home."

Declan felt the sense of inevitable fate closing in on him.

Daylon said, "When Balven and I revealed Hatushaly's true identity to him, he said he was the King of Ashes." Daylon poked his brother in the chest with his forefinger and said, "He was wrong. You are the King of Ashes, and you have a nation to raise up from the cinders of destruction."

Declan said, "What must I do?"

"Talk to Balven. I always do."

EPILOGUE

A NEW BEGINNING

The celebration in the king's makeshift pavilion on the island was muted. Despite a relatively easy victory, there had still been men lost, and Daylon and Declan were both left with a profound emptiness. Vengeance had provided neither man with a full sense of closure or accomplishment.

Still, an entire continent of enslaved people was now free of the Pride Lords, and that was to be celebrated. What little ale and spirits had traveled with the king was parceled out to those who had earned Daylon's notice and favor.

The new master-at-arms also provided a small cask of whisky he had somehow managed to pack away unnoticed.

Hatushaly looked around, feeling a touch of nostalgia for his days back at the Inn of the Three Stars as he sipped a small cup of the wicked and wonderful "water of life," as Collin called whisky.

Zaakara and Ruffio had been invited, but seemed content to remain in a quiet corner. Donte and Hatu had spent an hour sharing amazing tales and wondering what lay ahead, both delighted that the other was alive and well.

Declan had been pleased to finally see Hatu again and seemed amused by Donte. He found the entire recounting of his being sent to kill his best friend darkly amusing and enjoyed the way Donte narrated the story.

Hatu deciding to tell Donte that now he could have ended him with a wave of his hand, could wait. More than anyone, Hatu understood the dark arts the Sisters of the Deep had employed on him, and Donte was far less able to resist that power.

Hava luxuriated in the sense that her family had finally been reunited.

Donte had been filled in on what Hava had known about the Pride Lords, then Declan and Hatu had contributed their discoveries about the Dark Masters.

Donte shook his head. "So, these Dark Masters, these horrible creatures who came out of a rift in the sky, they destroyed armies and preyed on people?"

"Yes," said Declan. "But they were not invincible. The Hour Keeper, or whatever his title was, translated a story from a fellow named Nestor. Nestor said that iron harmed them and drove them off, and could even kill them. Still, they kept coming back and ultimately prevailed." He took another sip of whisky. "He said there's a story about a magical traveler who held them at bay and created the Curb, though others say the gods finally took a hand, but at some point, a balance was reached. People were taken but only on certain days and only a limited number."

Donte was working on getting drunk despite the limited supply of alcohol. "Can't eat all the herd," he said. "Got to leave some alive to breed, right?"

"An inelegant way to put it," said Ruffio from the corner of the pavilion, "but not inapt." He looked at Hatu and nodded.

Donte said, "So, with all this going on, these Pride Lords plotted to take control of the entire continent?"

Declan nodded.

Donte started laughing and looked at Hatu and Hava. "They convinced an entire continent of, I don't know how many nations, that they were the ones who finally defeated the Dark Masters? And I thought the Council of Masters was the cleverest bunch of criminals who existed, but I was wrong. This was a criminal undertaking of impossible proportions." He lifted his almost empty mug. "To the Pride Lords, you evil bastards. Burn in hell." He finished his drink.

Hatu saw that Zaakara was already heading outside.

Daylon motioned Declan across to him. "You saved my life, you know."

Declan didn't know what to say.

"I'm getting to be an old man. Next time, you go fight the big bastard."

Declan laughed. "Very well."

The king said, "When we get back, we have to get Balven busy finding you a wife. There will be no shortage of women who would adore being the Queen of Marquensas, and many of them will be very beautiful."

Declan looked alarmed, then said, "I loved my wife."

"As I did, in my first marriage, deeply. My second was selected for political advantage, but after a time I grew to first appreciate her, then . . ." He shrugged as emotions took hold for a moment. "Then I grew deeply fond of her. She was a good mother, and I cherished my children." His deep pain became briefly visible. "So, Balven will find you a suitable queen and all you have to do is find her attractive enough to father an heir. More than one is best. Now go, relax." He waved his brother away and turned to speak with Collin.

Ruffio rose from his seat in the corner, and indicated to Hatu they needed to meet outside.

After a moment, Hatu said, "Come with me, please." Hava looked a little surprised, but nodded, and followed him outside. Once they were a good distance away from the king's pavilion, he said, "I need to talk to you about a couple of things."

She smiled and said, "I'm listening."

"Those two"—he pointed to where Zaakara and Ruffio stood a short distance away—"they want me to go with them."

"Where?" she asked, her eyes narrowing.

"To a . . . place to study, to learn how to master my powers." He quickly recounted to her his ability to find her and others, and his part in saving Declan in the Wound and ensuring that the massive doors in Akena were burned.

As he spoke, her expression turned darker and at last, when he was finished, she said, "You're leaving me?"

"Only if you won't come, too."

For a moment her expression became stern. "So, either I give up being the best damn ship's captain on this world, or you leave me here alone!"

Ruffio and Zaakara were close enough to overhear their conversation and Ruffio said, "We have ships."

Hava's eyes widened and she looked from Hatu to Ruffio and said, "What?"

"I said, we have ships. If you need a ship, that is not a problem."

"Do you have pirates?" she asked.

"Too damn many," said Zaakara, "if you want the truth."

She brightened and said, "Sounds like my kind of place."

"But we have to leave now," said Ruffio.

Donte came out of the tent looking for them and walked up as

Hava threw her arms around Hatu's neck and said, "Of course I'll go anywhere with you." She squeezed him tight, then playfully pushed him away. "As long as they have ships."

"What is this?" asked Donte, starting to show the effects of Collin's whisky.

Hava shouted to Ruffio, "We're coming!" Then she threw her arms around Donte's neck and hugged him, only to have Hatu also come and hug him as well.

"What?" asked Donte.

"We're going on an adventure," said Hava. "We love you, idiot. Stay alive!"

Suddenly a huge oval of energy sprang into being, one Hatu felt as it manifested.

The sizzling sound it emitted caused Daylon, Declan, and the rest of the king's retinue to leave the pavilion and come outside.

Ruffio indicated that Zaakara should step through first, as Hatu shouted to Declan, "Say goodbye to Bodai for me when you visit the Sanctuary!"

Declan waved as Hava stepped through the silvery light and vanished. Hatu followed.

As Ruffio was about to step through, Donte sprinted to the oval, shouting, "Wait for me!" He dived through at the same instant as Ruffio and a second later the oval of scintillating energy snapped out of existence.

Sixto came to stand by Declan's shoulder. "Do you think we will ever see them again?"

Declan paused, and said, "I don't know, but I now fully believe anything is possible."

*   *   *

DONTE SLID ACROSS WET GRASS and hit Hatu from behind, sending him reeling as he turned and fell on his backside.

Hava and Zaakara were far enough away to avoid being knocked over. Ruffio was knocked sideways and rolled a few feet down a grassy incline.

Two men in black robes stood a short distance away. Both held staffs. The slightly taller man had pure white hair that fell to his shoulders, but his face looked relatively young. The second man appeared greatly amused by the pratfall and moved to help Hatu to his feet.

"Welcome," said the white-haired man. "I only expected one newcomer, but you are all welcome."

Hava playfully punched Donte on the arm. "You could have got yourself killed, you idiot."

"Ow!" he said. "You hit hard!" He looked around then turned his head so fast he got a spasm in his neck. Putting his hand up to where it hurt, he exclaimed, "Look!"

"What?" said Hava.

"Three moons!"

Above, a large moon illuminated the night, and in the distance two smaller orbs were rising.

The dark-haired man said, "When all three are high, it's almost like a bright foggy day."

"Where are we?" said Donte.

The white-haired man made a sweeping gesture. "This island is Sorcerer's Isle, and on the other side of this hill is our school, Villa Beata, which means 'happy home.'

"We are in the middle of an ocean called the Bitter Sea, and you are on a world called Midkemia. I am Magnus."

The younger man shook Hatu's hand and said, "My name is Philip, but everyone calls me Pug."

World of Garn